AMERICAN FEVER

Greed & Duplicity
by Frank Zirbel ©2007

See works by Zirbel & other artists at
AmericanFeverBook.com's Gallery

AMERICAN FEVER

A Tale of Romance & Pestilence

PETER CHRISTIAN HALL

For missing persons everywhere

INTRODUCTION

MORE THAN 'A BLOG OF THE PANDEMIC YEAR'

Welcome to the words of a digital zombie.

I barely exist under any name, having relinquished my own years ago. I can't say where I am. It's dangerous.

I was long supposed to be dead. Now I'm a *flugitive*, still pursued by the U.S. government for crimes I allegedly committed amid a collapse of order, justice, and sanity.

Yet I'm here—in your hands—breathing anew. *Thank you.*

A year ago I was miserable, hiding in a distant and unmentionable spot under an assumed identity. I was sprawled one afternoon in a dingy Internet café, yawning over a cheap stimulating beverage and scanning news of places I once knew. Playing Nostalgia for Dummies.

When I discovered that my former self had risen in spirit, it was hard not to jump up and scream, buy everyone a round. The flu blog I had cursed more than once—shut down by the Feds during the Great H5N1 Avian Pandemic—was suddenly a big-selling book. Its vanished author was being mourned as a tragic victim, a heroic and romantic American who had died on the run from the Feds.

Me?

I could hardly breathe. Would the others hear my heart exploding, see my eyes blazing? They ignored me as I clicked on, trying to picture a shop with my blog posts waving at passersby in the window. (Does Manhattan still have bookstores?)

I read that my humble rants had been preserved, as if in amber, by a program at the University of Auckland in New Zealand, where countless blogs from many nations were recorded during the contagion. By the time H5N1 bird flu followed swine flu, New Zealand was so well prepared that students and professors could play the role that Irish monks had fulfilled for civilization in the Dark Ages, safeguarding a world of restless outbursts.

A couple of years after killer H5N1 evolved into a moderate seasonal flu, an enterprising editor in New York had sifted Auckland's hoard and published excerpts from some American blogs whose authors had died in the pandemic. *Lost Voices* was a critical and commercial success.

My older brother turned up to demand royalty payments from the publisher.

Impressed by kind reviews for my entry and inspired by the prospect of cash, my brother set about publishing my entire blog. Typically, he corrupted it.

The rascal spun nonsense about how he had lovingly tracked my escape from New York to a lonely stretch in the Missouri woods where he and I once played together. (He never explained how I had crawled into that unmarked grave.) He doctored my blog posts, adding positive references about himself and removing factual mentions I'd made of him. As you'll see, I had taken pains to avoid revealing that the biggest wretch in my blog—worse than any torturing Fed flunkie—was my kin. Wary that a few survivors might recognize his sleazy self, my brother scrubbed my blog.

Worse, he added a really sappy poem he claimed I had left behind. Talk about defiling the dead!

It was this contaminated version—which he sold for a sizable advance as *A Blog of the Pandemic Year*—that drew sufficient acclaim to catch my eye. Subsequent communications with lawyers and editors from my hole in the known world can't be detailed here, but I'm grateful to all of them—and to some very courageous intermediaries—for their patience, fortitude, and discretion.

Now we have fully reissued my blog with introductory and closing comments as *American Fever: A Tale of Romance & Pestilence*. Amid what the world hopes is a permanent break in the political fever that gripped the United States during the pandemic, a bold publisher has invested in freedom—yours and mine. Editors have even restored my website at AmericanFeverBook.com. It contains every blog entry, complete with artwork, photographs, and live links to a universe of vivid information. I welcome you to contact me there.

I Blogged My Life To Pieces

My writing began humbly as an adjunct to a website I had created to peddle masks, gloves, and goggles to Internet consumers. I never intended to make history. I'd long planned to be far from New York City when H5N1 showed up.

Well, as so many individuals and governments proved with devastating incompetence, it's really hard to prepare for a flu pandemic, even if you're certain one is coming. I was still in town the day the first New Yorker succumbed, when I posted the initial entry, *Day 1: Sign Up to Fight Killer Pandemic Flu!*

I continued in that vein for more than half a year—through the second, shattering wave—until the government crashed my site.

I mainly intended to help people by offering advice and insights (and sure, blow off a little steam) as I sat, safe at home. Personal material quickly crept into my account.

Soon I was shocked to find myself entertaining strangers around the world. Like a kid who gets a kick when adults laugh at his manic antics, I went too far now and then. Some entries are embarrassing, even for a guy who barely exists. A few are funnier than I meant them to be. Frequently the joke was on me.

Some things I wrote have since proven to be scientifically incorrect. That's inevitable. Even today—five years after a pandemic that unfolded in front of our finest scientific minds—man's comprehension of influenza remains a primitive work in progress.

Looking back, I marvel at our hubris in attempting to contain a planetary process that's more like continental drift than the common cold. Try soothing El Niño with a shot and some pills.

You will see that many of my early certainties dissolved into questions, particularly after I made the acquaintance of a prior pandemic zombie. This was a deceased English doctor whose fresh thinking on influenza had been ignored, even scorned, during his century-long life.

As I write this (wondering, as ever, if footsteps I hear are coming for me) I try to keep in mind my original readers. These folks asked my advice, offered their own, mocked me, praised me, threatened me, consoled me. I have overcome the impulse—the compulsion—to update things, correct errors, smooth kinks, erase my idiocies. They're not mine any more, but yours. They changed hands once I posted them.

With one worthy exception, I'm also resisting the impulse to explain details in advance. Whenever you find a reference to "my very old friend" (whom I eventually coded as *Mark*), please program yourself to substitute "my *&@%$^ older brother," as in Mark *(of Cain)*.

You will find that this character relentlessly exploited and betrayed me. I wanted to like him, as I had when we were little kids and I didn't know better. You know how it is: Some relatives are like pesky bugs that came with the place.

As I wrote my blog, I sought to smooth over my brother's shortcomings out of respect for our family. Hoping my forbearance wouldn't seem stupid and contemptible to my readers, I dressed my big brother up, coded him as one of those pals we choose to forgive. His greed and duplicity—and our parents' deaths in the third pandemic wave—have liberated me from such consideration.

I invite you to read between my lines. I'm still discovering subliminal secrets, messages I couldn't have fathomed when I wrote them. I know I never would have started the blog if I'd thought my personal life would figure so prominently in it. That happened to a lot of bloggers when the Web was young and innocent. And free.

In addition to being accurate and complete, this restored edition contains a bonus: I've written an afterword that completes my account as much as my present legal circumstances permit. I hope to be able to explain much more in a future edition—one with a dizzyingly happy ending that I earned by falling so deeply in love amid such horror.

I dedicate this volume to *my mystery mailer.* I still—*and I will!*—love you.

Finally, I thank everyone I mentioned in the blog. I choose not to name a number of people who have helped me, lest they be tarnished and persecuted as my accomplices. Most of you know who you are. *Wink.*

DAY 1

SIGN UP TO FIGHT KILLER PANDEMIC FLU!

Call me Maskman. You might come up with worse names before we're finished.

I'm starting this blog tonight because I'm scared. Sure, I fear my writing will suck and you'll all think I'm a moron. That goes without saying.

I'm much more worried that we're all going to die because the last new flu that hit the U.S. laid an egg that still stinks. Americans no longer believe influenza can kill anyone but old folks—and maybe a few younger people crossed by bad luck, as if they got hit-and-run by a drunken virion. After swine flu's flop, who respects influenza?

There's a distant quality to the TV reports about H5N1's global spread, as if the problem were some volcano in Sumatra. Images are scarce, unaffecting. Nothing reads: Crisis!

Sure, the talking heads mention that mutated bird flu probably showed its teeth in New York today, after weeks of false alarms. They say it may have killed a yet-to-be-identified bus driver, but add that there's no proof we face a pandemic. We see video of the early alarm in 2009, when a New York high school erupted in swine flu when some kids brought it back from Mexico. The World Health Organization (WHO) and the U.S. Centers for Disease Control (CDC) are holding lots of meetings, urging calm in more and more places. Ho-hum. What's for dinner?

The stock market went down hard but recovered. Big-time traders don't ride buses.

I hear that eyewitnesses in Bushwick said the driver hacked up blood all over his windshield before crashing into a bodega. And that half-a-dozen other people are said to be lying in rotten condition in hospitals all over town, apparently quarantined as likely avian flu victims.

My neighbors aren't impressed. New Yorkers do more damage to each other on quiet evenings. I can already hear lusty students from Happy Hour U marching down Avenue B to a chorus of shrieks. The guy downstairs is bawling out his boyfriend's sister. This always excites the Doberman next door.

What would it take for a microbe to impress these busy, urbane souls?

This disease-of-the-week thing is old. Since 9/11 we've seen (more like: heard about) West Nile virus, SARS, the original, dreaded H5N1 bird flu, untreatable TBX tuberculosis, MRSA, dengue fever, and swine flu. Someone dusted midtown Manhattan with what the government claims was its own anthrax. So why should Gothamites care about some remix of a flopped avian flu that scared everyone silly in 2006 and then flew around afflicting (mostly) Egyptians and Indonesians?

Because this one's a Category 5 hurricane. *Welcome to the Ninth Ward, folks. (You do remember New Orleans, right? Katrina…?)*

I'm already watching conspiracy theories pop up all over the Web. The social networks are abuzz with cynical comments and theories. Most people who think flu is dangerous seem convinced it's a man-made microbe. Others think it's an overblown fraud. One way or the other, immigrants, pharmaceutical companies, Muslims, Jews, Christians, atheists, gays, and the United Nations are all suspected of duping us.

Doesn't anyone respect nature around here? Not all catastrophes are caused by humans.

We have to challenge this attitude—and not because the government says so. We must speak out because H5N1 avian pandemic flu has everything the Great Pandemic Flu of 1918 had and more. It's transmitting more easily every day and it looks to be able to kill a greater percentage of people more horribly than any influenza ever recorded. Far more than *anyone* ever predicted swine flu would kill. As shown in the movie, *Awakenings*, survivors can sustain nerve damage, even develop Parkinson's Disease.

Swine Flu's Secret Punch

Here's the problem. The so-called swine flu that surfaced in the U.S. and Mexico to cause such a stir in 2009 had a remarkable pedigree: It contained genes from birds, pigs, and humans. Before it faded in a backwash of popular annoyance and ennui, novel H1N1 left the world a monstrous memento.

True to its nickname, swine flu managed to get into Indonesia's pig population. There it encountered H5N1, the incredibly nasty bird flu that loved to get into mammals but was having a hard time getting humans to pass it to each other.

Nature doesn't care about irony. It's just a coincidence that pigs in a Muslim country hooked up the two flu viruses. Those who accuse 'Muslim bioterrorists' of cooking up this contagion are ignoring that experts warned in 2009 that Novel H1N1 and H5N1 might join forces.

After H1N1 gave up some vital genetic snippets—presumably through a process known as reassortment—H5N1 took to killing more Indonesians. Then Vietnamese. It popped up in Hong Kong, as it has done intermittently since 1997. In the last month mutated avian flu has struck four continents, killed at least 100 people. Some cases already show signs of picking up immunity to Tamiflu—the primary antiviral medicine in the world's flu arsenal. While H5N1 learns how to infect us, we're learning that mankind drew all the wrong lessons from swine flu.

DIY, ASAP

This is no time to be smug. Sure, I've got a lifetime supply of personal protection gear, which I sell on this site. I can't *prove* it makes much difference if we wear professional-grade masks, goggles, and gloves. (Experts in and out of the government are downright confused.) I wear it.

I got into this line of work because I was scared and wanted to fight this disease. By the time the threat is formally recognized, H5N1 will be upon us. It's already here, where I live. Coming soon to your 'hood. Get ready.

Oh yeah, I nearly forgot! Welcome to my blog. I haven't ever done this. Be kind.

I invite you to visit the flu bloggers and news sources I rely on. Most have been reporting and analyzing viral developments for many years. We're lucky to be entering this crisis with so many seasoned commentators at hand. I'm the no-name rookie.

DAY 2

CRACKS APPEAR IN OUR MEDICAL TEMPLES

With two New York corpses awaiting final testing results and 16 likely victims in intensive care, we're awash in flu news. It's about time.

The biggest story isn't the local contagion, however. It's in Vancouver, where a family of tourists from Szechuan who seemed fit when they landed five days ago is now in the ICU. All of them, plus a tour guide and a pizza vendor who served them. Coincidence? That would hardly be reassuring.

Not that some aren't still fiddling. While the WHO meets again to debate alert levels amid so many complaints about how quickly they raised them for swine flu, veteran flu debunkers peddle cynicism across our TV screens. They cite New York's past scares and promise this month's menace will pass, too. Sometimes I wonder if these guys would have sneered at the 1918 pandemic, too: *Hey, what's all the fuss? I feel fine. The Black Death was so much worse and we're all here, right...?*

Like Wall Streeters who insisted that dot-coms and real estate would pay off forever, the flu skeptics have been right for years. When they're finally wrong, the downside will be far worse than any stock market crash. (Financial Armageddon will be the least of it.)

Some fear H5N1. That sprawling fistfight streaming in various versions on the Web took place outside New York's biggest hospital. It hints at what's coming.

The riot squad looks ill-prepared. Sure, they've got plenty of weapons. But their paper masks look like a joke to me. Helmets and clubs and tasers won't protect cops from flu as they face off against flushed and furious New Yorkers desperate to get inside a building that's bursting with virions.

New York's hospitals are filling with frightened, sneezing people. It is reported that some doctors, nurses, and technicians are already missing in action. These professionals know what we face. Many were given paper surgical masks that I consider next to useless at blocking the tiny aerosol particles that erupt when people cough or sneeze.

The pros know that our surviving medical facilities—redesigned to shed excess capacity—can't cope with virulent influenza. Those who slashed medical personnel and resources in the somersaulting recession made no provision for <u>surges in demand</u>. As with dominoes, a systems failure anywhere may mean contagious collapse for all.

Nothing could lure me to a clinic tonight. Survivors will someday look back on today's emergency rooms with revulsion— as we now think of the notion that surgeons would ever slice into us with unclean hands and tools. (American hygiene still isn't what we prefer to imagine: Read some grisly studies about how few doctors wash their hands.)

It's safer to stay home with people and creatures we love, and who care about us enough to *hydrate* us in a pinch. In this regard, I'm a very lucky man.

Newbies to H5N1 can pass their early self-quarantine days reading copies of Dr. Grattan Woodson's excellent *The Bird Flu Preparedness Planner* and *The Bird Flu Manual* or download for free his *Good Home Treatment Of Influenza.* (He'll tell you all about hydration.)

My home is crammed to the cobwebs with boxes of the best respirators, masks, gloves, goggles, and disinfectant I could stockpile. (Plenty of water, beer, wine, and spirits, too.) I hope to save a lot of lives. Anyone who doesn't catch flu is someone who won't spread it, so I take pleasure in helping people who will never even hear of my wares.

DIY or Die

Surviving this thing will take more than protective gear. It will take wit and heart and luck. It demands the do-it-yourself spirit that animated the American settlers and New York punk rockers of yore. DIY can save us. It kinda has to.

As long as the Internet holds up, we're linked. There will be times the digital thread fails us—when electricity is cut, servers can't handle increased demand, or workers are too sick to keep the ISPs afloat. I won't be surprised if criminal botnets try to do more than sell phony flu cures and counterfeit Tamiflu. People still robbed banks in 1918; I'll bet those little gauzy masks everyone wore made it easy.

For now, we're joined in our isolation. We can safely trade insights to help each other survive. Contact me at this website and I'll post tips I like.

My digital bean counter says I've already snared some readers. I presume they came to buy and stayed for the bonus verbology (with a splash of virology).

Next, I'll have more to say about how we can defend ourselves. Hint: We need to infect society with rational fear. We need to go viral—no less than H5N1 has done. People far from New York must prepare. *It's not too late!* Yet.

DAY 3

A LIBERTARIAN WITH HOPES, FEARS & REGRETS

I'd like to apologize for yesterday's post. My friendly unofficial editor says it looks boastful, the words of a wise guy who saw it all coming.

I'm not here to lecture anyone. I don't have to blog to sell my products, which have certain nonverbal charms.

I hope it's clear that I'm more frightened than you are. I've built a lifetime hoard of masks and gloves and goggles and disinfectant, and I've been hiding at home for more than a week. My roommate and I withdrew from the world after H5N1 killed that vegan in Sweden. The authorities couldn't blame chickens or pigs for *her* condition.

I'm also sorry that some of you think I'm encouraging medical personnel to stay home. I agree that these times call for heroic acts, even if our first responders aren't properly equipped. But I respectfully—*violently*—oppose the idea that they should be arrested and prosecuted for dereliction of duty. These people are civilians, not soldiers.

A lot of states are calling up emergency legislation to yank licenses from medical professionals who fail to show up for work. If the government is going to approach this deadly emergency by punishing the living, we're worse off than I feared.

As for my politics, I can assure you I'm not particularly liberal. I am *libertarian* with a small *l*. I trust few politicians, no parties. No institutions. No tea brands. I haven't seen leaders do much I consider praiseworthy. I've watched the presidency amass powers that few who signed the Declaration of Independence would have endorsed. I've watched Congress turn into the world's most predictable game show. Our Supreme Court couldn't judge a music contest without displaying extreme prejudice.

It's nice to think that persevering civil servants in Washington will ensure we have enough food, water, electricity, and heat. But as this report from the American Civil Liberties Union warns, they're far better geared to lock us all up. Post-9/11 doctrine gives the U.S. military and the Department of Homeland Security the authority to force Americans to be medicated, quarantined, and vaccinated if the president declares it necessary. Today's Pentagon intensively tracks flu around the world. (Do the generals know that 'magic bullet' is a metaphor?)

This libertarian simply wants the government to function politely and effectively.

I'm overwhelmed by demand for personal protection items, so I have work to do. I'll return tomorrow with some useful information.

Meanwhile, I can report the failure of my neighbors' annual April Fools bash, though it's been a gorgeous night here. Normally the NYPD would have crashed the party by now. In lieu of guests, all I can detect across the street are empty thumping pop music and ripples of laughter. New Yorkers are lying low. Stay well.

DAY 3 (#2)

A HELPFUL GLIMPSE OF HELL

I've just returned from a kind of purgatory—a gateway to hell that's not quite open yet.

I should explain that I have a partner in this business, someone I worked with years ago. He joined up with me a couple of months back to sell personal protective gear. (He still has a job that demands focus, so he's basically an investor.)

Tonight a blue SUV with New Jersey plates swept through a Soho bike lane painted green and slammed my friend and his bicycle into a parked car, then took off. My headstrong friend tried to ride after him but his wheel was warped, so he didn't get far. That's all he remembers before he turned up here, bent and gasping.

Once inside, he started vomiting. He had a headache. No other flu symptoms. No apparent broken bones. I googled symptoms of internal injury and couldn't find blood in his barf. Still, he needed a doctor: an MRI, X-Rays, a proper inquiry.

After waiting an hour for an ambulance, we walked to the nearest hospital. He said it was a good thing nobody reads my blog because the staff would otherwise know I'd said hospitals are dangerous places staffed by filthy people. "Only the doctors," I reminded him. "Which would make the nurses extra-kind to you."

He wasn't convinced. He hates my blogging, thinks I'm going to annoy you all and blow his savings. "Why insult your customers? Have they insulted you?" (Well, no, but I haven't insulted any readers either.) I shut him up by pointing out that if you all link to this site, our products will achieve better visibility—with no advertising expense. Sales are booming anyway. Case closed.

Yeah, he's the mercenary one. I'm the carrot—who's really blogging because I feel like communicating with you all. He has to put up with me because I do all the work.

No Disease Permitted Without Photo I.D.

The cops almost didn't let us into the hospital. Not because it was too crowded or rife with contagion, which it was. They didn't like our ... masks and goggles. This may have been a matter of jealousy, but they said it was a security precaution. They wanted to see faces and ID. They keep records of all visitors.

I hated the thought of unveiling myself at the entrance to an orgy of killer microbes. My friend was incensed. I'm a libertarian, but I'm not paranoid; he is both. I worry about the potential for the government to track us all into virtual cells; he thinks it's been happening for years.

My partner thus told the cops to go to hell. Which meant: no help for him. I tried to explain that he was in shock, had been run over. They told us to step aside so others could jam the doorway.

Then my friend did what he always does—surprised me with a sudden theatrical turn that reboots a tense situation. He fainted.

His ideological incapacitation enabled some orderlies to remove his mask while I extracted his ID. They put him on a stretcher and processed him for four hours amid the kind of chaos I depicted pretty well yesterday. People inside were yelling, coughing, screaming, sneezing, moaning, dying. I didn't see any fights, but this is known to be a pretty civilized hospital. The medical staff looked exhausted in a motley array of masks—no goggles.

The young doctor we saw was probably an intern. She didn't really listen and we barely understood her mumbling. After poking my partner to assure there were no broken ribs or internal injuries, she ordered some tests and told us to come back for an MRI in a few days, "when things have calmed down." Fat chance.

DAY 4:

PANDEMIC PRESCRIPTION—
GENERATIONAL CONFLICT

I hate to sound like one of those flu debunkers, but *so far* most of the cases arising here in New York are false alarms. This is hay fever season, so the prospect that a sneeze could kill has driven thousands to the emergency room. The pictures of corridors and sidewalk tents crammed with anxious people, paper masks askew, are reminiscent of 1918. (Sick people sure dressed better then.)

Many cases are undoubtedly influenza-like illness, which accounts for most symptoms in most years. (There are hints that catching the common cold might help fight flu.)

Most of these people are fine. Those who are genuinely ill will get less care because hysterical allergy cases are disrupting the system. That helps H5N1 circulate.

So do toilets: Flushing infected waste aerosolizes microbes, churning them into a fine mist. Short people and children in particular ought to close toilet lids before they unleash clouds of nasty virions. (Don't even *think* about airplane lavatories—those cramped and smelly plastic enclosures, brimming with germs so violently and constantly stirred….)

Stores are emptying. Pharmacies are arming guards. People are bashing pigeons in the streets. (Not the best idea if the birds *are* sick—peasants in Southeast Asia long ago learned what H5N1 can do to people who slaughter infected chickens and ducks.)

Before we succumb to pointless anxiety—as opposed to the kind that might make us *prepare*—I'd like to point out that Americans of differing ages face different risk levels.

Influenza is tricky. It works much of its harm indirectly. Even though *seasonal* flu concentrates on the very old, half of the elderly wind up succumbing to unrelated, opportunistic infections, mainly pneumonia. The flu virus weakens them and pneumonia bacteria swoop in for the kill.

Though *seasonal* flu can harm the very young, whose immune systems aren't yet up to speed, it is easily repelled by teenagers and young adults, whose immune systems reject opportunistic infections, too.

Shelter From the Cytokine Storm

Pandemic flu brutalizes youth. It provokes a ferocious immune response that can run out of control—scorching a victim's lungs beyond repair and flooding them with white gunk. People can turn blue for want of oxygen. Scientists disagree as to whether this is caused by the much-discussed cytokine storm, by which "the violent and uncontrolled immediate response of the immune system ... destroys lung tissue by runaway inflammation." (Sure sounds like what happened to that bus driver; here's a charming video account of how a Deadwood, S.D., bordello madam saved the narrator's upright grandparents from a cytokine storm during the Great Pandemic.)

The elderly are not a prime target of *pandemic* flu. They've survived so much that their immune systems are tired—too relaxed to kill them. In 1918, people over 65 accounted for only 1% of excess deaths. The rate at which folks over 75 were killed by influenza and pneumonia *fell* that year.

Among H5N1 victims, 90% have been under 40. Half were under 18, and most of those were 10 or older. Younger kids tend to survive nearly as well as people from 50 to 70, probably because their immune systems are too immature to put up a suicidal defense. Those aged 10 to 40 have the most to fear.

The elderly face a different peril: They stand to lose things they already rely on to stay alive. Our health system won't offer much support or medication for such conditions as cancer, diabetes, or heart or lung disorders. A century ago there were numerous extra deaths during the pandemic from tuberculosis, whooping cough, and premature births.

Scientists have added obesity to the list of known flu risk factors that include asthma, pregnancy, and diabetes. That's progress for you: *In Flu: A Social History of Influenza*, Tom Quinn quotes a doctor's observation during the influenza pandemic of 1831 that "stout young men" and pregnant women were likelier to catch pneumonia.

For years, flu debunkers have proclaimed that our advanced civilization—our antiseptic society—could easily withstand an avian flu pandemic. I say sophistication cuts both ways: People didn't depend on kidney dialysis systems in 1918. There weren't millions living with cancer. This makes us *more* vulnerable to disruption, not less.

How will elderly Americans deal with traditionally fatal, chronic illnesses? Who will tend them? With what? In keeping with our just-in-time inventory system, the only stockpiles of medicine and ventilators are maintained by the Feds. I don't know where the stuff is located, but it can't possibly suffice. Heck, I hear *fuel* is already running out. Coffins and body bags will be scarce. The only products that seem plentiful are bogus flu remedies featured in spam emails, texts, NFC, and calls.

The elderly feel vulnerable and they vote. The young are vulnerable *to this flu* and they do not. Expect resources to be misdirected.

A final note: I'm receiving a lot of email for a blog that's only three days old. Some ask why I don't let readers post responses. Good question.

I don't want to have to monitor the site for *abuse*. Nor will I host debates about what politician would make a worse president, or which movie star or pop singer is doing more to fight bird flu, (Listen to the chorus of *Smells Like Teen Spirit*—lyrics & music about entertaining contagion here.)

I welcome email if you want to talk back. I'll respond to interesting points. Just don't expect me to publish them verbatim.

DAY 4 (#2)

BOOMERS FOREVER?

A study in England has claimed that people born before 1969 seem to bear some immunity to a virus that was never known to affect people until *1997*. In 2008 a panel of WHO experts reported in *The New England Journal of Medicine* that "approximately 15 to 20% of older adults have some baseline neutralizing antibodies to H5N1 virus...."

While I like Boomers (who could fail to cherish their childlike egocentricities?), it's a little creepy to think that nature may be contriving to help them outlast me.

For those few who might wonder *how* these lucky geezers acquired immunity to H5N1, the authors quietly added: "*The mechanisms leading to these antibodies are uncertain.*" The deeper I dig, the more I see how little the experts know about influenza.

DAY 5

Q&A AND FRIENDLY FLUBLOGIA

So many questions, readers, though some lack question marks. They read more like indictments of your humble servant. Is it the homebound audience? Feeling edgy? Oh heck, I asked for it.

1. Yeah, I'm sort of young. My most recent milestone was turning 30. Since then, I lost a job, ended a great relationship, and started preparing for epochal pestilence. Do I seem overly sensitive? (Maybe I should add that I've since managed to fall in love.)

2. I do indeed fret that my still-youthful immune system will blow me to pieces. I like to think that my darkened corpse would be recognizable to my parents back home, should someone find me in time. More likely I'll wind up in a lime pit on Staten Island.

3. I was born well after 1969, that hallmark year of Manson on the Moon that seems to divide geezers with inexplicable antibodies to H5N1 from the rest of us. I personally fear the cytokine storm and I might well resent that our few solutions are going to the elderly who are less likely to experience one.

4. On the other hand, I want my parents to have all the help they need. (*They wouldn't listen to me* and are unprepared.) My stepmom is in remission from breast cancer and my dad may have something that at least requires further testing. Like most men, he postponed it.

5. Aged Americans will die in great numbers from everything but the flu. Have you seen those idle ports on TV? China makes most of the world's penicillin, among other indispensables. *My stepmom's meds aren't even in motion.*

6. I never said I was noble. I'm not taking any chances these days. I researched flu, planned to survive it, then invested in the best ways to do so. What's wrong with that?

7. Sure, I like social networks. I use them. But I stopped haranguing my friends about flu years ago and I maintain strict privacy settings. Readers of this blog might recognize me only by some songs I post.

8. I'm no kind of medical person. I took biology in high school, never in college or grad school. But I love nature and I'm not stupid. I've studied bird flu's history and evolution for years and years.

I learned from books and from *Flublogia*, as the informal society of flu bloggers is known. Although they cover a compelling array of infectious diseases, influenza is their primary focus. I commend these generous souls, all linked on my Flu Resources Page.

None in any way resembles Alan Krumwiede, the venal, grasping blogger played by Jude Law in *Contagion*. (Watch the trailer.) Sure, they're quick-witted, enterprising newshounds who were first to grasp that swine flu was breaking out along the U.S.-Mexican border in 2009. Unlike the villainous Krumwiede, these voluntary reporters and analysts do not profit from their efforts. They won't accept advertising lest a Tamiflu pitch, for instance, pop up to erode confidence in their musings about antivirals.

For daily insight on anything significant that comes up, I look first to Avian Flu Diary. Blogger Mike Coston is a retired EMT and preparedness stalwart who covers a lot of issues as Fla_Medic. (Peek into his emergency "bug-out bag" and his list of preparedness gifts.) Coston's site offers one-stop shopping—an exhaustive flow of linked citations and thoughtful commentary, complete with earnest charm and flashes of wit.

Though I follow others, too, my short list of superb bloggers includes retired writing professor and dean of Flublogia Crawford Killian at H5N1, IT expert (and Computerworld blogger) Scott McPherson at Scott McPherson's Web Presence, Vincent Racaniello at Virology, and Maryn McKenna's Superbug at Wired.com. Good, newsy sites also include those of Arkanoid Legent in Malaysia and Flu News Network from Cottontop, an upstate New York mother and longtime flu forum commenter on the Flu Wiki bulletin boards. Many draw on timely reports from Dr. Michael Osterholm's CIDRAP and on the crowdsourced global disease surveillance that takes place every day at the excellent FluTrackers community board.

9. Finally, patient readers, I would *never* call the cops on a noisy party. I favor freedom and initiative. I'd yell at them myself if I felt it necessary. Or crash it, if I liked their music.

DAY 6

A HARROWING SNEEZE & HOME DECONTAMINATION

I ventured out today in driving rain. I couldn't get my products picked up and my partner was working his day job, so my backup 'flu buddy' insisted on driving me to the UPS shipping center in midtown. I felt like a draftee being hauled off to war by a cackling drill sergeant.

I've never seen New York so empty, not even on Christmas. Traffic is scarce. Drivers are courteous.

The mood was radically different at UPS. People were jammed together, nervous, venting at the understaffed desk. I was an alien—safe and distant—wearing what I consider pretty good equipment. As people stared enviously, I started to feel like a celebrity. I should get a t-shirt emblazoned with my URL.

Then a stocky woman sneezed. Flu circulates by annoying our immune systems until we cough or sneeze. Hers was a titanic launch. The room went silent.

All eyes turned to her, turned *on* her. She tried to keep her paper mask on, but she needed to blow her nose. In the middle of doing that—as people around her tried to back away without losing their places—she sneezed so hard, her mask blew off.

As she groped on the floor for the soggy piece of bent paper, I wondered how she'd kept her lipstick intact behind a mask. *Everyone wanted to kick her.* I could feel the rage through my plastic sheathing. I hated her, too. When she opened her mouth to mutter apologies, her lips festooned with slimy, dangling white blood cells, I felt sick.

The sound of a sneeze has become more jarring than chalk scraping a blackboard, scarier than a police siren erupting behind your car. It pumps the heart into overdrive. It's a loud reminder that invisible viral particles are scratching and clawing inside *the others* until they can burst forth to fling themselves at *us*, infesting the very air we gasp when we hear that sick, violent exhalation: *Achooooooo….*

Or *hatschi* in Germany, *atchim* in Brazil, *hakushon* in Japan, *apshkhi* in Russia, *atchoum* in France, and *han-chee* in China. Here's a nice <u>Web page</u> about this.

My roommate has been sneezing tonight. It should be cat allergies, though this is denied, probably in deference to the fact that it's *my* cat. To throw us off track, the cat sneezed, too.

Bio-Security Starts at the Door

Coming back inside was a pain—and not merely because my roommate has refused to talk for hours. Did I return with a mermaid tattooed on my forehead? The mirror shows nothing but concern.

The process of decontaminating is so bothersome that it's often easier to stay put. My cleansing area consists of plastic sheeting near the front door of my three-room apartment, which opens into the living room. I keep going-out clothes by the door. I wash in a temporary tub, using a makeshift shower head and a bowl of diluted <u>disinfectant</u> solution to clean parts of me that were exposed and then to soak goggles and gloves.

I worry that my cat will catch H5N1 from something I track in. It's interesting how caring for a helpless creature makes one more responsible. (Is this what happens to parents?) He is no longer allowed to enter the living room or kitchen. His vocal response to this catastrophic loss of territory has inspired a new nickname: *Mrrrowlin Brando.*

I like dogs a lot, but I'm glad I didn't get one. My smarter, dog-owning pals are building indoor litter boxes. Imagine a Doberman lifting his leg in a Manhattan living room. I still see a few people walking canines on the street below, which is risky. They can pick up bird flu, though not quite like cats: *Dogs shed it without becoming ill.*

I can only imagine how parents feel as they keep their children cooped up. Kids have fingers and voices. They can easily escape, or make you want to.

DAY 7:

MAIL CALL! GETTING PERSONAL....

I'm proud to be opening a plump digital mailbag after just a week of posting. I'll never understand why many of you are interested in my personal life. It's flattering, but I value my privacy. I will limit my responses. Sorry, but TBIMB.

No, I'm not a professional writer. (*But thank you.*) My degree leans toward the technical side, with some artistry.

I'm glad some people think I'm funny. Feel free to laugh with me—or at me, if you must.

I suppose I look like a white guy from the Midwest. I'm a bit taller than average, but not tall. I'm trim, but not thin. My hair is neither light nor dark; it's shaggy, but not what you'd call long. I'm clean-shaven. (My dad convulsed unforgettably at my early whiskers; he said I had "a baseball mustache—nine players on each side.")

Okay, I have a wide face and eyes that change with the weather. Mostly I wear dark clothes. I'm a moderate Bohemian, good-looking in a Germanic way.

I live in one of New York City's infamous neighborhoods, home to generations of immigrants. There's a nearby <u>Tenement Museum</u>. Closer is a big old-time *Jesus Saves* cross that advertises an active evangelical mission. There are lots of bars, world food. Sometimes the East Village feels like a small town full of college kids, but I like it.

All kinds of music appeals to me when it's performed with spirit and taste, but most pop bores me. Here's <u>a rock song</u> I'll never tire of—*Shotgun*, from Earl Greyhound.

I hate Internet jargon, and clichés in general. You'll have to get your LOLs and ROTFLMAOs elsewhere. I don't know what most of these things mean, and I don't care. I'm in no hurry, anyway. Unless I've miscalculated, I have loads of time to type.

The real words I won't use here are curiously known as curse words. Not because I don't swear when a taxi runs clean over my foot, as once happened (*without damage*) to me in London. I simply don't want censorious spider software to bar kids from accessing my thoughts. I welcome anyone who stumbles into my blog. *You'll never leave, hehe.*

Mahesh Pops the Big Question: Am I Gay?

Sadly, one question engages a disturbing number of readers—particularly an Indian gentleman named Mahesh. He lives in Mysore (which he kindly explains is near Bangalore) and he demands to know if I am homosexual. (I hope that word doesn't activate those danged spiders.)

Unlike some Americans who ask the same question, Mahesh didn't try to coat his query by saying the answer makes no difference to him. Obviously it matters to a lot of people. But Mahesh is desperate. My talk of having a male 'partner'—as well as a roommate of unspecified gender—has traumatized him. He fears they are one monstrous gay person.

"Please assure me that you are in no way one of these filthy, cursed buggers," Mahesh pleads so elegantly.

Will he disbelieve my comments about H5N1 if I say I like men? Will Mahesh toss his mask into the rubbish heap?

I'm tempted to stop blogging altogether and join my mysterious roommate in an orgy of strip poker and movie streaming. (Do they have that in Mysore?) Or I could do the politically correct thing and refuse to answer.

But some of you intolerant souls are evidently nice people. Some inquiries even come from people of various genders who seem to be trying to flirt with me. So I'll bite the bullet by declaring that my roommate is a woman who is indeed my girlfriend and *we are vigorously living in sin* because of H5N1.

This damsel took refuge in my cramped apartment two months ago. I was predicting a world depression from the effects of bird flu (*sure, that looks easy now*) and I wanted her safe with me for the duration. She tends to her job at a mega-global bank from this very computer during the day. Her iMac never sleeps.

She is no longer my unofficial editor unless she secretly reads my blog. Let's see if she complains about tonight's post. (I'll test her: Please brush those teeth, honey.)

Did I mention we're in love? I hope people respect this and stop bugging me about my personal life. I could truthfully add that my best friend is gay, but clichés are abominable.

So Mr. Mahesh, I hope you are not engulfed in *aak-chheen* or *aak-chhoon* over in Mysore. I gathered that Hindus have two ways of sneezing. Is one manlier?

I bow to any readers who figured out that TBIMB means *too bad it's my blog.*

DAY 8

FEARSOME FOMITES EVERYWHERE

The cat and I watch the neighbors—silhouettes outlined by big flat screens.

I make up lives for these human dolls. Earlier a bald man across the street looked like he was playing video games while a younger woman changed her clothes again and again. (She wasn't naked—just kept returning to the mirror in fresh outfits that were almost clownish.) I figured she was vying for her heartless lover's attention with clothes I might want to ignore, too. I watched with morbid fascination. Nah, more like boredom.

Regarding last night's experiment: Since my girlfriend is proud of her gleaming incisors—and would rightfully and righteously have erupted had she seen my suggestion that she isn't tending them—I'm certain she isn't monitoring my posts. *Sob.*

My flu buddy wants me to come to meetings about fighting H5N1 in the neighborhood. The organizers sound pretty liberal: They're planning a demonstration against the way companies have been laying off workers for the pandemic. I agree that cutting off peoples' health insurance and cash flow exacerbates the economic plunge and probably spreads disease. I hadn't realized layoffs were such a key item in corporate pandemic contingency plans. Still, companies have the right to fire people, just as the unemployed have the right to not buy their products. Nobody marched when they took my desk away.

I'd rather not strain my voice and lungs yelling at capitalists. My mask would muffle everything. My girlfriend would miss me. Ayn Rand would curse me from her grave. So thanks anyway, buddy. (In case he's keeping up here.)

Now, please, listen up. This is serious! Today's lecture concerns *fomites*—doorknobs, light switches, pens, ATMs, or anything else that accumulates germs and viruses. (Even prayer books: God may be *on* your side, but do you really want a sneezing worshipper *at* your side?)

The average person with a simple rhinovirus cold leaves contagious particles on 35% of the surfaces he or she touches. Healthy fingers pick them up 47% of the time. *Don't* rub your eyes in shock at this study. It's dangerous.

While bacteria can multiply on fomites (even dust particles), viruses such as H5N1 must lie dormant on surfaces, basking in a special coat of fat they nick from our cells when they replicate. The stolen fat protects them till we reach out, acquire them, and then touch the vulnerable mucous membranes of our mouths, noses, and eyes.

Washing your hands really vanquishes virus. Just don't fall for noisy ads pitching high-tech cleansers and antibacterials with impressively unpronounceable names. Some kill bacteria that keep our cells healthy, especially in our digestive tracts. Some contain Triclosan, which sunlight turns into dioxin after we rinse it into the sewer. In treated water, Triclosan also produces chloroform, which can make you dizzy and tired, damage your liver and kidneys, and perhaps trigger cancer. Specialized skin sanitizers aren't always reliable, either: Mike Coston blogged about a company whose skin-care products were seized for bacterial contamination.

If Your Soap Passes the Drug Test, It's Not Soap

Stick to the old-fashioned stuff, which closely resembles the soaps invented and manufactured in Palestine and in Iraq back in the Seventh Century. (They even developed a special soap for shaving!) Traditional hand soap is superior. But be warned that a drug testing kit commonly used by police officers falsely detects the so-called date rape drug (Gamma Hydroxy Butyrate) in soaps from Dr. Bronner's, Tom's of Maine, and Neutrogena; it passed on other so-called soaps, proving they consist of detergent.

As Dr. Michael Greger explains in his *Bird Flu: A Virus Of Our Own Hatching* (read it online for free) hand washing doesn't so much kill a virus as dilute it until it's no longer infectious. Cool water is healthier, doesn't dry out our flesh as much as hot water does.

So fight fomites! That's all the authorities tell us. Don't touch anything, wash your hands constantly, lest these fancy-sounding surfaces dose you. That's exactly what they preached in 1918. There wasn't much else to say. Oh yeah, *wear a good mask*!

And gloves....

And goggles. Your eyes are viral portals, too. Wearing this gear keeps you from touching your mucus membranes with unclean fingers. (Sure, it itches sometimes, and many public officials— such as this former New York City Health Commissioner—think flu can't enter through the eyes; read on.)

Wash things, too. All you need for a cheap, potent disinfectant is a tablespoon of chlorine bleach and a gallon of water. (Don't use it on plastic, though; for that you need a milder disinfectant.) Hard surfaces nurture microbes much longer than porous ones do—as long as 24 hours—however counterintuitive that might seem. In other words, surfaces that take good fingerprints are the most dangerous. Scrub them fomites!

I miss shopping carts and subways. But I must be safe here at home ... *doh*! The keyboard. My girlfriend uses it all day. It's hers. What a fool I am.

Then again, we've got better ways to trade germs.

DAY 9

A TRAIL OF IPODS TO HELL

Closing the schools was a great idea *on paper*. (Even though, as <u>a Brookings Institution report concluded in 2009</u>, it could cost up to $47 billion in parent-worker absenteeism—particularly that of health-care workers.)

Everyone knows children are prime flu vectors. Once infected, they can take six days to show symptoms as they traipse from the playground to your kitchen and back to school before anyone notices a problem. Look at the 1918 mortality rates in St. Louis, where they quickly closed the schools, vs. those in Philadelphia, whose authorities ignored the plague. Philly's peak was more than four times higher and ran far longer. <u>Nonpharmaceutical measures</u> made a difference.

Highs and lows in the pandemics of 1957 and '68 corresponded to the academic schedule, presumably because crowds of kids with fledgling immune systems help flu reach critical mass. Not to mention Wave II of the Great Influenza of 1918, when barracks of young soldiers exploded with disease, camp-by-camp, state-by-state. (Then they gave it to the German Army, which collapsed and lost the war.)

Today a ragtag army of bored students roams New York's streets, trading germs and viruses like ringtones. They can't shop in empty stores. There's no work. No one's organizing volunteers. (Everyone's too busy waiting on the government.) Teens hang.

Kids and cops are the only people I spot from my window. I'm like a retired shut-in, thrilled when some delinquent wanders past with a cranked-up boom box. Most whippersnappers wear earbuds.

So some spirited college students decided to put on a campus show, an outdoor hip hop concert that would deliver pandemic education in the form of handouts and a speech or two. Typically, the police cut the power before this *permit-less event* could begin. Some mischievous performers started rapping *peace* lyrics, without amplification. The cops stood by.

Suddenly one of the singers quietly collapsed in the sunlight. The silence that followed turned into a long whooping roar.

Before the authorities could figure out that the rapper suffers from asthma, the audience had scattered for miles. At least 26 kids were injured in the panic. (Two passersby on the street freaked out and got run over.) A sophomore tumbled over a wall, broke her neck, and died before anyone spotted her crumpled like a doll on a pile of cinder blocks. Count her as the city's (forever unofficial and uncounted) 37th bird flu fatality.

Lost iPods, tablets, and cell phones lay scattered across campus and down the streets, marking that sad stampede. Lots of shoes, too.

I fear it would be easier for New Yorkers to adapt if more of us were dying. All that's happened so far is that a lot of people are laid-off, schools shut. The viral pace is too slow for a city that likes to get down and move on, to *confront problems* fast. I feel it myself, and I've always predicted a slow climb to catastrophe. This was a sad warm-up.

DAY 10:

AN OUTBREAK OF HISTORY, MINE & OURS

There's lots of dangerous talk about mandating mass quarantines, which no credible experts think can fend off pandemic flu. Beware the kind of governmental exercise that makes uninformed people *feel* a crisis is coming under control.

Look at how quickly Florida's National Guard occupied poor neighborhoods when H5N1 broke out in Miami. Was that a health measure? A bid to intimidate the locals? A kind of coded reassurance to the (distant) general public—a message that order will be maintained by any means necessary?

You may find this hard to believe, but the U.S. government and press *ignored* H1N1 in 1918. Although influenza wound up taking far many more lives than World War I did, the state had already mobilized to fight Germany. One enemy was enough.

On entering World War I in 1917, Washington suppressed free speech and seized thousands of newspapers. A Federally sanctioned private gang called the <u>American Protective League</u> worked with the Attorney General to spy on people and stifle dissent. Lest the pandemic distract the masses from the War Effort, American health officials insisted there was nothing unusual about *that* flu. No one mentioned or reported that U.S. troop ships embarking with healthy draftees were unloading their corpses in Europe— if they hadn't already dumped them at sea.

Ah, but *Spain* was neutral. When H1N1 raged in Madrid—whose papers were allowed to report widespread death—the warring powers' press *discovered* that a *special* flu had erupted *there!* 'Spain' became code for things that couldn't be discussed. A global disease that may well have started in the fields and parade grounds of Kansas thus became known as *the Spanish Flu.*

From SARS to H5N1

A pathologist in Pittsburgh has asked what made me a flu bug.

It began with <u>SARS</u>. When the first case of Severe Acute Respiratory Syndrome was reported in New York, <u>where all diseases turn up</u>, I ordered <u>paper N95 masks</u>. The box didn't reach me till the scare was nearly over.

I started reading about viruses, beginning with Frank Ryan's *Virus X,* a striking exploration of microbes and how the destruction of rain forests may be uncorking nature's antipersonnel devices—viral bombs that defend species we've never even heard of. *Plagues and Peoples* by William H. McNeill taught me how disease has shaped and changed human society from the start. Jared Diamond covered some of this in *Guns, Germs, and Steel,* too. (These books and others I mention are now available for sale on my new <u>Cultural Merchandise Page</u>!)

I discovered that the doctors who first encountered SARS were terrified that it was something called H5N1, which I recalled had killed chickens in Hong Kong. (The story of SARS is vibrantly told in Karl Taro Greenfeld's *China Syndrome.*) After reading John Barry's excellent *The Great Influenza,* I realized that SARS had proved relatively easy to contain because victims showed symptoms *before* they went contagious. In the case of influenza, infectees spread it for days before falling ill—*if they become ill at all.* As many as half the people who carry seasonal flu may never show symptoms. They can pass it along with each breath and handshake.

Obscure Alarmist Makes Good—Finally

After my first year of investigating H5N1, friends stopped humoring me. People emailed articles disparaging *my* pandemic. Lefties said it was a <u>conspiracy by the Bush Gang</u> to profit from Tamiflu. (Successor <u>Barack Obama's portfolio</u> prospered by holding shares in the same company—Gilead—though this didn't bother anyone.) The right-wing John Birch Society called bird flu a scam "to justify expansions of government power and integration of nations." Still, my favorite political comment was that the moral failings of liberals would cause H5N1 to kill more of them. *Are party pollsters tallying fatalities yet?*

After a few H5N1 alarms, pandemic fatigue set in. Americans don't *like* to prepare for the worst; optimism *sells*. If you predict a catastrophe, it had better show up.

Then came the unexpected: swine flu. I stockpiled supplies, began filling orders, and got a <u>Pneumococcus vaccination</u>. (Half of all American seasonal flu victims die from pneumonia.) I took it very seriously.

Gradually scientists came up with lots of reasons why H5N1 would never turn contagious in the ways Pandemic H1N1 was thought to have done in 1918. Nothing fails like failure! Now that humans are finally receptive to H5N1, I look forward to the rush of studies that will explain why it happened.

Now click on Graham Parker's ferocious song about *Protection*.

DAY 11

BE AFRAID—PNEUMONIA FOLLOWS FLU

I'm sorry this comes so late. My roommate interrupted me with a mandate: We had to dress up as a couple on a blind date. She ordained no less than 150 minutes of uninterrupted improvisation while we drank. Excessively, I fear.

The first person to break character would have to spend a painful sum on anything the other wished to order online. No question she'd cash in. So, then, would I, *even if it never arrives....*

I wish I could remember the BS I came up with. She can fling it in her sleep. I fear I was predictable, an East Village guitarist trying to assemble a band. I wore sort of gothic clothes, black boots and cool hat. She began as a fetching, innocent out-of-towner, turned out to be a lass with a past. She loves to lure me to the dark side.

It was hard not to crack up, so she took the prize. Which she instantly spent downloading music. So I feel we both won. *Pandemic Playhouse*: A worthy game for quarantined adults!

I even found out why she doesn't read my blog: She prefers to get her flu information "from the source's mouth."

Now for what I wrote so soberly before she refreshed my mind.

The Puzzle of Pneumovax 23

Readers ask about the pneumonia vaccine I mentioned. I don't normally get flu shots because I prefer to rely on my natural immune response. The eggs in which they grow influenza vaccine haven't been so receptive to avian flu, so I'm not optimistic about a timely H5N1 vaccine.

Man is already striving to dispense with the chickens. Companies are making flu vaccine via something called cell culture. The tobacco industry wants to grow vaccine in a certain leafy crop that's losing its allure. And the corn industry wants to raise flu vaccine for humans and swine in stalks.

Maybe my youth makes me complacent. I share some of Bill Maher's suspicion that too many vaccines might weaken our immune systems. And I'm repelled by arguments such as this one, which compares people who decline vaccination to drunk drivers!

Still, I find Pneumovax compelling. Virtually every H5N1 case includes pneumonia, which is an inflammatory condition with many causes, not a disease. A third of all swine flu pneumonia deaths might have been prevented had the victims been vaccinated against bacterial sources of pneumonia. (The other deaths were caused by viral pneumonia, for which no vaccine exists.)

Since 2001, newborn Americans have been vaccinated against bacterial pneumonia, which globally kills two million kids a year. Merck's Pneumovax 23 shot for adults is stronger, fights 23 different strains with few side effects. Then it can be boosted, reactivated after at least five years. What's an adult not to like?

There's a mystery. The government's advisory committee recommends P 23 shots only for adults who are HIV carriers, are otherwise immunosuppressed, or are *over 65*. Merck's P 23 Web page recommends shots for immunocompetent (healthy) people *50 and older*, says the shot should last up to nine years, and then fuzzes over the question of revaccination.

Part of the problem is that the shots have been around only since the 1980s and the data on the usefulness of boosters is limited. The policy solution seems to be have been to hoard the shots for old folks.

That might be a waste. As this blog entry by Mike Coston explains, a study in Edmonton showed no benefit to people over 65, compared with those who had not received it. This dovetails with evidence that older folks don't show that much response to seasonal flu shots either. Maybe it's all academic. Few people among the recommended groups bother to get Pneumovax 23.

Since none of this makes much sense, I insisted on getting injected in April 2009, when the news broke about swine flu in Mexico. The doctor wasn't happy because I'm so young, but I'm pleased to have done it. P 23 is your call. Don't sue me....

DAY 12-13

A GOOD TURN GOES SOUR IN BROOKLYN

I'm sorry I didn't post last night. I won't lapse again, as long as I'm healthy enough to type and the Internet is up to carrying it. Even in a black-out, I could post by candlelight with a charged laptop; my DSL would function like a telephone landline, albeit without a router.

I went on a mercy mission to someone I've known all my life. He's a bit older than me. Without dwelling on the past, I'll explain that he used to have a lot of problems, which he solved by stumbling into New York's post-9/11 land rush. He found better highs peddling overpriced apartments than he'd ever nailed on the street. For a while, he was so manic his family suspected he'd gone back to dealing drugs after graduating rehab with multiple 'degrees.'

He turned out to be much better at legitimate commerce than he was at mooching and scamming. You can't snort real estate. Within a year he was dressing up to feed underweight models. He endorsed the kind of 'conservatism' that opposes state power except when *you* can use the government to confiscate people's property. He thought Goldwater was a health drink with bling.

My old friend took to lecturing me about the slimmer salary I was making in my own profession. He shrugged off my warnings about a real estate bubble and for a long time he was right. Not even a vertical interest rate chart could dampen demand for his services. When subprime collapsed, he laughed. He wouldn't have sold to *those* people anyway. He could move any high-end property. When foreigners stopped bidding, he caught a bounce doubling down on foreclosed homes in selected neighborhoods.

Having survived swine flu, the guy now sees the avian variety as a buy opportunity. He aims to grab some pricey apartments whose owners leave in a bag.

Even the carnage in the stock market fails to quell his bullishness. Bottom feeders, he says, will soon bid prices back up, as they did after 9/11. "Demand is demand," he grunts, "and I am *da man*." You get dizzy rolling your eyes around him. He doesn't even notice.

My old friend has always been the biggest H5N1 skeptic I know. To start with, anything he doesn't *want* to believe is plain wrong, and he couldn't see how a plague would facilitate his flight to respectability. When the first New Yorkers caught bird flu, he ignored it. When it spread through the city, he blamed *me*.

Then he stopped calling or emailing. Though my girlfriend savored the hiatus (she despises him), I've been trying to reach him for a week.

Yesterday he phoned to ask if I'd bring him some masks, gloves, and goggles. He was more frightened to leave his apartment on the Brooklyn waterfront than I was to leave mine. He wanted a lot of gear for his girlfriend and their closest friends. As a courtesy, of course. He's like family to me, as I guess they are to him.

I donned my protective gear and set out for the condo he acquired four months ago, a small space in a refurbished factory with a world-class view of downtown Manhattan.

On the subway, masked riders were trying to keep distant from those whose faces and hands were naked. Some can't afford to take precautions. Do they resent their shrouded neighbors? Class divisions grow painfully awkward when they become matters of life and death.

I saw parents and children wearing masks like the ones I sell, others with paper masks, and some with nothing. On one platform stood a young couple with a toddler; each wore paper towels fastened with rubber bands around their heads. *They knew and they cared.* I wish their attitude could protect them.

Putting on Airs, Underground

I had to look away, clutching my big opaque bag of masks and gloves and goggles. I had even packed children's masks for my friend's girlfriend's sister's kids.

Adults avoided one another's glances in those swaying cars. Only the children looked around. It was sad to behold their eyes; kids are rarely fooled. The defenseless ones knew the others had something they can't have, something more *important* than a branded shoe. They looked about curiously, politely, helplessly. I wondered if the masked tykes had drippy noses, too. I wanted to make a speech.

There was nothing to say that hasn't been said before. Nothing I believe could have made much difference to them *now*, on that train.

I wish I had quietly taken the rubber-band family aside and given them some gear. When the heart calls, it's best to answer quickly. Or risk hating yourself all night. (In the morning, Ayn Rand will tell you it's all right.)

I reached the condo late. Hard to imagine, but subway service has degenerated.

A House Infested I Couldn't Stand

My friend's girlfriend had been replaced. The one I knew worked for AmEx in human relations or resources or whatever they called personnel last month. She was pretty in a non-descript way (*blonde-descript?*), wore khakis, and left all controversy to my friend. I don't think I'd have recognized her next to me on the subway.

The woman who greeted me at the door was memorable. She was younger, dark-haired, clad in a minimal lace bra. She sustained a pair of his boxers with willpower and cheek. A huge ink angel adorned her naked back, tattooed wing tips dipping to a place I tried not to stare at.

She had never heard of me or my charitable mission, though I'm sure she's heard of American Express. My friend had gone out. She hoped he'd return soon. After about an hour, I realized she didn't know him very well.

I regretted having taken off my gear. I couldn't find soap in the bathroom. The kitchen was full of moldy cardboard takeout cartons and bugs you can see without a microscope.

My friend's cell phone wouldn't answer, but I couldn't leave. Worried, I watched TV from a hard designer stool while she sprawled and slept fitfully on the giant leather sofa. She sniffled a lot. He never returned. At sunrise, I left the bag and went home.

As I scoured my flesh of microbes, scrubbing myself raw, I heard an eerie wailing. It wasn't my cat. He was crouched on his sill in the bedroom, listening warily to what must have been a woman down the block, moaning in musical scales.

My girlfriend explained she's heard it several times, always around 8 a.m.—unless I'm snoring. (A *lie!*) She's lacked sympathy of late. This morning she was icy. Still is.

DAY 14

IS THE THEATER ON FIRE YET? SHHHH....

I was awakened by a *Bring Out Your Dead* parade led by a mad bearded monk with a flute and featuring carts hauled by chanting people dressed as donkeys. In better days, I might have tossed eggs or fruit, but I can't afford to waste any. I confess that I considered dipping into my cornucopia of cat dung. Imagine watching someone die of H5N1 while your neighbors stage public jokes about the murdering microbes. Sounds like something gays went through in the 1980s.

The jesters are lucky they didn't try dancing in Phoenix, where the sheriff's department has been shooting people who won't stay home—or who won't *leave* their homes. (Frankly, the orders did sound confusing, and I'm a native English speaker.) That's after *12* confirmed cases in the whole city.

I'm never been a big fan of government. (To me, Original Sin is that we need it.) I do accept that researching and fighting disease are reasonable state functions. I was sad to realize years ago that the U.S. Centers for Disease Control & Prevention might not be much use in an old-fashioned crisis.

The CDC was the world's premier disease-assessment institution until it refocused on terrorism after 9/11. (The same thing happened to FEMA, the Federal Emergency Management Agency; after 9/11 it was made part of the Department of Homeland Security, which in New Orleans turned out to know or care little about helping civilians after a natural disaster.) The CDC's budget was reduced. Shrinking slices went to 'disease control.'

Soon after the anthrax mailings that followed 9/11, the CDC managed to convince Florida to embrace its Model State Emergency Health Powers Act, which entitles bureaucrats to order the examination, medication, isolation, and vaccination of private citizens—even if they aren't ill. The law exempts aggressive officials and medical personnel from being sued if they, for instance, *kill* you. Other states chose to ignore the proposal. (New York's legislature considered MSEHPA a few times, then lapsed back to sleep.) Now legislatures are taking up statutes like it with ghastly enthusiasm.

Fight Flu, Not People

I do not—and will never—endorse mandatory vaccination for anyone.

Be warned, in fact, that great drama will surround efforts to devise H5N1 vaccines. The research and development always takes longer than experts predict. The government will promise too much, too fast. The vaccine will be late. Any shot addressing such an unfamiliar flu strain might contain unpopular side effects.

Antivaxers around the world are already organizing to denounce the shortcuts governments and corporations are preparing to embrace in the rush to cook up vaccines. That fuss over swine flu immunity was *nothing* compared to what's coming.

Finally, flu shots are less effective than the public thinks.

Next: a scary lecture on why no one should be getting pregnant.

DAY 15

SORRY, FLU IS RISKIEST FOR THOSE PREGNANT

I've spooked women of childbearing age. Even my pregnant cousin in Washington wrote to express alarm. (Didn't know she was pregnant or reading this thing!) I'm sorry, but flu foils the fundamental mechanism by which women manage to contain fetuses. Pregnant women ranked first among 1918 pandemic flu casualties. Almost 70% who caught H1N1 died. Many flu survivors lost their babies.

The problem is that in order to conceive and carry an alien fetal entity—a baby—to term, the mother must <u>allow her immune system to suppress any response</u> that might harm it. Once this defenselessness allows influenza to infect her, the flu stirs up an immune response that damages the fetus.

Schizophrenia is one of the greatest risks to surviving fetuses. A University of Wisconsin study found that the offspring of monkeys infected with mild flu developed brains with "features similar to those seen in people with schizophrenia, including less gray matter in the cortex and enlarged ventricles," as <u>reported in *New Scientist*</u>.

A lot of embryos endured 1918, but went on to suffer lifelong physical and mental damage. A <u>health study</u> showed that people born—or conceived—during the 1918 pandemic tended to be plagued by terrible problems, regardless of class, race, or gender. Compared with people born earlier or conceived later, the Great Pandemic's babies proved less likely to finish high school. They earned less money, used more public assistance, and matured as sicklier adults. One fifth more of them contracted diabetes by age 61.

Not that nature can't be unpredictably kind. <u>Maurice Hilleman</u> was born on August 30, 1919—conceived between pandemic outbreaks and borne as a fetus through the Great Pandemic's third wave. Hilleman survived the immediate deaths of his twin sister and mother, then spent the next 85 years inventing dozens of vaccines, including those for mumps, measles, hepatitis A and B, meningitis, chickenpox, pneumonia, and the *Haemophilus influenzae* bacteria.

All influenza varieties seem capable of damaging embryos. <u>Britain's leading charity for parents dove into hot water</u> when it urged women to postpone having babies during the swine flu outbreak. H5N1 pregnancies documented by the WHO have entailed fetal destruction; in most cases the mother died, too.

Exposure to *seasonal* flu during the first trimester of pregnancy has been <u>reported</u> to make people up to seven times more likely to suffer schizophrenia or autism. A <u>University of Minnesota study</u> of mice found that H1N1 influenza caused genetic damage that significantly shrank the fetal hippocampus.

What's good—or bad—for mice often fails to register in people. But <u>another study</u> showed that H5N1 passed right through a Chinese woman's placenta to damage multiple organs in her fetus, including its brain.

Short of shunning all intimacy with men, the only protection for women is reliable birth control. Steely abstinence can be tough in close quarters.

Toxic Kitties?

While looking into those issues, I coincidentally discovered that exposure to cats can be risky for pregnant women, too. I knew that felines could catch and probably spread bird flu, but I never knew they could also give babies schizophrenia and/or bipolar disorder. Then I spotted a <u>passing crack by top flu fighter Robert Webster</u> in an old interview.

In disbelief, I googled *cats & schizophrenia* and found a mother lode of reports. <u>Pregnant women should shun cats that might recently have caught a mouse or rat</u> that carried the protozoa toxoplasma gondii. Exposure can cause brain damage, even death.

<u>Toxoplasma</u> is a tricky parasite that spreads via a protein that rodents

pick up from eating cat dung. It <u>makes them fearless around felines</u>—first by unwiring the part of their brain that responds to fear and anxiety and then by using <u>dopamine</u> to make cat urine sexually attractive to them. When our cats take advantage of the brazen mice, the little killers catch, replicate, and shed the protein for a brief time. Though cat fur seems not to carry active eggs, and *most humans catch the parasite by eating undercooked meat*, it can be dangerous to handle infected kitty dung that's been lying around for more than a day. (Cats that already contain the antibody are safe.)

Infection causes flu-like symptoms and sometimes damages the eye. Any creature with the parasite will forever contain cysts. These were long deemed not to cause symptoms.

Now I see that <u>a Czech scientist</u> claims toxoplasmic men tend to be more aggressive and *dumber*—not to mention slovenly and suspicious of authority. Infected women are said to be more aggressive and *smarter*, friendlier and more promiscuous. The condition is said to slow human reactions, contributing to car crashes. More than 80% of all French and Germans are infected, about twice the American rate.

My daddy loves rare meat, and my stepmom's a closet catlady. Do I come off as a rebellious psycho? Huh? *Who says?*

DAY 16

SURE, I'M A FLUNKY FOR FELINES

Last night's scribble triggered the biggest response yet. Women were appalled at the thought that—all birds and virions aside—*Fluffy* could turn embryos into trailer trash.

The solution was to shoot the messenger: me. My assertion that someone's furry bedmate could set her fetus on the path to psychological and economic ruin was too much for an astounding 11 readers. *Hit those links, folks.* I make sure to post them when I expect people to think I'm crazy, which proves that I'm not, doesn't it? *Hehe....*

I am extremely fond of cats. Yet I'm no sycophant. I know kitties for what they are—our narcissistic masters. It's become clear in recent years that <u>cats teamed up with us</u> 10,000 years ago—they volunteered to keep our granaries and towns free of rodents and we respected and fed them.

No other mammal *initiated* its domestic relationship with mankind. (Some say dogs came in from the cold, too, but others contend that canines were captured and bred selectively to perform tasks; <u>bone traces found in human dung</u> show that pre-Texans probably bred dogs to eat 9,400 years ago.)

My resident feline is gray with black stripes and a broad white chin. For all his splendor, he's a mutt I recovered from a Brooklyn junkyard. He'd never tolerate the words *rescue* or *save*; the greater pleasure was mine. For all I know, he thinks he was catnapped.

He sports a big nose and a calm, frank gaze that belies an aptitude for scheming. It wasn't without provocation that I named him. I'll blow a smidgeon of my cover by telling you: *Sneeky Pete.*

When you bring a dog into your home, it wanders about, looking back to see if you approve. The tiniest kitten will explore a new domain with eyes only for entertainment and food. It looks back to see which of these you intend to provide first.

Sneeky disdains my advanced degree, the student loans I'm still paying, the efforts I make to keep house. He watches me sift his litter with fascination and disgust. I think he considers me a useful pervert.

Cat Lovers: The New Litterati

I owe it to my blue-eyed lord to keep him inside, distant from anything that might bring H5N1 into the bubble he kindly shares with us. (Some cats and dogs caught swine flu from their keepers.) While it gnaws at me that *mice can catch H5N1, too,* I count on Sneeky's unnatural disinterest in rodents to keep us out of trouble. Our historic symbiosis means little to him.

Cats don't shed H5N1 in enormous quantities. It might not take much if you sleep with one that hunts. You owe it to your pets (dogs, hamsters, guinea pigs, ferrets, etc.) to keep them safe until animal vaccines for H5N1 are developed and distributed. With seven billion humans praying for a people vaccine, that will take years.

Your pets never needed you more than they do now. Even if they'll never admit it.

DAY 17

DIY, A CAUSE THAT REFRESHES

I've received an unsigned email I'd like to answer. A reader from *my own neighborhood* wrote to question the assertion by the Czech scientist that toxoplasmosis makes men slovenly and rebellious. "If 80% of Germans have it, where did all those scrubbed Hitler Youth come from? Wasn't obedience the problem there?" A good point that any Czech should know well.

The message went on to challenge my statement a week ago that no one was organizing volunteers. "Right under your preachy nose we've started distributing food and medical supplies to people who can't help themselves. If your feet still function, you will find our tables at Tompkins Square Park and Astor Place. You should get some exercise and share some of the equipment you thoughtfully accumulated. Donate masks to your neighbors. Especially children."

The writer is apparently a woman, to judge from her conceptual handle. A spirited one.

I was delighted to read about her group, the Lower East Side Do It Yourself Committee. I instantly googled and found notices for meetings and handouts at historic St. Mark's-in-the-Bowery (actually located on Second Avenue). The idea that some of my neighbors recognize the peril and are taking care of themselves seemed revolutionary. I was inspired to venture forth.

This took willpower. I wasted two hours. Tidying up. Trying to start conversations with my girlfriend, who thinks it's risky. Petting Sneeky. Choosing from the limited selection of excursion clothes by the door. (What's this week's New Black?) Poking my phone for incoming orders. Eventually I wondered if I'd developed agoraphobia. *That* got me moving.

DIY in the Sun

A blast of sunlight blinded me as I descended to the vestibule. My heart thumped wildly. Not from fear—more like a four-year-old kid's at first light on Christmas. I tore off my jacket in the doorway and floated down the street in the warmest rays I've felt since the February thaw. I felt blessed by the sun. Imagine the tan we'd get wearing only masks, goggles, and gloves.

The LES DIY has potential. Some of their literature blames the government for whatever's gone wrong, but that's how most people think around here. Once they get past yearning for Big Brother to do more, they get down to business—which assumes we need to do just about everything for ourselves. Yay!

The group is enlisting volunteers to help folks obtain food and medicine. There were so many people surrounding the table at the park that I couldn't reach the woman tending it. *What I don't touch or breathe can't kill me.* At Astor Place I encountered a table manned by a drummer who used to shake his hair with various bands at the Lakeside Lounge when he wasn't shooting pool around the corner. Today, he was friendly and efficient under a gleaming tattooed skull.

The LES DIY sells Dr. Grattan Woodson's *Good Home Treatment Of Influenza* (<u>free download</u>) for little more than the copying cost. They have a signup list for people who've recovered from H5N1 and who feel safe circulating. There were few names. I offered to donate some masks for the volunteers.

Then I bought some fish. Small wonder that seafood sells at black market prices these days. *Certifiably free of bird flu!* But wild salmon for $42 a pound? The vendors shrug impressively. I found some farmed tilapia at the old free-range salmon price. My moody roommate marinated it in a decent white wine while we guzzled the rest of the bottle.

That proved relaxing enough for me to tell her about my stroll. I'm thinking we should take walks together, enveloped in protective gear like lunar explorers as we mutter sweet nuffings. *A small step for man, a giant step for romance.* My cute alien seems intrigued.

DAY 18

KATRINA HITS ST. LOUIS?

My neighbor wailed all morning. It's really disturbing. I arose hung over, discovered the news stories from St. Louis. I have family thereabouts. I haven't been able to reach them by phone but I hear they're okay. *So far.*

The media sucks at explaining what's happening there. Web sources indicate that the case fatality rate has shot up to something like 20% in some areas. Bloggers say there's looting in blacked-out areas—even in the suburbs, where an SUV carries lot more swag than a shopping cart. One says immigrants are being rounded up and dumped in camps, which would demand a ridiculous diversion of public safety resources.

Let's hope these reports are inflated and that the Missouri National Guard can stabilize things without making them worse. The images of those kids in paper masks clutching loaded M16s were the scariest I've seen since the pandemic started. I was reminded of an early scene from George Romero's _Dawn of the Dead_, when young Guardsmen prepare to storm an inner city housing project whose tenants won't give up their living dead. (What follows—trailer here—chased the _New York Times_ film critic out of the theater.)

These are moments when society gets naked. Knots of power are stripped bare, exposed as incompetent, inadequate. We see the agents of order lost and frightened as the citizens in greatest need are forced to fend for themselves. We've all heard those New Orleans blues, seen people on American rooftops waving from another world: the land of _Katrina_.

DAY 19

VIRUSES? THINK MOTIVATED INFORMATION UNITS

My parents interrupted this morning's mournful cries to say they've escaped to a summer cabin in the Ozarks, so I've resumed breathing and sleeping. For once I understand how people feel when their own lives pop up on news screens, sensationalized by idiots. For too many hours the media made Missouri sound like the 10th circle of hell.

While I was freaking out about my family, my girlfriend offered some 'reassuring' observations that made me realize how poorly viruses are understood. We wound up arguing frenetically about stuff I didn't comprehend so well myself. Cabin fever fosters hotheaded debate.

When she started hurling my collection of H5N1 books at me, I took refuge on the Web. In addition to some wretched virus jokes, I found out that viruses might be the missing link! Read on....

Influenza may be a fancy-sounding name, but it hides a primitive medieval belief that the sickness was caused by the _influence_ of the planets on our bodily fluids. We now know it as a virus first isolated in 1930 (*that* one was a swine flu) and then in 1933 (the human kind), long after top scientists had spent the Great Pandemic seeking a bacterial cause.

Our understanding of the physical forces of life is still arguably medieval, reminiscent of when any returning Crusader could become a local expert on foreign policy, geography, and cuisine.

Back in those flat-earth days, the word *virus* connoted a slimy, offensive, or poisonous liquid, taste, or odor. The vagueness of the description fits an entity that is far tinier than bacteria and which no man could see until the electron microscope was invented. Much the way man's understanding of earth's geography was limited—then enhanced—by the tools to explore it, technology defines our progress in charting the viral universe. Here's <u>a glimpse of painstaking progress</u> by Dr. W. Ian Lipkin, a pioneering microbe hunter who later helped devise the killer virus for the movie, *Contagion*.

Humans harbor an unfortunate tendency to *think* that what we know is sufficient. People who admit they don't know what to do about our problems rarely get to pontificate on TV. It's expensive and unpopular to concede ignorance.

When it comes to viruses, we're still flying in a thick fog.

For one thing, viruses don't please us by fulfilling the <u>positive functions that bacteria perform</u> in soil, in air, in our stomachs. Try googling for *benevolent virus.* You'll find loads of entries debating the merits of computer bugs. And a handful about research efforts such as a 2008 breakthrough in which scientists in Japan and Pennsylvania managed to improve the sight of some blind people by injecting their eyes with <u>genetically engineered adenoviruses</u>. A second genetically modified virus was used to create metallic wires for a <u>working nanoscale battery</u> that might power solar cells.

The Joy of Herpes

Some viruses may shield us from unwelcome bacteria. Scientists in St. Louis have established that the <u>family of herpes viruses protects mice</u> from bacteria that cause bubonic plague, as well as a type of food poisoning. Might herpes protect people too? The symbiotic virtues of viruses aren't so easily established. Anyway, most American adults have already caught herpes, which is associated with blindness, deafness, cancer, encephalitis, itching, and acute sensitivity to disclosure.

An interesting possibility that surfaced during the swine flu pandemic is that catching a rhinovirus—a primary agent of the 'incurable' common cold—may protect against pandemic influenza. From Philadelphia to France and Sweden, doctors noted <u>delays in flu's onset</u> among populations struck by an aggressive rhinovirus. One virus is fascinating; the interactions of two are downright obscure.

Some scientists contend viruses blew in from outer space. Others say they're malignant parasites. A bold few claim viruses are the source of all life on this planet. Experts tend to clear their throats before they try to explain—unless their problem is a *rhino*virus. (Human metapneumo virus, a different agent of the common cold, <u>diverged from birds</u> a mere 120 years ago.)

As Frank Ryan details so well in *Virus X: Tracking the New Killer Plagues*, a virus is a tiny molecular entity that flourishes amid the stuff of life—DNA and RNA—without conducting any of the activities we regard as normal. Viruses don't even have tails. They require other entities to move them (*achoo!*) so they can keep replicating, which is all they do. (*A Pope's wet dream!*)

Amoral Operating System Seeks Hard Drive

Viruses are hardly primitive. They are as Darwinian as an entity can be.

Ryan takes pains to emphasize that what he calls their "genomic executive intelligence" has no moral values. They are *amoral*, much the way a digital virus doesn't care whose PC it infects or how it affects us. A virus is an operating system in search of a hard drive.

Most viruses seem to display no dismal effects in their hosts. (Influenza briefly gives young ducks a mild stomach disorder.) Many viruses fall apart quickly without a carrier. Others can float dormant in nature until they sense an appropriate host at hand—a cell in which they can copy themselves. Then they swing into play. <u>Varicella zoster</u> causes chicken pox and can then go dormant for many years until it erupts as <u>shingles</u>.

Given its need for a host, influenza has to be regarded as a pretty 'smart' virus: People and birds circulate extremely well on our planet and must be regarded as brilliantly chosen hosts.

Scientists fight over how to classify viruses. They're constantly trying to neaten up the tree of life as our infant tools for genetic analysis force the reconsideration of links among various plant and animal groups. (They've found a <u>close kinship</u> between *Tyrannosaurus rex* and our humble friend, the chicken.)

Again, the confusion reminds me of a map of earth, where my own continental mass is named after a lesser explorer who arrived late. (What *did* *Amerigo Vespucci* find?) Other names that once made sense stopped doing so long ago: *Greenland* is icy (this year) while *Iceland* is green*er* (this year).

Our tree of life hasn't included trunks or limbs for these molecular clusters of protein-coated DNA or RNA. By our standards, viruses are neither alive nor dead. They don't replicate through cell division.

Lacking the structures and practices that mankind generally accepts as the basis of life, viruses operate like pirates. They hijack cells, inject their own genetic material, and start generating copies. They don't leave fossils, so we've barely begun to study how they mutate over time.

Thus far, we've classified some 4,000 viruses. There are *billions* on this planet. Pioneering genetic researcher J. Craig Venter mounted an expedition that doubled the number of known genes in earth's biosphere during a single sea voyage.

Mimivirus: Our Long-Lost Mother?

Until very recently, it was comfortably assumed that viruses were subordinate to—dependent upon—the three official branches of life. These are: organisms whose cells have a nucleus; single-celled bacteria that may or may not possess a nucleus; and a very old line of microbes with no nuclei.

Then a stunning viral specimen turned up inside an amoebic bacterium in an industrial cooling tower in England. The sample wound up in Marseilles, where scientists were thrilled to discover a gigantic virus three times the size of any other. It was larger than some bacteria.

Dubbed mimivirus because it was deemed to mimic bacteria, the discovery turned out to contain more than 1,200 genes that can do all kinds of things scientific classification had reserved for the 'superior' life forms. More significantly, mimivirus shares seven genes with all three of life's primary domains (the ones with and without nuclei).

Some very sharp scientists have come to think that a virus such as mimivirus might have provided the missing link in the formation of life on earth. *Forget monkeys*—mere tools. We may have descended from viruses that drifted in from outer space, invaded primitive cells, and stirred the infamous primordial soup. Unless even *those* cells descended from viruses....

Everything I just wrote should be outmoded, discarded—deemed laughably ignorant—in 20 years. Or two. *That's* how much we know about viruses.

It's a lot more than my girlfriend knows. She's still storming around, kvetching about the weeping woman, and pressing me to vacate her keyboard. *Done.*

DAY 20

AN AMERICAN DREAMER'S BEST-LAID FLU PLANS

Some country folk ask how we manage to share such confined territory. I should explain that under normal circumstances—Sneeky and I occupying three rooms and a bathroom—my home is relatively spacious for Manhattan. It shrinks dramatically when you factor in the loving roommate and the boxes of provisions and protective gear.

It takes your breath away when there's no leaving it. We change when we're locked up.

My girlfriend is by nature outgoing, an adventuress who instinctively engages strangers. She loves to find out what makes people tick, what they're good at, how they can amuse. If all else fails, she launches terrible puns, which at least make people laugh nervously.

On the two occasions we left the city together, she was unforgettably lively company. She tells good stories, gets people to open their doors and minds. She dreams of a life well traveled.

I love to take trips, but I don't mind staying home, reading, researching, playing games, goofing off together. She likes to read, too—on the road.

Now she has contracted a nasty case of claustrophobia. She tries to deal with it. As do I.

I hope the pandemic takes its inevitable break before it strangles her. I reckon the first wave will end in a month or so. In the meantime, I wish she'd stop being rude to my partner. His visits are unbearably tense. They snap at each other's comments the way lizards zap flies. All that cringing hurts my neck.

Some city folk ask how someone who knew this pandemic was coming wound up trapped in Manhattan. Great question! I always intended to rent a place upstate, not far from a UPS center and not close to many people. I acquired an old car so Sneeky and I could ride out the plague in rural comfort. Solitude has its charms.

I was confident I could make a good living by saving lives—selling protective gear from a prudent distance. Still, I arranged some remote work in my profession. (It quickly fell through when the pandemic broke out: Projects were frozen, contractors eliminated.)

I Fell in Love Instead

You'd think someone who was planning to withdraw from his known world would have enough sense to practice isolation in advance. Well, I *did*. I wooed the Internet.

I founded a site about the music and life of <u>Gene Clark</u>. (Here's <u>a site that deservedly outlasted mine</u>.) Clark was the coolest member of the original <u>Byrds</u> and he wrote most of the songs that weren't rented from Dylan. (Watch his great <u>live vocal performance</u>—amid go-go dancers—on the Byrds' second-ever appearance on TV.)

Clark was taking home the hottest women and the bulk of the publishing money till the other Byrds made him unwelcome. Clark wrote most of <u>the lyrics</u> to *Eight Miles High* (hear <u>the band's original, better, unofficial version</u>) before leaving to pursue a solo career that went unthinkably unappreciated. (My site was unseen, too, but I think I'll add his music to <u>my already legendary Cultural Merchandise Page</u>.)

I also spent hours every day on the flu boards, signed onto friends' networks, all that. I might as well slap clichés together—I explored <u>social distancing</u> via social networking. Call it 'Safe Friendship.' All those buddies would come in handy on the distant rural pandemic nights when Sneeky didn't feel like talking.

I encountered a woman in Los Angeles, a friend of a friend of someone or other. She posted smart and funny and unpredictable things and seemed bored out there. We were headed in opposite directions, career-wise. Neither seemed to think the other was wrong.

After pursuing art dance for years, she was developing promotional software for a big bank. I was abandoning my professional avocation to commit to my own dream, my own business. (If I survive bird flu, I'll reenter that profession with enough to live on for a couple of years while I try to do it my way.)

My new correspondent delighted in mocking my obsession with H5N1. Early on, her grandparents coincidentally sent her some of the masks I sell; she accused me of bamboozling the aged and demanded a refund—in person—in LA.

Banned in Austin

That caught my eye. Which she then pinned to the screen with a stream of peculiar emails, IMs, and photos she hadn't posted for the public. (They weren't obscene, just brimming with character.) Her eyes were dark and suggestive in a wise, angelic face that could otherwise adorn a Jane Austin movie. She'd been cursed with smoldering black holes in a mask of enlightened and accomplished femininity.

She was proud of her refocused ambition and she wanted a lot from her new life. She liked that I was fanatical, too.

By the time we started calling one another, interest was keen. Her voice was breathy, suggestive. I remember dreaming that we met by a river. Rushing waters drowned out what we were trying to say, so we swam together. She was light and shadow in liquid motion. I was happy.

Soon we met here. It turned out she'd been planning to leap to a bigger bank in New York. I hosted her while she cased the institution, which had cheated me badly on credit interest after the first crash.

She left my apartment only to eat and to be interviewed by ever-more-prominent players in the organization. Those bankers loved her as much as I did, although they got more sleep. (I was busy adding color to her cheeks.) She won the job, though it took a few extra days to authorize the salary she was demanding. I was awed by her confidence. She was a high-performing virus who'd found a good cell in their operating system. "A good start" is how she put it.

We celebrated their surrender till after dawn. (Hung)over brunch, it became obvious that I should invite her to live in my apartment while I prepared to head upstate to ride out the plague she didn't believe in. The longer H5N1 took to cross over from the chickens and pigs, the more I'd visit her here.

She hinted at fleeing with me if H5N1 did break out. But she isn't the type to run. (She admires Ayn Rand, too.) I turned out not to be the type to run off on her. Here I am.

Heck, let's call her Nina—short for _Ninotchka_. She'd like that. She turned me on to the old Greta Garbo comedy when she moved in.

Our isolation began like a low-budget romantic adventure flick. This is the first time I've lived with a lover. It's been exciting.

DAY 21

LIFE IN THE CARDBOARD MOUNTAINS

When H5N1 actually sprang, I think I was a little dazed. How could I leave Nina? I stayed put, started the blog weeks ago. That's where you all came in.

Nina's bank planned for a lot of employees to telecommute during the emergency. Until the dust settles, she'll work on state-of-the-art marketing ploys from my walkup in a recovered crack house. It's not as if they're going to launch this year.

A month of enforced intimacy has been tough. I suspect we're each accustomed to prompting others to leave us alone when we don't feel like communicating. That's not possible in three cramped rooms occupied by that many strong-willed creatures.

A more recent complication is that Nina hates it when I go out. I don't understand why it makes her so nervous. (She's not overjoyed when I'm home, either.) She denies that she minds my occasional forays into the real world, but coming home is getting strange.

We take turns working in my living room under looming stacks of protective gear. Nina uses her iMac during working hours; it's 'mine' all night. I cook in the kitchen under piles of household supplies. (She's accustomed to eating out or ordering in.) Joined by the cat for family hour, we dine in the bedroom under a mountain of boxes she brought from LA. I've run out of exciting recipes. Alcohol is no longer much consolation. It's merely necessary.

I meet the shipping people in the hallway and reenter to scrub off as she taps away on her iMac.

We have principled differences, of course. Nina loathes Sneeky's array of empty cardboard boxes, calls it *Kitty Waco* in honor of the Branch Davidian compound that the Feds attacked in Texas. She doesn't get Gene Clark at all, says there's no beats. At 19, Clark and the Byrds brought Dylan to the masses—and all she cares about is *beats*?

Nina finds my breakfast of granola, rice milk (keeps till you open it, no nasty hormones), and dried fruit (tasty, nutritious, and easily stored) unthinkable. Perhaps because she's got some Russian blood, she favors a diet I call *Cream of Bacon*, tough to fulfill these days. Does she slip out to forage for bootleg fried chicken while I sleep?

H5N1 has hideously weakened her impact on the bank. My city can't entertain. Her friends are in California and Europe. She's working through our wine supply faster than I had anticipated.

He Who Detected it....

Nina had barely heard of bird flu before I mentioned it in an email, had it mixed up with SARS, probably chicken pox, too. I remember her asking if I was a "movie-of-the-week freak." She loathes hypochondriacs—maybe people who are genuinely sick, too.

I fear I am *The Father of H5N1* in her eyes: *He who detected it infected it.* Subconsciously, she blames me for the whole crisis.

She's lost interest in chess. She sets romantic comedies up for me to view in bed. I watch actors fall in and out of love and wonder what she meant to suggest as she snores through happy endings. Eyes ablaze with borrowed pixels, Sneeky stares at us from the windowsill. Our neighbor's dog cries out to distant shut-in pals. Pets on my block want to know what's gone wrong.

Living with a person is challenging. Having to stay with them 24/7 is deadening, especially when it feels as if they don't like you.

This disease will turn us into cellmates. *I hate it, too, Nina.*

DAY 22

COFFEE AND A SMILE CURE ME

I couldn't sleep all morning, certain Nina was reading my sad account of love in the time of H5N1. I cascaded through clicks as she worked, or interfaced, or IM'd her pals. I expected to wake up to a harangue, a torrent of accusations. Or worse, alone.

She greeted me in a good mood, bearing a big mug of my favorite health drink, <u>coffee</u> (which <u>fights liver disease</u>, among its many benefits). I've learned to appreciate a happy Nina without asking questions.

We even went for a walk. I've been thinking she may be depressed for want of sunlight.

We enjoyed our escape, although the East Village looks shabby and lots of places are closed. I ran into a friend who talked so fast we couldn't wait to get away. It was *almost* a relief to discover that everyone else has gone nuts, too. Nina smiled a lot. Gleaming dark eyes lit up her goggles. She took my hand. We couldn't wait to get home but we took our time anyway.

We bared our teeth and lips, kissed all over the East Village. I'd completely forgotten the thrills of public microbialism.

I shouldn't have posted all those things about her yesterday. We barely knew one another when we got into this. When the First Wave subsides, I hope she and I recover our souls during the hiatus. We can learn to explore better, trust more, take more pleasure surviving Wave Two.

It really was an excellent day here!

DAY 23

APOCALYPSE? YOU AIN'T SEEN NOTHING YET

Prolonged rain has turned my abode into a dank sarcophagus. It reeks of still, dead air. There's no point in sneaking out, nothing to gaze upon below. There's little news. We've stopped talking, meowing, grunting, snoring, playing music. Even the sad woman has lost her voice. Silence reigns. And rankles.

A propitious time to consider Doom!

Odds are that, whatever you believe, you personally *feel* that the problems we face today are far worse than usual and that some kind of ruinous reckoning impends. You could be religious, secular, Green, Lavender—or Red, White & Blue. Your toilet paper may derive from recycled newsprint, or your SUV might sport a sticker that says *Out of Work and Hungry? Eat an Environmentalist!*

You may be a born-again Christian anticipating the Rapture, a New Age devotee of the Mayan calendar, an expansionist Israeli Jew, a Muslim awaiting the Mahdi, or a hardcore materialist watching icecaps melt.

You think the end of the world is coming. *Soon.*

A lot of people have pitched cataclysms over the years. In 1831 an Upstate New York preacher named <u>William Miller</u> started heralding the Second Coming. People sold their businesses and homes to await Christ in accordance with Miller's Biblical arithmetic. When 1843 failed to yield the Apocalypse he'd predicted, Miller announced that his count was off by a year. October 22, 1844 brought 'The Great Disappointment.' As many as 100,000 spent the evening on hillsides awaiting the Light. Miller spent years explaining he'd fixed on that date because his followers had done so; it seemed a sign from God.

The Bahai think the Savior did turn up that day, but in Persia.

More recently, Sun Myung Moon predicted that the Kingdom of Heaven would begin its reign in 1981. Moon was an honored guest at President Reagan's inauguration that January. Things must have seemed awfully promising for the self-styled 'Savior' till the Justice Department threw him in prison for tax fraud. Ronald Wilson Reagan had *three sixes* to his name....

None of the forecasts have come true. So why leave Apocalypse to the professionals? Ordinary folks wish to play an active, democratic role in the process of terminating our pathetic existence.

So it is that missionaries trawl New York's subways in search of Jews to convert to Christianity because *The Book of Revelation* says 12,000 Jews from each of the 12 tribes (good luck, *most of those tribes haven't been seen for millennia*) must accept Christ in order to facilitate the Apocalypse. Some Israelis want to blow up the mosque complex that lies atop the wrecked Temple of Solomon so they can rebuild the latter.

The End: Our Only Friend?

Christian American farmers are trying to breed perfect red heifers whose ashes are needed to purify the Jews who would pray in that new temple. Why such ecumenical charity? These dispensationalists think it will bring on the Antichrist.

I know that sounds counterproductive, but it's supposed to *force* Jesus to return in the Second Coming. Perhaps annoyed that His followers are so pushy, He is expected to liquidate any Jews who don't convert. (At least Christians and Jews agree on the first, uh, *constructive* part.)

Not to be left out, Muslims concur that Christ will reappear, but as an Islamic prophet betokening the Final Judgment. So if Christ does return, either a billion Muslims or a billion Christians will be disappointed in His religious disposition.

It's easy enough for secular folks, if any still exist, to laugh at all of this. But Karl Marx was an outspoken atheist, and his most positive predictions reek of prophecy and Apocalypse. (After certain tribulations, eternal justice for workers!)

Today's atheists, agnostics, humanists, and whatchamacallits preach that The End Is Near, too. Secular Apocalyptics assert that their own exciting views of catastrophe are rooted in science and measurable observation. ("But Glacier National Park used to feature *glaciers!*")

My favorite path to secular meltdown is as big as anything the Evangelicals embrace. Referring to a quantum physics principle that says particles function differently when we measure them, two Midwestern professors suggested that by noting the existence of dark matter in 1998, mankind may have drastically reduced the odds that the *universe* will ever stabilize from the Big Bang. (Yeah, it's complicated.) Since aliens somewhere are gauging matter, too, I'm thinking this particular End won't really be *our* fault.

Human society can't have known many times in which *everyone*—from religious fanatics to logical materialists—agreed about doom. Bird flu freaks don't even rate. We regard H5N1 as a passing phenomenon, horrific but endurable (if you're lucky).

The Book of Revelation does mention four horsemen of the Apocalypse, and one of them is often said to be *Pestilence*. But only Death is named in the text. The identity of the other riders is, um, guesswork, divination.

So what can it mean for a society—for the *world*—when everyone but Buddhists and the occasional atheistic Republican who disbelieves in global warming agrees that the game is over?

More on this next time … *if there is a next time.*

DAY 24:

C'MON OVER, THE WATER'S GREAT

The little woman across the street plays piano while the man gazes at a screen, light flickering across his gleaming face. She plays classical stuff I hear faintly if I watch very closely. Her bald guy can't hear it because he's wearing earphones. Is rudeness a new avian flu symptom?

I shall now respond politely to some questions.

First, we all speak a little Yiddish in New York, the world's biggest Jewish city. It's lively and expressive. You need to know what people are calling you. Even a hick like me learns some. TV viewers everywhere do, too: Tell me *you* don't know a *schlemiel* from a *schmoozer, spiel* from *schmaltz.* (Jewish humor was born amid a three-year massacre in Ukraine in the 17th century, according to a Berkeley professor.)

As a child, my closest exposure to Jewishness was playing Joseph in the Christmas Pageant. (It *sounded* like a big role.) So yeah, I was raised Catholic and I'm entitled to make cracks about the Pope. I earned the privilege on my knees, serving mass.

Third, I love dogs. Nor is my "absorption" with my cat unhealthy. *Enough!*

Fourth, I'm not "rooting" for bird flu to kill anyone. I don't need calamities to sustain my ego. I'm spreading information that can help people survive, whether or not they buy anything from me.

Fifth, the emails that do not threaten me display an unexpected and unwholesome interest in my personal life and views.

Still, I'm grateful for the positive reviews of my report about bringing my old friend some protective gear. I haven't been able to reach him since. I'm not sure he ever got home. I think it must be easier to buy narcotics than legal drugs. (*Wrong powder, dude!*)

I did write short stories in college. My teachers admired them. Friends and family were enraged. (*Of course I changed their names!*) I thought it best to learn a proper profession. Now look at me, antagonizing my customers.

To the nice ones, I apologize, as always. For the man who asked for my personal information, I reiterate that my lover is a woman. For the woman who asked for my personal information, flattery will get you nowhere. See above.

For the woman who said she'd rather see her lungs dissolve in bloody paste than put a penny in my pocket, I've sold 256 masks since you hit *send*. I hope you survive.

More practical readers inquire about safe drinking water. In the best of times, that's a scary topic. You should know that 49 million Americans were exposed to significant levels of dangerous substances in their drinking water from 2004 to 2009. Few water system operators were exposed, let alone punished. A 2010 study found hexavalent chromium, a probable carcinogen, in the drinking water of 31 out of 35 American cities sampled.

If your tap features arsenic (even 'acceptable levels,' as many do) you should consider that mice have been shown to be more likely to catch influenza after drinking water with arsenic exposure equivalent to what's found in many private wells in New Hampshire.

A Swimming Pool in Every Tap

Some municipalities have been declaring turbidity alerts. When your system tells you to boil water, it's breaking down. Take it seriously—especially if it's one of those that now recycle sewage, as they do in Orange County, California.

I barely notice these issues. New York City's water isn't perfect. Our showerheads tend to contain "a particularly high dose" of a tuberculosis-related microbe that can cause hot tub lung, lifeguard's lung, and Lady Windermere syndrome, according to the *New York Times*.

Like water all over the country, my tap water arrives brimming with medicines and toxins. Still, it's plentiful and it runs downhill from the Catskill Mountains. Raw water will reach my apartment even during a long blackout. My toilet will affirm civilization with every flush.

I also use a reverse osmosis home filter system, which clears most contaminates found in municipal systems—even the omnipresent weed killer, atrazine—but people in areas short of water shouldn't get one because RO wastes an enormous amount of water.

Power is the biggest vulnerability. Most U.S. towns and cities need electricity to get water delivered. Power stations stock only a three-week fuel supply. Thirst, catastrophic fires, and dangerously bad hygiene are a few possibilities.

Surface water is full of bird droppings, dead fowl, human sewage, and Tamiflu. H5N1 can survive in it. Chlorine kills H5N1, but many water plants stock only a week's worth of it. Factories that generate chlorine can fail. Transport can break down.

Will we always know what's in our water? Let's drink to our iodine pills and hope we'll never need to eat them.

DAY 25

TURN ON, TUNE IN, TERMINATE....

My theories on religion struck a legion of nerves. *Excellent!*

I've been wondering if our ideological frenzy dates to the 1960s, when hippies and New Leftists brought a kind of religious fervor to movements against war and for broader rights. Did conservatives then apply that ferocity to religion?

Now everyone agrees that the end of human life on earth may be nigh. But they vigorously debate how and why *Homo sapiens* is doomed.

The Religious Right tends to believe in the *End Time*, a period of tribulation from which a minority of the best Christians will be chosen by God to escape early. *There will be human chaos followed by physical chaos.*

The Secular left tends to believe that nature has been systemically overloaded and that civilization will be destroyed in a chaotic, long-running series of ecological catastrophes. *There will be physical chaos followed by human chaos.*

For Apocalyptic Christians, doom will sweep them off to heaven, where they will finally learn the answer to an age-old question: *Do pets join us in the Afterlife?* Not to mention an unmentionable curiosity: *Does anyone have fun up There?*

For Eco-Apocalyptics, there isn't much to look forward to. Escape isn't really possible—the best places to hide and maintain a decent lifestyle will become battlegrounds and fascist enclaves against desperate losers. The nice ones hope that some of the species we've come to love will survive our self-destruction (even if that entails learning to thrive on PCBs, mercury, and plutonium).

Suddenly I see a giant light bulb glowing over the American educational system. I have an idea! Are we engulfed in conflict over how the end of the world will be interpreted *as it happens?*

Are all those fights about Darwinism vs. Creationism really just a war over who's responsible for this mess? Will America's children be taught that they are doomed by man's compulsively sinful nature or by man's compulsively sloppy nature? Sounds like *Homer vs. Simpson....*

Is the agent of our doom a Supreme Being? Or is it Nature? Who owns the morality of our destruction? Does it matter?

Since bird flu is a passing tribulation, those with protective gear and some luck get to see the next act. Bear in mind that not a single apocalyptic prediction has ever panned out. *Yet.*

DAY 26

THE COOL GANG THAT DELIVERS

I had a surprise encounter with the Lower East Side Do It Yourselfers. I like that they picked a klutzy name instead of some contrived words to spell an acronym like S.U.R.V.I.V.E. or MERCY. LES DIY sounds like some kind of women's separatist gang, decked in leather and cool caps and sneers (directed, of course, by <u>Katrina del Mar</u>).

But the group has plenty of male members (that was innocent, *hehe*, so I'll leave it). I'm embarrassed to report that one of them is my best friend (and previously mentioned flu buddy), who's just begun hosting their daily meal giveaway in his restaurant. I'm proud of him. Let's dub him *Ric* because he's a <u>Bogart</u> fanatic. He'd feel and look at home in <u>*Casablanca*</u>.

I haven't seen Ric since he harangued me into letting him drive me to UPS. And I haven't heard from him since I told him to stop nagging me to support what sounded like a gang of left wing hipster rabble-rousers. We're both sensitive. My friend is arguably smarter.

Ric sure listens! Having heard me pontificate for years about the impending emergency, he encountered the LES DIY weeks ago and volunteered to put his assets where my mouth was. Now he and a chef are devising and preparing tasty lunches from whatever is donated by competitors, stores, or individuals. For those who are immune-compromised or unable to walk, the LES DIY will make deliveries.

When he called, I was inspired to emerge from my pit with masks for the active members. (Ric had already gotten some for himself and his restaurant staff.)

The LES DIY is an eclectic crew. Deliveries are managed by an efficient and pretty elf who grinned, wide-eyed, when I turned up with a box of protective gear. Her minions are a lively mix of East Village generations, from undead ex-rockers to indefatigable Sunday School teachers to guys in hats—berets, fedoras, caps, and Stetsons. There are Latinos, Ukrainians, WASPs, squatters, and yuppie workaholics ravenous for labor to perform in a flu-frozen world.

Even in a pandemic, my community feels more like *home* than my hometown ever did. (Let's play Santigold's <u>*L.E.S. Artistes*</u> in honor of the LES DIY!)

Where I come from, people drive everywhere. The friendly ones honk and wave. In normal times, East Village sidewalks teem with people chatting, arguing, flirting, plotting. Everywhere you see old friends, enemies, lovers—people you met once and liked, but can't remember why. Memory loss is not uncommon.

Obscure Alarmist Makes Good—Finally

I hope my contribution has answered that local woman who wrote again yesterday, demanding I give money to the LES DIY. I've provided something more precious—tools with which the organization can safely pursue its mission. Let's hope she's providing more than lip service.

The LES DIY boss generously packed some private-stock *Penne alla Puttanesca* for me to take home. She even included a dab of pastry! My girlfriend found the entrée too spicy. At least it prompted her to mutter something at me.

For a few weeks, my new love and I had a ball behaving like kids freed of supervision. It was fun playing chess and backgammon half-naked in a room full of blues and jazz and smoke, pretending we were marooned in a far-off land. I don't think I've ever been so happy with someone.

Now my place feels all too close, real—airless. Not a complete sentence since I got home. She has a way of exhaling that makes me feel I've just been expelled.

Nina hates my blogging, too. I took it up to give her a break. I'll go surprise her, share a movie, try to stir a pulse.

DAY 27

MUSICAL CHAIRS WITH ANTIVIRAL MEDS

We must all be on guard against pharmaceutical panaceas: As John Barry points out in *The Great Influenza*, desperate doctors in 1918 shot patients up with typhoid vaccine, quinine, even *hydrogen peroxide*. If half the subjects survived, any abomination was hailed as a breakthrough.

Today every Web hustler is selling antivirals—mainly Tamiflu and Relenza, though sometimes Adamantanes. A lot of people are buying them. Sometimes the stuff is *real*. Most is for the birds: counterfeit.

What are these things?

First, let's trash the Adamantanes. Not only are they *not* members of a trippy New Wave group's fan club, amantadine and rimantadine probably won't even be useful. The Chinese fed them to poultry for so long that H5N1 thinks they're chicken feed. (I can't hold back: Here's *Ant Music* for you.)

Then there's Peramivir. This newbie intravenous antiviral took the field during the swine flu pandemic. A mixed record, countered by Washington's avid interest in the success of anything that would add to the antiviral arsenal, has kept it in the game. Experts haven't yet cheered conclusively.

That leaves Tamiflu (oseltamivir) and Relenza (zanamivir). Neither kills flu virus, but each can slow it down while your immune system powers up. They *can* make infected patients feel better, faster—if they medicate at the first sign of sickness.

Tamiflu in particular faces questions about the process by which it was approved. Its use has been associated with some disturbing side effects (detailed below).

Tamiflu is cheaper, comes in pills, and works throughout our bodies. Relenza must be applied directly to the lungs— inhaled as a dry powder through a breath-activated plastic device called a *Diskhaler*. It can't be given to small children, as Tamiflu can. Relenza is dodgy for asthmatics and others with diminished lung capacity. It can *cause lung problems*. If you're already too sick to breathe well, you'll never get it down.

Unfortunately for those who need it, avian flu made Tamiflu trendy and then swine flu got everyone to take it. Chinese farmers may have fed it to their poultry. The WHO has been slathering Indonesia with it for years, much the way various states and cities have lately thrown pills and powders at contacts of isolated H5N1 cases.

Tamiflu fever can conceivably be dangerous—particularly for kids—according to the U.S. Food & Drug Administration. Use of the antiviral has prompted scary side effects in young people in Japan, where 25 patients under 21 had died as of 2007. In Britain, 18% of schoolchildren reported "mild neuropsychiatric side effects." The FDA has inelegantly warned about "post-marketing reports (mostly from Japan) of delirium and abnormal behavior leading to injury, and in some cases resulting in fatal outcomes, in patients with influenza who were receiving Tamiflu."

Resistance to Tamiflu crept in during the 2008-9 flu season, when our old pal seasonal H1N1 suddenly mutated to acquire immunity to it. (Here's

Dr. Racaniello's technical analysis.) A longstanding theory that influenza would have to give up some bite in order to defeat Tamiflu turned out to be wrong: Resistant seasonal flu proved no less nasty.

Still, when swine flu came, Tamiflu seems generally to have helped. Against H5N1, it shows some signs of faltering. A lot of the Tamiflu stockpiled by governments and corporations has passed its expiration dates.

Relenza: Less Charming, More Effective

Relenza's cost and complexity may have helped maintain its effectiveness against H5N1. Chickens can't use Diskhalers. The WHO didn't hand them out to peasants. Unless you're pregnant, nursing, or over 65, we still have Relenza. (*I know I do.*)

Could this antiviral lose its punch? Optimists stress that its molecular structure differs from Tamiflu's. Because Relenza resembles the very sugars that influenza must target in order to spread, experts hope H5N1 won't be able to reproduce well if it stops binding with Relenza.

It's crucial to take it within 48 hours of showing flu symptoms. (The first 24 are optimal.) Refrigeration is unnecessary, but don't store it over 85 degrees (30 Centigrade).

Know your flu symptoms—the rapid onset of fever, chills, aching muscles, cough, weakness, and fatigue! *Memorize that list.* Know, too, the common cold, which lacks the flu's fever, muscle pain, and fatigue.

Beware psychosomatic illness: A hypochondriac with hay fever is a terrible thing to behold. Twice a year, in spring and fall, New York is stuffed with them. I don't want to see my neighbors inhaling white powder unless they really need it. (Let's rephrase that: unless it's really good for them.)

Relenza's side effects seem less dangerous than those of Tamiflu, which (again) is associated with suicidal impulses and attempts. Reported cases of confusion, delirium, and impulsive behavior among Relenza users—none fatal—may stem more from patients' reaction to flu than to the drug, which doesn't easily enter our central nervous systems. Let's hope none of us ever needs to use it.

DAY 28

PROGRESS DOES NOT MAKE PERFECT

The flu debunkers are back on TV, gracelessly hailing numbers that indicate a lot of old folks are dying. Since pandemics are thought to feature markedly lower mortality rates for the aged, the skeptics claim this proves our global emergency can't be a pandemic. This is pathological hairsplitting that rejoices in what amounts to terrible news for senior citizens. It proves nothing positive for the rest of us.

H5N1 fatality rates are indeed falling. Avian flu used to kill two-thirds of its victims. Now the debunkers cackle that it's down to a few percent— mostly fools with <u>underlying health conditions</u> or foreigners who don't eat as well as we do. No worries! Pass the fructose.

Here's the truth: No 'flu bugs' expected H5N1 to keep killing more than half of those who caught it. That would have wiped out more than three billion people. Not that our bird flu can't do that. It could do *worse*. It most probably won't.

The skeptics' argument goes like this: Because viruses exist only to reproduce, they need to maximize contacts with potential hosts. This is why influenza hides in your system for days while you shed it. (Like a horrible date, a smart virus attacks you after it's charmed your friends.) So any disease that quickly kills off its vectors cannot thrive.

That's crap. <u>Smallpox</u> never relaxed. There's <u>no proof that virulence limits a virus' effectiveness</u>.

Dying Like Rabbits

An oft-cited example of a virus that quickly moderated its effects is the <u>myxoma virus</u> that almost wiped out Australia's rabbits when scientists introduced it in 1950 to control the lapine population. Confronted with the prospect that it would have to find a new host, the virus swiftly stopped killing as many rabbits. The optimists rarely explain that myxomatosis moderated its bite only after slaying more than 80% of its hosts. Now it only kills *half* of them. Are you reassured yet?

A further issue is that influenza isn't fundamentally a human disease. It began in ducks and reproduces in countless birds and waterfowl. It may be incidental to the virus that it can infect people and certain other mammals—we're just bonus hosts, easily dispatched. Indeed, all humans that catch flu turn out to be dead ends, one way or another—they either die or develop immunity. Does it matter to the virus which of these takes place?

So of course I welcome that the case fatality rate seems to have fallen to 1.25%. But these numbers are necessarily incomplete in a crisis. Even if the change turns out to be more than a temporary aberration, 1% would be dreadful—10 times greater than normal. And that's just the first wave. Suppose the next, likely-to-be-worse wave registers a paltry 2.5%. That wouldn't be so bad, right? It's merely the 1918 pandemic death rate.

I'm assuming half of all Americans will be infected within the next three years, so a 2% case mortality would kill 1% of our population. Click up your address book and reckon how many friends and relatives you'll miss if the flu erases one of every 100 people in your life—especially the young and healthy. Whom would you least miss? Whom would you most miss? Would your losses be a *"non-event?"* That's what one professional skeptic just labeled the pandemic.

A Peace to Start More Wars

The Great Pandemic killed the brilliant Austrian painter Egon Schiele and his pregnant wife in their twenties. Many think it wrecked President Woodrow Wilson's physical and mental health, causing him to let the Allies sabotage Germany's economic future after World War I, which paved the way for Hitler, the Nazis, World War II, the Holocaust, and the Cold War.

Pandemic flu famously comes in waves. In early 1918, the first wave moderated so sweetly that most Americans regarded the flu season as a mild one. H1N1 returned globally and very unseasonably in August, grew ferocious in September, killed hundreds of thousands of Americans in October, and tore though November before subsiding. It came back in a third wave in 1919.

Scientists still do not know if people who survived the second wave were immune to the third wave. *That's how little is known about pandemic bird flu.*

DAY 29

GO INOCULATE MYSELF

All hell has broken loose. I'm completely confused. Enraged, too. I don't trust the combination, so I'm afraid to write. Tonight's sermon was going to be about the messy quest for a vaccine and the startling movement that's sprung up to oppose the effort. The only shots I saw were aimed at me, my work, my soul.

Nina was out for most of the day. She came back without explanation—just accusations.

She barged in without decontaminating, knocked down a stack of boxes full of gloves, then locked me out of the bedroom. Silence lasted till I knocked two hours later.

"What?"

"What's wrong?"

"What?"

"What's wrong?"

"I can't hear you."

"Open the door."

"What?"

Her ears were probably enfolded in music, so I went back to googling the vaccination wars: Do you know how many governments are saying they might not buy vaccine? Last time it was merely Poland, which turned out not to be much of a problem. (I have no links because I can't find articles about the aftermath, which indicates there was none.)

When the empress emerged, I said nothing as her eyes bored through my spinal cord. I tried to type. It's hard to fake wisdom when you can't think of anything but the person over your shoulder. Then it occurred to me that Nina might be joking—this could be her biggest domestic theater piece yet.

I typed that I loved her. I meant it.

"Better write fast because I'm taking that thing with me," she said of this iMac.

I asked why, on screen.

"You know."

I still don't. I turned around and asked her why she was so angry. She said there was no need to explain anything to me. "You know what you've been doing."

Um, no.

"You're the only one that ever gets to leave this place."

I've been trying to get her to go out more frequently.

She responded with diatribes about 'Ric,' my partner, my old friend, and my old girlfriend, none of whom she's ever much liked. Her buddies don't seem to favor me, either: She made one friend at work—a woman from Tennessee who seemed pleasant the two times I met Nina after they'd been hanging out—but her forever-best pal is downright rude. She constantly invites Nina to join her for weekends at her boyfriend's house overlooking Woodstock, but I'm pointedly not welcome. I guess the pandemic put some of our vexing issues on hold—though one resurfaced when I began stepping out to see my friends.

"Who else do you see?" she asked. I shrugged. The UPS guy?

She ordered me away from her computer, started making dinner for one, consisting of things she knows I hate—split pea soup, dried Parmesan, stale crackers, and Scotch.

I'm posting this from my old PC, which I retrieved from the bedroom closet while she was simmering.

Not sure how long my immune system can sustain this level of inflammation. Where was Nina all day? Was she drunk? Where does she get off hating me like that? Is she serious about leaving?

DAY 30

WHO VANQUISHED THE VIRUS?

I was channel-surfing earlier and spotted a text on one of those hyperactive financial channels: *Is Avian Flu a Buy Opportunity?* Greed is immune to H5N1.

Things do sound calmer. Midwestern power 'failures' that weren't quite blackouts have subsided. The troops patrolling various cities look relaxed. Lovers of old war movies can't help but expect them to start handing out candy to the kids and cigarettes to the babes.

The utilities rationalize the outages as flukes. Liberals see them as moral failures by private enterprise. TV 'conservatives' view them as proof that we should let the government seize our property and hand it over to corporations for power lines. *Heckuva discourse.*

Our system isn't designed for prolonged emergencies. A problem should whack us hard and fast. We freak out, roar into position, and then jaw mindlessly till no one can remember what specifically happened.

After windy Congressional hearings, we watch movies about someone's valiant struggle, invited to imagine that *we* are heroic. Or would be.

Sometimes I think we suffer from *Schindler's List Syndrome.* Everybody wants true stories with happy endings. No fiction, no downers. All's well that ends well. Pass the popcorn.

The public is looking for reasons to doubt that H5N1 is much of a killer. If people react as if this were some late October hurricane that missed the coast, we will be toast.

DAY 31

DID HEALTH CANADA SEDUCE A YANKEE MOM?

I'm *sort of* delighted to report that most of you claim to be bearing up better than we are. A certain number of outright failures wrote in, too. I can't say they made me feel better. How did so many find the *chutzpah* to cheat on their lovers during a pandemic?

One guy reported that his wife ran off with their kids to Canada, presumably with another man. He didn't have a particular rival in mind, so I have to wonder if she left on her own. What makes this guy certain she ran off with a dude, or even a woman?

Her choice isn't very patriotic, but things might be better in socialist Canada: If you can't get doctors to look at you, they may as well be free.

Since the insurance from my last full-time job ran out, I've paid doctors as needed. I have friends who fork out $1,300 a month to HMOs that can't guarantee they'll get treatment for anything. Should they stop paying? No way! If they survive, they'd have to get insured all over again and any active medical problems would be pre-existing conditions *not covered* till the government effectively mandates it. (That's my status, of course: I'll never recover financially if I catch the flu and need hospitalization.)

To be fair, Canada's government has reportedly been decent to foreigners caught there when the pandemic broke out. They have access to medical attention and food, both of which are said to circulate better than they do here. Canada domestically produces more than enough vaccine for its population and it orders vaccine the instant a pandemic looms. That's because the U.S. completely stiffed our Northern neighbors back in 1976 amid panic about a swine flu emergency that never quite materialized.

Perhaps my reader's errant wife hooked up with Dudley Do-Right, his Mountie saddlebags laden with Relenza and caribou jerky.

No-Spying Zone

I have received sinister emails about my own circumstance. Not the Ayn Rand followers who scold me for committing the crime of altruism—giving personal protective gear to people I don't know. That's easy to defend: The transaction was in my pure, selfish interest. I live here. *Chaos is bad for me.* Not to mention that if everyone dies, who'll buy my masks?

No, it's advice about Nina. One guy urges me to check the surfing history on Nina's iMac. I won't say it's not tempting.

But listen, *see*—for me to assume that no one is spying on me, I have to leave other people alone. That's my *Silver Rule*: Don't do unto others what you don't want them to do unto you. Kindly shove those suspicions up your cache.

I'm truly glad the flu seems to be abating. Demand for my products will remain keen as people reload their stockpiles—or expand them. Don't cry for me, America.

Nina does plenty of that. I remain clueless. I sure wonder where she went that day.

DAY 32

ANGELS CRY WHILE WE RECOVER FROM FLU

Only half a million dead globally. Cynics compare H5N1 to Y2K. Some hint that fat people deserve to die anyway. (Is the phrase 'American civilization' an oxymoron? *Who ya calling a moron, creep!*) My neighborhood wailer has gone silent. Is she sick or tired? Both?

Yet things are decidedly improving. The LES DIY is experiencing a fall-off in visitors at my friend's restaurant. The faces that show up look more like homeless and less like hapless East Villagers.

A lot of people starved in 1918. Not for lack of food, but because healthy people stopped circulating. No one would go near the sick with food or medicine. Surviving children were abandoned. I wonder how many lives the LES DIY has saved.

Ric's Place normally features superb, underpriced French food—not generic *Chez Oignon*. To those who sneered at gays when I started this blog, let me point out that he's openly homosexual, though I don't think he does much about it these days. Ric's too busy nourishing the entire community, compounding pandemic losses by keeping his once-chic restaurant open for people who can't pay.

I've always thought him to resemble a hearty young Mediterranean *patron*, with a sharp goatee and demonic flashing eyes. His slight paunch used to hint at prosperity. All gone.

Ric still thinks he's funny: He introduces me every afternoon as *El Bandito Plastico* because of the masks and goggles and gloves I wear. Today he gave me an orange water pistol, which I filled and emptied to good effect, distracting Do-It-Yourselfers from their duties. They look so serious in those masks!

I wound up sitting alone for a while in a green patch behind the restaurant. Took off my mask and goggles, *breathed*. A glass or two of red wine and some passing smoke had relaxed me. I fell asleep in a lawn chair, woke uneasily to the sound of someone gasping.

It was the interesting woman who runs the LES DIY's food service. She was huddled on her heels, cheekbones cradled in her hands, sobbing softly in a pool of light. She hadn't noticed me. I wasn't about to shock or embarrass her by declaring myself as she grieved.

I remained 'asleep' till she arranged her goggles and went back to work. She was piling plates when I attempted to slip unnoticed through the kitchen. When she saw me, she jumped, broke a dish. I bumped into a chair, kept moving.

When I got home, Nina looked like she'd been crying, too. She's wracked with hay fever. She's flushed and looks hot (the wrong kind). Her voice is scratchy, eyes sticky. Her nose is a busted faucet. She refuses to take any allergy medicine or even to discuss what's wrong. Is silence galling? At least it leaves the door open.

It used to be endearing that she never agreed with me. Civilized conflict can be sexy.

It hurts that she won't let me take her temperature.

DAY 33

LOVE, PAIN & THE VIRUS OF SELF-DESTRUCTION

I apologize sincerely to the guy whose wife left him. I'm a dolt, whining about my own problems, sneering at those of others. That's what bad bloggers do. Or creeps.

Now to vex more readers.

I've received a propaganda barrage hailing Gram Parsons, a later ex-Byrd universally regarded as *the* lost genius of country rock. He founded The Flying Burrito Brothers, wrote some brilliant songs, and taught the Stones a few things before overindulging to death at 26.

I like Parsons' music a *lot*. Heck, he invented my devilish Nina (*Christine's Tune*). My cat is named after Sneaky Pete Kleinow, the Burrito Brothers' steel guitar player (who played in Gene Clark's final master recording session). Some of Clark's best work might never have happened had the Burritos not invented what Parsons called "cosmic American music."

But Parsons' great works are no secret. His legend has come to verge on cliché. There are books about him, even a movie. Too much of his mystique derives from his having died so young (and mysteriously) in a California desert motel, after which his corpse was stolen by a close friend and burned in Joshua Tree National Park.

The brutal truth is that Parsons was a good 'ol Harvard boy, an epochal underachiever who wasted a lot of people's time screwing up. (Yep, I read one of the books—good and sad: Ben Fong-Torres' *Hickory Wind: The Life and Times of Gram Parsons*.) I think Parsons was a gifted musical formalist (with a limited attention span) who related best to pain—and how to counter it pharmacologically.

Gene Clark's work is far less cynical. It's heartfelt and it asks better questions. I can't explain why he failed so abysmally in the music markets once he quit the Byrds. John Einarson's detailed biography, *Mr. Tambourine Man*, relates how the pioneering country rock poet grew up without plumbing in a family of 15, part Native American in a tiny Missouri town so small-minded that Clark pretended his dark looks came from Chicano blood. He was terminally shy till he started making music.

A superstar at 20, Clark drank too much, took drugs, and could be impossibly insecure, staggeringly arrogant. He got into lots of fights, tried to physically attack both David Geffen *and* Bob Dylan. Parallel fears of success and of failure kept him careening violently betwixt them until his body fell apart at 46. Once his yearning baritone turned into throat cancer, a few further binges finished him off.

Clark worked relentlessly for many years with artists who kept coming back for more, and he left a gigantic catalog of sadly underappreciated songs. His collected works outweigh Parsons' and his voice was immeasurably stronger, keener. Ask <u>Chris Hillman</u>, who co-founded both the Byrds *and* the Burrito Brothers.

Harold Eugene Clark sure believed in love and pain. You hear it and you feel it.

Since I'm now selling his music here, I think I'll add some of Parsons' stuff, too, plus both books. Let's put on <u>a show</u>!

DAY 34

FROM THE FOOD GODDESS TO ELIZABETH TAYLOR

The world outside strives to look normal. Nina stayed in, responding in 'normal' fashion to calls from her office. The bank is reanimating, even if she's not.

Ric will reopen his restaurant when things settle down. The LES DIY members have put aside their protective gear and are debating whether (and how) to keep their soup kitchen going if (and when) he clears them out.

The woman who runs the food operation looks on grimly as her volunteers grumble. Two of them are calling Ric—*their mentor*—the *&@%$^ embodiment of greed. Some religious members are complaining about some of the spoken words.

I've learned that the food czar lost her daughter in the first onrush of flu. That would be a month ago—or even less—which explains the anguish I witnessed in the back garden. I don't see how she manages to work so hard.

I guess it makes her feel better to help people, a wonderful kind of functional grieving. I applaud from afar (as other Randians call me a fraud).

Like so many East Villagers, this woman looks great in black—light, airy fabrics.

She can be tough: Faced with a colorful and contentious gang that never shuts up, she periodically roasts everyone, then whips up a feast for the survivors. Her dove-gray eyes miss little, even when streaked with red. Yet she always looks startled when I go to Ric's, as if she's seeing me for the first time.

Let's call her *Anna*, for <u>Annapurna</u>, the Hindu goddess of food and cooking. It's fun renaming everyone! *Don't try this at home.*

Outside, there were lots of naked faces. The streets are filling with grinning souls, though lots of conversations are conducted at more than arms' length. A few unlucky souls will regret discarding their masks so quickly.

For once, I didn't see anyone spit. Ordinances passed from coast to coast may have had some effect. They arrested spitters in 1918, too.

The sidewalks were lumpy with dog crap. New Yorkers usually clean up, but the citizenry has devolved.

There were rats aplenty, sunning in the park, waiting for a junkie Pied Piper to finish tuning his guitar. It reminded me of a story an old timer told me about seeing Gram Parsons perform at <u>Max's Kansas City</u> in the '70s. Parsons was so ripped he dropped his guitar and teetered on his stool till a spectator handed it to him.

Meet 'Mark'

I headed to Brooklyn to visit my very old friend, who has surfaced to plead for more masks. I will justify my patience by explaining that he and I grew up together and I will save y'all the trouble of trying to figure out who he is by honoring him with the pseudonym, *Mark*.

It was my first trip underground since a homeless guy was pounded into a coma for sneezing on passengers in a rush hour No. 4.

Even with a mask and goggles, the rush of air when a train enters the station is intimidating. Particles of soot, pigeon waste, and scraps of litter swirl furiously as you hover by the track. Even after avoiding subways for so long, the primitive urge to secure a seat at any cost reboots in seconds.

I saw fewer masks, generally of higher quality than on my last trip. Only middle-class folks wore the type I sell. I don't know if poor people understand the differences: Mine are cheaper if you use them properly. To make people feel better, the media pretend that a t-shirt over your nose and mouth can make a big difference. It's true to the extent that the gullible *feel* much safer—till they keel over from the tiny virions that bounded through the cotton.

When I reached Mark's loft, an altogether new woman opened the door and left before I could take her measure. The place was cleaner, but smelled like melted plastic. If you don't know what that stench can indicate, I'll leave it at that.

I brought only a few gloves and goggles because I'm certain he sold the masks I gave him, or traded them for things that won't help him survive H5N1. Let's hope a flu hiatus will give him the chance to rebuild his life. Again.

Typically, Mark kicked back and started lecturing me about profiting from fear and warning that I'd better come up with a more secure income stream. Our real estate mogul's revived arrogance was kind of reassuring, the comfort of an old, familiar pain.

Then he asked me for money.

I generally like to imagine that I'm patient. Still, I'm delighted to report how vividly I told Mark what a dung-slinger he is. I haven't yelled like that in years. I thought he might belt me, as he used to do when we were kids. (He's bigger and older—no longer the advantages they once were.) I bet I could pound him.

Civilization prevailed. He insisted the aroma was from skunk. He knows I favor the libertarian line on marijuana (which in no way invites him to con me out of money for it).

We wound up getting wrecked, drinking a lot of beer, watching *Butterfield 8*. Elizabeth Taylor is one of his better habits.

I feel guilty when the birds chirp so innocently at dawn. (Yawn.)

DAY 35

THE SOLITUDE OF SICKNESS

My girlfriend is truly ill. Nina has barely spoken since I got home 16 hours ago.

Since I've never seen her under the weather, I don't know how she usually deals with it. So far, I'd guess she starts out in denial and then nukes her symptoms in hopes that no one will ever notice she was sick. It's scary and unnatural. Where I come from, we welcome loving tribute; no matter what ails us, ice cream has healing properties.

To Nina, mere witnesses are unacceptable, *verboten*.

She's been vomiting and crying and behaving strangely. Her stomach is a mess. She won't answer telephone calls from anyone but her employer. Her best friend 'Growly' texted *me* to get Nina to call her back. Debussy and thumping sounds emanate from the bedroom, as if she were trying to dance. It's been a while. I hope she doesn't hurt herself.

Every cough sounds deeper.

Nina pulls together heroically for the criminal bank. I can hear her saying how much she misses the office. I picture the smile she fakes for good measure. Apart from the nice blonde executive from Tennessee, Nina had barely met her desk when the flu struck. Sometimes her voice grows inaudible, as if she's saying something confidential. As if I care about their marketing schemes. I'm hardly the target audience.

The boss wants her to show up Monday and she's desperate to oblige. I doubt smallpox could keep her home, but she looks bad: She's both red and pale. Her little dark orbs are inflamed. I tried googling her visible symptoms, got nowhere.

She refuses to discuss her malady. I don't believe she has bird flu. Where could she have caught it?

Her symptoms seem like a kind of virulent hay fever—headache, fever, runny nose, cough, dizziness, fatigue, even stomach upset. I'm just a mask-vending typist, not a doctor. She may have something.

A doctor would probably advise her to head for an emergency room, which I still consider dangerous exposure. I haven't been asked.

She won't call a doctor. Her eyes tightened at my suggestion.

Instead she asked me to sleep in the living room, ostensibly to spare me from exposure to her symptoms. It's absurd. Everything in this apartment smells of disinfectant. She's polished every <u>fomite</u>.

Has Nina caught the American plague of <u>presentism</u>? Fewer than half of our workers get sick pay; the rest can't *afford* to stay home. Not even a third get time off to care for ailing children. Part-timers and contractors fear they'll be fired if they don't show up. So people crawl to work, where they can infect their bosses.

A senator pointed out during the swine flu pandemic that only five nations in the world lacked mandatory sick leave: Lesotho, Liberia, Papua-New Guinea, Swaziland, and the U.S.

The deeper you look into the work chain, the worse it gets: Fewer than one-fourth of the lowest-paid workers get sick pay; maybe one-sixth of restaurant workers get it. *What do you think happens to viruses in those kitchens?*

Some so-called libertarians blame illegal immigrants for spreading bird flu. But there's no native immunity for Americans. U.S. passports are fomites, slathered in germs and viruses. Just like paper money, which can harbor influenza virions for hours, even days. (Up to 2 ½ weeks if coated in mucus, according to Swiss bankers.)

Did I mention that Nina is wearing a mask *inside*? It's not one of the (better) masks I sell, but a run-of-the-mill N95 like those reporters wear on-camera so they can look like common folks. What is she trying to tell me?

DAY 36

ONLY THE SILENCE IS PREGNANT

I've received some arresting emails about Nina's condition. Some suggest she's pregnant. The first notes came from American women, who worry that I am a dimwit. This may scare them because they come here for advice.

How would I know if Nina's breasts are tender? The question pains me.

Several women who sound like Europeans and another from Hong Kong were more critical of Nina but reached the same conclusion. I googled and googled and came up with nothing more definite than general symptoms: Headaches, fatigue, fever, grouchiness, stomach upset, a sudden aversion to coffee, and a reluctance to communicate with the man who might have caused it.

I can't believe she could be pregnant. It's the worst condition one can acquire in a pandemic. I've never impregnated anyone. This is unthinkable.

She could have bird flu. Or several hundred other serious conditions. I was betting on hay fever but I think I lost.

Your humble profiteer thus spent his morning sneezing on an old futon coated with cat hair amid piles of boxes in the living room. At least

Nina wasn't typing nearby. She didn't log in until her bank called late in the morning. I'd like to think she was being considerate about my sleeping near her iMac, but I think she was too sick to get up.

I'm quarantined within a quarantine. My home shrinks by the day. Am I living an Edgar Allan Poe story? I await the pendulum.

Nina looks feverish. That room smells bad. I tried to think of ways to slip a thermometer into her. Thank you for your thoughts and wishes.

DAY 37

MY LIFE—FOR THE BIRDS

Did you know birds used to hunt people? Scientists at Ohio State have assembled compelling evidence that scratches and holes in the skull of an immortal little girl were caused by local raptors the size of our bald eagles. (Is *that* what happens to 'reformers' in D.C.?)

The ape-like Taung child was a very significant 3½-year-old. Her discovery in a South African cave back in 1924 was the first indication that *Homo sapiens* had evolved in Africa. The impressions on her skull were thought to have been made by ferocious cats. Turns out they match marks on comparably sized monkeys devoured by birds of prey.

It's comforting to see feline innocence affirmed.

Some cats can't get off the hook so easily. Mine got loose in the kitchen today, tore open a big bag of granola. Sneeky doesn't even like cereal. When I told him that wasn't very nice, he looked at me and shrugged: "Nice rhymes with mice, dude."

Maybe he missed me, was tired of being cooped up with my cranky girlfriend. He'd gotten accustomed to a kind of rotating exposure to whichever of us was sleeping in *his* room. Since I'm no longer welcome, Sneeky busted out to surprise me with a breakfast avalanche of human kibbles.

My own happy family.

Nina wouldn't let me enter the bedroom to return him. She wants him to stay out here from now on. This exposes Sneeky to my decontamination zone—and robs him of the window he loves.

The doctor we need here may be an old Austrian. *Paging Sigmund!*

I should make clear that Nina has many of the *apparent* symptoms of pregnancy with one big difference. She has indeed gained weight and has turned chunky, cranky, dizzy, sleepy, and barfy. (Which dwarves did I forget?) Her stomach is horribly loose, though.

The Web says she either has some virus or is indeed pregnant. I tried to feed her rice and applesauce and toast (<u>yes, we have no bananas</u>), but she snarled like a prehistoric feline. She won't even take Imodium.

You'd think I made her sick. She seems to.

I wish she would talk to me. I am striving mightily not to express myself. Sneeky knows I'm losing my mind. I hope he doesn't lose respect for me.

DAY 38

LOVE IN THE TIME OF BIRD FLU

My shadowy correspondent from the East Village has written a long and thoughtful email to help me grasp why Nina would be so distressed: She has a new job unsuited for instant motherhood and she *thinks* she hates the presumptive father. Made me feel rather sorry for Nina myself.

We've never even talked about children or abortion or pregnancy. Nina's eyes double in size when she details her dreams of promotion, travel, exploits.

What should a man say? What say should a man have? Doesn't she have to talk to me?

What should I do? I'm feeling grumpy and dumpy, too. Maybe *I* should be having the kid.

NOTE: I replied to two emails from the correspondent in question and I even filled out the form to get cleared for acceptance/delivery (as 'Maskman'), but her account still bars my email. She might wish to look into this.

Finally, I did snoop to see if Nina has searched for information about any revealing medical symptoms. I wanted to see if she shares my concern or has a better theory.

She evidently erases data when she signs off. I feel like a rat for looking: It's her computer and she uses it to plug into the bank's internal network. There's nothing quite like failing at doing something you knew was wrong anyway.

I rub my stubble and wonder if I should have sniffed her keyboard when

I had the opportunity. There's a truism that keyboards are filthier than toilet seats. Not this one: Nina regularly scrubs it with the disinfectant I sell. Is she making fun of me?

I wonder, wonder who wrote the book of *love in the time of bird flu.*

DAY 39

SOCIAL DISTANCING BEGINS AT HOME

Someone died across the street. I watched them remove the corpse. There was no hurry, no face.

Nina and I are quarreling about whether she should go outside. If she wanted to see a doctor or meet up with her friend from Knoxville, fine, but I think she just wants to roam around. It's cloudy, chilly, windy. The last time she went out, she came back in a homicidal mood and promptly turned sick.

I wish she would get help. I wish she'd talk to me.

I recognize that bird flu is less risky to most people this month than it was last month (or may be next month), but pregnant women need to avoid any flu, let alone this one. I wouldn't want our child to be damaged before he or she even has a chance.

Of course I couldn't say that. Didn't dare try.

So I'm sorry to report that I can't follow any of the advice that so many of you offered. I've failed to "charm her into sharing." I don't really want to "kill the [*]." I feel paralyzed.

I offered to cook us a special dinner. Nina insisted we order in. She didn't want spicy food—another symptom of pregnancy. (*Instant expert here.*)

We compromised on a Thai place neither likes and ate in silence after I disinfected from my quick trip outside to pay the Mexican guy. Nina rolled her eyes as I re-spiced my share of dinner. I was the only one watching her performance. Sneeky sat facing the closed bedroom door.

The loneliest people in the world must live with others who don't talk to them.

Social distancing begins at home. We communicate so little that *I almost addressed her as Nina.* She is more real to me as a character on my screen than she is as my lost soul mate. Is that some sign of denial? Our song must be *Tainted Love.*

Nina's voice is for her iPhone, mine is for my cat. When she talks with friends, she speaks in hushed tones. When she's talking to someone at work, she sounds like she's just conquered Deutsche Bank. I wish she'd try to fool *me* by acting warm.

I'd hate to have parents like us.

DAY 40

A WORLD OF PREPARATION—FOR WHAT?

I stopped by Ric's Place for relief. The mood wasn't much happier there than *chez moi*, though Ric was pleased to see me. When I entered the kitchen, he warned Anna to take care lest *El Bandito Plastico* (that's me) steal the air from her lungs. She tried to smile. So did I. She looked as if she might burst into tears again.

We commiserated silently until Ric abruptly decided to show me things he wants to change for his restaurant reopening. I don't remember anything he said. Anna was glancing at me sadly while she rinsed dishes, as if I'd tripped over a nerve no one knew was there. I still don't know what upset her, but it's still active, churning. I feel it.

Why are all the women I know suffering relentlessly?

If Nina is pregnant, Sneeky ought to be tested for toxoplasmosis. Is that why she expelled him from his/my former room? Nina's procedures are a mishmash of things I've said, as if she's memorized every third word I uttered about bird flu.

It's extremely unlikely that Sneeky killed any sick mice recently. He's not that sort of feline. If he found one that refused to run away, he'd meow in peremptory outrage until I dealt with the intruder.

Whatever the truth is, I wish to help. If Nina plans to bear a child, that's her choice. I would go to any length to help our baby survive with full physical and mental faculties. She must know this. I don't understand why we can't discuss it.

I'm going to confront her condition in the morning, when I hear her turn on my TV. I haven't prepared a statement—or even the question—but this has drifted too long. If she's pregnant, she needs special nutrients, a doctor, lots of luck. Less wine, for sure.

I don't communicate well when I'm so uncertain. I'm trying hard not to resent Nina's attitude and behavior. I'm failing.

It's a daunting time to be breeding, even if our baby turns out well. I wonder if bird flu is nature's way of striking back at mammals. Our evolutionary line is devastating a world that's far more active than we like to think it is. How *reactive* is it?

This disease may dramatically rearrange life on earth.

Bureaucrats everywhere are responding with plans to *take control* by doing it themselves—slaughtering birds. New York City has announced a poisoning campaign aimed at common street fowl. I suspect they hope the burgeoning rat population will eat the corpses and die, killing multiple 'pests' with one toxin. The law of unintended consequences will take dogs, too. (People and their pet canines get electrocuted here, just walking wintry sidewalks.)

Widespread avian slaughter will unleash a global fog of insects that are already flourishing amid rising levels of carbon dioxide. Bugs we can see and feel will thrive without birds to check their population growth. With bats, too, dying in vast numbers from a little-understood fungal plague known as white nose syndrome, insects will freely feast on people and crops. Sicknesses such as malaria, dengue fever, and chikungunya—surging northward as the climate heats—will surpass those Biblical scourges. Famine will kill hundreds of millions. Wars will follow.

I can't resist noting that houseflies can carry avian flu. Along with dump flies and dung flies, they are known to have borne H5N2 in Pennsylvania during a huge, lethal outbreak in 1983-4. Twenty years later, the Japanese found "highly pathogenic" H5N1 in some blowflies near a stricken poultry farm. It's not yet known if they can *spread* bird flu.

DAY 41

SPEECHLESS, FOR ONCE

I'll post tomorrow.

DAY 42

DUMB

The sun was high and bright. Looks like an early summer. More tomorrow. I promise.

DAY 43

VITAMIN D—A GORGEOUS STEROID THAT FIGHTS DISEASE

I'm sorry about the last two days. Call it *functional difficulties.*

Today's regret is that I've never paid tribute to Vitamin D. Being locked up has inspired a greater appreciation of the sun. It's no surprise that people get depressed in the winter, when the sun is distant and low. It drives me to google....

Which is how I discovered that Vitamin D is a profoundly useful natural hormone, essentially a *steroid.* (Yup.) The Vitamin D Council maintains an informative site.

Vitamin D boosts your immune system. It's a biocide that seems to kill bacteria, fungi, and viral particles by stimulating white blood cells to produce more cathelicidin, an antimicrobial compound. Studies show that it fights rickets, osteoporosis, diabetes, breast and bowel cancers, and other cancers.

Vitamin D is even considered helpful in repressing immune over-reactions. It seems to support heart health and fight high blood pressure. *Aging*, too.

A deficiency of Vitamin D in the womb may contribute to making the unborn child schizophrenic. *Just like the presence of flu.* It is suspected of causing autism.

Our need for Vitamin D—think of it as a substance that rich sunlight inspires inside us—may even explain the seasonality of influenza. A lot of people lack adequate Vitamin D, particularly in late autumn, winter, and early spring.

In the really old days, we ran around at least half-naked and worked outside when there was light (indoors being a stinky, smoky cave). Even those in temperate climates got plenty of D much of the year. Nowadays people work indoors, overdress, and use sunscreen. We are told to fear any exposure to the sun.

But it's nearly impossible to obtain enough Vitamin D through diet.

Milk is not the answer, at least not the *whole* answer. It doesn't come with D naturally; the dairy industry adds 100 international units to *fortify* an 8-ounce glass. Studies show that most retail milk fails to contain as much D as the labels claim. When it does, you'd have to drink almost a gallon a day to get what many leading Vitamin D experts consider necessary—up to 2,000 IU daily. (Some recommend 5,000 in the winter.)

Twenty minutes of full-body exposure to the sun in summertime generates 20,000 IU within 48 hours. That's how much our bodies are geared to handle from nature.

We Come From Fish

Our need for Vitamin D reflects human evolution. We originated in oceans rich in calcium and then crawled onto land that didn't offer it. Mammals developed Vitamin D to keep blood calcium at levels critical to maintaining heart, brain, and muscle functions without having to dip into the calcium stored in their bones—at least 90% of human calcium is stashed there. (Forget the monkey talk; read *Your Inner Fish: A Journey Into the 3.5-Billion-Year History of the Human Body*, now available on this site.)

Because *Homo sapiens* emerged in tropical Africa, where sunlight is plentiful and rich in Vitamin D, we evolved dark protective melanin, pigment to guard against melanoma. Then some of us marched north into Europe and Asia, where our skin bleached to absorb more of the invaluable hormone.

Today most of the world's economic activity takes place above the 35th parallel in the northern hemisphere, where winter sun isn't sufficiently intense to keep residents healthy. I could stand naked on a heated Manhattan rooftop through a bright and clear New Year's Day and derive next to no Vitamin D. In the U.S., the 35th parallel runs from just north of Santa Barbara through Albuquerque and Chattanooga to Cape Hatteras.

All of Europe lies above the 35th. It runs just under Tokyo and most of South Korea, with much of China happily below it (though air pollution blocks much of their D). In the southern hemisphere, far fewer people live on the polar side of the 35th parallel—residents of Melbourne and those who live south of Buenos Aires and Valparaiso.

Black people make very little vitamin D, so those who dwell in the north are thought to suffer more prostate and pancreatic cancer for want of it. Tuberculosis, too.

This applies to all non-whites. In 2007 a <u>University of Toronto</u> study found that 85% of students who had originated in East Asia lacked sufficient D, as did 93% of students from South Asia, and all those of African descent. <u>A Harvard Medical School</u> study said 97% of African Americans and 70% of white Americans are deficient in Vitamin D.

I must point out that I found a <u>study of studies</u> by the National Academy of Science's Institute of Medicine for the U.S. and Canadian governments. It concluded that few people lack Vitamin D and there's no need to take supplements. The report ignored most of the best work on the subject. I disagree, respectfully or not. So did these <u>experts at Harvard's School of Public Health</u>.

There's no question that, as we age, our bodies produce less D in response to sunlight. An 80-year-old needs four times as much rich sunlight as a 20-year-old. A black octogenarian needs eight times as much as a young white adult. The arithmetic leaves older folks plundering their bones for calcium, causing osteoporosis.

There's a certain elasticity of supply if we proceed wisely. (To thwart skin cancer, avoid more than 20 minutes of naked sun between 10 am and 2 pm in the brighter months.) If we achieve sufficient exposure in the sunny months, we store Vitamin D in our body fat and then draw on it.

Tomatoes, Coffee & Exercise Fight Skin Damage

Unless we use too much sunscreen (which <u>may accelerate</u> cancer). Children are so sensitive to Vitamin D that sunscreens won't prevent them from getting what they need *if* they circulate under the sun. (Rickets is coming back, so some kids obviously aren't getting enough D.) But a sunscreen with an SPF of 8 is enough to turn adult Vikings into the equivalent of Black Alaskans—heavily inclined toward D deficiency. To help protect your skin against sun damage, <u>eat tomatoes</u> and <u>exercise and drink coffee</u>. That's a regimen I could live with, if my gym were open.

In the darker months, people can eat oily, fatty fish like mackerel and sardines, drink fortified milks (including rice milk or soy milk), eat egg yolks and such organ meats as liver, and take vitamin pills. Cod liver oil has some D, but a teaspoonful is worth a mere 400 IU and contains a lot of Vitamin A, which can be very toxic.

Many folks supplement daily with pills containing from 2,000 to 5,000 IU of cholecalciferol (D3). *Be careful*: One can overdose on D in food and pills.

Have your Vitamin D level tested if for any reason you think you might be deficient or overdosing. Many advocates think everyone should be tested because we all have different absorption rates.

Stay strong: Get naked outside, somehow.

DAY 44

THE PROBLEM WITH VITAMIN D

A lot of readers demand to know things I'm in no mood to discuss.

Two admirable individuals ask why they haven't heard much about Vitamin D, our most plentiful nutrient. That's easy: *It's free.* The companies that profit most from Vitamin D are those that lure us to sunny climes in midwinter, offering to dry up our cold, soggy blues. Or fly us there.

There's a healthy logic in waving your mammaries at drunks during Spring Break! Or visiting Key West, or Granny in Lake Havasu City, or what's left of the Big Easy. Retirees heading for the Sunbelt don't need canasta tournaments to justify the move.

Few sell Vitamin D to us up north. Bottling it is a minuscule business— maybe half-a-billion dollars—compared with marketing sunscreens and osteoporosis pills that might make your jaw fall off.

To get a substance approved for therapeutic applications, you need to conduct big clinical studies with controls and lots of subjects, as this article from the *Financial Times* explains. Pharmaceutical companies have every reason not to pay for expensive testing that might establish an inexpensive—even free—rival for their products against a stunning range of medical problems. Governments don't seem to like the idea either.

I also wonder if our way of dealing with illness reflects our society's obsession with control. We go to doctors to get simple things that make us feel in control of our problems: pills. Writing prescriptions helps those harried professionals feel in control, too. *Take two pieces of paper and don't call me.*

Consider <u>Lyme disease</u>, which defies easy testing, diagnosis, and treatment. It's a dangerous condition that's out of control, spreading relentlessly through North America. With no brand medicine to counter Lyme, it is more profitable—perhaps even comforting—to worry about <u>restless legs syndrome</u>. There are pills for that.

If I could only think of a kicker....

DAY 45

I AM NOT INFLUENZA

Okay, okay. I hear you.

Record email has prompted me to check my page hits. This blog is more popular than I'd imagined. Evidently the world cares about my existence in this cluttered hole. Or is at least amused.

I'm still here. The joint's gotten more spacious.

So I stopped in at a library. It was full of chattering kids pretending to read while staffers worked to get the place back up to speed. Revelation came when I saw a sign that read *Biog* and misread it to say *Blog*. I flashed on the error of my ways.

I am not bird flu. H5N1 is not me. *Mea culpa*.

I initiated this blog to report on how people could help themselves and secondarily, to comment on what was going on around me. I didn't mean in my kitchen or bed. Or even across the street. How does that help anyone?

My partner was right: Like a lot of bloggers, I've succumbed to talking about myself most of the time. A waste of all our lives, I assure you.

I've stopped. I hope my further ideas aren't boring. I shall continue to express myself about things that are important. Stay tuned.

DAY 46

BROKEN GODS & THREATS OF LITIGATION

I acknowledge blame for the world's interest in my existence, though I don't get it.

I was served with a legal notice that I should cease writing about 'Nina' because I was making her a public figure. *She must have finally read my blog!*

Ric steered me to a lawyer who assured me that nothing I've said about her is litigable. So long as I remain obscure, she can't be identified. I salute your ignorance and apathy.

So here's what happened. We broke up a few days ago, when I discovered she was sick from *taking Relenza*. She'd gotten word to come back to the office soon and had started inhaling antiviral powder because she decided she was coming down with bird flu and wanted to be 100% present on her first day back at work.

It's not as if I'd never mentioned to her—okay, *ranted* might be a better word—that I expected ignoramuses to take Relenza and Tamiflu for hay fever. I've warned that when they conduct pandemic post mortems, it'll turn out that most antivirals were wasted.

This is what I posted three weeks ago:

"Know your flu <u>symptoms</u>...!

Memorize that list.

A hypochondriac with hay fever is a terrible thing to behold."

She used about a third of my stash before I happened upon a used Diskhaler under a pillow while she was off on a mystery stroll. I had gotten up early to confront her about her apparent condition, but she had already slipped out. It seemed a good opportunity to wash the sheets.

Finding that plastic thing dumbfounded me. It's risky for pregnant women to take Relenza—another point I had posted. Even if it works, embryos that survive bird flu can be damaged for life.

At first I hoped she was out visiting a doctor. I longed for her to come home and tell me what, if anything, was wrong. I imagined she was keeping silent until she could confirm that she was pregnant, sick, or both. *Or neither.*

She returned wearily at sunset, marched wordlessly to the bedroom. When I followed her inside to ask about the Relenza, she dumped the window screen on the floor so she could sit on the sill, facing me. (She knows I oppose this because I'm afraid Sneeky will fall out the window—a common, fatal horror in New York.) I tried to ignore her transgression while she readily admitted having taken Relenza.

She glowed in the soft pink light as she refused to explain why she was so convinced she'd caught bird flu. Or why she hadn't warned me that *I* must be at risk. She said something weird to the effect that I was probably "safe" because I was the source. I told her I wasn't ill and she said maybe someone in the LES DIY is and I happened to get too close to her and started carrying flu without symptoms. My perplexed expression amused her for a moment. Then her eyes turned into lasers, firing contempt.

She started ranting about things she didn't bother to explain. I realize now that she assumed I understood them because she knew I was guilty of whatever she was implying. She was speaking in codes she thought I had written. Madness.

Airborne Antiviral Assault

When I said she was poisoning herself and our child, she went volcanic. She was outraged that I had thought she was pregnant. She asked if I was confusing her with someone else. Now her eyes were wider, accusing.

She was certain I had cheated on her the whole time she lived here. With lots of women: Mark's playmates, the wailing woman, my old girlfriend, even the weird emailer. She had Ric playing a central role in my perfidy—the gay wingman nefariously hooking me up with the sad woman who runs the LES/DIY food service. (With whom I've never spoken.)

Soon she was on her feet, hurling what was left of the powder disks at me. I scrambled to find them before Sneeky could start swatting them around, sampling them. She sneered as I crawled.

Then she started throwing bigger objects. One was a brightly colored ceramic of <u>Ganesh</u>, the elephant-headed Hindu god of wisdom, knowledge, and plenty.

I can fling stuff like any angry guy with an opposable thumb, but I've never attacked anything that belonged to someone else. If I lose my temper, I smash my own things. I don't doubt that such eruptions can scare and/or violate other people. I try very hard not to get crazy, but at least it's *me* who loses stuff if and when I do.

Maybe she always hated my little Ganesh because my old girlfriend gave it to me. I treasured it. She cracked it.

I placed injured Ganesh on a bookshelf. She laughed and threw him out the window. I heard the statue shatter on a car parked below. An alarm started whooping and beeping.

I went hot and cold, stunned that she hated me so. Furious, I told her to find another place to live as soon as possible. She agreed, smiling for the first time in what feels like weeks.

She insisted on sleeping in the kitchen that night, probably so I couldn't post anything to my myriad illicit lovers—you.

After a long night of cycling thoughts and regrets and shock, I walked all the way to Central Park. It was a lush afternoon to feel so desolate. I mulled things over on a big, greasy boulder while high school kids courted and texted and smoked cigarettes around me. Nothing made sense.

I decided to tune up my bicycle soon. She never wanted one.

Peace arrived when I relaxed into the sun's warm, inspiring glow and discovered Vitamin D. Talk about *revelations*. I should build a pyramid to <u>Aten</u>.

Two days ago, Nina disappeared. The iMac was gone when I arose yesterday. Late afternoon she returned with a pair of men in ties to pick up her other things. They didn't look like Mormon missionaries, so I reckon they work with her. Nina's stuff was evidently moving to the home of a guy with thinning black hair, a lunar forehead, and a hyperactive iPhone with a ringtone from Pink Floyd's *Money*.

None of the bankers disinfected when they stomped in, so my apartment got contaminated. I hope it's okay. Hardly any new cases were reported this week, few of them serious.

I feel as if I've lost two people. Y'all really had me going with that pregnancy business.

DAY 47

WHAT FLU? (& WHERE'S THAT VACCINE?)

The prevailing local strain of H5N1 seems to have mutated to infect a lot more people in Georgia. I bet it's thriving in lower cell temperatures than it used to require. Noses are cooler than bellies.

The death rate hasn't climbed much, even with influenza spreading like Sherman's fire. Every hospital is out of ventilators. Atlanta has shut down. Water supplies from Lake Lanier have been fouled by some kind of chlorination glitch. They didn't have much water to start with: <u>Georgians have long been praying for rain</u>.

But Atlanta's *so* far away. In New York, we're wearing '*I caught H5N1 and all I got was hot!'* t-shirts. We're attending so-called fever parties, where I doubt the powder is medical. And we're dancing in every bar (which is actually illegal here—check out our bizarre cabaret laws).

Baseball says it's coming back, but I'm certain H5N1 will win the playoffs. The season had begun well for this Yankees-hating, Mets-loving, Cardinals-worshipping fan. I'll wait till next year and hope my teams survive.

I still wear gear when I go out. Who wants to be the last soldier killed before a truce is declared? At least 60,000 Americans have succumbed, though it's always difficult to quantify flu fatalities. History says the second wave may be far more intense.

Who cares? Everyone expects a vaccine by then.

The U.S. Food & Drug Administration says we might see a shot by late July. Others think September far likelier. After what happened with swine flu, you'd think the Feds wouldn't want to promise more than they and the pharmaceutical industry can deliver.

Unless Americans add adjuvants—which heighten a single dose's effects by supercharging our immune systems—the developed world's pandemic vaccine capacity will fall way short because two shots are probably needed. Rumors circulate that the FDA has quietly approved a batch of experimental processes and additives that haven't been fully tested for efficacy and adverse effects. Among the controversial adjuvants is squalene, an oil accused of triggering autoimmune disorders in test animals. While it has never been approved for use in the U.S., European governments embraced adjuvants, particularly squalene, during the swine flu pandemic. Mike Coston makes the case for adjuvants here.

I'm not certain I want to be vaccinated, even for pandemic H5N1. This article sums up my problems with seasonal flu shots. I'm not so impressed by a supportive study claiming that the swine flu vaccination worked in 72% of adults under 65; it had a lot of holes and that's not even three-quarters of the poorly collected subjects.

The Cochrane Collaboration, a respected global network of health-care personnel and institutions, has published devastating assessments regarding the usefulness of flu vaccines. A review in 2010 found that even when flu shot components perfectly match the circulating strains—a rare triumph— "vaccination had a modest effect on time off work and had no effect on hospital admissions or complication rates."

I do not in general oppose the concept of vaccination against disease, though I think we've gone overboard. Even in this year of mortal threat, I'm not convinced I want to mess with my immune system. I've gotten this far in life and hope my personal protective gear sees me further. I feel blue enough these days without changing color.

The 1976 Swine Flu Vaccine Meltdown

The vaccine business is kind of shaky. Nineteen of 20 U.S.-based vaccine manufacturers quit the business after the swine flu debacle of 1976. A national inoculation program (watch some of its strange and colorful public service announcements) broke down after a higher-than-expected number of recipients came down with Guillain-Barré Syndrome. When that pandemic failed to materialize, American flu vaccine production collapsed. It took massive subsidies to restart it.

Which leads to something that bugs me. In a typical year, elderly subjects are herded by the busload to get seasonal flu vaccines. But in 2009, when swine flu vaccine seemed in short supply, the authorities shoved the old folks out of the line. Sure, young people were hit unusually hard by that flu, and some of the old-timers showed immunity to Novel H1N1 (possibly from so many prior exposures to influenza), but most of them evidently did not. Without much fuss, it was conceded that the elderly don't respond all that well to flu shots. You know, those tired immune systems....

The problem is that if no one gets annual shots, pharmaceutical companies will stop making the stuff. So once the pandemic receded, the authorities revived the 'get-out-the-old-folks' routine. Even my stepmom grew suspicious—and she loves doctors.

Still, I reserve the right to change my mind and stick my arm out for a *properly tested* H5N1 shot. That's asking a lot. Washington is teeming with lobbyists seeking *emergency* federal support for any products and processes their corporate clients conceive. Congress long ago immunized vaccine manufacturers from most lawsuits that might result from nasty reactions to their *formulae*. The men of the Supreme Court unanimously approved in 2011. (Of three female Justices, two opposed the ruling and the third recused herself because of prior involvement in the case.)

Even if they do maximize production—and enough sterile chicken eggs manage to survive avian flu to make doses for all—millions stand ahead of you and me. The prime guinea pigs will be cops, soldiers, nurses, and firefighters. I won't envy those human betas baring arms for Uncle Sam. I'll wish them minimal side effects as I pore over test results from around the world.

At best, it will probably be *four or five months* until ordinary people begin getting vaccinated. We're on our own.

DAY 48

PLASMAPHERESIS: THE GREAT RED HOPE?

Public health partisans have flayed me all day for admitting I'm not dying to get vaccinated against H5N1, even though I haven't told anyone else what to do. Antivaxers are screaming because I didn't tell people not to get vaccinated. Of course I know about the mercury in flu shots; people should worry more about all the other ways we consume mercury, starting with fish and coal burning.

Folks, you can all take those threats and shovel 'em where the sun don't shine. I'm a free man in a free Village.

My partner disagrees. He says I work for him in a corrupt society and that the antivaxers are right. What shall I do?

Hey, I've got it! Let's call him 'Fitch'—as in Ezra. H. Fitch, David T. Abercrombie's associate.

Then we'll discuss a slightly more natural way to gain immunity to H5N1. I've been wondering if any recent flu victims were given <u>transfusions</u>. People are mobbing hospitals for procedures they wanted to undergo in April. What if the blood supply is awash with H5N1?

In 1984 a baby who had received blood in San Francisco came down with AIDS. Even though a local blood donor was known to have died from the mysterious condition, authorities paid no attention. Doctors who warned that the blood supply might be tainted were denounced as alarmists. HIV entered the nation's blood reserve and 35,000 Americans were transfused with it.

No one panicked. The CDC's budget was reduced. Federal AIDS researchers were told to cut back on spending for laboratory equipment and conference travel. In 1984, you see, they expected a vaccine within two years for whatever caused AIDS. They didn't feel like fussing over short-term details.

There's still no vaccine for HIV/AIDS. But some scientists think blood extracted from avian flu survivors may contain <u>useful antibodies</u> that could help sick patients recover. A few studies from the 1918 pandemic imply that <u>plasmapheresis</u>—also known as therapeutic plasma exchange—might work. I wonder how long it will take survivors to auction their blood on eBay? (I can't imagine a dumber, riskier purchase than buying injectables from an online stranger.)

Some hospitals claim outstanding results. Others say the difference is marginal. <u>China keeps trying plasmapheresis</u>. Exposure is not reported to have killed anyone.

DAY 49-50

FLU 'DEFEATED,' PARTY ON!

Last night the streets were full. For once the East Village celebrated a speech by a president. They heard that "strong American hearts and clean hands" had licked H5N1.

I loved the warning that the second wave has historically been far worse in pandemics. I doubt it will be necessary to call in the Army, but I'm grateful and impressed that the nation's all-clear was qualified.

No one paid heed to the disclaimers. My neighbors were too busy partying, making out—all genders, styles, ages. It was as if the president had shown up on a flatbed in a toga, flashing flesh, popping corks. But our splashy <u>Mermaid Parade</u> doesn't happen till June, in Coney Island.

I was impelled to go downstairs and join the throng. Of course I kept my gear on. Some of the revelers had undoubtedly just caught H5N1 and were incubating it, unaware. *Probably* their cases will be mild.

I'm torn about exposing myself now that the virus has lost virulence. I wonder if catching it might confer immunity on me later, in Wave Two. No one knows. Some are holding flu parties to spread "harmless" microbes. But any acquired immunity might fade fast.

To come back and kill 10% of humanity—a not impossible prospect—the RNA would keep changing as H5N1 explores our world. Then our bodies might not recognize it as that bug we celebrated surviving three months earlier. We might catch it again.

I felt lonely without Nina and silly wandering around in goggles like the

Ghost of Plagues Past, so I headed into a bar famed for its happy hour. I was too late for discounts, but no one was leaving. The bartender couldn't hear me over Ozzy, so I had to lift my mask.

It was my first naked exposure in a public space in more than eight weeks. It was intoxicating to breathe stale suds. The bar smelled like people—not so bad, really.

I fixed the mask back on and perched on a stool.

Someone tapped my shoulder, a guy in a dark sports jacket. He asked me to join his friends at a table. I started to decline, but why not?

There were three guys and a girl, all really buzzed. They each shook my glove and we shared a round of tequila and beer at their expense. I lifted my mask for sips. They ignored me till they ordered another round and then the one who'd fetched me reached woozily for my goggles.

I leaned back and shook my head and checked them out more carefully. Were they trying to pick me up or pick a fight with me? Both? New Yorkers are probably weirder than ever now.

'Tinker Tailor' Tequila Table

The girl was younger than the men, with long blonde hair, green eyes, and a pudgy expression I found intriguing because she looked dumb enough to fool people. There was something alluring. I wondered if this was her show. Had she made them summon me?

The man who thought he was the ringleader was a young corporate lawyer—short hair, high school athlete, probably a pothead then and now. He was flanked by a round-faced guy in glasses, who turned out to be a freshly minted anesthesiologist on a fellowship at a nearby hospital, and by a darker man with a mustache and elegant hat, a Wall Streeter.

They weren't dangerous but they wanted to mock me. Maybe I embodied the deprivations they'd suffered. I wasn't even quitting. I was still dressed to die.

The doctor was smug. He didn't know much about bird flu and thought the system had performed well. He supported the others without adding anything, like a hack rent-a-witness in a courtroom. Perhaps he was exhausted from working a lot harder than his friends. Or maybe he'd lost his mental edge on a long break because there was so little surgery to support.

The lawyer asked if my gear made me feel powerful. Did I feel invisible to viruses and germs, shielded by a microbial firewall that scrambled my biological IP address? A fair question, imaginatively phrased. He'd be good before a jury, if that's what he does.

I replied in muffled voice that I felt like a geek then and there, but that I'd felt super-secure weeks ago. There were times when I strode down a sidewalk full of frightened, confused people, feeling invulnerable. Far from invisible, though—I carried cards to give people who asked about my protective gear.

I ordered a round.

The Wall Streeter was from London, the son of Brahmins—arguably an Indian Chief to complement the Doctor and Lawyer. A human rope-jumping rhyme had sprung up to toast my first night out in months. I thought that was pretty cool. We quickly agreed that the Beggar Man would be greeting newcomers out on the sidewalk as the Thief lifted wallets at the bar.

I started to take out my cell phone to photograph them as they toasted me. It was jolly in a barbed way.

So was I the Rich Man from selling all those masks? I answered that I would be the Poor Man until Wave Two, and then I'd be in pretty good shape.

Blame the Humble Flu Messenger

When I turned to the girl to ask her if she planned to jump rope for us, she splashed her tequila in my face. "You want this to come back," she said, adding words I can't post, or my site will be banned as unsuitable.

One by one, they tossed their drinks at me, shots I'd painstakingly paid for. (It's hard to count money with gloves on.) The men didn't speak as the girl blessed each salvo with a shiny-eyed nod.

Sticky booze coated my goggles. I could hardly breathe through the soaked mask. My phone was wet. I considered flipping their table over, but what was the point? I wasn't even drunk.

I pulled the mask aside and predicted they'd all turn black and blue from lack of oxygen. Shuddering with wrath, I cursed them. I described each of them leaking blood from every hole and I asked them to remember me when their genes pull the plug on their vital organs.

Raggedly, they lofted their empty shot glasses and gave me the finger.

I smashed a plate when I got home. That felt swell, but I resisted the impulse to keep going, to smash whatever 'Nina' had left intact.

Strange that they attacked me after I said I didn't have much money. What was that? Gene Clark had it right when he sang about people spreading infection through pain in *Echoes*.

DAY 51

STRING UP THOSE FLU PROFITEERS!

Antiflu partisans are in disarray everywhere. Stocks that rose on H5N1 have imploded. Chicken stocks are soaring. Financial newscasters mock profiteers who blew their exits. People with no sense of history chant 'Y2K, Y2K,' cynicism bubbling up like the contents of a broken toilet.

The LES DIY has called off their activities. I looked in vain for their table.

I missed the volunteers at Ric's Place, too. Between bird flu and Nina, I lost contact with a lot of people—friends, acquaintances, bands, artists, even job opportunities. I shared my home, my trust, my dreams with an angry mirage.

Fortunately, Ric is in very good spirits as he scours and paints his restaurant. I helped some and will attend his grand reopening in a few days. Ric's getting great press for his humanitarian efforts. With luck, he'll be out of debt by the time the second wave materializes.

I can't wait to taste the truly excellent grub he will dish out!

I hope the LES DIYers are proud, happy, and resting. Can't wait to see them again.

DAY 52

MY BLOODTHIRSTY READERS

I'm amazed at how many people wrote in to say I am lower than soot in a fireplace because I didn't kill those yuppies. Fitch lost all respect for me. Sneeky looks away when I call him. Nina's probably twitching in extrasensory disgust. Even some women say I should have tossed my glass in the girl's face.

I'm more the Jimmy Stewart type. Don't forget who wins the lady in *The Man Who Shot Liberty Valance*.

I didn't see much purpose in a fistfight. The president may feel safe from H5N1 in the White House, but I don't fancy a night or two in jail. If the pandemic still flourishes anywhere in Manhattan, it would be in the Tombs, as we call the local hoosegow. It's rumored that lots of prisoners caught the flu. The sorriest victims have to be those Mexicans they locked up in Arizona, then forgot to tend: two-thirds *muerte*.

DAY 53

A PERSONAL PANDEMIC POSTMORTEM

I'm worried about Nina. She wears tension, needs to be coaxed out of it like a turtle from a shell that fits too tightly. The first few times I saw her get worked up, I reckoned she'd calm down after we settled things logically and lovingly. Forty-eight hours later, something else would rattle her. When she's inclined to freak out, it's like trying to stifle a geyser. And she hates to suffer alone.

Maybe I ran out of reassurance.

I think the prospect of fatherhood under those particular circumstances scared me numb. I was trying to be rational and responsible. I can get a little clinical in a crisis. I retreat to logic. It's not the worst response, but it can seem cold.

Oh hell. What can you say when the woman you love would rather *turn blue and die* than spend another day with you? I hope she's okay.

DAY 54

ADVICE FROM BEYOND

My mysterious emailer has come up with a cogent explanation of Nina's behavior. She writes that Nina might have felt she caught the flu through some exposure I'd consider unacceptable. She could have been seeing someone who had it or hanging out somewhere that turned out to contain the virus.

She felt guilty. She wanted to cover it up, get rid of the illness, the symptoms, as soon as possible. *She wanted to take control.* So she raided my Relenza.

To spare me from her presumed viral particles, she decontaminated everything in my apartment and banned me from interacting with her—

from sleeping, touching, even from entering my once and future bedroom. Sneeky could've caught it from her, of course, but she couldn't think of—or manage—everything. Ultimately she evicted him, too.

Even her use of an N95 mask makes sense in that light. They protect others from the wearer. I thought she was trying to protect herself from me, which would require one of *my* masks. On the other hand, she seemed pretty sure I had given it to her after catching it from some vixen, so nothing really makes sense.

In any event, thank *you* for your thoughtful letter. (*Please send the text of your appeal; I'll post it if it seems suitably broad in scope, as opposed to a local notice.*)

DAY 55

HOWARD ROARK MAKES ME WRITE FUNNY

Nina writes to say she relished my account of the yuppies throwing drinks at me. She says I should tell you all how I gave her bird flu by cheating on her. Okay, I confess: Sneeky and I had a three-way with a stunning, long-necked pigeon. It was a one-night stand only because Sneeky got carried away and decapitated the poor creature.

For his part, Ric says Nina once accused him of fixing me up with women he knew. (He kept it to himself.) Her suspicions are evidently why Ric and I lost touch after she moved in. "I didn't want to say anything because I'd never seen you so happy," Ric explains. Now that I'm miserable and helping him reopen his place, anything goes.

The rest of you aren't much comfort, either. You think I'm abnormal because of how I write. Let me explain. I'm not a freak—merely an *architect* who cares about detail.

So when I find myself reading that a neighborhood in New Orleans was *decimated* in the flooding that followed Katrina, I know the writer is referring to the Roman military punishment known as decimation (which means *to remove a tenth*). This drastic penalty made every 10 legionnaires draw lots to choose which individual the other 9 would club or stone to death. I'd expect to see 90% of the buildings standing in a decimated neighborhood, with 10% of them wrecked.

Most people who know anything have come to think that 90% of the buildings were ruined, which is what today's writers usually mean. That doesn't make it right.

I was the kind of architect that aims to get everything correct. I will do that in every dimension at my disposal. Ever read *The Fountainead?* Or see the movie? (No? Well, buy them here!)

Not that I don't care what others think. Keep telling me what you want me to write about, but please confine future queries to matters of Health or History—just no more Herstory, okay? I've posted enough about Nina.

I might skip tomorrow's post—big party! I'll do my best to enjoy it on all of your behalves.

DAY 56-57

AT LAST, EVERYBODY GOES TO RIC'S

My excellent friend reopened his restaurant with a smashing event that turned out to be several different parties, sequentially. I tried to arrive late because Ric had warned me that the first phase would be critics and celebrities, perhaps even politicians. The critics are said to have been delighted. The first write-ups were very positive. *Boffo Blogging!*

The place was crammed with yuppies. Avenue C was full of smokers and hangers-on, just what you want to see at an opening.

When I managed to squeeze inside, I found a lot of women smiling compulsively and trying not to eat hors d'oevres lest food stick to their teeth or they gain weight or something. The men were happily digging up the gourmet trough, using as few utensils as possible.

I found myself standing in a crowd of masticating Uptowners, reluctant to pull exquisitely concocted bundles of food out of a tray in the middle of the worst disease mankind has ever faced. On the demand side, I faced the ever-cumbersome mask problem. How to drink that Nebiolo the host slipped me?

Even worse, how to flirt with goggles on? I have Nina's accusation to live up to.

I began poorly. It's hard when your consciousness still belongs to someone, but I had to start somewhere. The women in black dresses ran off one by one, claiming friends were waiting for them in the other room. I'm lucky they didn't fetch pals to throw drinks at me.

I met a reporter from a local paper—a rascally sort of guy with eyes that wink without moving. I think he widens them to seem sarcastic when he says anything that sounds idealistic or gullible. He was pretty well informed. Before heading home to the wife and kids, he arranged to buy some masks.

Then I hung alone, as if from a string. I hate that.

Ric spared me by explaining that my protective gear was scaring people and that the hip crowd would be coming later. I was wondering what had happened to the LES DIY.

The (Wet) Sidewalks of New York

I strolled the Lower East Side, which seems to have shrugged off the recent unpleasantness. Street corner entrepreneurs again hiss drug names at passersby (ignoring New York's ignoble status as what <u>NBC's local station called</u> the "marijuana arrest capital of the world"). The sidewalk crust of dog dung has cracked, revealing time-honored urine trails.

When I returned, the swarm was younger, louder, counter-cultured. I spotted numerous locals and members of the LES DIY stuffing themselves. They had hung up their masks, which made me feel even more out of place but allowed me to see their faces.

Many sported the infamous scowl that veteran East Villagers turn into a permanent sneer, but they looked happy to be relaxing together: a gang of do-gooders who did really well.

I wondered if my wise and persistent correspondent were present. It seems clear from her texts that she's a DIYer, a woman (duh), and a night owl like me. She has never offered clues to her age or style, though she's pretty savvy about how men and women relate. She has never referred to meeting or seeing me and has made it impossible for me to reply to her emails except publicly, in these posts. She might be older, offering flu support from behind an email screening service and a door lined with Multilocks.

Sifting the possibilities taught me something virtuous about wearing goggles: It's easy to scan a roomful of women without being obvious.

I began with someone I've suspected—Anna, the food czar, who normally works as a event planner and lost her job when the pandemic broke out. She's a diminutive princess with luminous skin and high, elegant bones. There's a little tomboy in there: She could poke you in the arm, *hard,* if you annoyed her.

Anna was dressed in black cling that left a lot exposed. This surprised me because her smile was as distant and sad as ever. I don't know if it's because her volunteer gig has ended (temporarily, I fear), or because she lost her little girl to the flu. Probably both.

I took off my mask and goggles to commence our first-ever conversation. Seeing so much of me may have frightened her. Her wide gray eyes darted around like mourning doves in hunting season.

Then she asked when I expect the next wave of bird flu to commence. *A girl after my own heart!* It could start tomorrow or in six months, I began. No one even knows why there has to be a hiatus. Is it the eye of an epidemiological hurricane?

Ayn Rand: Communicable Discomfort

Anna asked what I thought of the government's response to the pandemic, then looked bored when I said that anyone who needs the government has made at least one mistake. (Which she'd know if she were a faithful reader, right?) I raved about the LES DIY's work, and she thanked me for helping. Would I join them? *Never*, I said, <u>Ayn Rand</u> would kill me. I was joking, sort of. (Rand is dead, but I'm pretty sure she'd disapprove of the LES DIY).

Our conversation imploded. Discomfort is so communicable.

Somehow my brain overheated. I wanted to know more about her, so I asked about her daughter. I don't recall why or how I phrased it, but the best adjective must be: *badly*.

Anna looked confused, then suspicious. She went impossibly pale, fixed her eyes on an empty chair. They grew moist. I wanted to comfort her. I stuttered an apology.

A DIYer who co-owns an organic bagel shop abruptly engaged her in a one-way conversation about someone I don't know. Maybe she was protecting Anna. As she started rubbing Anna's neck and shoulders, I felt like a grain of sand stimulating an oyster in all the wrong ways. There'd be no pearl for me.

Red-faced, I moved away before Anna spoke again. I tried not to look at her after that, which took some effort. Her bare navel shimmered like gold, a testament to the wealth of Vitamin D in Ric's backyard. It hurt that we had felt closer in this very place, amid microbial menace, than we could feel now.

The LES DIY women ate a lot more than the previous female guests.

Their bodies and characters were fuller. The most arresting was Vanquisha, a retired transsexual nightclub personality who tends sick rescue animals for a shelter. She joined out of friendship, knows little about bird flu, is unlikely to be one of my readers.

The next activist I probed turned out to be a socialist bike rebel who thought I was insane to have spent years anticipating a virus.

A woman with powder blue eyes and a hard expression was intriguing and seemed to be watching me closely. She decided I was a creep when I asked if she had written to me.

No one, in fact, mentioned my website or blog. Where was my fan?

I was tempted to ask Ric who she might be. But I never seek the inside story on a woman. Even close friends are usually wrong: A little knowledge is a dangerous invitation to misjudge. Best to follow your instincts.

Then came a DIYer I'd never noticed—a medical student in epidemiology. She hadn't had much time to volunteer because she was working in two clinics, but she seemed cool. She's a true believer who aims to help society prepare for the second wave.

Rise of the Valkyrie

Henceforth she shall be *Val*, for Valkyrie. She's a tall, vital blonde with hazel eyes, exactly my height and wider in the right places. *A perfect 'write-in' candidate.*

Val had been impressed with my mask, which DIYers had given her. She wasn't allowed to wear it at work, where everyone was forced to use the same protective equipment. Ayn Rand wrote all about socially ordained mediocrity.

Val wanted to step outside for a smoke. I'd have walked a mile for one if it might establish that she'd been writing to me.

She had something nicer in mind. We walked in what I eventually realized was a pattern of one-way streets whose traffic was always coming at us. No cops were going to sneak up behind this lady. She was pleased to let go after months of tension and overwork, regaling me with things she'd seen at hospitals.

The public health system came closer to snapping than I had suspected. There's a desperate global shortage of ventilators, which I'd predicted. A lot of equipment failed from overuse, which I hadn't considered. There aren't enough needles to vaccinate many people.

If the second wave commences soon, the medical industry will collapse. Staffers are fed up. With vaccination mandatory for New York State medical professionals, many worry about the prospective H5N1 shot. People are tired, dispirited.

"The problem is that we did well enough going through the motions in a mild pandemic to let everybody think the system works," Val said, "which was probably the worst thing that could have happened."

She was warming up when I realized I felt dizzy. I'd drunk too much wine and had stupidly eaten little. Val's smoke was especially thick.

She kindly located a stoop so we could talk some more.

It was gloriously unthinkable when we kissed, like unsafe sex would have seemed a year ago. However clumsy I felt, it was delicious to explore a mouth other than Nina's. A warmer, deeper, softer space welcomed me.

Then we heard the voices, a chorus chattering in our direction, wherever we were. Soon they were upon us—the women of the LES DIY—and we were embarrassed. At least I was. Anna looked up at me, then away, as usual.

After greetings, Val left with them. We didn't even get to trade email addresses. I'm convinced she already has mine.

DAY 58

NO FEARS FOR TEARS

I'm watching the body count rise in India, where so many died in 1918. Could this be the start of the Second Wave? It's way too early. Dread the thought.

To its credit, the New York City Department Of Health & Mental Hygiene is reminding people that a second pandemic wave is inevitable. They've posted ads on subways and buses telling people to keep scrubbing their hands. (Unfortunately, these alternate with NYPD placards <u>urging us to turn each other in</u>, anonymously, for whatever.)

New Yorkers don't want to read about microbes while they rock along, clinging to dirty poles and breathing one another's breakfast. The overhead blurbs about hemorrhoid surgery and how to learn computers are nasty enough.

Torture comes in waves, too. You can be heroic the first time. It's when the brutes come back with tongs or electrodes or hoses that your imagination starts to work against you, anticipating whatever they haven't done *yet*. You torment yourself on their coffee breaks. By the third round, you'll invent anything they wish to hear.

Romance also circles back. It was so cool kissing Val that by the time I got home, I was drowning in memories of Nina. I was stirred and sad after a few moments of intimacy with someone. Still, I think knowing Nina was good for me. No regrets.

I do feel wretched about having upset Anna at Ric's reopening. As much as anyone I know, she's earned the right to relax, rejoice in her own survival. Having seen her cry twice, I can report that it's an impressive sight. Tears assemble atop her cheekbones like imperial phalanxes, ready to wash away any rebels below.

Fortunately for Anna, crying reduces tension. A study compared the chemical content of tears from women who cried for emotional reasons with that of tears stimulated by onions. The emotive drops contained high levels of neurotransmitters and hormones linked to stress. Shedding tears lowered blood pressure and pulse rates, smoothed brain waves. Crying supports the immune system, memory, and appetite.

My stepmom always says men stew in our own juices. Now I think she means we don't cry. According to this report, it turns us off when women tear up. (That hasn't been my experience.)

I always wish I could comfort Anna. I hope something—or someone—does.

DAY 59-60

CRUSOE VS. ROARK, ROUND ONE

My mystery correspondent has resorted to snail mail to send me what she insists in an unsigned typed note is no joke—Daniel Defoe's novel, *Robinson Crusoe*. She sent the paperback *Priority* two days after Ric's party.

The note says Defoe 300 years ago was a fresher writer and thinker than Ayn Rand was 50 years ago. I'll check it out, however doubtfully. Of course I've read Defoe's *Journal of the Plague Year*, an extremely realistic account of the Black Death in 1665 London. (Buy them both here!) Some suspect the British government paid him to write propaganda to stir public support for unpopular measures they were taking against plague.

Face it, lady: Ayn Rand wrote good yarns. Sure they're simplistic, but they're driven by ideas and they're fun to read.

Today I contacted the LES DIY's coordinator, a woman who sang a New Wave hit in the 1980s and now runs a big community garden. She says the gang is hard at work preparing for Round Two. I pledged to keep them shielded in protective gear until this pandemic is resolved for real—and not merely obscured by social euphoria and willful ignorance.

She agreed to pass my contact information to the medical student I met. I suspect Val may already have sent me history's first English-language literary classic. I want to know for sure.

I'd like to send her *The Fountainhead*. Then we can compare notes—she on copious rum, me on martinis.

I'm pleased to report that the LES DIY has officially asked me to join. Of course I'd never enlist in a collective organization, but I'm grateful for the recognition. I'll continue to back their efforts. Now for some reading....

DAY 61-62

NO MAN IS A (HAPPY) ISLAND

Robinson Crusoe turns out to be a great, brisk text. It involves risk, enterprise, failure, fear, more hazard and enterprise, and then comfort, all in vivid cycles. The hero hurls himself into the sand after each shipwreck, wishing he'd been content with his previous lot as a survivor, vowing to settle down and serve God if only He will grant *one more chance*.

Each time the protagonist gets a break, he's gripped by a fresh ambition. The first great realistic novel is about one of fiction's biggest-ever workaholics. In a way that Defoe never formally admits amid all the god-fearing rhetoric about hubris and greed, work is his hero's true Grail, his salvation.

Ayn Rand would agree. She never bothered with religion, though she was a big-time moralist.

In the present context, *Robinson Crusoe* also addresses the anguish of loneliness, isolation, the possibility of dying unfulfilled, even unnoticed. In a pandemic, all men may wish they were islands, but there's a downside to solitude.

Imagine being the only survivor of H5N1, or at least the only person you ever see again. For decades, Crusoe could see only himself—in a watery reflection, at best.

I'd be forever hearing Gene Clark sing *Here Without You*. (Watch it.)

DAY 63-64

GRATITUDE

Finishing *Crusoe* made me feel clear, at peace. Thanks, generous one. *A heck of a read!* Feel free to quote me.

Then I emailed Nina to tell her I understand why she was so upset. I appreciate that she tried to spare me her fanciful virus. She meant well.

Because of her work and my pandemic, we never got to travel—something we felt could sustain our romance. When this is over, I hope we bump into one another at that café we both like in Madrid. She can make a fool of me on the dance floor, as we always expected would happen there.

I don't want anything from Nina, but I respect our months together. Enough readers have written in about their own personal problems to give me a better sense of how people who are cooped up together can substitute fear and mistrust for their better feelings.

At least we've *each* survived bird flu, so far.

DAY 65-68

RADD—A PRE-EXISTING PANDEMIC DISEASE

Sorry about my little hiatus. Friends lured me upstate for my first escape since February. I underwent digital purification by keeping off the Web. (Fitch took care of orders and shipping.) It was hard at first, but I rekindled friendships among great conversation, lively dogs, brilliant cook fests, and challenging music-making. (I'm a force in percussion.) I got soaked during a long hard rain in the woods. I began to forget what words look like.

I returned to some jarring ones. Mystery Mailer wrote to inform me that she is not a medical student and that the latter is engaged to a doctor. The plot thins. I hope he's not one of my readers.

Who sent that book? How does she know my name and address? I hope she explains herself soon. Shall I dub her *The Stalker*? She's been too nice for that, so far.

Meanwhile, Nina emails that her bank tested everyone and found H5N1 antibodies in her blood, so she *did* have bird flu. *Not certain I believe her.*

She adds that her work is going very well and that she's seeing someone who is less tense and more fun. I presume she means to say *than I am.* (I hope she means *than she is.*) I do hope it's not the suit with more ego than hair.

Nina thinks she's a forbearing soul. Hers is the kind of patience that lets her stick a knife in, then let it rest. Now and then she adds a new blade. Eventually you're a voodoo doll with a weighty assortment of hardware. Mere pins would be a blessing.

Perhaps she suffers from Romantic Attention Deficit Disorder. I miss Ganesh.

DAY 69

GENE CLARK CHANNELS MY CONFUSION

I've gone whole hog on Gene Clark (best anthology: *American Dreamer*), rotating through the stages of romantic withdrawal with my ears in his hands. Clark's voice is plaintive but never lacks dignity.

First there was <u>*Set You Free This Time*</u>. Well, not quite, but it felt good to think that's what had happened. (Watch an old TV <u>video</u> of this masterpiece)

Quickly followed by <u>*I'll [probably] Feel A Whole Lot Better*</u>. I (sort of) did. (<u>See the Byrds play it wholly live</u> on *Shindig*, a '60s TV show.)

Then came some inevitable self-pity: <u>*The World Turns All Around Her*</u> and <u>*Because Of You*</u>.

Finally, my dimwitted attempt at amiable contact: <u>*Tried So Hard*</u>. Swell, now I know … something.

Harold Eugene Clark was a far more miserable bugger than me, as you'll find in that excellent <u>website</u>. He was a real Missourian—a hard-luck player who never bellyached, even when a trench ulcer was pitting his stomach.

Watch him struggle in this <u>late-career performance of *Tried So Hard*</u>. Somehow he manages to come through. An inspiration to all damaged Americans who try hard.

DAY 70

FASHION & LITIGATION FOLLOW THE FLU

Proof that society has recovered from bird flu: Ambulance-chasing lawyers are already campaigning to squeeze the survivors! On the subway today (yeah, I still wear my mask underground and in dense crowds) I saw a sick poster. No, it wasn't my reflection.

The placard screeched: *Did you catch bird flu at work?* The graphic showed workers huddled like galley slaves under a sneezing overseer. What if you instead caught it from a cute contractor you weren't supposed to be hitting on?

As if anyone knows *how* or *where* they caught H5N1. But employers have money, so why not trade your job insecurity for some tacky litigation? Maybe they can't fire you till your suit is concluded. Call it *The Banality Of Survival.*

The ones destined to clean up in court are those who can make a reasonable case that they were sickened by a flu vaccination their employer mandated. Forcing people to get shots rubs me the wrong way.

I was more inspired by the *Los Angeles Times* fashion article someone kindly emailed me about *Q Zone Style*, with tips on how to turn protective gear into nightlife accessories now that the pandemic is "over."

Watch for my website overhaul! I'll be selling *Mystery Mouth*, *Digital Vigilance*, and *Epi-EyeShades*. For a nifty markup, of course. That stuff you bought from me is gonna redefine coolness.

I came home to find Sneeky rollicking in a sunbeam, his eyes alight with Vitamin D and feline fervor. As if nothing had changed in six months. I'm free to sing bits of hearty doggerel to my cat without minding that I look like a schmuck to someone who finds it hopelessly endearing only 28.2% of the time.

DAY 71-72

FAST TIMES & FLU TALK WITH WISE GUYS HIGH

At last, some fun. My old friend Mark is in much better spirits (evidently not *that* kind). He invited me to a hot nightspot on condition I not wear a mask or any other "embarrassing" gear. (He must have missed that fashion piece I blogged about.) I consented because I'm bored now that life approximates 'normalcy.'

That would be a state of anxious boredom. Some dare call it depression.

Mark readily hops social groupings in the best of times, so the guys he was with were new to me. I tend not to have much in common with his friends.

The use of one of their names enabled us to sweep through a mob of elegant people to enter the place. We were shown to a big, central table where about a dozen men and women sat, drinking champagne and vodka.

The guys were twentysomethings of undefined substance. I assumed they had real estate interests. Most of them wore dark office clothes under neat hairstyles, no face fur. They could have been seminary students on a quiet bender, somber about everything they did. Even when they humped women while dancing, they looked distracted.

I was shocked to discover they were into bird flu. They knew about the masks I sell, wore them during Round One. (Was that where my emergency gift delivery went?) I didn't ask, but they took care of me as if I'd gone to Brooklyn just for them. They bought me good beer all night. (I didn't want the multicolored vodka things they were mixing.)

The alpha male was of medium height, black brushed-back hair, and intense brown eyes. When he spoke, the others shut up. When he left, I was surprised to see another guy pay for everything.

The young boss knew about pandemic waves, wanted to hear my view of what will make H5N1 come back. I explained this flu's lethal ferocity, the variety of animals that catch it, the different ways it destroys them—all factors that distinguish this pandemic from say, the one that laid an egg in 1968, or swine flu.

He wanted to know what I thought of news reports heralding a vaccine. I explained that each claim of progress contradicts the others (an epochal discovery every week!) and that there's no way to produce enough vaccine quickly to stop the disease.

Every "breakthrough" comes with caveats no one wants to consider. Fine print makes terrible sound bites. Will candidate vaccines be carefully *tested* to see if they're safe? A public desperate to regain complacency doesn't wish to hear that today's rumored miracle never underwent proper trials; they'll scream for quick approval and sue everyone in sight if it turns out to be toxic.

Quack Alert: Don't Inject Peroxide

In 1918 people claimed typhoid vaccine worked against influenza. Others said mega-doses of aspirin did the trick. Or quinine. Citing statistics they gathered from their own caseloads, American doctors gave patients heroin, atropine, oxygen, strychnine, epinephrine.

Europeans indulged in vivid concoctions, too. In *The Great Influenza*, Barry tells of an Italian doctor who claimed success after injecting people with mercuric chloride. Some French physicians rhapsodized about arsenic. A Greek who injected patients with a blend of morphine, strychnine, caffeine, and their own fluids boasted that his subjects improved rapidly and that only 6% of them died.

I came close to clearing the table with that tirade. I captivated them anew by predicting that tens of millions of Americans will refuse to be vaccinated and will want other ways to fight flu.

It wasn't long before we were discussing a big protective equipment sale that wouldn't involve shipping. No commitment, but I may have sold more gear in four hours than I did in the whole first round. I'll do my instant best to replace them.

By the time I noticed a little vial making the rounds, we were discussing Relenza and how much of it must have been wasted by now. (Nina's dementia proved illustrative.) They wanted to buy Relenza, too, but I couldn't help them.

Dancing on the Edge—of What?

Gradually I realized these guys were operators, black market types, scammers. Mark must savor exposing me to them. He has always hitchhiked on dark roads and would be a master criminal if he weren't so lazy. He's one of those tall, good-looking guys who seem shifty and proud of it. Some people extract charm from corruption.

By then I was watching the gang socialize. At least 50 girls must have dropped by. Most took at least one drink.

A pair of women marched up wordlessly to partake of champagne. They poured and poured into their cups, pausing to let the bubbles subside before resuming. The cute one bore the harried look of a stray canine poaching on a bigger dog's turf, while her less-gorgeous friend mooched with confidence. She was big-boned, big-eyed, and fearless.

While the men circled the prettier woman, the bold one struck up a conversation with me. She didn't know or care who was hosting the table and she turned out to be a heck of a dancer. Unlike men who blandly stare into space as they dance 'erotically,' I enjoyed her pale eyes, full of light and wit.

The music was modern oldies mixed with synthetic hip hop and no one really cared about any of it until some immortal chords stuttered forth and froze everyone while they tried to figure out what had changed. It was Nirvana, *Smells Like Teen Spirit*, and it was vital and riveting and momentarily cleared the air of empty irony.

Mark wanted to split those women with me. In the past, I've always gone out after breaking up—taken stock of the world as a single man, brought home at least a headache.

Blame his smarmy attitude or the sappy dance music that followed Nirvana. I wound up feeling toxic, sad, as if something horrible were happening somewhere. I left that hearty babe free to find someone who's all there. This blogger's no fun.

DAY 73

SO HOW DO PEOPLE CATCH FLU? DON'T ASK!

A reader sent me some shocking quotes and allegations. At first I thought it was a hoax, but he sent links, too. He was responding to my consternation about my ex's claim that she caught H5N1 while barricaded in my apartment. He didn't try to explain, but it seems anything is possible—or at least, *not impossible.*

The first shocker was a quote from—and link to—a 2005-6 research solicitation by the CDC, wherein the Feds offered tax dollars to get scientists to conduct some pressing research:

"The biological and genetic basis of transmissibility of influenza viruses among humans, and mammalian species in general, remains poorly understood."

Huh?

Then he quoted and linked to <u>a reprint of a paper</u> co-authored by leading global flu researchers, including legendary flu-fighter Robert Webster, a New Zealander who was first to figure out that influenza originates in birds:

"A key feature of a potentially pandemic influenza virus is its ability to spread efficiently from infected to noninfected hosts (i.e., its transmissibility). The molecular basis of influenza virus transmissibility remains unresolved."

The CDC and the man who helped develop the method by which flu vaccine is now created are saying that the *biological, genetic,* and *molecular bases* of flu transmission among people are *not understood.* Not even for seasonal flu!

And I thought it was a slam-dunk: Someone sneezes and we breathe it in, or touch the active residue. (You know, on fomites.) *Nope.*

I spent the day trawling deep science on the Web. Thanks to the University of Toronto's website, I found <u>a faint photocopy of a 599-page work about the 1918-19 pandemic</u>. An extremely respected doctor named Edwin Oakes Jordan wrote the book for the American Medical Association's Chicago branch, which published it in 1927, when experts were still trying to determine if the pandemic had been caused by a virus or by a bacterium.

Strangers on a Plane—Proof of Flu Transmission?

In *Epidemic Influenza, A Survey,* Jordan reports (pps. <u>441</u>, <u>442</u>, and <u>443</u>) on three distinct attempts in 1918 and 1919 by the U.S. Public Health Service to transmit H1N1 from numerous sick people to healthy volunteers. They failed to demonstrate a single impeccable transmission, even after rubbing fresh, hot sputum into volunteers' throats. And that was a fearsome flu.

In only a handful of studies have researchers claimed to have observed direct flu transmission. The <u>most commonly cited paper</u> dates back to 1979 and concerns an airplane stuck for four hours on the tarmac in Alaska. A very sick passenger is said to have transmitted the flu to many others while the air filtration system malfunctioned.

That, folks, is an anecdotal report. There were no controls. Ventilation was down and passengers wandered on and off the plane. I'm not saying it didn't happen. *But a decades-old cause-and-effect observation is the best they've come up with to prove what we all 'know.'*

As Dr. Michael Gardam, director of infectious disease prevention and control for Canada's Ontario Agency for Health Protection & Promotion, told the *Los Angeles Times*: The only thing the study proves is that it was extremely unpleasant to be on that plane.

Heck, I was stuck next to a woman sneezing from Madrid to New York at the peak of last year's flu season. I was sure she'd infect me. I could *feel* her fever radiating at me as I leaned away, into the window. What did I get? *Nada.*

I can't explain the alleged Alaska flu carrier. I don't disbelieve it. Maybe it was a 'superspreader'—as happened in several cases with SARS transmission. But I'm flabbergasted that it's all they have. I don't understand how I failed to notice that the science of flu transmission is so incomplete.

Have you folks ever heard any of this?

I've been selling masks and gloves and goggles on the assumption that sick people spread the flu. I think I'll keep at it—and continue wearing them. I'm not going to risk my life or anyone else's on the gaps in popular flu theory. Hey, it *feels* better to wear a mask. Might help. Who knows?

The more I learn about bird flu, the less I know I know.

DAY 74

A LIBERTARIAN FLU BLOGGER'S POLITICAL DEVOLUTION

I woke up to a nasty message from *she who doesn't relent.* "The liberal enemy Rand puts forth in *The Fountainhead* is a cartoonish shinyheaded intellectual who is feminizing the man's world with his squishy socialist tricks," she writes. Even her italics sneer as she asks: "I always thought you were cute, but arrogant. Are you simpleminded, *too?*"

Boy, am I.

Some of what our shadowy friend says is true, and she says it well. But who can resist Rand's lurid tales of high principle and hot sexuality? Not I. It looks like fun to tell all those predictable mediocrities to stuff it.

I should hook our hectoring correspondent up with the devoted libertarian who wrote in to denounce Jimmy Stewart for having starred in *It's a Wonderful Life*. Not because the Christmas classic is sentimental. It's "col-

lectivist, bank-bashing propaganda" aimed at *"robbing the fruitful to enable failure."*

I'd have snapped to attention for such rhetoric until 2008, when America's megabanks stirred up so much havoc that they extracted grand subsidies from the Feds to stay in business and charge us more. (Shades of 1933, after which they at least kept a straight face—and books—for a few decades.) In 2009, the bank Nina works for bounced a credit check it had just sent me, then charged me a bad-check fee! I wonder what Rand would have said about such an enterprise. (Sadly, she never warned that borrowing money is the ticket to credit serfdom, as too many Americans have learned.)

I see now that I must be devolving into a *moderate*. (Our malcontented correspondent doesn't get it, but hey—I'm still waiting for her to finish composing the voluntarist manifesto she asked me to post.)

Mom would be thrilled that I'm mellowing (*girls hate all that talk*), Dad sullenly disappointed (*real men don't care what girls think*). Please don't tell them.

DAY 75-76

ROUGH SEX—WHO OBJECTS TO AYN RAND'S STRUGGLE?

If emails could maim, I wouldn't be able to type. I received a very strange message from Nina, who thinks I've been calling her and demands that I stop. I replied, asking if she needs help. I don't know what to do. The voice mail at her office sounds fine. Is she playing games with me?

On top of that, my friendly reader has seized on my reference to the sexuality in Rand's novels to ask if I believe women need always surrender to the men who won't admit defeat. She's referring to the bottom billing embraced by Rand's leading ladies when they encounter the Heroes Who Resist Mediocrity & Collectivization.

I confess, Madame! The first time I ever thought much about S&M, I was a 13-year-old holding a big fat book, Rand's *Atlas Shrugged*. Dagny Taggart was leaving Hank Reardon's rail car the morning after with a bloody lip, some bruises, and a smile I couldn't comprehend. Miss Railroad Princess sure didn't seem to mind that Mr. Steel Baron was a clumsy kisser. Weeks later, reading Howard Roark's epic rape of Dominique Francon in *The Foun-*

tainhead confirmed my confusion.

Yet I survived. The books helped make me a libertarian while leaving me a gentleman, confirming the virtues of unadulterated free speech.

Our crusty commentator also ripped my um, subtle joke about the LES DIY as a 'voluntarist' association. They're *altruists*, as she goes on to emphasize: "We help people because we believe it's in our interest to do so. WE ARE *&@%$^ [my special code] HUMAN BEINGS."

Then came another swing at your wretched blogger. "If you want your girlfriend back, maybe you shouldn't publish reports about your public makeout sessions."

Finally she tried to turn Gene Clark against me. She attached <u>Death in Vegas</u>' cover version of one of his greats, *So You Say You Lost Your Baby*. It features a booming vocal from Paul Weller of the old Jam as he taunts a guy who's moaning about a lost love when in fact, *he's* the real baby. Uh, I get it.

Clark's versions of the song are far richer (<u>here's one</u>). (For Death In Vegas, Madame, I prefer *Dirge*, or *Aisha*, the serial killer song Iggy Pop recorded with them for their cd, *The Contino Sessions*—on sale here, of course.)

Oh heck, I get her point. I've been whining. I hate that, too.

She followed that with the first Web icon I've seen her use—a blue frowny face. Which effectively spells B-A-B-Y.

DAY 77-79

DON'T JUST DRIFT INTO THE FLU'S SECOND WAVE

I finally got the residents of my building to discuss the pandemic. Representatives of a third of the apartments gathered in the laundry room. (There's no lobby—and no way I'd invite so many vectors into my home.)

I don't think any of them understand bird flu very well.

A fifth of those who came are trying to organize a rent strike, albeit for unrelated reasons ('kill the landlord' being a general theme around here), another fifth are so lonely they'd attend anything they don't need to go outside to get to, and two-fifths believe bird flu embodies some kind of conspiracy, though they differ vigorously as to whether it's a hoax or a genuine threat. One fifth nodded a lot when I spoke—-my bobble-headed peeps. A heck of a flock!

I ain't much of a shepherd, but I got most of them to consider the likelihood of famine, riots, plague, and bedlam. New Yorkers are surprisingly open to apocalyptic visions, so long as you're addressing the near future and you don't invoke conventional religion.

They wouldn't consider buying protective gear or Relenza or getting pneumonia vaccinations. We did exchange gmail and yahoo and hotmail addresses. I hope my secret—that I have ... health stuff—is safe with them. I know that survivalist readers will hurl at the thought that I told neighbors about my pandemic safety stash. What was I thinking?

Nice things, I guess. I even befriended my next-door neighbor, a Ukrainian gentleman whose children live on the West Coast. Long before I moved here, he was this building's super. He's a vigorous old man whose immune system could tell tales. He'd probably empty a bar washing down some borscht.

I'll try to find someone to keep an eye on him when Round Two begins. He's agreed to get a Pneumovax 23 shot, for which he's way overdue.

We should all make something useful of our hiatus. Don't forget this is the first pandemic in history that followed years of warnings. The others came 'suddenly.' What does it say about our civilization that we've chosen to remain unprepared—even as H5N1 circles like a big shark, tearing into us from time to time? Just sampling, *so far.*

Blabber & Smoke

People are already making fun of the government for what little effort it did make. In my view, the Feds wasted billions on pre-pandemic vaccines and antivirals when what we needed were hospital beds, ventilators, and nurses. Others loudly argue the reverse. Let's agree that, whatever we need, there ain't enough of it.

A lot of atrocities took place in our brief first-wave crisis. We're now hearing how people took the law into their hands—or out of the hands of others. (Some cops surrendered without much fight.) Mayors jumped to seal off their communities at any cost (not that this helped much) or deployed cops, deputies, and guards to divide their constituencies by race and class. For years we'll be hauled off to sit on juries assessing criminal charges and civil damages from that month of uncertainty. How much hardship will *three months* of chaos wreak?

This is our chance to ensure that frightened citizens don't need to steal food and medicine—or kill their neighbors—in Round Two. If a hurricane slammed into Miami, tore it up, and then froze offshore for months, would everyone just go swimming till it made landfall again? Won't anyone prepare?

DAY 80-82

ALONG COMES EVELYN

Mail call! My cranky correspondent says I must be drinking too much to have so miserably misunderstood her critique of Ayn Rand. "The coolest aspect of Rand's novels is her distinctive sexuality. Her taste for antagonistic sex must have embarrassed right-wingers in the 1940s and '50s," she says. "That took some guts and a sense of humor, which you [meaning *me*] evidently lack."

Hmm. I thought I made it clear that I had nothing against Rand's sexuality. When Rand couples her characters, she invests *all* of their power, to the max. *The Fountainhead*'s Dominque uses her newspaper column to deride Roark's work, even as she invites him to plunder her body. She's hardly helpless. Their violent lovemaking embodies their work, their war, their passion for so much that isn't sexual.

I believe in purity of expression in all dimensions (short of serious injury), as long as the doings are *consensual*. Dagny and Dominique are strong-willed women bent on draining the cup of life with a worthy partner. They know what they're doing. Unlike my stalker, who's just earned the name 'Evelyn,' for the character in *Play Misty for Me*. (Hear Orson Welles narrate the lame movie trailer!)

Rand wasn't the first writer to say love hurts, but she primed the pain with socioeconomic and sociopolitical issues. When her leads consummate the buzz, history feeds their need. Talk about compelling unions. Compulsive might be the better word.

I do agree with Evelyn's observation that Gary Cooper turned in a lame performance as the idealistic violator in the movie version of *The Fountainhead*. Cooper played the scene like a George Romero extra who'd lost his teeth. Jimmy Stewart would have been *driven*. (Watch him take Kim Novak shopping in *Vertigo* or knock Doris Day out with pills in the second *Man Who Knew Too Much*.)

A number of normal readers write that they've been organizing their communities all along, but that the public suffers from flu fatigue. "It was easy to get my neighbors excited about bird flu until it showed up," says a Wisconsin woman. "Familiarity has bred contempt," reports a student in San Jose. "We've lost them."

I was afraid of this, and not because my personal protective equipment sales are negligible. (Fitch is never far from my thoughts.) I don't doubt that demand will return aplenty in October, at the start of flu season, even if H5N1 is still lying low.

After all, I'm selling a solid mask technology and everyone knows we defeated bird flu with *technology*. Never mind that America's hospitals locked patients out, that there were disturbances and blackouts and shortages. Who cares that Tamiflu failed frequently and that Relenza doesn't always work—and was impossible to get when fear broke out?

It's as if a thriller called *Pandemic* bombed with critics. I'm afraid the fans will wind up catching it anyway, Word-of-mouth gets around, you know.

DAY 83-86

HOPE-SIMPSON SHEDS LIGHT ON FLU

A retired Scottish doctor has emailed from Buenos Aires, Argentina, to tell me that answers to my questions about flu transmission have been staring me in the face for months. "You need to go back and look into who discovered the role Vitamin D plays in influenza. *Follow your own links!*"

That's all he said.

So I've spent days compiling information about the thoughts of a deceased English doctor named R. Edgar Hope-Simpson (1908-2003), who spent his final decades challenging and rethinking everything that was known about influenza. A *true* debunker!

Not that anyone paid much heed. Hope-Simpson's research was published before the digital age. His papers and his book are out of print. I've stumbled on the Gene Clark of viral research, a once-famous man whose greatest work is ignored.

Devoted readers will recall my Round One post about Vitamin D, wherein I noted that flu epidemics correspond to seasonal declines in exposure to sunlight. I failed to digest a Scott McPherson blog entry about Hope-Simpson's work way back in 2007. Apart from abstract summaries of Hope-Simpson papers once presented in Britain's *Journal Of Hygiene* (now *Epidemiology & Infection*, which has published more recent research on it, too), Hope-Simpson's work is best accessed via the Vitamin D Council's excellent and intriguing summation of the actual papers.

R. Edgar Hope-Simpson was a country doctor who riveted the medical world by proving *on his own* in 1965 that childhood chickenpox virus reactivates in adults as the painful condition called shingles. The British establishment was charmed and impressed that a general practitioner could conceive, research, and demonstrate something important that had eluded research labs and universities. (It brought Nobel prizes to others who followed his work, though a shingles vaccine that hit the market in 2006 isn't selling because it costs too much.)

Hope-Simpson could have spoken at banquets for the rest of his life, the establishment's pet exception to the rule that proper research is conducted in well-heeled institutions.

So Who Does Spread Influenza?

He was just getting started on another virus he suspected lurked in seemingly healthy people, as he had shown chickenpox does. While maintaining his practice, Hope-Simpson spent the rest of his life arguing that *seasonal flu isn't spread by sick people!*

That's no misprint: The good doctor surmised that seasonal influenza is activated by an unidentified force that circulates among people whose paths don't need to cross during flu season. *People who are not only symptomless— but entirely well.* (Hinting at the mystery is a *New York Times* story on the peculiarities of swine flu transmission in a Pennsylvania community.)

Like all great thinkers, Hope-Simpson started with good questions.

What makes influenza roar into our lives every year, only to depart abruptly with so many promising subjects yet to be infected? The Black Death didn't do that. The measles don't. Disease normally spreads as fast and as far as it can until it runs out of carriers or creatures to infect.

What brings influenza back so regularly? How does it explode across continents and oceans faster—when you consider the necessary incubation period—than jets can carry it? And how did it do this before the Wright Brothers?

Why is the second wave of a pandemic supposed to be worse than the first? How does a disease come to kill more people after it's made a run through the populace? Shouldn't people become immune to it?

For that matter, what makes change such a constant feature of all influenza A strains? Why do they inevitably mutate—*evolve away from our control*—so that health authorities have to *guess* which varieties to fight against in each new vaccine?

Hope-Simpson began by noting that his hometown in Southwest England came down with epidemic influenza at the same time every year as Prague. (They share the same latitude.) He pored over ancient church registers showing that influenza spread just as quickly back when Britain's roads were impassible.

He further observed that tropical flu breaks out in the rainy season, when the inhabitants' sun exposure plummets. This was confirmed in a study published by others the year Hope-Simpson died.

'Solar Radiation'—Vitamin D

He also detected patterns involving sunspots, which reduce the quality of rays that reach us. He surmised that a drop in solar radiation levels triggered seasonal flu in Europe's dark months and in tropical rainy seasons. Vitamin D's immunological properties weren't known yet.

Essentially, Hope-Simpson concluded that epidemics spring up as Vitamin D levels plunge in the population, activating *symptomless carriers* who caught flu the previous year and then repressed it with natural antibodies.

He also said the flu vanishes broadly every year because carriers stop being infectious after six to eight weeks.

Since many people are known to spread influenza without showing symptoms, Hope-Simpson's claim isn't as radical as it seems. Until you consider that he also asserted that *active* influenza sufferers do *not* transmit seasonal virus as much.

His studies of communities in Wales and England showed that in most families, only one member catches flu in a given season. He opined that *this individual* becomes the vector that spreads flu to his or her uninfected kin during the next epidemic—not the schoolchildren we customarily blame for transmitting flu.

Seasonal flu hides quietly, evolving inside the previous year's victims and mutating to trick its way past their immune systems. Then it competes with other active flu strains to infect potential hosts. They all play hopscotch in us, among us, competing to replicate. Each year's flu victims select the viral variety against which they have the least immunity; the winner becomes the new season's hit strain. That's why the medical establishment must gamble on which strains to batch into each annual vaccine.

It's not clear if carriers can spread seasonal flu in July—or if they simply harbor it in an inactive form until their Vitamin D levels drop low enough to let the virus circulate. So I won't be selling masks on the beach.

Next: What this means for *pandemic flu*....

DAY 87-89

WE'RE ALL ANIMALS ON THIS LEAKY ARK

I've aroused a tempest of protest. I'm shocked that the furor wasn't motivated by my enthusiastic and succinct account of Dr. Hope-Simpson's theses. Readers seem charmingly open-minded about that.

You'll thus be pleased to learn that someone is sending me some old Hope-Simpson papers. Others are being kindly faxed to me by the kind folks at *Epidemiology & Infection,* the Cambridge University journal. I can't wait to read and digest them.

First I must wade through a river of indignant emails about my defense of sexual freedom. I wish I could quote them at length but the exciting ones are, um, unprintable.

I'm not going to turn my blog into a debating forum about sexual aggression. I do, however, deny I'm a *pervert.* I'm proud not to judge other peoples' sexuality and I'm danged if I'll be judged for Ayn Rand's. Some of you people should take a long look in the mirror, naked. We are *all* animals.

That's why we get *sick.*

DAY 90-91

MY BABY WROTE ME A 'LETTER'

I received a very strange Valentine's Day card from Nina. (I presume she knows this is July.) It was beautifully put together, probably with the best creative gear at her bank. The cover read, in splashy colors: "How many Valentines does a man need?"

Inside was a photoshopped image of me biting into a heart, adapted from a photo of me grinning as I opened up for some pie she enjoyed trying to make three months ago. A big bowl next to me was full of juicy cardiac treats. She signed it 'Heartless.' That part makes sense.

DAY 92-95

FLU VIRUS 'SEEDS' HUMANS

Sorry this took so long to prepare. I want to get it right.

R. Edgar Hope-Simpson was 10 when the 1918 pandemic struck England, so he never had the professional opportunity to observe an influenza strain that crossed directly from another species, the way H1N1 is commonly thought to have done in 1918—and as H5N1 has done.

The pandemics that Hope-Simpson lived through as an adult were minor affairs—strains that conquered the world by mixing genes from preexisting human varieties, as H1N1 swine flu did. Many people had vestigial immunity from exposure to precursor strains.

I'm guessing that Hope-Simpson would concede that species-jumping strains are so intense, so virulent, that they can and do leap from the sick to the healthy. Leaving aside the curious, almost incomprehensible resistance in some elderly people, no one has any immunity. These strains rage through the population like fire. We've all seen it this year.

I think Hope-Simpson's theories can explain how and why H5N1 percolated for so long before it went global. *The virus had to seed us* to reach a kind of biological critical mass.

H5N1 killed most of the Indonesians, Egyptians, Vietnamese, Chinese, Indians, and Africans who caught it from birds or other animals. A minority of victims survived. Many weren't logged as H5N1 cases. Many survivors probably thought they had outlasted dengue fever or some other tropical disease.

But *bird* flu had found a home in them, if Hope-Simpson was correct. After falling ill, their bodies suppressed the symptoms and the virus proceeded to lie dormant inside them for a year or two.

Now, according to Hope-Simpson, the microbes were desperate to replicate. This entailed further evolution so they could jump past their carriers' immune systems to infect other people. When their recovered hosts' Vitamin D ran low, H5N1 would power up, mutate, and attack new subjects.

At this stage, H5N1 became a *human* disease: An *avian* virus that had learned to survive in one human being became capable to spreading to other human beings. This explains the early cases in which no animal or human vector—a sick chicken or person or cat—was identified. One person had encountered another who harbored freshly minted human H5N1. *Without symptoms.*

Each low-light season (rainy season, in the tropics) would bring a wavelet of human cases that would recede after spreading just a bit more. I begin to wonder about the rumors of experimental H5N1 vaccines based on human survivor antibodies. Could they have helped it circulate?

The 'First' Flu Wave is Second ... or Fourth

I've also located strong evidence that the so-called springtime *inaugural wave* of the 1918 pandemic wasn't the first. A noted U.K. microbiologist named Dr. John S. Oxford makes a very good case that British soldiers garrisoned in Étaples, France, were felled by what looks to have been <u>pre-pandemic flu in December 1916</u>. They turned blue.

<u>Mortality studies</u> from New York City at the start of 1918 indicate an undetected pandemic wave that took the young, spared the old. <u>Helen Branswell published an article</u> that raised similar questions during the swine flu pandemic.

Did the spring 1918 pandemic follow a series of *herald waves* that no one noticed? Each would have left more carriers embedded in a seemingly healthy populace. One wave's survivors would quietly inspire the next until the tide of illness rose so high that it could be ignored only by monarchs and politicians bent on world conquest.

If I'm right, we can catch H5N1 from just about anyone. We could catch it from sick people because pandemic influenza trumps the seasonal pattern. We might get it, per Hope-Simpson, from recovered latent carriers. Or it can be spread, as everyone knows, from infected people who aren't yet showing symptoms.

This may explain why the first wave of pandemic flu is weaker than a later one. The second and third waves are spread by both freshly sickened carriers and by seemingly healthy veterans from earlier waves. Sources of contagion abound. Because the virus is *mutating* to leap from recovered victims, later waves are likelier to entail evolutionary gains in virulence as the unstable RNA virus tries new tricks.

Which could in theory render any vaccines generated from a first-wave virus obsolete!

No one is safe until the deadly strain loses its punch. We knew that, didn't we? Now we know *why*.

DAY 96-97

ULCERS ARE FOR HECKLERS, NOT 'CRACKPOTS'

My relentless correspondent (no, not Nina, whose emailed accusations mount like the snows in her native South Dakota) reports that the LES DIY is still holding well-attended meetings and that morale is strong. She suggests I shuck off my "romantic egotism" and attend a meeting tomorrow night. Drink is pledged afterward, even for "snotty self-indulgent Randian nonmembers."

If 'Evelyn' had promised to reveal herself at said meeting, I'd be sure to attend. But I don't think she goes to these things. So instead of driving Anna to tears again, I'll just hope she's feeling better—sunbathing, swimming, cooking tasty grub for her friends,

I'll head upstate early in the morning to find refuge. It's what Crusoe would do. Now that I think the earth is well sprinkled with human H5N1 survivor 'bots colonized by virions, Round Two should really suck.

I'll post sporadically until I'm settled. I've arranged for someone to fill orders for personal protection equipment that come in while I'm gone.

A final note regarding the fabulous Dr. Hope-Simpson (for those who email that he and I are crackpots): When a couple of Australian doctors, J. Robin Warren and Barry J. Marshall, tried to tell the world that peptic ulcers were caused by a bacterium named <u>Heliobacter pylori</u>—and not booze, spices, and insufferable spouses—they were <u>scorned for years</u>. That must have made winning the <u>Nobel Prize</u> more fun.

Hope-Simpson took lots of honors, but never that one. Two scientists who separately followed up on his work with chickenpox (varicella zoster virus) and herpes zoster each won a Nobel.

Hope-Simpson was a gutsy man whose Quaker faith made him resist fighting in World War II. He was lively enough to remarry in his 90s. His obituary shows a balding, bespectacled man with an amiable expression. It bespeaks that he maintained a good sense of humor and professed to love life, even as he was leaving it.

DAY 98-100

MY DREAMY HUNT FOR A FLU HAVEN

I'm posting on the fly from a friend's house way upstate, where a big sun burns off the mists every morning. It's all trees, few people, and yet so huge that the population adds up to seven million upstaters—lots of them libertarians.

After Round Three has concluded or a good vaccine has penetrated me, I'd like to buy land up here and design a gorgeous house I could execute inch-by-inch, like a vine. That's how immigrants to the U.S. do it back in their home countries; they add a room every few years.

Mine would be a palace shrouded in nature, camouflaged among trees and rocks and water. Not very Howard Roark-like. Still, Rand's point is to fulfill oneself without superfluous references: There are different ways to clear out postmodern sludge.

I'll try the Finger Lakes next. Meanwhile your humble correspondent can recommend Jose Saramago's *Blindness,* a great disease novel about a virus that causes its victims to see only glowing whiteness. Stock it for Round Two. I can't believe I just touted a book by a lifelong communist, but it's that good: *Superb.* Guess I'll sell it. (The movie wasn't bad, but the book is sublime.)

While you're at it, read *The Viral Storm: The Dawn of a New Pandemic Age.* Global virus hunter Nathan Wolfe's exploration of the world of invisible life forms we've only begun to discover is enjoyable, comprehensive, and scary—and available here.

DAY 101-104

MEET JANE DOE—A DIY FLU MANIFESTO

Our pal Evelyn says she brought the following manifesto to the meeting I skipped. Did she intend to hand it to me and declare herself? Bombard me with paper planes while I was dozing?

I like what she says and I like how she wrote it. Reminds me a little of Gary Cooper's populist speech in *Meet John Doe*. (Watch the speech here; read it here.)

Evelyn wrote two distinct messages—a preface to me and an appeal to the world:

Dear ____, I wasn't very aware of bird flu before the pandemic hit. I thought it was a hyped up monster story. I've learned a lot, thanks to you and your blog.

You said you didn't personally know anyone who died in your Round One. I did. This isn't a survival game for me. I'm not trying to profit or prove anything.

I believe in what I'm doing. It keeps me alive. More people need to do more while there's still a chance. It's not just about breathing. It's about the world we want to live in. I'm sorry we didn't get to meet, but that shouldn't keep you from posting this. I bet you can think of a selfish reason to do what your heart wants to do anyway.

Here goes:

We are little people who have lost someone or who fear that we can and will lose someone. We are the immune system of this society, standing up and banding together to fight something we don't recognize or understand, but which threatens all of us.

We are little people united by the fact that we breathe together and we hope to breathe together next year, no matter what we think of each other.

We are not alone. We are tens, hundreds of millions of Americans, billions of world citizens, and we must stand up together to fight for our survival.

Meet with your neighbors. Learn from them. Teach them. If they're sick, help them. If they're hungry, feed them. Meet with others who feel as you do, no matter what they think they think. Band together to do more than you can accomplish on your own. Save others. You may just save yourself, too.

Create your own DIY. Call it anything, in any language. Do it for yourself and for others and for the future we all want and need to have. It only needs teamwork and a sense of humor. If you don't have one, team up with someone who does.

Evelyn ends with a private note: "Guess which one I'm missing?" Hard to tell. Personally, I'm missing both. Guess I missed her as well. Too bad: She sounds interesting again.

DAY 105-107

EVELYN'S SWEET SUCCESS

Our anonymous contributor's appeal went over awfully well. Other blogs linked and/or reposted, and I've spent a day poring over emails about it. Apart from a few loyalists who angrily defend my sense of humor and generous spirit (*shhhh!*), most laud her message. Some want her to keep posting here. Many ask questions.

They want to know how she is now, what she does, who she lost, how she deals with it, and if she herself caught the flu. More than a few ask why she doesn't simply introduce herself to me. (Good one!)

She has stirred people. I'm delighted to have provided the venue.

For her part, she thanked me and says the LES DIY is setting up a website to take contacts directly from other DIYers. "But we're going to stay local," she assured me, signing off as Evelyn.

I think that's wise. Thanks for writing, Evelyn.

DAY 108-114

A NEW YORK (UP)STATE OF BEING

I'm posting this from a Wi-Fi café in a town whose name I forget because it's so weird. I haven't seen much news, unless you count TV. I see that H5N1 is kicking up here and there. Happily there's no pattern yet.

I've been in—or at least driven past—Rome, Naples, Geneva, Waterloo,

Phoenicia, Poland, and Norway without ever leaving New York State. Or being far from Wal-Mart. The big box is *the* cultural contribution from my neck of the woods, now that Budweiser is brewed by Belgians.

The natives here are New Yorkers of a different sort. They have the trademark intensity and they worry a lot, but they can be nicer. The city dwellers are busier, more optimistic—and rotten listeners.

Upstate isn't prosperous once you escape the city's monetary spill-zone and that of the capital, Albany. Bird flu doesn't faze upstaters. They cock an eyebrow if you mention it, curious to see if you have something new to say.

Where I'm from is more interesting to them than my views on H5N1. Few have visited Missouri, but it makes me a country boy, which they appreciate so long as I don't seem dangerous or freaky.

The local papers can be fun. The crimes up here are pretty dramatic. Every time I pass through an old industrial town and then glide by one of thousands of lakes, I'm reminded of Theodore Dreiser's *An American Tragedy*. The book starts in Missouri and ends up here—from a storefront revival house to death row. The precedent keeps me on my toes. (Yes, it's for sale here.)

New York City is a monstrous distant rival. Upstaters fight to the death for government money and attention. In some counties job growth comes only from prisons that house convicts from the city. Upstaters are tough on crime.

They sure do sell a variety of rolling papers in service stations. Real choices greet the roving consumer.

DAY 115-116

RAISE—FEDERAL FLUREAUCRATS

Sorry for being so slow to pick up on America's leap into community organizing. She-who-never-sleeps emailed me a news story about it, but I didn't realize how weird it was until I stopped to read and google.

Since the hiatus struck, I've felt there are three dimensions I can inhabit. There's the popular zone in which H5N1 is dead and bells resound in celebration. There's my world, where gongs are for warning people. And there's been the Federal world, which seems unusually, uncharacteristically, *remarkably* similar to my own. From the president on down, we are told that disaster looms unless we prepare.

Now the Feds have actually done something—just days after I helped issue Evelyn's DIY Manifesto—though I am *not* claiming credit for the Department of Homeland Security's decision to set up its own volunteer group. (DHS had already been <u>recruiting Girl Scouts</u> to fight terrorism and microbes.)

The ornately christened *Restore America's Independent Spirit & Enterprise* looks to be a grand expansion of <u>National Voluntary Organizations Active in Disaster</u>. NVOAD is a Washington–based group of national, state, local, and faith-based volunteer organizations. Its board members have included the Federal Emergency Management Agency—<u>FEMA</u>, already part of the <u>Department of Homeland Security</u>—and the <u>American Red Cross</u>.

I confess I don't see how creating RAISE can ever constitute the dramatic innovation so eloquently trumpeted by the president. Sure, the acronyms can make you dizzy and some people enjoy that sort of thing. But why do religious groups and charities need to be paid by Washington to do what they always said they wanted to do—and for which they constantly solicit vast sums from kind people?

Evelyn writes that she isn't enthused, either. I'll stick with her Do-It-Yourselfers, unsullied by taxes and bureaucracy. The LES DIY worked very well with our local churches and synagogues in Round One.

RAISE doesn't need our help anyway. It's already a hit in Congress, winning promises of big bucks from pols in both parties. It's rapidly staffing up with candidates who flopped when they ran for elective office. I'd rather take soup from people who really want to dish it out—and who don't work a clock, as these hacks will.

The Feds say they intend to contact the groups that coalesced so helpfully during Round One. They should bring guitars—and big amps!—when they come to my Village.

DAY 117-119

HOW I BUILT THE HOLE IN MY CAREER

I banged up the bottom of my car cruising a bumpy back road in too good a mood, so I've been inactive and incommunicado for a few days. I'm back at my friends' house in the Catskill Mountains, rediscovering garlic and ginger. I'll need a hydroponic spice farm to get through a long quarantine.

An architect wants to know why I quit the profession. Evelyn does, too, so here goes: I got fed up with the tech race. Designers have elevated software above craft. Me, I like a blank sheet of paper. It glows and frightens. It provokes.

But there's more to it. My breakthrough career crisis came after the first real estate crash, while swine flu was menacing America. I was working as a young drone at a boutique firm that was excited to have landed a plush gig planning a McMansion in Westchester.

That was when I met my partner Fitch, a more-seasoned architect with a sense of humor that's so dry it feels like sandpaper. We couldn't be more different: He writes architectural software for kicks, dreams of hitting it big with a killer modular design. Fitch's droopy eyes never fail to spot trouble on a project—something he probably picked up when one of his early designs installed an elevator backward. "Treat every assignment as your last," he counseled me in what seemed the infancy of my promising career. "One of them will be."

The project that did me in required the removal of several structures—a gorgeous 19th Century Robber Baron manor, a rocky hill, some ancient maple trees, and a timeless, towering oak. The dream residence was to be a showpiece of gadgets, colors, and shapes ripped by the client's wife from fashion magazines (and revised monthly with much fussing).

Fitch explained that the spouse's inability to marry any design for longer than eight weeks made this project a slow-motion rush job. "We could be in a hurry for years," he exulted over free tequila one night at a dive bar he'd designed on the side five years earlier. In a wretched economy, he said, the client he called 'McMissus' would fund our lives indefinitely.

Transcendently Trashed

I worked hard, staying at the office later and later at night, drinking more and more to recover from it. One Sunday, I made the mistake of smoking a joint when no one was at the job site and I had to check a detail. The place's beauty smote me. What Fitch called the *Trash Mahal* wasn't funny.

Suddenly the owner drove up in a blue Porsche, alone. The guy turned out to be more of a techie than a hedge funder. He was a rather nice, slightly abstract quant with spiky hair that was prematurely frosting as he designed his firm's trading programs—its essential identity, I guess. I wasn't supposed to communicate directly with clients, but he wanted to show me the old mansion. As we toured it like kids in a haunted house (complete with a secret passageway), he volunteered that he hated to tear it down.

My mind exploded with ideas. What if we repurposed the mansion as a classic annex to the modern palace his wife wanted? History could survive by bowing to her gleaming, glass manse. Our client yearned to keep contemplating that oak from the gray stone tower, which turned out to be an ideal spot for contemplative smoking.

At work the next day, I told Fitch I intended to pitch an alternative—a contemporary structure that could coexist dynamically with the old one. He lurched out to smoke a cigarette on the corner—never a good sign—and returned to show me a URL for want ads: Architects were clearly not in demand. Cowed, I decided to wait, possibly forever.

The client was less discreet. He told his wife about my idea. Her excitement was lethal.

I was fired a week later, when I showed up 35 minutes late after having toiled till midnight the previous evening. My boss, a dreamy eyed hypocrite who had regarded me "like a son," accused me of betraying him by trying to exploit our client for side work. He surely knew that was never my intention.

I wish I had pulled a Howard Roark and marched out, denouncing my profession for its immoral mediocrity. (Watch the Roark speech that Ayn Rand forced Hollywood to film in full when they shot *The Fountainhead*.) I can't stand being falsely accused—it makes me crazy. My brother framed me for lots of his transgressions when we were kids, and my parents too often believed him.

I left my office quietly, in shock, and then had to fight my way through lies for months just to collect unemployment. I've been a lowly contractor ever since. When there's work.

DAY 120-126

QUICKIE CRUSOE—MY CRASH FLU COTTAGE

Just in time, I've found and rented my haven, a bungalow in a hamlet about 100 minutes' drive north of New York City. This place is rural with *two* capital *R*s. Not even a stoplight. It makes my hometown seem *trés* cosmo.

Mark has been uncommonly useful. He's handled sales and fed Sneeky while I'm away. Sometimes he helps me pack the car so I don't get ticketed for double parking. It's good to get along. I admired him a lot when we were young and he had answers for everything. (He still thinks he does, but it's easier to fact-check them.)

After each trip, I return to an apartment full of empty beer bottles, smoldering ashtrays, and an iMac loaded with strange software. I can't tell what the programs do and Mark is lax at explaining. (MacWorld is lush with bootleg programs.) I'll figure them out in the backwoods, where I've arranged satellite broadband service, the best I can get in my chosen cow town. I need sleep.

Instead I just went to that bar I like for a public drink. The place was more subdued than when the yuppies attacked me. I recognized the drummer from the LES DIY and we shared a few rounds.

'Bruno' has a haunted demeanor—sunken eyes, deep cheekbones, a haggard grin—but he turns out to be a pretty funny refugee from Buffalo. He'd rather croak than hide from Round Two upstate, but he said this without judgment.

I was horrified to learn that Ric's business has been failing. My friend hasn't mentioned problems when I call him. Bruno thinks diners don't want to eat there because they associate it with "that depressing old disease." *Has helping people cost Ric his dream?*

DAY 127-131

I FEEL FEVER COMING & IT AIN'T YELLOW

I've made three further trips upstate, reckon I'm half-resettled. I've transferred canned food, rustic clothes (read: too worn for Avenue D), tools, and utensils. I've stocked decontamination supplies and filled oil tanks and gas canisters. Foul weather gear and books and music and movies. Satellite service is up. Crusoe would envy me.

My home is taking on a desolate air. Sneeky's comments have begun to echo. Nina doesn't even write any more. I reckon she has settled into her job and her new yuppie friends. No need to dredge up confusion from our old life.

Last night I went to a club to watch a band of once-famous, ever-in-famous East Village old-timers for whom Bruno plays drums. I stood in a packed basement full of wriggling hipsters coughing from what I presumed was too much smoke of one sort or another.

I was watching the group play a jolly, lilting—yet somehow nasty-sounding—song that goes something like "*I don't know me and you don't know you/Maybe we both got reflecting to do/Let's get started now….*"

Suddenly I started feeling *pandemic.*

I could smell it through the fog of illicit tobacco. I heard it in the desperate throat clearing that rivaled the band's roar. I saw it in wheezy dancing moves, jittery bloodshot eyes. I tasted it in my beer. The mug was open to every passing breath.

I fled that simmering, oozing, viral pit. This was a full-on premonition, not my customary logical conviction that disease is coming back. I felt I could touch it, that those people are doomed. As I may be, too.

I was all elbows, all the time, all the way home. Empty boxes greeted me like hungry hatchlings.

Tomorrow I'll start transferring masks and gloves and goggles. Last will come the rest of the food, my stereo, and Sneeky.

I'm staying up too late, reading a novel I bought for a buck from a sidewalk vendor: Josh Russell's *Yellow Jack*, about a revolutionary photographer who documents a series of <u>yellow fever</u> outbreaks in New Orleans in the 1840s. Those folks knew how to party during an epidemic. They even paid to have images taken of their beloveds' corpses, dressed up with dolls, toys, books, and sabers.

It's fascinating that Yellow Fever now occurs only in South America and Africa, even thought the <u>*Aedes aegypti*</u> mosquito that best spreads the virus is common in the Middle East, Asia, and the Pacific. Another *how-can-this-be* viral moment, brought to you free—by nature.

DAY 132

SWAMPED BY THE FLU'S SECOND WAVE

I blew it, horribly—worse than you can imagine.

I hope you're all safer and better prepared than I was when Wave 2 slammed New York. I'm stuck here indefinitely. A bunch of my goods got stolen in the panic. I have more.

DAY 133

GOING NOWHERE, ASAP—FLU IN NYC

Who'd have guessed the public would run amok at the first word that H5N1 is back?

Even as they joked about Swine Flu II, the masses must have been listening to us. Not that we convinced them to take any useful measures, but we evidently scared their daylights out. People responded with passionate denial until the news came yesterday that seven Brooklynites had caught viciously fatal cases of bird flu, with dozens more cases suspected.

As it happens, I was obliviously loading my rusty old VW Fox with protective gear. The sun was shining, the street quiet. I smiled at some kids and their scruffy dog. I packed so many boxes I couldn't see much in the rearview mirror.

Then I drove off without checking the Internet for news. I've been trying to be less compulsively informed lately and the radio in my car was stolen years ago. (I just sing Gene Clark's _Radio Song_, about how every tune they play is about his lost love while he drives cross-country to find her.)

Traffic was weird, intense. It thickened by the second and people were unusually hostile. They were yelling, gesticulating, honking, ignoring cops as they pressed through lights of any color. I've never seen worse gridlock, a deafening, throbbing muddle of sirens going nowhere.

In midtown I decided there must have been a terror attack—that the safest thing was to keep going and get the news at a gas station up north. When I saw people wearing masks, I put one on. Any kind of barrier might help against whatever, right?

It took three hours to cover 10 miles to Washington Heights. Access to the George Washington Bridge was frozen, as if it were closed. Unimaginable. Had someone blown it up? Emergency lights and sirens were fired up in all directions.

I opted to head north through the Bronx and Westchester, as did most everyone else.

The End of My Road

Somewhere above 190th Street, near the bottom of a long hill, a Hummer pressed out of a side street and into my car. He tried to push me out of his way like a stray garbage can. He crushed my right front wheel, backed off, and inched away.

I got out to chase the behemoth, pen and pad in hand. He sat in the block ahead, revving his engine and bumping cars. His windows were smoked. I don't think that's legal here. I banged on his door. No response.

I headed to the Hummer's rear to log the license plate. The side burst open and a fist slammed into my face. A hand snatched my notebook.

I looked back through broken goggles to see people pushing *my* vehicle out of the road. An old red van rammed my trunk, causing the Fox to lurch into a teenager. I think it broke his leg.

Next thing I saw was a younger kid running off with a box of my masks.

The crowd pushed my car to a bus stop and dispersed. The injured kid vanished. I still had no idea what had set the city off. My nose was bleeding.

I tried to call my insurance company for a free tow to a repair shop, but cell service was jammed. I know the New York Police Department wanted the power to shut down mobile phone service in the event of a terrorist attack. Whatever they did wasn't quelling public anxiety.

No one would talk to me. They kept their windows rolled up. I closed mine, stood by the car door, hoping someone would pause to explain things.

The End of My Load

Instead three guys showed up with shopping carts and the youngster who'd stolen the masks. As they emptied my passenger compartment and trunk, they let me notice they were armed. No one directly threatened me. Nor did anyone grope for the wad of cash in my pocket. They pretended not to notice I was trembling. Does everyone do that when they're being robbed?

A short man with a big head explained the furor as best he could: Bird flu was back, unstoppable. This he registered by flapping his hands and coughing with a fatal expression. He took pains to tell me they needed my gear for their families. "*Todos para los niños*," he said, holding a box of children's masks and taking snapshots of little ones out of his wallet.

He pointed to my cracked goggles questioningly, then to my gloves.

I pointed to the empty car and shrugged. I had packed it mostly with masks and some personal stuff, which they let me keep.

As if to prove his honesty and good faith, the man handed me an old taser. He frowned when he saw me wonder if it might be useful on the spot. He grinned when I put it away.

I had to get home by subway. I don't remember making my way to the station. I was flat-out terrified—of people, the air, noises. I mostly rode between the cars, a crime here. I kept my eyes closed as clammy, sooty August air whipped around me in the tunnels.

I was in shock. *If* I made it home, I would be trapped there. My lungs were burning from disuse by the time I got my door open and gasped for air. I still haven't eaten much.

Don't worry—I have plentiful supplies to sell you. *But no car, little money, and a refuge I can't reach.* We'll all need better luck than I've had.

DAY 134

FEAR & HOPE TEAM UP TO TORMENT

I've tried in vain to rent, borrow, or buy wheels. I offered friends free shelter in the second bungalow, but no one is interested. They sure want masks though.

I'm on half-rations until further notice because I stashed so much food upstate. Sneeky is noisily aghast at my failure to pinpoint Round Two's arrival after predicting it for months. I paid for this with a black eye and a very sore nose that remains indented from the mask's edge. I feel like a cop who got mugged on duty.

The city seethes with fear. A lot of people are sick. There has been looting almost everywhere, though the streets sound quieter tonight. There probably isn't much left to steal … in the stores. I've come to hate the sound of footsteps and voices in the corridor. Silence never sounded so sweet.

My audience has mushroomed. Welcome back! I'm sure to be more entertaining and informative *tomorrow*.

I feel so alone. I don't know what I'd do without Sneeky, my loyal friend. While he senses the disturbance, his gaze says: "We're still here, relax."

I'll be OK. When I was a kid my parents dragged me to see what I expected would be a terminally dull operetta, <u>Dialogues of the Carmelites</u>, about nuns who wind up getting their heads chopped off during the French Revolution. I liked it. That night I dreamed that everyone I knew was lined up at the guillotine. When I tried to join some kids I knew, the guards told me to go away, I wasn't supposed to be executed. I felt really left out, dejected. The way Crusoe did on bad days, I guess—condemned to survive alone.

Maybe I'm destined to outlast you all.

DAY 135

NEW YORK MET NEW ORLEANS ON A BRIDGE

My neighbors bang on my door at all hours, seeking protective equipment, advice, and assurance that someone knows what's going on. They want to hear that they'll be able to get their medication, that there will be food.

How could my responses be heartening? I'm just a masked and goggled face grunting across the seven-inch chain that safeguards my door, keeping one hand out of sight so they can imagine I'm armed. I spend my free time (is there any other kind?) looking out the same windows they have.

Their expressions turn sour. Some hold their ground in the hallway, staring, challenging me to admit that things aren't really so bad. I know this trick: It can get store clerks to look *again* for what you want.

I have nothing positive to say.

A very good friend of mine—a onetime love who gave me the lamented Ganesh ceramic that Nina smashed on her way out of my life—may have caught H5N1. 'Lisa' left a ragged, fearful message while I was sleeping this morning. When I returned her call, I reached the Irish guy she lives with, who was sick for a while in May. I dined pleasantly at their new apartment a week ago. I get along well with her boyfriend, who knows that neither Lisa nor I want to revive our old romance. (Nina seems to have thought we wanted to.)

I've never known Lisa's confidence to falter, but two people at her workplace are sick. One has vanished into a medical system that can't or won't account for him. The other was afraid to try a hospital and doesn't answer her phone.

I had already provided Lisa and her boyfriend with protective gear and I've offered to visit if it might help. He's open to the idea, but Lisa won't hear of it. She's feverish and uncharacteristically high-strung. She's afraid to miss more work because her company is firing people. I felt terror in their voices. I'd do anything to keep her breathing.

I emailed them links to the best sites, including Dr. Grattan Woodson's *Good Home Treatment of Influenza*. And I recommended that Lisa start taking Relenza immediately.

Hydration: Key to Surviving Flu

Woodson offers very good advice about resting and hydrating flu patients. Lying down reduces our need to breathe deeply, so we don't draw viral particles deeper into our lungs. We must drink a cup of nonalcoholic liquid at least once an hour when awake. This helps cleanse our system and replenishes fluids we lose to fever.

Patients who cannot eat must consume electrolytes. A quart can be made from clean water, two tablespoons of sugar, a quarter-teaspoon of baking soda, and an equal amount of salt (or half a teaspoon, if no baking soda is on hand). Dr. Michael Greger, who literally wrote the book on bird flu (free at his site), further suggests adding orange juice and mashed banana for potassium, if such luxuries are available. The electrolyte drink must be dripped into a patient's mouth if necessary. Precision is very important in how much sugar and salt you use, says Mike Coston.

Dr. Greger emphasizes that *fever is a good thing*. Viruses don't like heat.

Fever is our way of inhibiting replication, effectively curbing the enemy's reinforcements. Greger warns against tampering with fever by taking acetaminophen and/or ibuprofen unless a temperature surpasses 104 degrees. If it does, he recommends both, along with cooling cloths and tepid water sponge baths. Aspirin should never be given to children (good thing my stepmom doesn't read this blog or she'd feel inadequate) because it can trigger a rare side effect.

Otherwise, I don't know much more than you do. The Internet is still up, so I know New York City is the epicenter for Round Two in America.

I scoff at the notion that someone brought the virus from that prison in Sao Paulo (where the pandemic reignited in the Western Hemisphere). People are desperate to identify a foreign flu vector, as if no American could have brought the virus back from a business trip, a sinful escapade, or both. The preferred narrative is that an alien brought H5N1 here. It invites us to blame both outsiders *and* the government (for letting them in).

Hope-Simpson would have smiled politely and said that nothing could have prevented Round Two. We were well-seeded months ago.

Barricades on the Bridge

I'm astonished that New Jersey closed the George Washington Bridge the day flu came back. I was stuck just blocks from that hysterical parade of pedestrians trying to cross, including drivers who had abandoned their cars. Thousands of New Yorkers managed to reach the dense suburbia that tops the Palisades.

Then a line of New Jersey State Troopers blocked the bridge with shipping containers, tear gas, clubs, and tasers.

You've all seen the streaming cell phone videos. The worst was posted by a *flugitive* while masked cops took turns bashing wads of blood and flesh out of his friend's head. (How did this brave guy grab and post those shots so near the action?) The troopers' savage defense of the Garden State against the late Columbia University sophomore who happened to be from Montclair, N.J., was playing on hundreds of thousands of screens around the world before the brutes could catch their breath.

We still don't know if a tourist from Las Vegas tumbled over the side of the bridge while the crowd ebbed and flowed. She'll wash up or she won't.

Protesters are enduring a defiant vigil in high winds under the great suspension cables, surrounded by cops from two states who don't want to touch them. Suburban police in Long Island blocked the Long Island Expressway until New York's governor threatened to send our state troopers after them. The media find it inconvenient to cover any of this in person. I see only copter shots and talking heads. Are reporters afraid to go there—or are the cops blocking them?

I think of Gretna, La., whose cops fired toward Hurricane Katrina refugees on a bridge as they tried to escape New Orleans. (On a different bridge, police shot and killed people.)

As for the president's national military alert, I want to know if it's intended to help us or lock us in. A little clarification is in order. All we hear are orders amid so much disorder. It sounds like dogs barking furiously at phantoms.

DAY 136

A PANDEMIC WORLD—WITHOUT MONEY

New York needs money. No, not a traditional budget blowup: We're suffering a life-threatening liquidity crisis on the simplest level.

WE HAVE NO CASH HERE!

The whole city shut down at once. A lot of people are getting fired for the duration, many without severance. I count seven friends whose jobs are gone, including the calculating Fitch. He wants to know how people are supposed to file for unemployment benefits at offices that are closed. What about welfare payments? Or food stamps? Sure, do it online. Let's hope those servers are sympathetic. I doubt many workers are tending incoming applications.

For those fortunate enough to remain employed, who will process their checks? We see gleaming, empty towers. The suburbanites who staff offices either got out or are still trying. They're not tending accounts in an enterprising spirit.

Bank service looks pretty spotty on my TV. ATMs ran out of money the first day—not counting the ones that were pried open.

There can't be much for sale in stores. We won't even be able to get a black market going without cash. Do we have to invent our own scrip? Even I'm starting to miss my nearest *Chasebucks Coffee Bank*, at least conceptually.

DAY 137

FLU SOLUTIONS ARE FAR FROM MY WINDOW

I'm still holed up. Thanks for your concern. I appreciate that a gun might feel useful, but I wouldn't have shot the guys who took my masks. They weren't threatening my life.

Sneeky and I are back at our windows. I wish he would talk. Or trade views with me. (Mine overlooks the fire escape.) He's good at spotting things. When his neck extends, I crane mine, hoping it's more than a pigeon. My block has started to smell like Naples. Not far away it sounds like Kabul on a slow night.

The bald man is back to his games. Perhaps he never quit. The woman he lives with plays louder now, or my hearing has sharpened. They inhabit different dimensions of the same space. I've never seen them communicate or share. It looks and feels like science fiction...until I recall living that way not long ago.

Our local correspondent reports that the LES DIY is setting up shop again. She asks when I'll come around to help. She and some of you inquire about Lisa's status. I'm not sure. Her boyfriend says she seems weaker but feels better. He is giving her Relenza and hydrating her. He's way more reliable than any hospital staff would be right now. The problem is that he doesn't have a ventilator. He'll call me if Lisa starts gasping. Not that I have a solution.

I watch public service ads on TV, broken up by inane specials like *Avian Flu: Are We Flying Blind?* Paid commercials are scarce. Locally, they push only stuff that can be consumed at home by history's biggest captive audience. The Mormons are back with free Bibles. (I ordered one; it's as good a time as any to catch up on a colorful credo.) And of course there are innumerable quack infomercials about bird flu.

Sold in Britain: Counterfeit Meds

The Web pulsates with spam for Relenza and Tamiflu. The best pitches come from vendors in Britain, a center for informal pharmaceuticals— many of them counterfeit—because taxes, greed, and contempt for the citizenry make Brits pay more for medicine (as with most goods). Not only do the natives comprise a big market for discount meds, they speak English with verve. So they sell lots of them.

Most counterfeit drugs are manufactured in China (which also makes most of the vitamins Americans consume). Much of the rest is made in India and Egypt. *Many* contain the required chemicals, though not necessarily with the ordained proportions. In normal times, it's good business to keep bootleg pill-heads alive and clicking.

But Relenza (or Tamiflu) buyers aren't likely to come back for more.

They'll soon either be immune to H5N1 because they've just survived it or they'll be past needing anything. So the Internet antiviral is frequently 100% bogus. When it's only partly fake, it's likely to speed the flu's resistance to these shaky weapons. Let's hope it's not harmful or deadly. (European Union inspectors once nabbed 'heart attack' pills composed of brick dust that was painted yellow and glossed with furniture polish.)

At home, startup companies announce research breakthroughs as fast as they can get our hungry media to publicize the*m*. How many different technologies have claimed to vanquish H5N1 since March? *Where are they?*

Down on Wall Street, trading electronically in fits and starts. Fitch awaits confirmation on a sale he made days ago; the shares vanished from his account but the cash credit never appeared and now he's getting margin calls. The financial community is a mess. How does a firm ensure regulatory compliance when its entire workforce is telecommuting? Inside information is flowing through private email accounts and calls on unsecured phones. Documents that need to be shipped and papers requiring a signature must be quarantined—even irradiated to kill microbes—before they can be delivered to the telecommuters.

The market is in a grand dive punctuated by euphoric upsurges that seem to flop as soon as the smart money has cleared out. Even when investors are healthy, programs account for most trades. I wonder where their sell triggers are set. It might not take much to flush the market, erase trillions of dollars in an hour.

DAY 138

FLU YORK CITY—WE'RE ALL FOREIGNERS

They're taking the big view on network TV, trying to suggest H5N1 can be contained in the Big Apple: *Our* very own pandemic!

Too bad for them there's a growing list of other infected places. Is it poetic justice that New Jersey's capital just announced a swath of likely flu victims? I sincerely hope it's a false alarm that gives Trenton more time to prepare for our reality.

There are sinister suggestions that the new strain reached New York City via illegal immigrants, as if the Department of Homeland Security screens incoming viruses. (More likely, Hope-Simpson's *seedlings* are sprouting—Americans who were infected over time by latent carriers are becoming active spreaders.)

Nevertheless, some out-of-town radio chatterers persist in hailing New Jersey's rudeness as a timely move that may have saved everyone else. *Sinful New Yorkers will take the hit from God for y'all.* Danged nice of us, I say!

Without actually *doing* anything, the Feds hold secret teleconferences with various governors who want to bar each other's citizens. (Might they postpone elections?)

Every day people die by the tens of thousands overseas, and Americans dream of avoiding the bug. There are people all over this country who don't know they're carrying H5N1. Most were born here.

Domestic travelers have panicked. Roads are full, flights rerouted, planes, trains, and buses jammed. (Looking for reasons to stay put? Watch that video of the Chicago cops tasing the hungry women besieging a donut stand at O'Hare Airport.) If you live in a quiet zone and want family members with you during Round Two, you'd best gather them fast. I've blown it so badly that I'm tempted at least once every seven minutes to try to head home to my folks. It's too far—and far too late.

Friendly Words of Warning

My Fellow Americans, New York's travails are your future.

Consider a longtime buddy who sorely yearns to join us (little suspecting he'll merely wind up in my blog under a cute pseudonym if he makes it). He was researching species extinction in Kenya when the flu reignited. He has bags of protective gear, but can't travel. He's alone and frightened in Mombasa, hoping to snag an illegal berth on a boat to a place with better international links. The U.S. Embassy in Nairobi has washed its hands of Americans who ignored the warnings. No food, water, medicine, transport, or *advice*.

I hope for my friend's sake that Kenyans don't start blaming foreigners.

Here, the usual suspects stage demonstrations against the city, state, Feds, and various businesses. Their demands are shameless: They want a freeze on layoffs and they want more medicine, hospital beds, ventilators, food, funeral services, and garbage collection. They even call for more cops, though the response hasn't been uniformly grateful. Today the cops bashed and busted people at City Hall while they let others yell in Times

Square. One reporter tried to question the inconsistency. The police commissioner ignored her. Maybe he thinks chanting spreads particularly dangerous microbes.

DAY 139

DEAD PRETTY—MY FRIEND LISA

I can hardly see to write. My friend Lisa is gone. Her boyfriend called to tell me she had darkened and died while he slept. He was hysterical, had no idea she was so ill. I wish he'd called me.

Sure, it's *his* fault. I should have known, must have known. It's obvious that she didn't want me to visit because she thought she was dying, knew I wouldn't keep my mask on if I saw her like that. I stayed home, typing for myself and a bunch of strangers.

Lisa's the best woman I've ever been with. Anyone she dated would agree. She was beautiful, smart, fun, loving, and kind. Not that Lisa was a Girl Scout—she could be earthy and hot, too, a garden of delights with a macabre sense of humor.

I didn't know what to say to her boyfriend. I resorted to technical support, tried to be *useful*, probed to see if he felt ill. He merely feels like death, doesn't sense any brewing inside. Even as she lies cold in their bedroom.

I didn't know what to tell him to do with her corpse. Call the city, sure....

Her *corpse*. How can I type that? The word is a hallucination, an abomination.

He sits near her as I cry for both of them. I've broken a bunch of things—cds, dvds, dishes, a book about wine she gave me years ago. I can't put it back together. The binding split open. I liked the book. I loved her, always would have.

Sneeky watched without judgment or fear while I freaked out and cursed myself. When I began to relax, he padded over to forgive me with a lingering head rub to my calf. That broke me down all over again. He was sad when Lisa and I broke up.

DAY 140

PIGS & BIRDS DIDN'T COOK UP THIS FLU

My world was bleak enough. Now the windowsills on my block are sprouting spiky metal strands, bird barriers that bristle in the sunlight. What's the point? I prefer to keep a clear view of my former world. It's bad enough that Sneeky claims the best window.

Worse, New York is full of pigeon corpses. The birds are generally impervious to avian flu. *Most are being poisoned.* (Others were beaten to death.) Sick morons, who may or may not believe they are achieving something, have thrown millions of New Yorkers into panic by poisoning these scrappy birds. The carcasses are a genuine threat to our health whether or not the birds had flu. No one dares go near them.

I think I see a dead pigeon rotting on the fire escape across the street. Earlier I thought I could smell it, but an eastern breeze spared me.

Few wild birds would have gotten H5N1 if it hadn't festered in chicken factories.

No Big Deal for Ducks

In East Asia, big chicken farms include lots of ducks—for millions of years the source of influenza viruses that had little effect on other species. As Greger points out in *Bird Flu: A Virus Of Our Own Hatching*, humans invited the flu to cross the species barrier when we domesticated ducks 4,500 years ago.

Most ducks can carry the virus without symptoms, shedding billions of infectious doses in days. As China expanded duck farming in recent centuries, it forged the reservoir from which most avian flu has been leaping to chickens, and then to people. It's no coincidence that China has kicked off so many pandemics, not least <u>the Black Death</u>.

The most common transmission mode is the commercial shipping of diseased birds—as edibles or exotic pets—to distant locations. Then, when industrial poultry catch and ferment a virus, migrating birds can pick it up from one pond and drop it into another. The world's big poultry factories are the equivalent of munitions depots that exchange bombs with passersby (which won't surprise anyone who believes that swine flu was cooked up in <u>gargantuan, unnatural pig factories</u>). Curious? <u>Read on.</u>

Less than a century ago, the average American ate half a pound of chicken a year. (The Republican Party was really talking big when it boasted that it had given Americans "a chicken in every pot" in the 1920s.) Prices tumbled after Maurice Hilleman at Merck came up with a vaccine to counter a cancer-causing poultry virus known as Marek's disease. Now we eat an average of a quarter pound a day. To turn this rare luxury into a staple, we created factories in which broilers grow so fast that their legs can't keep pace. Some become too heavy to walk—not that there's much space to move—and the weakest are trampled to death when their desperate mates flutter into a panic.

It's instructive that when H5N1 started killing turkeys at a huge British establishment, no one noticed. As Ben Bradshaw—Britain's *animal welfare* minister—put it, the death rates were "nothing out of the ordinary."

In fact, flock fatalities are a welcome indicator. When a few chickens suffer heart attacks, growers know that nutrition is going to the edible parts instead of being wasted on organs the birds won't need because they'll never be functional creatures. Broilers subsist in piles of dung—immobile, unable to groom themselves, vulnerable to any pathogens that penetrate the big sheds. Egg-layers fare little better. Growers stuff them with cheap antibiotics. This helps train bacteria to resist our miracle medications, giving rise to superbugs that gobble our flesh.

A study in *Emerging Infectious Diseases* found that 80% of raw chicken in stores in the southern Netherlands carried multi-resistant bacteria identical to those found in hospitals. While the Dutch consume very little antibiotic medication, their farmers dose them through poultry.

In the U.S., *Consumer Reports found* that 83% of the packaged chicken it tested in stores carried salmonella or campylobacter. The packaging itself teems with microbes. (Attention shoppers: Don't touch your eyes or noses after comparing weights and prices!)

Avian Flu Subtypes Lined Up for Us

Bird flu is an even greater threat. Since 1999, at least four additional subtypes besides H5N1 have afflicted humans. Human beings are 'immunologically naïve' to at least 13 avian subtypes. From a menu of eight genes, flu sure knows how to dish up variety. In fact, some top scientists have suggested we view any influenza virus as a "gene team" that constantly trades with other varieties and other subtypes for new players that can strengthen it.

Even if H5N1 were to vanish tomorrow, we could soon find ourselves coping with an H7N7 pandemic; in 2003, that little bug killed a veterinarian and infected 1,000 poultry workers in the Netherlands. Another one, H7N2, infected four people in Wales in 2007. H5N2 caused the deaths of 17 million Pennsylvania chickens in 1983, turning its victims into what a researcher called "bloody Jell-O"; 23 years later, 77 people in Japan were found to carry antibodies to this "mild flu." (How would I know how they got them? No one does.) In Hong Kong, meanwhile, they worry a lot about H9N2.

Never heard of those strains? That's no accident. In 2002, as Greger explains, H6N2 popped up in California's San Joaquin Valley. Instead of reporting the outbreak, growers packed sick chickens off to markets in trucks that spewed feathers and virus, infecting neighboring farms. They couldn't wait to sell those tainted legs and eggs.

As a libertarian, I distrust state intervention in commerce. But it makes sense that businesses should clean up the mess they make and charge enough to make a profit doing so. Poultry farmers are operating like the mines and factories that long spewed toxins into our waterways and streets because they didn't feel like paying to dispose of byproducts.

No one keeps tabs on the medical costs and losses in productivity that result. Heck, the way economic metrics are designed, deaths *add* to America's gross domestic product by necessitating economic transactions— when undertakers, coffins, plots, and gravediggers are available.

So lay off the pigeons! Stand up for our free, feathered friends. The virus has already crossed over. *H5N1 is now a human disease.* We must protect ourselves from other people, not birds. (Masks, anyone?)

DAY 141

MY LOST PIGEON

People are screaming. First, that I've raised prices. We're still cheaper than the competition, but yeah, we lost a lot of masks. Plus Fitch lost his job—like half my customers.

The loudest complaints concern the poor dead bird whose photo I ran.

Let's be clear: I like pigeons, though I don't feed them. So what if the French rather stupidly brought them to North America? (At least they got other Europeans to use soap.) Bear in mind that Shakespeare fanatics brought starlings here. These shed more H5N1 than pigeons or sparrows, though they seem better at resisting it.

A pigeon once shat on my head at the start of my first and last date with someone who didn't regard it as good luck. Yet I admire them. When I was very young, my dad rescued an injured pigeon. He built a coop in our basement and freed the lucky bird after her wing healed. I hate the vans that come to New York's streets to kidnap our pigeons for live-target shooting (see video and story) in Pennsylvania. I oppose the chickensh*t shooting of animals sprung from boxes no less than I oppose gun control.

In the Near East, ancient pigeons were cultivated so their dung could be used for fertilizer, and later for gunpowder. The finest can fly hundreds of miles at 60 mph. Their still-mysterious homing instincts won wars. The CIA once developed a pigeon cam. Pigeons are cooperative lovers, monogamous for life and rarely brutal. Some are truly beautiful—gleaming white with green and violet highlights. Here's a nice one I photographed last summer in Tompkins Square Park.

Meanwhile, I've discovered that Nina has vanished. I wanted to make sure she was okay, but she didn't respond to emails. When I found her cell phone disconnected, I called her office and wound up speaking with someone who started to say she had left the bank, then clammed up when I admitted my interest is personal. I called back to leave word for her blonde office pal from Tennessee, whose name came back to me after two hours of concentration. Her honeyed voicemail message said she was working remotely and would get back to me. Nothing so far. She could be dead by now.

Nina's email and social network accounts are down, too. (She had defriended me before she moved out, but now she no longer exists for anyone.) I don't know where she was living since then. I even contacted her condescending old friend 'Growly,' who said she hasn't heard from Nina since they argued about something six weeks ago. She has no numbers for Nina's family members, none of whom I've met.

I know Nina's mother lives in South Dakota, but "Dustville" evidently isn't the town's real name. (Yes, I checked.) Nor do I know her mom's last name, which reportedly changes frequently. I hope Nina was telling the truth about having antibodies to H5N1.

This is what it must be like to live in a war zone. Imagine not knowing for years if someone you care deeply about is alive or dead. It hurts to picture Nina out there—jobless, out of touch, surrounded by desperate people.

Management Of Dead Bodies In Disaster Situations

Lisa's corpse still awaits pickup. The Irishman called for counsel but wouldn't let me come over. I directed him to the Pan American Health Organization's *Management Of Dead Bodies In Disaster Situations*. You can download the PDF, which assures that corpses do not pose epidemic health risks. (Since dead people don't breathe, they tend to be less dangerous than we, the living, are.) Still, he can't leave her there.

The death toll must be soaring. In 1918 they covered up the mortality rate to keep Americans focused on the War Effort. The Irishman puzzles over our government's nonperformance. He politely mentioned that his contacts in Ireland and in the U.K. say they haven't heard of anyone left to rot over there. *As our chosen city has forsaken our dead love.*

Typically, like some parody of a Jewish mother, I urged him to drink lots of water and to eat at least soup and crackers. He's fed up with the flu diet. Probably sick of us, too.

DAY 142

LATEST PANDEMIC CASUALTY—FREE SPEECH

New York City has banned demonstrations and imposed a curfew from dusk to dawn. I don't think it's legal, but few seem to care. From what I've gathered, the cops were already making pedestrians unwelcome at night. They do that a lot in good times here.

There are exceptions: Anyone with identification confirming that they work in health care, transportation, utilities, food delivery, social services, finance, or information technology or provision (which can include couriers) may sample the darkness.

They will hope not to run into anyone looking for emergency medical care. The desperately sick-but-mobile are restrained only by their frailties.

I kinda feel for the masked men in blue charged with keeping folks off the street. They'll be sifting through business cards that list strange tech occupations for companies with snazzy, meaningless names, trying to figure out if the bearer should be seized and exposed to other unfortunates in the Tombs. *Listen up, youse guys: we need volunteers to frisk self-proclaimed flu carriers!* The city intends to set up email accreditation, which might someday be useful.

A new local blog, The Tribulation Beat, says makeshift prisons are being created in the Bronx, Brooklyn, and Queens. At least one consists of tents. No concentrated camping in *my* yard, says Manhattan! (Hurts real estate values.) No word from FEMA as to plans for those camps people are always going on about.

So help me, I did find a U.S. Army "Civilian Inmate Labor Program" that authorizes creation of labor camps and prisons for civilians on Army bases; if that's not freaky enough, Halliburton subsidiary KBR was contracted to support "establishing temporary detention and processing capabilities ... in the event of an immigration emergency, as well as the development of a plan to react to a national emergency, such as a natural disaster." So said KBR's PR. Best of all, there are jobs to be had: Become a U.S. Army Internment/Resettlement Specialist (31E).

Need I mention again that experts always agree that locking people up won't stop the pandemic? In 1918 the flu broke out fastest and worst in crowded military bases.

Rejecting calls to criminalize the shaking of hands or cheek-to-cheek, kiss-kiss greetings, a city council majority urges us not to touch and jacks up penalties for spitting. The latter took guts: A lot of New York voters expectorate with conviction.

Turning to the demand side of human circulation, the city has banned sporting events. Also *verboten* are political rallies and assemblies, instantly the subject of free-speech lawsuits. Elections are big business. Politicians who support postponing them are playing with fire. They could lose TV face time for threatening to deprive the networks of lucrative attack ads—and television and the Web are all that remain to campaign on during a pandemic.

I don't see how this can be enforced, but the subways are closed to riders who lack surgical or N95 masks. The city's stockpile frequently runs out at individual stations. Crafty folks have apparently started selling used paper masks to wannabe riders. *Not recommended*, but New Yorkers are always in a hurry. (Getcha masks here, *used only by great-grannies who survived the Great Pandemic.*)

Schools shall remain closed until further notice. Precocious kids will live off the land. There are mountains of garbage and brigades of rats. The sewers are clogging up.

Churches, synagogues, and mosques are *requested* to close, with mixed results. Some are setting up videoconferenced services on the Web. Others continue to assemble the faithful. How can elected officials stand up to the religious establishment when even agnostics are praying for the flu to relent?

Funerals 'Discouraged' as Corpses Proliferate

Funerals are still permitted, though "discouraged." Web ceremonies will become standard procedure, so long as the Internet holds up. Soon there won't be coffins. I hope New York has enough body bags. I wish I had one for Lisa.

Weddings are effectively banned; the city reassigned the clerks who give out licenses.

Homelessness is more vexing than ever. It might amount to state euthanasia to cram vagabonds into the Tombs. Might as well give them tainted blankets and let 'em die peacefully in the useless ATM parlors.

The commercial interests closed fast on Round Two's opening day. Bars, restaurants, gyms, and most stores remain shut.

A lot of the city's police, firefighters, sanitation workers, and paper pushers live in the suburbs and couldn't get to work if they tried. Wisely, the city is sending fleets of school buses upstate to pick up suburbanite public workers. Some don't seem to be home.

I gather that only drugstore chains and food markets and hardware stores are welcoming the rare passersby into rooms of empty shelves guarded by extremely large men who are presumably armed.

I have no idea what anyone is doing for money. I haven't left my apartment.

It feels hot and sticky and hopeless tonight. The city pleads for us not to use air conditioning unless we are feverish. Who can tell the difference? Some of us dread what a blackout might bring. Others keep their AC going; you can tell by the closed windows and the *drip drip drips* from above.

Tomorrow will be hotter, stickier. Part of me is relieved that I don't have to share this sweatbox with my crusty Ninotchka. The rest of me fears for her. I pity anyone who's alone—no Sneeky, no blog with lively readers—in this city. It's so bleak here.

DAY 143

TOAST TO FRIENDSHIP—& FOOD

I apologize for overlooking the hospitals. It is *said* they are okay. An acquaintance who works for a newspaper reports that this isn't quite true. You wouldn't know it to read his paper, which incessantly hails the medical system's inspirational performance.

I don't doubt that most nurses, doctors, and technicians are giving their best.

Hospitals operate at 80% to 90% capacity in the best of times. The last numbers I saw, the city had 3,000 ventilators and not much more than 1,700 intensive care unit beds to serve more than 8 million residents. The hospitals were trying to get more of everything but patients. Guess what grew fastest?

Security! There are armed guards everywhere.

So far we have hundreds of flu deaths per day here, publicly noted. There are undoubtedly others moldering alone, at home. Half of Manhattan's apartment-dwellers live alone. Solitude is a staple of our lives. The other half is getting dangerously crowded. Each economic downturn since the one that began in 2008 has caused more families to jam together in single dwellings.

In a pinch, we're supposed to call hotlines staffed by people who don't know much because the professionals are in the trenches. Fitch's sister reached a woman who confessed that she normally takes cash in the hospital cafeteria.

A lot of communities have resorted to automated distress lines. A RAND Corporation report in 2008 deemed message systems starkly inferior to live lines that connect callers to public health professionals within 30 minutes.

If you're lucky enough to reach sentient operators, make the most of it. Don't abuse them. It's traumatic responding to hours and hours of frantic pleas, especially when you haven't much aid to offer. (Watch the Constantines perform *Hotline Operator* in tribute to those whose mercy we'll all need someday.)

Evelyn has written to express her condolences about Lisa and Nina and to say that the LES DIY will try to spur the city to pick up Lisa's corpse. The Irishman and I have been calling every few hours. I think an operator recognized my voice today, before hanging up.

My Ukrainian neighbor seems to have mastered how to wear the mask

I gave him. (The others are griping about having to pay because they know he didn't.) I'm not sure *"Stefan"* cares enough to wear the mask each time he goes out—or to return for it if he remembers he forgot—so I visit him in fully protected mode when he rings.

Stefan's quick to hoist two glasses of vodka (*not* shot glasses) and goad me till I take one. I suspect he's a terminal fatalist who won't just get sick. He'll either be very lucky or he'll blow to pieces. Either way, he'll never run out of vodka, which he calls *horilka*. He's prepared for a Second Flood.

He humors my medical lectures so long as I drink with him. It's a worthy cause that gives us both a kick. Having lived through three winters of the Nazi occupation that killed 7.5 million Ukrainians (counting Jews), Stefan calls our pandemic "a spring wind."

It's strange and wondrous how being kind can be so rewarding. I think Ayn Rand would smile on his vigorous speeches, and on my *choice* to help him. I'm lonely. He's my bristle-browed man Friday, though assuredly retired from work.

Stefan is running out of the canned fish that sustains him most nights. *Choose To Send Food!* We who are about to starve implore you.

DAY 144

SAD PORTRAIT OF A FAILING HOSPITAL

Tonight I present an email from a nurse who explains why she will no longer report for duty at a big medical center in Brooklyn. She asks not to be identified. I'm withholding the hospital's name, too. (I slip sometimes, but I try not to promote or make examples of institutions, companies, individuals, or products.)

"*Thanks for trying to tell the truth but you don't know the half of it.*

"_____ *has people piled in corridors. The cafeteria is jammed with patients. They all say they just came down with flu no matter how long they had it because the [city's] guidelines say Tamiflu and Relenza only go to people who went symptomatic less than 48 hours ago. We ran out of ventilators the first day and what we have are breaking from overuse and use by people who were never trained to operate them. There's hardly any oxygen left to operate them with anyway. We use throwaway masks over and over, marked with our initials.*

Nursing assistants are running ICU beds on their own.

"Management is totally mixed up. They suspended regulations and quali-fications so they don't know if the people they're talking to know how to do anything right. Doctors are losing it. Nurses are dying. My best friend turned purple yesterday. She's stuffed in a freezer. She was 29. I heard there's no more room down there. Where would they put me?

"My kids need me more than I need the money. School is closed. How is my 9 year old suppose to watch the others? I didn't sign up for this mess. My husband's a cop risking his life in a million ways wearing a paper mask they gave him. They don't want either of us to wear the ones we got on your site because they violate standards by being better, for God's sake. Anytime my husband could bring bird flu back with him. I'm going to stay home from now on to back him up and give our little ones a fighting chance.

"That means at least the end of my career if they don't arrest me for deser-tion or something. Under the emergency, we have to stay here til they say we can go. They do anything they want with regulations, the unions, professional practice, "ethics," whatever. Lucky they have no place to sleep us so I get to see my kids. What if I make them sick?

"I didn't accomplish much in 15 hours today anyway. Lied to patients sur-rounded by people leaking blood and gasping to death. Told them help was coming when it was going to be a dental student who hasn't had any sleep.

"They should have planned better. It's all a wreck, everybody for him-self. I'm for my family. Keep warning everyone to stay home. Did I mention the MRSA?

I have nothing to add to what she wrote. Readers who live in areas not yet affected should yell at their authorities to prepare FASTER! Any talk of heading off the pandemic is nuts. *Sick.*

She referred to <u>MRSA</u>, which can come with influenza. As with bacterial pneumonia, staph infections are taking advantage of flu-weakened bodies—<u>particularly in children</u>—to infect people. Hospitals are hotbeds of MRSA transmission….

Earlier I saw the bald guy stomping around his living room, waving his mantis arms like semaphores. I couldn't see what his friend was doing. But he saw me and slammed the curtains so hard I could just about hear the fabric flap. He's an insect version of the guy in *Rear Window*.

Stop telling me to go out! What's the point?

DAY 145

WASH, PRAY & WHIP IT GOOD

A city truck fetched Lisa today. I'm sure it was because the LES DIY prodded someone. The dispatcher asked for me when she called the Irishman. Thank you, Evelyn! (By the way, who are you?)

The authorities now admit that flu has popped up just about everywhere. Maybe idiots will stop going on about illegal immigrants (I'm sorry to say some self-described libertarians are spreading dumb rhetoric, too) and start focusing on how we can all survive this thing.

The Feds coughed up a speech from the character who runs the Department of Homeland Security. Not a very good speaker. The result seemed at once liberal and paranoid, fussy and grandiose. Are they trying to reassure us or arouse us?

If I remember correctly, albeit painfully: "Wash and pray, and support those who want to help, not hurt, our nation through this historic challenge." *Yawn.* "The American Family Comes First!" *No comment.* Words fail me, too. I smell dreams of a presidential run.

Help, of course, is on the way. That new Restore America's Independent Spirit & Enterprise is already doing something or other (besides wearing out my fingertips). Vaccine coming … *Testing, testing* … patience … Americans special ... determination ... resolve ... solution ... be patient ... God bless.

I'm trying! I've been unable to ship packages of personal protection gear. UPS vows every day that they will visit. First guy I see in a brown uniform gets a free mask! Unless it's a <u>stormtrooper</u>.

I reckon UPS will reach me before the vaccine does. As the whole country becomes like New York, things here will actually improve. Get ready for your part of that adjustment.

You might soon spot an odd group of medievalists flogging one another bloody on the steps of your parish church (St. Patrick's Cathedral, in our case). They come in crimson robes, bare their chests for penitential abuse. A few strip down to loincloths. The Catholic Church is neither amused nor heartened by their devotions, which makes sense when you consider that they claim the Church invited contagion with *"pedophiliac iniquities."*

The police want to vacate the cathedral steps, but the brass is evidently stymied by the thought that the NYPD's customary thrashing would only reward the fanatics, who were known as <u>flagellants</u> in the Middle Ages.

I wonder if we deserve this. Is nature whacking us before we can finish wrecking the planet? While holed up here, I've looked into deforestation, extinctions, hydrocarbons, and waste. My mirror shows me an animal that no longer knows itself.

The Natural Storm Man Cooked Up

Around me, I see a swirling mass of ever-more lethal strains of diseases that we extracted from our favorite creatures. As Dr. Greger explains in his book, epidemic diseases are harbored by animals that cluster together in dense flocks (like us), or are forced to do so (like the protein sources we cultivate—pigs, chickens, cows, and ducks).

The tuberculosis that now infects a third of us likely sprang from our domestication of goats. Cows seem to have given us some tuberculosis, along with measles, and probably smallpox. Farming pigs gave us whooping cough; raising chickens brought us typhoid fever; taming water buffalo induced leprosy; and breeding horses (or cattle) introduced the common cold. Milking sheep is thought to have circulated the bacteria that trigger ulcers, even cancers.

You're welcome to believe that God must have countenanced this catastrophe. My humble mission is to help you flout His will.

Here we are, stocking little arks of real estate with our families and threatened pets and food stocks, then defending them with masks, gloves, goggles, bleach, bootleg pharmaceuticals, semi-automatics.

But we are the beasts that caused this storm by corrupting chickens into filthy, dysfunctional critters so we could eat cheaply and blow the difference on video games. Or porn. Or *hey*, drive-in churches where they preach delirious consumption.

So how fair can *the culling of mankind* be if some of us can stave off retribution? Banks, government agencies, and insurance companies have prognosticated for years that Western countries will emerge from a pandemic in far better shape than poorer nations. We own the vaccine makers. We have doctors, satellites, the latest weapons of mass—or minute—destruction. We even have a few ventilators for people with clout.

Boy, do we have medical technology. The <u>British lab</u> that brought us Dolly, the cloned sheep, aims to start mass-producing medicinal protein for humans ... in *chickens*.

DAY 146

FLU IS UNKNOWING

Today was a gorgeous concept that hurt—a painting that felt more real than my dried-up skin. When you're locked indoors, ears conditioned by canned, compressed air, even the colors seem like a mirage. You watch someone pass on the street below, seemingly immune to fear. Dazzled, jealous, you open your window. A bracing hint of autumn fills those blue skies. Someone calls out nearby and you pause. No problem: It's a child, laughing.

Nostrils piqued by fresh air, I impulsively climbed onto my fire escape. It creaked, as always—a familiar, even comforting sensation. Then an ascending gust brought a whiff of reality: My street stinks like a slum in a tropical country. I swear I could hear rats scratching and chatting below.

Next I heard glass shattering as some malevolent kids swept down the block, throwing rocks at our windows. Women howled at them. Fortunately the delinquents were clustered on my side of the street. They wrecked half the windows opposite my building. Shielded by the fire escape above them, I imagined pouring molten oil on the mob, as if in a medieval siege.

This reminded me of the grim flagellant procession that terrorizes a country village with whips, chants, and sermons in Ingmar Bergman's _The Seventh Seal_, a magnificent old movie in which a weary but defiant Crusader plays chess with Death to save a young family from the Plague. ("I am unknowing," says Death, rather modestly.) I used to play chess with Nina, who was neither knowing nor modest.

I'm pleased to know and report that somehow, amid our ruins, the LES DIY has fully resumed its services. Again working out of Ric's Place, the group is dishing out meals and delivering them to the weakest. The plates are smaller, though; certain stores that donated generously during Round One are holding back. (They must be losing a lot of money this time; newly unemployed, little-subsidized consumers can't afford whatever goods they have to sell.) Evelyn reports that Ric seems listless, depressed. She urges me to visit my best friend at home. Does he know her?

I'd happily visit Ric, but I must wait every day till the curfew takes effect at dusk, in case UPS shows up. Ric sounds okay on his voice mail, but he never calls back. Trying not to be annoyed, I've been reckoning he was busy helping folks. I called him again. Left a message telling him not to make me leave my home. That sounded dumb, I'm sure.

Notwithstanding Fitch's orders, I've invited the group to fetch some masks. I'm proud of my community. Their name says it all—*Lower East Side Do It Yourself Committee.*

Do It Yourself has a fine resonance. The East Village may not be what it used to be before I got here, but these people couldn't be much better than they are.

DAY 147

FEAR STEALS THE LIGHT

A banner day for the flu resistance! A saint from UPS saved me. He took every package that was due to go out, even waited while I raced to seal everything. (I was so shocked to see him that I wasn't quite ready.) I caught up with raging demand.

The guy was wearing a mask that was worn and torn and barely covered his grin when he saw how happy I was to see him. I gave him a couple of masks and goggles and gloves.

His arrival would have allowed me to visit Ric's Place—and Ric's home, if necessary—but some neighbors turned up to trade plywood for protective gear. A lot of people are barricading their windows in the wake of yesterday's assault. They'll have no natural light, not even indirectly. No sights. No hope. I'll never do that.

The bartering visitors in the hallway wouldn't shut up.

I've returned to the purple twilight of my porthole, where I listen to a symphony of alarms from cars and stores and apartments, punctuated by shots and shattering glass. The city sounds like a haunted house in a techno amusement park.

Edgar Allan Poe, New York's poet laureate of personal doom, would celebrate our mass hysteria with a chilling story about the comeuppance of some pompous idiot who thought he was above it all.

DAY 148

COOPED UP WITH SICK MEMORIES

I've missed the boat on the trend toward pet abandonment as the pandemic spreads. Except for dogs, New Yorkers keep their pets indoors. (That's not a bad thing, given that scientists think <u>cats scare urban songbirds</u> out of reproducing.)

Readers have sent me links to stories about stray dogs, cats, guinea pigs, parakeets, ferrets, anything—all tossed out of doors, or cars, or hearts by beings who no longer rate the adjective human.

It's people that make me sick at times like this, not virions. Please read this <u>Humane Society page about disaster planning for your pets</u>!

Meanwhile, Evelyn warns that I'm exhibiting *dangerous* signs of <u>agoraphobia</u>, a panic disorder that manifests itself as a fear of being in public places. "You have to take control fast," she exhorts. "Please don't let yourself get locked inside. Who's ever gonna get you out?"

And here I was, thinking I felt <u>*claustrophobic*</u> as I watched my neighbors' windows go dark with sloppy patches of plywood, heavy plastic, even furniture. A strong wind could hurl some of those sharp-edged slabs into peoples' heads. The rampaging teen vandals seem to have put Rome over the edge.

Listen, friend, I *hate* being cooped up in here. I long to walk in the streets again, take in some sunlight. (I rise early to try to catch direct D rays in the window.)

I'm dying to taste fresh fruit. An apple, an orange—especially a banana. I'd beg for a stalk of broccoli. Shuttered inside with no fresh nutrients, no place to exercise, how much resistance can anyone offer this virus?

As a kid I was quarantined with <u>whooping cough</u>. (AKA pertussis; evidently my vaccine wore off, which can happen.) When I wasn't wracked in bed, I'd stand at the front door, wishing *anyone* would come to visit. I even missed certain teachers. A sign told visitors not to ring. My older brother was trapped, too. He blamed me for our incarceration, made sure I couldn't access toys *or* the phone. One day I made it to the corner in my pajamas before a neighbor called the cops on me.

In *Justinian's Flea* (about the first known pandemic, a bubonic plague outbreak that may have broken the back of what remained of the Roman Empire), William Rosen notes that the people of Constantinople took to going out with their names fastened to their necks in case they fell ill and died before they could get home.

I'll step out when it seems wise or necessary. Fully clothed, with <u>dog tags</u>. *Promise.*

DAY 149

THE GANG'S ALL HERE

Surprise visitors today! First came Bruno, the drummer from the LES DIY. He said they all worry about me because I told someone—he says he doesn't know whom—that I hadn't gone outside in more than two weeks. Hard to believe it's been 17 days since I got robbed.

I must have come off like a psycho in tin foil. To start with, I couldn't let him in. We chatted *sotto voce* in the hallway, our voices muffled by masks. I almost called him Bruno.

I presumed he had come to pick up protective gear, but he brought me a big hot meal. I'd eaten a late breakfast, but *roast pork with potatoes and greens* was a scented mirage made real. I had to ask if this is really what they deliver.

He said the woman you and I know as 'Anna' created it specifically for me. Does Anna know the benevolent stalker? Is *she* the stalker? I had just finished concluding for the hundredth time that she can't possibly be Evelyn.

Bruno says Anna is eating more, talking more. Sounds good, looks good. I haven't seen her since Ric reopened his restaurant three months ago.

All this made me fat and happy till I read that Los Angeles gangs are engaging in formal military maneuvers. There were maps of an area that's turning into an American Bosnia as young black, Hispanic, and Asian criminals strike at one another's home turf. Inhabitants are being driven out with the expectation that they might never return.

This has evidently been happening for years between blacks and Hispanics. (Hollywood never noticed?) With Asian gang membership rising quickest of all—and less geared to specific localities—the H5N1 crisis is said to have prompted paramilitaries in LA and the valleys to draw their heaviest weapons. Encouraged by politicians and media to blame immigrants, they've all taken up ethnic cleansing.

The LAPD is accused of working hard to keep them all out of white 'hoods. Are the Russian and Armenian gangs gratified or insulted?

Is this for real? Is someone sensationalizing minor events? It's hard to tell from here. I wonder what the residents of LA think of their latest terror trigger.

Not that we don't all have scary issues: I was googling LA gangs when someone banged on my door. I didn't open up.

It was the bald guy I've never met from across the street. He's heard rumors that I possess medical supplies. His wife is suffering chest pains, has a history, and the hospitals are inaccessible. He called an ambulance *yesterday*.

When I explained I had nothing for them, he waved a gun at the peephole and threatened to blow my lock off. The 911 operator didn't speedily comprehend where I live, asked if I'm on the Upper West Side (*East* is the first part of my street's name). It felt like I'd called Turkmenistan tech support. When I held the phone to the door so she could hear him, she hung up. Did his cursing affront her moral sensibilities?

I fetched a cast iron pot with which to mash the man's cranium if he broke in. He yelled and pounded and bellowed and then vanished quietly. I don't think he knows I'm the guy who used to watch his wife play piano before he nailed plywood over his windows.

I'm feeling sorry I tried to help my neighbors. All it did was blow my cover.

DAY 150

MY STORM TRACK

LA isn't so bad. While a few readers say it's worse than I reported, more say I slipped in melodramatic muck aimed at justifying martial law, or at least distracting Angelenos from *the real issues*—whatever those are. I'm told the celebrated flanking maneuver at Harbor Gateway was merely the accidental arrival of a bunch of well-armed gangsters who were fleeing from the cops when they saved their lucky allies from a bloody defeat. How reassuring!

I'll stick to writing what I see from now on: The bald guy's windows are sealed, silent, funereal. Has his wife died yet? My block is asleep or cowering silently.

Sneeky is licking his belly far too much. I see hairless patches with red sores. No idea what this could be.

Ric called. He sounds worse off than I am. Still, I bet his house is neater.

I'm watching Hurricane Luke on TV as I write. Reporters in foul weather gear stand manfully in rising winds, suffering for *us* in front of Disney World. Viewers seem delighted to kick back and experience Luke, an old-time disaster, on their big flat screens. We all know The Mouse will make it. This will be a comforting spectacle.

DAY 151

FROZEN FRUITLESSNESS

I'm extremely sorry for my light-witted comments about Hurricane Luke. Orlando is in pieces. The looting is relentless. Local reporters pose before phalanxes of masked Guardsmen framed by flames. Will Disney World burn? Melt?

I could use some power, too.

Early this evening I heard a woman screaming below. I leaned out of Sneeky's window to see a woman in green backed against a car. I couldn't see what she was scared of, thought it might be rats. Then she started pleading with someone human to leave her alone, a high-pitched spoken wail that conveyed real terror. It sounded like *she said she had the flu*, probably to frighten an assailant.

I grabbed a metal bar I keep handy and ran toward the stairs, putting on protective gear. I was 'safe' by the time I reached the last flight. She sounded about 20 feet from the door, bleating for mercy—desperate, deranged, maybe both.

I charged down the stairs, rod in hand.

My world imploded. I couldn't breathe, realized I was choking on lunch. My heart went into overdrive. Hunched over, drenched in sweat, I shook for so long I forgot about the woman I was trying to rescue. By the time I remembered her, I felt better, clearer. I took another step, became horribly dizzy. I vomited into my mask and all over the stairs. Had I somehow caught H5N1?

People ran past the front door, shouting as they chased someone. They sounded like good guys, volunteers.

It must have been something I ate. I'm not a coward.

DAY 152

PANIC BECOMES ME

I woke up to a volley of concerned emails. A lot of you think I've developed an <u>agoraphobic panic disorder</u> whereby my body freaks out if I try to go outside. But I read that this usually *results* from panic attacks; you don't want to go outside lest someone see you suffer an attack. I'm basically extremely, um, reluctant to go outside because death is in the air. I undertook all this preparation so I could stay home.

Anyway, I just tried to step out. I get sickly near the door. Evidently it's from resisting an overpowering adrenaline rush as my mind tells me to run away from danger. Fighting to go outside is maddening, like forcing yourself to walk into a fusillade of bullets. That can lead to <u>post-traumatic stress disorder</u>. The most famous American foot soldiers of the first war with Iraq are <u>Timothy McVeigh</u> and <u>John Allen Muhammed</u>. Whatever happened to them in the Middle East, each brought the war home—in mass murder.

I'm just trying to get to the corner. Whatever my little problem is called, it's the kind of thing that can turn syndromal. You're right: I need to take a hike before I lose my mind.

Walking is what makes New Yorkers so healthy. A newborn resident can expect to live nine months longer than other American babies, and the difference grows annually. Since 1990, the average American lifespan has gained 2 ½ years, while that of New Yorkers has grown by more than 6.

<u>Read all about it</u>: We walk more, move faster. I'll never forget the man in black I saw charging through a crowded Times Square sidewalk last year, roaring at tourists: "Outa my way, this ain't *&@%$^ Kansas!" He was indeed thinner, cut through those people like a knife.

I need sunshine to cleanse the mold that afflicts my brain when I stay inside too long. Tomorrow I'll get out, sheathed in plastic like a walking condom. Whatever it takes.

The White House Flu Prescription

For now, I'll question the president's wisdom in having waited so long to speak out and then delivering a kind of verbal coup d'état. The military is going to start assessing the nation's needs on a regional basis. For now, troops will start checking ID on streets and in malls throughout the Southwest.

"Americans want to know that their nation's resources are being used to help their fellow citizens, and it's our job to show them this is true," said the president. Washington will prove it by tripling the budget at RAISE and rounding up illegal immigrants.

How will that put food in our stores and water in our fire hoses? How will it reopen cemeteries? Clean up and resupply hospitals?

For more than 130 years the military was barred from conducting civil police activity. Now <u>20,000 soldiers are trained and equipped</u> to do anything they're told to do—on U.S. soil. I'm sure glad I live in the Northeast.

What followed was laughable relief as the president told anecdotal stories about resolute survivors and steadfast public servants saving the day in what must have been the 26 states with the most electoral votes. "Meanwhile, on the Colorado prairie, a paraplegic schoolteacher named Patience Pureheart crawls daily to her church to...."

Help!

DAY 153

ANGEL WITHOUT MERCY

Bruno woke me without notice at noon. I was slow to fasten the chain as he explained he was on special assignment to get me to Ric's apartment. He barged in and started making me put on protective gear as if I were going to visit Stefan next door. Then he marched me to the stairs.

I quibbled, but it was embarrassing to argue with a guy who was trying to help me get over something so *stupid* till we got to the bottom set of stairs and I started to flip out. My brain was climbing the walls as if I could just slip away and leave my useless shell with Bruno.

When he pulled me onto the stairs, I started crying, gasping, hyperventilating. I'm pretty strong, but Bruno locked me in place and muttered friendly and supportive comments while I struggled and begged him to let me go back upstairs, home.

Then he told me *she* was waiting outside. I knew he meant *my mystery emailer.* Evelyn.

For the first time, I looked down. The door was bursting with light, broken by a shadow in the shape of a face and torso.

I still couldn't move. But I wanted to, even though this would be a rotten way to meet her—pathetic, tearful, needy.

When my adrenaline ran out and I tried to sit down, Bruno half-lifted, half-dragged me down the stairs and out the door. He didn't care that I was retching, drooling. No one else did, either. No one was there but a rat. Coincidence?

Bruno's incredulous look told me that he had expected her to be there. He didn't look happy, but wouldn't explain anything. When we reached Ric's building, he asked if there was any chance I'd get stuck in there. He wanted to go back to the restaurant.

I swore I'd make it home, thanked him lavishly. I was relieved to be outside, albeit furious. What had happened to *she who confuses everyone*? This was some kind of game. Am I the only player who doesn't know Evelyn's identity? Do they joke about me? I hope Bruno gave her hell.

DAY 153 (#2)

GOOD & SAD MEETINGS WITH RIC

I burst into Ric's apartment, hungry for explanations. The air was stale, with none of the normal scents of spices and flowers. I was embarrassed about my weeks at home, but not at all certain he knew about my problems. It turned out his are *real*.

I've never seen Ric drink cognac at 4 pm. He was intently watching a lurid Edgar Allan Poe movie called *Masque of the Red Death*, which presented rationalism as something evil and demonic that only love can defeat. From what I know about Poe, he didn't believe love could subdue a newborn kitten. For him, love was likely to be buried alive.

I got Ric to talk, though he could barely look at me. He can't cover the restaurant's rent. The problem is that the business was successful so briefly that Ric never sorted out his finances. Had Round One struck months later, he'd be in pretty good shape. A tsunami of personal and commercial bankruptcies will hit the civil courts when they reopen.

Businesses just don't have money coming in, even as they must continue paying rent, insurance, salaries. The banks may have put some cash in circulation, but we all know millions on millions of workers are being put out of work.

I had no idea that the pandemic master plan for corporations called for mass firings if the flu came back. Some state governors are dismissing public workers, too—by executive fiat. We're diving headlong into what could be a Depression. No one will be able to buy anything. How will people eat, even when there's food in the stores?

"The bosses are all quoting Ayn Rand," complains Evelyn. She's right, but it's not Rand's fault. *Atlas Shrugged* presents a society drowning in so much mediocrity and inertia that its workers walk away from pointless jobs. That's not what's happening now, when people who claim to be Rand followers are shutting private enterprise and government down just when Americans most need them. That's objectively anti-social and stupid.

Faced with a choice between paying his employees or the landlord, Ric is backing his people. Rand probably wouldn't have done that, but I think she would have respected the entrepreneurial impulse. Ric wants to keep his dream alive.

I should explain that he's always been an optimist. Hey, he tried to romance *me* once.

A Date to Remember

I forget how we met. We wound up talking for hours at some party I crashed. I didn't like the other guests and he was worth knowing—informed and irreverent and pursuing big ideas. I guess each of us assumed that the other shared his own sexual direction. Men do that about everything.

Days later, Ric invited me to dine with him. He surprised me by choosing a pricey French joint, his treat. I can be generous, too, so I just reckoned correctly that he had more money than me. I let him lead on the wine and appetizers.

As we built a buzz over some excellent Burgundy I never would have ordered, we talked about our roots and our ambitions and our politics. Of course I mentioned Ayn Rand and he pointed out that she never acknowledged the problems of race or religion or sexual issues in her novels. He was right. But a lot of writers used to skip over that stuff. 'Deep' thinkers, too: What did Marx or Keynes ever say about gays and minorities?

Ric thought that was funny. He hates ideology. I get a pass because I don't mind his mockery; he's good at it. Opposition sharpens the mind.

Socially, I wasn't dating anyone and didn't feel like discussing it. He said he was solo, too. I didn't think much about that. I certainly wasn't looking for a 'wingman.' I prefer to circulate alone, forgoing the buddy talk and prospects for competition. As it happened, the waitress struck up a conversation with us about the wine, lingered after dinner to pour free cognac. She was attractive and I like attention, but I thought it was cool that neither of us tried to pick her up or get her email.

Later we sought out a bar for drinks on me. He led me to an unfamiliar lounge full of guys, with one cute woman who came over to greet Ric. She was buzzed and lively and very fond of him. He introduced us and watched us talk till she ran off to greet someone.

Did I want to date her? I said no, thanks. She wasn't my type and I silently wondered if she was a lover of his. Was he testing me? Suggesting a threesome? I make my own arrangements.

Almost imperceptibly, his hand came to rest on my naked forearm. It was then that I realized the other men were gay. We were on a *date.* I felt terrible, reckoned I must have led my new friend on by being supremely dense.

He watched my face carefully. I was frozen, as if in a high-stakes round of poker. *What the hell to do?*

I raised my other hand to offer a toast to *diversity.* He cracked up. "Hey, are you straight?" I confessed I had just figured out that he wasn't.

We swiftly agreed we'd each suffered worse dates with 'appropriate' partners and decided to continue becoming friends. It wasn't long before Ric fixed me up with Lisa, whose brother was an old friend of his. I reciprocated by introducing him to an architect pal whom I suspected was out when he wasn't at work; they dated for a few months. Ric and I hung out less after Nina moved in, but that always happens when a friend falls in love. Real friends are still there when your romance hits the fan.

I wish I could help Ric now. On top of his business woes, he imagines he has bedbugs—until recently New Yorkers' greatest fear. He showed me three round, raised welts on his back, but I saw no bites. They looked like hives. But it sure made me want to go outside.

The Oracle of Inaction

As I stood at the door, wishing I could ask him about the disappearing trickster, Ric shocked me by saying he's been enjoying my exchanges with the LES DIY woman. I tried to grill him, told him 'Evelyn' had just duped me.

He didn't care. "She's a special prize," he said. "She got you out of that place. She did it for both of us. Keep at it." At *what?* I've been around those people for almost five months. The food's good, but something's missing.

He just laughed. "All in due time," he said. Given Ric's track record—Lisa was my longest, greatest love—I should be intrigued. But Evelyn is all bluff. She should have met me when she had her chances. *Round Two has dealt solitaire for all.*

At the door I flat-out asked if Anna is behind this. I know he's very fond of her. Ric looked pained, said she's still getting over her daughter's death. Back to zero. He doesn't even know 'Val.' "Just hang on," he said. "No one's going anywhere." Not exactly inspirational, but at least he didn't complain—yet—about any of the stuff I've posted.

I got home to find a neighbor on the top floor failing. She had hip-replacement surgery the day the pandemic recommenced, and they cleared her out of the hospital too quickly. It probably saved her life to be spared all that exposure to H5N1, but something's gone wrong and she's in screaming pain. I probably shouldn't say this, but one guy has gone out to look for street heroin to give her.

The pharmacies aren't working and her painkiller ran out. It seems that few residents stocked legitimate pills—a claim people neither believe nor challenge. Someone coughed up Tylenol with codeine. I hear it failing.

Two years ago, this woman fussed endlessly to our slumlord about my practice of chaining my bicycle in the rear of the ground-floor hallway. Ever since, I've had to carry it down and up three narrow flights when I wish to ride it—far less than I used to.

East Villagers tend to live and let live. Or die. I never complained about the hip-hop my upstairs neighbor blasted 12/7, when he wasn't working or skateboarding. I've missed that manic thumping since he got run over.

I hate to be so certain that this poor, howling woman took pleasure in seeing me lug my bike. In that weird way silly things pop into our minds, I hear a Gene Clark line from *Some Misunderstanding* about everyone needing a fix at times like this. He suggests it feels good just to keep living. It's easy for a dead artist to say that.

DAY 154

'THANK YOU, MASK MAN'

Without explaining, Evelyn has *apologized* for taking wing while I was being dragged down the stairs. "Call me crazy if it makes you feel better," she writes. "I had my reasons, even if they aren't any more rational than yours were. At least Bruno got you out."

It's the *other* readers who are slamming me (though the site's hits keep coming) because I was snippy about the president's oration and because I've stopped commenting on general pandemic news.

What am I supposed to say about the blackouts and rioting in Los Angeles? I already got burned blathering about stuff out there. I trust the media are exaggerating. Even the LAPD couldn't shoot that many people without making waves.

New Yorkers typically shun mob violence. We revolt as *individuals*.

So I'll focus on what I see and hear in my Village in Manhattan. I'll try to get out more—no point in wasting the *evil emailer*'s time and efforts.

I sure hope never to see the innards of the schools that are being turned into clinics and triage centers. The only draw I envision is that warehoused patients can be fed and kept warm when the weather turns. Not least, they can be given Relenza. Which *might* help.

I forced myself out the door today, strolled briskly around the block. My sortie proved that things look better than they sound but smell a lot worse than they look. Few people on the street want to hurt anyone, much less kill. The war zone atmosphere is more a matter of grim filth and shortages, once you get used to plywood façades on your local shops. Kids must have busted every window they could reach through the security gates they couldn't rip down.

People are sullen. Vendors and consumers contemplate one another with suspicion. Stores seem empty—some because the consumers took everything, others because shopkeepers want special inducements to show their wares.

There's no good food out there, unless you're in the clutches of the LES DIY. The thought prompted me to stop in at Ric's to sample the day's offering—a toothsome lasagna.

Praying For Cash in Washington

The gang was in high spirits, denouncing the government in a muffled chorus as they whipped up food behind masks. The latest conspiracy theory is that the government wants to crack down on community groups that aren't affiliated with religious institutions via the DHS's RAISE. The churches and synagogues that worked with the LES DIY in Round One have bonded with the Feds, who are reimbursing the religious institutions for their um, good works—as I now discover FEMA did after Katrina. Even God has a paid gig in Washington!

Charity, of course, begins at home. With the churches now offering competitive meal services, our colorful Village boasts contending *cantinas* for the needy. It's safe to say the meals and conversation excel at Ric's. Traffic is down, though.

I tried to take the opportunity to thank Anna for sending Bruno to save me. Would she confess? She blushed and mumbled that Bruno had volunteered because they were *all* worried about me. It was nice to see some color on her translucent flesh. (*Don't you think, Ric?*)

Later I caught her staring at me with those heavenly orbs, streaked with sorrow. Too quickly, they ran away, never to return. Again I found myself wishing she were my *addled adversary,* Evelyn. Then I realized they *all* stare at me—I'm that friendly right-wing nut who loathes the DHS and RAISE no less than they do.

Even my daily one-way communication was fruitful when I got home. She-who-is-neither-reliable-nor-Anna buttered me up with a link in response to my provision of children's masks to the LES DIY. It's an animation of an old Lenny Bruce riff called *Thank You Mask Man*. Watch it!

I don't know much about Bruce, who overdosed in the 1960s after being arrested and persecuted for uttering 'obscenities' we now hear on cable every night. (Dustin Hoffman played him in a hit movie.)

The cartoon is very funny. Made five years after Bruce died, but using his voice (thanks Google, for the show and background info), it's quite primitive. And eerily familiar. I'd bet a box of masks that the guys behind *South Park* loved it when they were just potheads with impossible dreams.

Thank You Mask Man starts with locals on the range marveling at the Lone Ranger's altruism, then questioning it, resenting it, and finally forcing him to explain how they might reward him. His solution is controversial.

I'm not above accepting gratuities. I love that Evelyn sent me this 'toon.

I'm a proud Mask Man in a pitiless, flat world. *Thank You, Mad Mailer.*

DAY 155

FLU YORK CITY ON TWO WHEELS

I'm watching my city mutate from a mobile perch. At times the air I bicycle through is inexplicably smoky. I see grim lines at stores, especially pharmacies—some a block long. People try not to mingle. But New Yorkers still hate waiting: I saw one column erupt like <u>a murder of crows</u> as someone tried to cut ahead.

Today I came across a young woman hacking her lungs up on 14[h] Street, evidently suffering the early stages of an immune system meltdown. Passersby watched her helpless red face and distended neck as she clung to a rusty fire hydrant, but no one had a solution. Most moved a little faster.

I reached a guy at 911. He was coughing, too. He said they already had the woman on a list to be picked up. "When?" ASAP, which could be hours, he explained candidly: A death sentence he neither intended nor denied.

Someone found cardboard on which to rest the woman in front of a closed luncheonette. The Samaritans thinned fast when blood began dripping from her mouth and nose. The effusion was dense, mixed with mucous in pink and red chunks and strings I've never seen. *Were they strips of lung*? It looked like a <u>cytokine storm</u> to me—as if her body had turned against itself, inside out. She was fighting infection to the last bloody cell.

A shabbily dressed man with a ragged turban, maybe homeless, looked at us as if we were chicken dung. He bent over to help. I watched, ashamed, as he spoke to her. When she tried to respond, a thick red blob spewed forth to paint his face.

Everyone ran away as if a bomb had gone off, leaving the man dripping horror. He was yelling—his hands bloody, outstretched, like an Aztec high priest.

I handed him a t-shirt I carry in my pack for emergencies, marched away before he could wipe his mouth to thank me. What else could I contribute?

I rode away as the sun emerged, wondering what to think of all the efforts to produce a vaccine. The longer it takes to deliver one, the more antagonistic the antivax activists are becoming. Poll results that once showed

Americans eager to take a shot have turned around, even as more people die from avian flu. Conspiracy theories abound. Even Fitch is up to his neck agitating on the social networks, which at least keeps him busy.

Fortunately, I soon discovered that New York has turned into a bikers' town. (Not motorcycles—we lack fuel.) Cyclists and skaters, even scooters, have taken the streets. I'm not sure it's such an improvement for pedestrians, who can't hear us coming.

Proceeding north, I saw bent storefront grilles, plywood windows, scorched façades. Mountains of garbage feeding more rats than the Pied Piper ever bargained for. Sidewalks flooded by waters whose storm drains are jammed with refuse. A city adrift in tawdry anarchy.

On a busy corner, I saw church volunteers handing out food to people who didn't look poor but sure were hungry. The charity truck was marked with a big RAISE logo advertising that odd new branch of the Department of Homeland Security. When I approached for a look at the sandwiches and pickles, I noticed the deliverers were wearing white shirts emblazoned with the logo, which made them look like airport screeners.

Speaking of Washington, I wonder how the government will respond to the anti-vaccine rally that's been called by Nation Against Toxins Under-Researched Everywhere. (Yep, N.A.T.U.R.E.) The march to the White House has already been banned on health grounds, but organizers vow that thousands of mostly mothers will drive to Washington with their children to demand that no vaccine be allowed to contain mercury, adjuvants, or anything that hasn't been thoroughly tested.

The authorities will never agree to any of these conditions. First, mercury (thimerosal) still comes in flu shots for people over six because each shot would otherwise have to come individually packaged; you can imagine how much more trouble, time, and expense it would entail to inoculate the entire planet. Second, while they were lucky with swine flu because only one shot was needed to render immunity, H5N1 will require at least two (possibly three) normal vaccinations because so few people have ever encountered anything like it before; adjuvants that boost the human response can stretch out supplies. Third, none of the emergency vaccines for the new virus strain will be thoroughly tested. That would take until after Round Two ends. Time is short.

So is gasoline. I doubt many protesters will make it to Washington. N.A.T.U.R.E. may call, but few will risk getting the flu to fight a solution most people can't wait for. This Million Mom March ain't gonna happen.

Fitch will hate me for saying all of the above. I've come to realize that he didn't invest in my mask business to make money—though I fear he intends to make more from it than I do —but because he hates vaccines. More than I (who might opt for a flu shot), he believes masks and protective gear offer the only way to survive H5N1. There's always more to Fitch than I had suspected.

DAY 156

MY DAY IN THE MEDIEVAL SUN

I biked today through a remarkably gray and lifeless midtown Manhattan. It looks as if no one is working. The food trucks are missing. There were empty parking spaces, few taxis. I don't know how the big companies function. All businesses need maintenance, contact, live flesh.

Plenty of skin was displayed on the steps of St. Patrick's Cathedral. The mad medievalists are still whipping themselves red over our shortcomings. Their leaflet offered the usual catalogue of misdeeds by the Roman Church (in which I was raised), plus man's general immorality and lack of penitence. That's reassuring: During the Black Death, hordes of flagellants marched around Germany, inciting people to destroy the Jews they blamed for the Plague.

The more restrained contemporary version was hideous to watch— or hear. The men beat themselves in stark rhythm, beginning with a *whoosh* as the knouts swept through the air, then a collective *whomp* as they ripped into human tissue, and finally the *tcchh* sound of tiny barbs being torn out of them in unison. Did some of these men used to wear suits in nearby skyscrapers?

Lest we be spattered by gore, the audience kept distant. Some baited the flagellants. Others cursed the hecklers. The police looked dangerously unhappy, though it's all apparently legal as long as no one flogs anyone else and the men don't lose their loincloths (or insult the mayor). They evidently don't enlist women.

Then I biked to the top of the island to see what's become of my car. First I pedaled along a path up the Hudson River to the tallest part of Manhattan Island, just north of the George Washington Bridge. A <u>mockingbird</u> was riffing in all directions over the old train tracks. Those critters inspired jazz.

I felt lucky to be exploring the city, rediscovering movement. My hamstrings haven't forgiven me yet, but I'm absolving them with ice. I won't pretend it isn't a drag to bike hard while wearing a serious mask, but I grew accustomed to it. There were long stretches where I was alone and could breathe nakedly, the sun on my face. The air was clean, the skies blue.

I coasted down Broadway into the 190s, 10 miles north of my home. My sense of menace dissipated as I realized no one cared to harm me. New Yorkers are spooky and angry and needy—their gait is slower, confused, wary—but there was none of the malice or viciousness I'd anticipated having to flee. Manhattan was more like an afternoon break on a <u>George Romero</u> set, with the zombies content to relax, stretch, smoke.

The streets up there were filled with cyclists. Even surrounded by contagion, the riders were friendly, almost exultant. People on bicycles seem convinced they're not ill. They must believe their exertions confirm it, the way some churchgoers think pious behavior proves they're destined for heaven.

I Hope They Recycled it

I felt like a double agent. Bicyclists in New York tend to hate cars. But I was using my two-wheeled Green Dream to rescue my four-wheeled Toxic Public Nemesis from the bus stop where the panicky crowd had left it.

The corner was vacant.

My old VW Fox had vanished, crumpled axle and all. With so many stranded Acuras to steal, why would anyone want a dented, busted, four-cylinder German sedan that was made in Brazil before the millennium? All the plastic stuff had long since snapped off—not least, the door lock buttons.

A shopkeeper who looked as if he maintains an arsenal under his counter remembered seeing it. Didn't know when, flung his hands as he shrugged. (I guess he trusted me.) The man actually had grub to sell. I was hungry, but it wasn't fresh.

I called the police tow garages in Manhattan and the Bronx. Each answered after long delays. One cop sounded surprised that anyone had waited for him to pick up. "You know the problems these days," he mumbled. *Sure, I predicted them.*

Tired, I followed Broadway south for five miles until I realized I was near

Central Park. There I found a strange world of *flugitives* camping peacefully enough, interspersed with mounted cops rousting people who didn't look like they were camping. No one bothered to yell so I couldn't tell what activity the police were discouraging. It looked like a jerky silent movie without title cards to tell you what's happening.

Sticks, Stones & Dead Birds

I pedaled up a steep hill to Belvedere Castle, next to the Central Park Weather Station. The courtyard was strewn with paper, deserted except for a couple of men barking into cell phones in foreign tongues. One had a little girl with him. She gazed at the battlements as if she wished a prince would come down to entertain her.

A frog croaked in the pond far below. I was tempted to tell her about the amphibious route to royalty.

Instead I bounced my bike down some stone steps into the Ramble, a wooded labyrinth famed for nighttime activities I won't describe here. I'd never been there, but it was scandalously pleasant to be surrounded by tall trees and chirping birds. The woods were deserted by humans, which was fine with me.

A trail led me onto a peninsula that jutted out into the lake, toward the big fountain on the other side. In better times, the water would be full of tourists rowing rented boats, but it was empty—except for ducks and geese that blithely pretended to know nothing of any plague. One honked at me like a native New Yorker of yore: *"Boid flu, wazzat?"*

As the sun began setting, I made my way to a bridge over the lake. On the shore below, I saw a pile of geese that hadn't died naturally. Some jerk had gone to a lot of trouble to catch and torture them. Need I repeat that whatever strain wild birds have is not the one people are giving each other? *We* are our problem.

In a secluded patch of magical, fading light not far from the carousel, I paused to watch a circle of hippies. At first I thought they were partying like it was 1969, trading tokes and blues on pipes and strings. But they were chanting for the dead. I sat by to admire their rich, heartfelt harmonies as I thought of Lisa, her big brown eyes, her serene smile.

As the sun set, the group invited me to break innumerable laws by smoking with them. (It's illegal to smoke anything in a city park.) A friend in Virginia had died of bird flu, and this was his memorial. I started to talk about the pandemic, but they stopped me after I mentioned that nature might be targeting mammals. "Dude, the other critters are collateral damage. It's *us*." No point in arguing with that.

Before I rode off in the dark, I traded a pair of masks for some herbal supplies. (Mine await a lucky intruder, upstate.) Nothing like finding a vendor who so enthusiastically uses her own. In my neighborhood, they favor harder stuff these days.

A patrol car stopped me on my way home. I told the cop I'd just delivered masks to a doctor in the West Village, showed her my remaining sample. She was pleased to accept it and told me how to obtain a permit to break curfew. I asked how dangerous it is at night. She shook her head and murmured: "*Pretty dead.*"

DAY 157

BEDBUGS THRIVE, WE DIE

The Feds have leaked an enterprising plan to fire doctors, nurses, and technicians who don't toe the line. That'll reduce America's health while breaking independent spirit. RAISE be praised.

I rendezvoused with Ric in Tompkins Square Park. He wouldn't let me visit his apartment because he's captured two specimens in a bottle and wanted to spare me any exposure. I had inspected an excellent bedbug site so I'd know what they look like.

He's got 'em—rust-colored insects the size of watermelon seeds. Bedbugs aren't known to spread human disease, but they can live in cracks and folds all over your home for as long as a year without blood. It's very difficult to outlast them.

Pigeons, sparrows, and starlings can carry bedbugs, which can also travel on bags, shoes, clothes, buses, taxis, and subways. I haven't sat on a wooden subway bench for years because the parasites love cracks in wood. I'm guessing Ric dragged some charming piece of infected furniture home after someone left it on the street. (We do that a lot here.) Or hooked up with someone who had one in his clothes or bag. Some people don't react to bedbug bites and can carry the insects the way asymptomatic carriers spread flu.

He can't get anyone to kill the pests. In the best of times, extermination takes patience and money, if you can find someone to pay enough visits. Often they bring dogs trained to detect the insects. Ric has no cash. Now he's afraid to visit his restaurant lest he infest it. As someone who nearly lost his mind a few days ago—and whose loving roommate apparently went mad several months ago—I worry for his sanity.

Even so, I sat away from him on the rainy bench. Of course he noticed. That's why we were out there.

Ric had the look of a bank robber on the run. He was gaunt, alert, poised to dash. His dark eyes were restless, taking in a world that no longer felt like home. When I squeezed his shoulder from afar, he kept his gaze on the squirrels. "Better not touch me." His voice was strangled. He sobbed quietly as I kept my hand there.

I wouldn't know about the LES DIY if it weren't for Ric. They wouldn't be nearly as effective without him. A lot of New Yorkers owe this man. I don't know how to help him.

Everything's going wrong. Sneeky is licking himself compulsively. His belly is a red splotch and I can't help but wonder if he's got bugs.

We hear rumors that H5N1 has turned more virulent, is killing more New Yorkers. All they tell us is to stay home and wash our hands. It makes me nauseous—but that's just another flu symptom.

I put together a business card and visited the 9th Precinct to get a Health Security Certificate so I can go out at night in my capacity as a provider of public health equipment on an emergency basis. Evidently my papers must be sent to Washington for approval by the Department of Homeland Security, something no news reports had indicated. But the desk sergeant appreciated my needs—and samples—and gave me a temporary permit that should keep me out of trouble for a while.

DAY 158

DIGGING PANDEMIC, THE HARD WAY

What am I supposed to say about the imposition of martial law in LA? Obviously it's a nightmare, but I'm not there. Nor do I know what to make of the announcement that RAISE is helping enterprising states set up recruitment centers to hire and train medical, fire, and security personnel for emergency service. Anyone whose blood test shows antibodies to H5N1 (and who lacks a criminal record) will be hired, uniformed, paid, and given priority for related jobs after the crisis ends.

The official statement mentioned U.S. citizenship as a possible reward, so DHS—which runs immigration—must be hoping that foreign cops, fire-fighters, and medical professionals with flu seasoning will jump ship for our troubled shores.

Evelyn chastises me for forgetting she was the person who first told me about the LES DIY *"when you were nesting happily with your banker."* Yeah, yeah. She says the group is overworked and divided over how to dispose of the burgeoning supply of corpses. They hear that scores, maybe a hundred, fester behind apartment doors in our corner of New York.

I'm wondering if the cops I saw in Central Park were chasing people who were trying to bury flu victims. (*Did they make the ones they caught carry their corpses away?*) An email just popped up to report that stray dogs were spotted unearthing human bodies in nearby Tompkins Square Park—just three blocks square, mostly concrete.

The LES DIY's coordinator runs one of the biggest community gardens in the East Village and she resolutely opposes the members who want to turn the verdant lots into impromptu cemeteries.

The city and developers have never accepted that the gardens—survivors from a time when residents planted greenery and built fountains in rubble-packed lots to enliven blighted blocks—should remain in community hands. The properties are now priceless and she thinks the city will grab them if residents are caught using them for unauthorized activities. Imagine how the media will portray illicit burials in two years, when everyone is feverishly trying to forget what things were really like *now.*

She's probably correct about the long-term peril. For the moment, I'm sure the police appreciate the LES DIY's activities, which help maintain order. Desperately famished folks can make trouble. The group has even enlisted doctors and nurses who have withdrawn from the organized chaos of Public Health to help people in a more accessible setting—a back room at the restaurant. Why should the cops oppose that?

Still, residents with dead roommates and relatives are frantic, and the group is fracturing. My correspondent didn't state her position. Ric has gone inactive. He writes to explain that the bedbugs must've joined him via a book he found in the lobby of his apartment building. Ric worked hard to keep his restaurant free of the parasites, but a novel called *Cloud Atlas* proved too intriguing. I remember when Ric texted me to praise it.

I sure hope the LES DIY can bear up. Nothing else works around here. Brownouts are becoming frequent around the country as utilities hoard coal and oil. Even writing at night, I save my text every few words. Count Blogula can't afford to waste thoughts these days. They could dry up.

In Lieu of Coal: *Breathe/Don't Breathe*

We must be close to running out of vital supplies. Power plants generally stock three weeks' worth of fuel. If, as we were promised, the authorities spent the hiatus preparing for Round Two, why are the shops so empty?

Fortunately, I've realized—*doh!*—just how much my protective gear is worth. (No, I'm not raising prices, although shipping costs have risen because it must all be *insured* for so much more; my cleverly disguised packages have started to vanish.)

Whenever I go out, I wind up making sales. I can't let people come here. Like a crack dealer, I meet them in the park or on street corners. I have yet to be robbed. I've managed to restock a little survival cash.

Storekeepers seem happy to barter food and kibbles for my goods, so Sneeky and I are plush with dull sustenance. I could trade for a car but I'd never manage to switch registration or insure it. Most bureaucracies remain shut.

The media tell us that New York's trend-setting Quarantine Culture is hot, so long as we consume it digitally. However slowly the pipelines move it, money flows to the ISPs and vendors of downloadable games, streamable movies, and songs that do both. The runaway hit theme of Round Two is *Breathe/Don't Breathe*, by Uncle Monkey. If you listen carefully, the song has nothing to do with bird flu, but who can resist something both ominous and cheerful? Let's hope we all get to dance to the post-pandemic nostalgia remix.

The overworked and understaffed gendarmes of the 9th Precinct spend precious hours pursuing me. I've heard from a dozen cops who want free protective gear. After agreeing to a couple of requests, I took to throwing things again. I could never satisfy the world's biggest municipal police force.

A call from "*Sergeant Petruca's nephew Cazimir*" was the last straw. Of course Poles and Italians interbreed; it just sounded farfetched in the moment. I told him my stash was fully committed to doctors and politicians.

And to *you*, my loyal patrons.

Let's hope they don't yank my temporary Health Security Certificate. The security of my health is nothing to sneeze at.

DAY 158 (#2)

'OUR' BIRDS—A SCARY DRAMA

I'll post this bonus entry and then I'll sleep.

I was restless after I wrote, wanted to walk, breathe, *ride*. I stuffed my curfew permit, a water bottle, and a couple of masks into a backpack, biked north in darkness. There were more people circulating than I'd expected. Everyone moved silently—walking without conversation, driving without music. Traffic is scarce, with few cops. No one asked for my papers.

I made it to Central Park not long before sunup, tried to pause on a ghostly Fifth Avenue to await the light. The park looked as it always does at night—forbidding. Impatient, I entered it to ride north on the East drive toward the Ramble, reckoning that the people who go there at night were finished.

Once there, a gorgeous faint light lured me into the woods, empty but for some early birds and a few squirrels posing like prairie dogs. It was exciting to see life stirring afresh, independent of man, in the world's capital city.

Lisa would have cherished seeing the cardinal that gently and persistently chased the blue jay from tree to tree. I couldn't figure out which of them was what gender, or why the red bird was so intent on being with the blue one. They looked like forbidden wannabe lovers who'd come to the Ramble to try their luck.

I went to the promontory I like at the lake. Ducks and geese floated around preening, oblivious to the terror they inspire in the planet's top dogs.

In his book, Dr. Michael Greger says that ducks catch waterborne flu for a few days when young. They don't fall ill, merely shed billions of doses of a digestive virus that gives people pinkeye at worst.

Then the innocuous duck flu drifts into our stinking chicken factories, where the virus must move up from the stomach to the respiratory tract to replicate among poultry. Once airborne, it can infect humans.

A gram of ordinary chicken dung contains enough viral particles to infect a million birds. China harbors huge multispecies farms in which chickens defecate onto pigs that eat the poultry dung and then void their own into waters that sustain commercial fish. When healthy, migrating ducks drop in for a drink and a bath, they can pick up enhanced virus and fly it to distant chicken factories—if shipments of infected poultry don't bring it first.

Thus can a mild disorder mutate into a versatile plague that infects pigs and chickens—and *you-know-who.*

We're not just talking exotic locales. In 2011 kids in Indiana and Pennsylvania contracted cases of H3N2 influenza that had been circulating only in swine—until that strain picked up a gene from the pandemic 2009 swine flu virus that had affected people.

A Man-Bird-Pig Virus in Missouri

In 2006, a variation of 1957's H2N2 pandemic strain (to which people born after 1968 have no immunity) turned up at separate pig farms in Missouri. This H2N3 subtype contained genetic material from a swine virus, a human virus, and at least three different avian viruses. (Raccoons can serve as influenza mixing bowls, too.)

That was three years before everyone was shocked, *shocked* that an H1N1 subtype with genes from swine, human, and avian viruses broke out in North America and became infamous as swine flu. In the midst of that pandemic, Mike Coston blogged about an article from a veterinary news site that detailed how the pork industry was resisting testing for influenza because it didn't want to lose money on infected herds.

Coston's post came just two months after pork, chicken, and beef producers told the government they opposed any effort to stop them from using antibiotics to grow their animals faster. The freewheeling use of antibiotics in factory farms is spreading MRSA, as problems in the Netherlands have made clear. (Read this *New York Times* column about an Indiana county with lots of hog farms and loads of MRSA; it was published six weeks before the 2009 swine flu pandemic was detected.)

Nothing changes. No one remembers anything. We just get sicker.

But our viral vulnerability is greater and deeper than that sparked by greed for cheap food and dirty profits.

As Frank Ryan posits in *Virus X: Tracking the New Killer Plagues,* we are squeezing natural life out of the planet. Every road we cut into virgin rain forest seems to trigger some kind of unusual outbreak. Each creature going extinct seems to harbor a virus that needs to leap *fast* to another species. In killing off our primate cousins, we wind up with mysterious maladies like HIV.

As the dominant global species asserts its primacy over air, land, and water, perhaps it's only fair that we acquire all the diseases. They migrate to the strongest carrier: us.

Bugging Viruses—Because We Can

We charge in and wreck these viruses' habitats, killing the hosts with whom they coexist and forcing them to adapt or die. It's as if we barged into a cave full of armed psychopaths and chased them into the Mall of America to seek new victims.

Pandemics are *natural*, and the conditions that foster them are spreading just as fast as we are.

So I sat in the morning sun, sucking up Vitamin D, listening to birds warble. My face and hands were naked, my mask and gloves and goggles arrayed on a rock. Some squawking crows reminded me of a rainy autumn night years ago, when I watched *The Birds* screen in a park behind the New York Public Library.

By then I was tracking H5N1's evolution. I marveled that Alfred Hitchcock had captured nature's fury long before it became clear that we could actually kill off the world's birds. Wetlands International said in 2007 that there were only *half* as many wild waterfowl as there had been five years earlier. Half of U.S. songbirds are thought to have vanished over the past 40 years—a growing problem because of summer habitat destruction in the north and the use of banned pesticides in the southern climes where they winter.

When the eradication of wild birds leaves us to the mercies of mosquitoes, will we feign surprise? I can taste the outrage—the bile of hypocrisy—as the public seeks culprits.

DAY 159:

A PLAGUE OF BUREAUCRATS

I can't sleep. The LES DIY has split. The singer who runs the community garden resigned with threats for anyone who might contemplate using her turf for corpse disposal.

Anna has become acting coordinator, as if she weren't overworked. She has already weathered a surprise inspection from the city Department of Health & Mental Hygiene. I'm told they found little to complain about: The clinic had moved into an adjacent storefront, staffed in part by medical pros fired by the city and/or their employers for alleged failures during the pandemic. They don't mind working for free.

My brief old friend 'Val,' whom I met at Ric's reopening, is one of them. She says that some big contractors are offering the hospitals foreign workers and trainees to fill gaps left by the purge. "All I did was question why we were wasting resources dumping good people who stayed home sick or needed a couple of days to care for their families," she told me. "Next thing, my grant dissolved."

Which raises another question: *How can a city without the means to pick up moldering corpses dispatch health department officials to harass volunteers who feed the starving and sick?* I'm surprised I haven't heard from Evelyn.

Outraged, I called my newspaper friend. I hoped he might look into it, ask questions, back the community with some coverage. He astonished me by explaining that the Department of Homeland Security is hunting for terrorists who might exploit the pandemic.

After the Pentagon, DHS is the biggest federal agency. In addition to running such security functions as Immigration & Customs Enforcement (ICE), the Transportation Security Administration (TSA), and InfraGard (a weird 'partnership' between the FBI and America's private sector), it directs the national pandemic response. DHS is in charge of FEMA and the startup, Restore America's Independent Spirit & Enterprise. I've seen complaints that executive jobs at RAISE are going to career *Federales*, rather than to FEMA or Red Cross-type relief professionals.

Public Enemy #*What?*

My newshound pal said DHS and RAISE are leaning on municipalities to document independent groups that have sprung up to fight H5N1 (preferring institutional, faith-based initiatives). In his best Bart Simpson undertone, he lazily suggested the city inspectors might have been detectives. Then he pleaded deadlines and hung up.

I replayed *Bart's* last quote in my (biological) memory several times before I realized my heart was pounding. His blasé comment scared and shocked me. The Feds have the time and interest to crush secular self-help groups?

I fled to my little peninsula in the park. Getting there is half the fun—maskless, wind in my face, legs pumping. Then I take out the excellent binoculars I got from a photo supply store in exchange for some gear, or I doze on a big rock that slants to the east in the early light.

I'm happy there. Lusty, too, in a lazy way. Life feels hot and promising so far from reality.

Escape in New York

Sometimes I imagine sharing my bubble with someone who loves life intensely enough to fight for it unconditionally: A survivor with heart and soul. Showered with light, surrounded by waking creatures of like mind, I can almost feel her with me. Of course we'd wish we were at a real lake, in a real forest, *really* safe. Till then we'd escape to my secret world, full of wonder even as human society dredges up pain, fear, and suspicion.

I guess the Ramble's nocturnal visitors feel the same way. They seemed creepy and exotic at first because they're after quick, casual sex with other men at a time when I can't *talk* to a pretty woman without a plastic coating. Some of the denizens wear masks, stalking the woods and paths in high Q Zone fashion.

None of this is particularly novel, reported the *New York Times*: In 1904 a well-dressed young foreigner shot himself at a cave by the lake, 18 years before an artist was sentenced to three months in the workhouse for trying to pick up a man there, and 25 years before *The Times* noted that 335 men had been arrested for "annoying women" in the park, particularly near the cave.

Whatever goes on these days takes place silently. The scariest sound I've heard was a vicious, hacking cough that sounded like someone was on his last cruise. I did happen upon a violent act—someone being struck by another—but it was a moonlit spanking performed for gleaming eyes in the bushes. Phone cams lit up like fireflies.

The taser I carry is for roving packs of canines, not people. I walk like an Indian, as they used to say, noiselessly rolling my feet heel to toe, one just ahead of the other. I think I learned it from reading Mark Twain.

Today I watched a tabby cat attempting to shadow sparrows in the reeds near where I sit. The kitty was trying to learn how to feed itself. It was scrawny and dirty, one of numerous feral felines I've spotted in recent days. That's bad news for the lake's residents; the toxoplasmosis that some cats shed can poison fish and amphibious creatures. (Frogs are already dying around the world from a fungus called chytrid.)

That hapless kitty was still wearing its collar and license. I trust the flu has killed its owner. If any healthy people abandoned this creature, I hope they die soon in a manner no less painful than the fate their desperate cat intended for those sparrows.

DAY 160

RELENZA & I GO UNDERGROUND

Count Blogula has much to report, some of it surreal, some scary.

The evening began with late bartering—masks for herbs. I set out for the Ramble from the West Village in high spirits. As I approached Penn Station, I noticed a vehicular armada parked on 8th Avenue, lights flashing in a way uncharacteristic of New York cops these days. I hunched with my bike against a dim porno storefront to watch the distribution of a consignment of boxes that must have arrived by rail during curfew hours.

When I saw the NYPD standing back deferentially, I reckoned it wise to freeze. Armed figures in blue DHS jackets were supervising lesser beings as they forklifted pallets into some trucks. The process took an hour. Ordinary folks would have done it in 15 minutes.

I had to urinate grievously by the time the trucks started off in various directions, heedless of traffic regulations. These were evidently *very important boxes*. I felt like the protagonist in *Invasion of the Body Snatchers* (the original one—watch the trailer), witnessing a shipment of alien pods. It was a dark and misty night....

When the last truck passed my hiding place, how could I resist tailing it on my old blue bicycle, in my old black clothes? WWJD? That's *What Would Jimmy [Stewart] Do*? Why, shucks, he'd follow them!

The truck didn't get far. It meandered west and north till it pulled into a parking lot near a shuttered diner on 11th Avenue. There stood a similar truck peopled by identical types in blue windbreakers that didn't say DHS. The new guys used their hands to lug boxes from the first truck to their own.

DHS merely watched. As did I, huddled by a bus parked in a corner of the lot, my bladder throbbing.

The DHS men left first, having handed off half a pallet's worth of boxes. Their unidentified colleagues drove directly west to one of the idled party boats berthed near the Circle Line on the Hudson River. It took five minutes to shift the packages onto the vessel—enough for me to bike up, across, and down the highway to a point from which I could use my binoculars to see what the boxes said: GSK.

GlaxoSmithKline makes *Relenza*.

The U.S. government is thought to maintain a Strategic National Stockpile (SNS) of antivirals in 12 secret depots for use in the pandemic. This was apparently a shipment from one of those facilities. I had just watched the diversion of half a pallet to an alternate location, presumably in New Jersey.

Those boxes would each contain thousands of powder disks worth hundreds of dollars apiece on the black market. *Priceless*. The pictures I shot ain't much, but they're mine.

I cell-phoned my newspaper pal, woke him with a whisper. I was hoping Bart could track the boat, an absurd idea at 2 a.m. He said he'd ring back in the morning. *Nothing*. He's stopped answering my calls. I hope he's okay.

NYC's warped dreamscape was hardly finished with me. When the boat had motored west and the truck driven east, I pedaled north along the Hudson.

Lust in the Weeds

Under the West Side Highway, where I'd planned to relieve myself, I happened on something no less shocking—an outdoor disco.

As I urinated in fogbound shadows, my binoculars revealed a speakeasy with lights, thumping beats, and dancing girls, surrounded by a multicultural crowd of dancers with naked faces. I heard whoops and howls and shattering glassware as people partied with abandon.

Then I detected an undercurrent of moans and grunts. People were having sex around me on the lawn and grasses by the river, a lot louder than gays do in the Ramble. Heterosexual New Yorkers are tossing caution aside, too. I wonder what sex clubs must be like. *Profitable beyond belief* is my guess, even after deducting for bribes.

A libidinous upsurge during the pandemic would make sense. It would mirror the activities of the particles that seek to invade us.

Influenza replicates with amazing speed. When two viruses infect the same cell, they can swap genes in an evolutionary process called <u>reassortment</u>; each can contribute units of the eight genetic segments needed to assemble fresh flu particles. <u>Dr. Robert Webster</u>, who suppressed a 1997 H5N1 outbreak in Hong Kong, calls it "virus sex" when influenza A *mutates* by drawing on the 16 H genes and 9 N genes in its hereditary arsenal. Reassortment is how <u>those little piggies</u> in my home state wound up with an H2N3 comprised of genes from birds and swine (with a dollop of humanity, too). And that was before Novel H1N1 swine flu popped up from the same hodgepodge.

Genetic Flu Passports

<u>Dr. Henry Niman</u> pursues a more aggressive theory called <u>recombination</u>, by which two moderate strains of the same virus can contribute to a new killer subtype by swapping genetic information from snippets of the same gene. Niman says this entails a quicker promiscuity, and he backs it up by posting <u>genetic strings</u> that detail where selected viral strains have roamed, like stamps in a passport.

At least the viral exchanges are voluntary. Humans aren't so civilized. Tribulation Beat, the Brooklyn blog, says New York's women are being sexually assaulted. I've seen nothing in the regular media, beyond reports from cities that endured sustained looting.

It could be that a greater percentage of women on the street are being attacked but that fewer are venturing out, so the number of actual rapes is falling. Or that women attacked in their homes aren't calling the police for fear of being exposed to further potential flu carriers. Who knows what goes on in a city whose population is hiding? What would the police know or do?

This must be a prime time to settle scores, knock off enemies. How many autopsies can the city be conducting? It could be tempting to poison unloved family members with prescription medications. How many detectives would be spared to grill an unhappy couple's contacts? Would neighbors even answer the door?

After so much skullduggery, it was a joy to reach my innocent avian pals. They fluttered happily and sang that I should let go, enjoy the rising sun and wind and critters. I sat in a bracing breeze for two hours as I contemplated what to say about what I'd seen. Now I know.

And so shall you: *Save & Enter.*

DAY 161

OUR REVOLTING HERO

I'm posting early because it's raining and I have a batch of instant emails.

It seems that I have two kinds of readers. One type attacks me for implying that DHS—or anyone, really—has done anything wrong. Emails call me "traitor," "renegade," and best of all, "human sunken retrovirus." That one's a little obscure, but it's fun to break down. The gist here is that I should never have … *what*?

I reported what I saw, added no judgments. Those who condemn me as a "quisling"—in rather obscure reference to a Norwegian Fascist who administered his occupied country for Hitler—betray their own dark thoughts as to what it *means* that I saw what I saw. Hey, maybe the State of New Jersey *needs* to send plainclothes goons to pick up federally distributed antiviral medicine in a Manhattan party boat. Heck, George Washington used a far shabbier vessel to cross the Delaware and surprise the Germans in New Jersey.

The second group thinks I should drop everything and run, that I have dangerously vexed the military-pharmaceutical-industrial complex. These folks say I'm "brave" and "insane." They counsel me to lie low till the pandemic has long concluded. Wouldn't they miss my bloggings? I'm insulted!

If I believed the government capable of executing much of anything, let alone an obscure, dissident mask vendor, I could sweat. But these clowns can't even deliver boxes. I doubt my fate is of much interest to them or anyone else. My buddy Bart never called back, so my little tale has concluded in a blink.

Believers in both groups contributed religious spin. One branded me an "atheistic scum who wouldn't see the truth if God painted it on [my] eyeballs." Conversely, a reader commiserated that this godless society ought to get what it deserves, but said he hopes I "will be spared, God willing."

Then came variations on my bread and butter. The *patriots* threatened not to buy masks and gloves and goggles from me; the *paranoids* warned that no one else would buy protective gear from me because I'm too outspoken.

The good news: There were a lot of paranoids, so my business will easily endure any drop off in demand from the *Washington Rules* gang. To welcome the alarmists. We've cut prices AND added a new line of less-expensive disposable masks.

DAY 161 (#2)

RIP

Ric is dead.
I can't even read that.
I've failed him. And Lisa. Who's next?

DAY 161 (#3)

CENSORED

THIS *&@%$^ IS TOTALLY *&@%$^ UP. (*Yes, I went back and changed it.*)
I am fed up with everyone—EVERTYTHING—including death and cowardice and lies.
Go to hell LES DIY and take the city of New York with you.
The SOONER THE BETTER.

DAY 162

REVIVED

I am *heartily* sorry for the previous post.
I can only explain that I was intellectually and emotionally shredded. I had just discovered my best friend's corpse. Then things got worse.
I've just returned from the strangest night of my life—Halloween come alive. It ended in a bold sunny day. I'm trending normal again. I need sleep. I'll post when I wake up.

DAY 162 (#2)

KILLER BUGS & PEOPLE

I've slept four hours, injected iced coffee, and can address the confusion I've stirred. Thanks go out to those who sent alarmed emails that weren't abusive. I feel as if I've been drawn and quartered by positive and negative forces, hung from earth's poles to roast on the equator.

Bits of me are dancing, others are paralyzed. The good stuff is rich, spectacular.

The bad commenced when I went to Ric's apartment.

He had sent a disturbing email asking me to visit, wearing a good *hat*. When I got there, the door would be unlocked and I should take plastic bags from his door and secure them around my feet and legs while I was inside. Since bedbugs track us by the carbon dioxide we emit, I should not sit anywhere, or even stand still. I was to leave fast and thoroughly shake the hat outside in case any bugs had climbed along the ceiling to dive on me. Best to vacuum it.

Since he didn't answer when I called for an explanation, I reckoned he had fallen into a disturbed state. I raced to his apartment. '*Ric's place*' isn't funny now.

It was unlocked. As promised, plastic dangled from the doorknob. The apartment was neat, as ever. I called out to him when I entered, fancied I heard a welcoming grunt over the music. That was a cruel illusion.

Ric was stretched out in bed, wearing silk pajamas and a relieved expression. The pill bottles he'd emptied were already in the recycle bin for plastics. Bach was playing low, on repeat.

I had to keep reminding myself to stay in motion. Finding your best friend dead makes you want to sit down.

In shock, I called 911, which asked me to confirm that he was dead and then to stay put till "somebody" arrived. If it was the same *somebody* that was scheduled to pick up Lisa's corpse for days, I'd be dried-up bedbug waste by the time they arrived.

I gave them my contact info. I took Ric's final words (*Never Surrender* were two I'll try to honor without judging him) and his financial documents, along with $132.72 he had stacked on them. I left the door unlocked, with Bach still playing. My goggles were soaked and smeared.

When I got home and drove the idea of bedbugs from my mind, I realized I'd be checking his flat for days, monitoring the city's response. I was sickened to have left him to the pests. How long will they suck his blood before it becomes too ripe? They are known to travel on corpses, if not feed on them.

Great disease novels all present a moment at which death ceases to affect the living. Souls glaze over. How many corpses must I see before I feel numb? So far I merely feel selfish, stupid, and sad as hell.

The Best New Yorkers Are Moldering

I haven't done much for those I've loved. Lisa and Ric died without even a visit from me. I was busy chatting with ducks, empathizing with strangers, pontificating online.

I wanted to call my parents last night, but it was too late. They've learned to expect little but words from me anyway. If they get sick in Round Two, *words* are all they'll get. I texted Mark, who still hasn't responded. I felt I deserved to be alone anyway, to die solo. Poor Sneeky, stuck with me.

I started throwing things, halfheartedly. I couldn't punish myself more than their deaths had done.

Then I realized Ric was a non-practicing Jew far from his family, who would have wanted to honor him by sitting shiva for a week. I started to telephone them, but how could I say I'd left their son to be exploited and dishonored by bloodsuckers? His dad's number in Seattle sits here, on my table.

I decided I should take it on myself to bury him. Here I was, waiting on a government whose services are certifiably dissolving. Me. So many things I predicted are taking me by surprise.

I determined to bury Ric *immediately*. Somehow. I telephoned Anna, the new head of the LES DIY, whose number I've had for months. I've seen her cry twice as many times as I've engaged her in conversation, which I botched by bringing up her dead daughter. I am utterly clumsy in the presence of death.

I've wished for a chance to start over with Anna. Dreaded it, too. She's an *Iron Angel*, a sprite with an unnaturally calm way of imposing her will on others—amid bouts of tears. I've never encountered anyone so appealing, yet so off-putting.

I knew corpse disposal was going to be a sensitive subject in view of the controversies the group has endured over the question. But I needed and deserved help. Certainly Ric did. The LES DIY is still using his restaurant.

When Anna answered, I made the idiotic mistake of talking around his death. I said I knew that corpse disposal was a controversial issue for them, but I needed advice regarding a very special case....

I heard her gasp. She snapped that the LES DIY has nothing to do with dead people, recited the city's special number for pickups—and hung up.

I could hardly breathe. Why did this woman hate me?

When I called her back, I reached a recording that gave the address and LES DIY service hours. (At Ric's restaurant!) I didn't leave a message. I posted that SCREAM OF OUTRAGE (which I've just *censored* to placate the spiders) and took off.

Hell Comes to My Haven

I pedaled furiously around the entire park before heading into the Ramble. I remember thinking murder was inevitable if anyone tried to mug me. I didn't know which end of the transaction I'd wind up at, but I was boiling. I yearned to encounter one of those bullying bird killers.

After chaining my bike to a fence under a lamppost, I followed the path onto my peninsula. With only a crescent moon, it was hard to see. Though I'd arrived earlier than usual, the woods were quiet. *Good*: I intended to grieve by the water till dawn, then glower and mope and reason my way back to sanity in the sun.

After sitting for a while, I rose to relieve myself. Then I thought I heard metal banging, back where I'd locked my bike.

I made my way over an informal trail between some rocks till I could see the lamppost. The streetlights outside my apartment are broken, but this one functions—just where nightly passersby probably wish it didn't.

The chain was intact, the tires full, the taser in my hand unnecessary.

Two men were walking east, down toward the restaurant by the lake. The short one coughed harshly and I wondered if he had contracted H5N1. So many people don't *get it* when they catch it.

I waited for a lurker to pass, then walked toward my spot. When I reached the main path, I heard someone behind me. I shifted to a dirt path that runs along the water and paused to see if I were being followed.

On the central path was what looked like an adolescent female wearing one of the masks I sell, complete with goggles and gloves. (I wish more New Yorkers sported my full product line.) The kid wasn't tailing me. She was striding confidently toward my lair, where the land thrusts furthest into the lake. I felt a twinge of possessiveness, then alarm: What was she doing there so late at night?

Then I heard a muffled cough and a *shhhh*. The men I'd spotted near my bike were following her. I don't wish to stereotype anyone, but they didn't seem gay—not even sardonic-trucker gay. They looked mean and aggressive. Was it their malevolent presence that had cleared the woods so early?

I watched them split up to flank her, and then I followed the tall one up past the reeds. Gripping the taser, my ears pounding with blood, I watched him reach for her.

She cried out in fright as he grabbed at her mask.

I can't continue. I'll have to resume tomorrow. Sorry, but I've barely slept.

DAY 163

RUMBLE IN THE RAMBLE

I'll pick up where I passed out yesterday:

Late at night, in Central Park's Ramble, a big, menacing guy had just grabbed what looked like a teenage girl in a mask and goggles and gloves....

I declared myself in what sounded to me a very shaky voice and ordered him to let her go, waving the taser. The guy cursed me loudly, waving his hands, till the back of my head exploded in bright flashes.

The little one had clubbed me with something. I turned around and without thinking punched him in the face. He was the first person I've hit since high school, and he flew. The weapon in my hand must have added heft.

I turned around to see the big guy holding the girl. He pointed a handgun at me, demanded I drop the taser. I recognized her just as I let it go.

It was *Anna*, the LES DIY's new coordinator. After hanging up on me, she had somehow shadowed me to the Ramble. *How had she known I'd be there?* Do the LES DIYers actually read my blog? (I thought you were all out-of-towners.)

The thug told me to empty my pockets. I slowly reached inside and managed to unleash some mace. Anna got sprayed, too. I should clarify that it was the classic CN tear gas originally sold as *mace*, not the pepper spray sold today under the <u>Mace</u> brand. The canister was a gift from an old-timer, and I wasn't sure it would work.

The muggers choked and gasped enough for me to recover the taser and the big guy's pistol. I was armed to the teeth. *Now what?*

The small one smacked me hard in the back with a rock, then leapt upon me. He turned out to be a vicious wrestler. The letter I won in 9th grade didn't save my mask or goggles. The big guy still couldn't see much, so he kind of helped me by kicking both of us. My best move came when my opponent's lungs seized up, but then I became easier to kick. Soon I was pinned.

They pounded me with fists and shoes, aiming to cripple me, at least. I hoped Anna would steal away while they stomped me. Would the city pick up my corpse if these guys finished me off? Would feral cats eat me while Sneeky starved?

Then the air vanished. My face caught fire.

By the time I understood I'd been gassed, the thugs were on their knees, coughing and spitting and drooling and pleading for Anna to stop. I crawled down to the lake as she emptied the can at them. *How could she even see them?* I had just gassed *her*.

I washed my face in the filthy pond. I could smell the water. The chemical effects were waning fast. *The canister was indeed obsolete.*

I looked back to see Anna rinsing her face with bottled water and tissues. Even in the dim light, her cheekbones gleamed. Deliberate as ever, she had gathered the weapons while the thugs sniffled and moaned.

She tried to explain about the telephone call.

Castle Dangerous

I couldn't listen. We needed to get away. Even the freshest tear gas isn't supposed to work well on drunks or drug users. Every time I moved, pain erupted.

We staggered toward my bicycle, but took cover by the rocks as the men stormed after us, coughing and cursing like madmen. I was through fighting if I could help it.

Somehow they knew the bike was mine. We huddled while the tall one used a small knife to wreck my Kevlar tires and my seat. Anna squeezed my hand (!) while he savored his rampage, using rocks to flatten links in the chain, bend the brakes, crush the gears. The little one spewed ropy phlegm as he watched. I couldn't see blood.

We slipped away while the maniac stomped my rims, grunting in a vengeful dance. We hadn't gone far when the clamor ceased. I heard a deep hacking in the woods. They were after us.

I handed Anna the taser. I had lost our way in the darkness. The thugs could hear us snapping twigs, stumbling over branches, so we opted to out-run them on a path. We ran till we reached some steep steps, then climbed up past the weather station.

Suddenly we reached Belvedere Castle. Had we found sanctuary in a fairytale?

Not that we were safe. Somewhere behind us, men were locked in rage. One of them probably had bird flu and nothing to lose. They'd gladly spend what remained of the darkness trying to kill us.

Instead of climbing onto the castle itself, where we could be trapped while they telephoned for reinforcements, I chose to hide in a stone cupola, a blockhouse set over a cliff to the castle's side. We'd see anyone approaching, just as their eyes would be drawn to the battlements above. I could tase the men in the courtyard, gun them down if necessary. Their loaded semiauto-matic was in the hand of a country boy who could fire it with confidence.

It was cold up there, so we whispered for hours without looking at one another, our eyes pinned to the entry path. It took a lot not to inspect her vaulting brows, so near.

Anna couldn't wait to explain why she'd hung up on me and then pur-sued me to Central Park in the dead of night. It was far more than I've ever heard her say. Her voice was cool and husky from the tear gas.

The LES DIY's view of the government resembles that of my more anx-ious readers. They think the city wants to shut them down, break up the group—possibly to please the Feds: The DHS and RAISE don't want com-petition.

It's ideologically enticing—downright fulfilling—to hear this from left-wingers. It strikes me as absurd, given that we're in the midst of a flu pan-demic. America needs all hands on deck to help fight the pandemic. Yet I must respect their convictions.

'The Inevitable Collision'

Here's Anna's explanation: When I called her about illegally disposing of a corpse, she presumed her line was tapped and refused to discuss it—or even to let me dig my own legal grave by spelling out any hopes of doing it on my own. She hung up, bent on breaking curfew by running to my apartment to explain.

When she found I had already left, she trekked four miles further to explain her rudeness. Her reward was to find out that Ric was dead.

She cried softly for half an hour. I was afraid to comfort her. I began to wonder how *the Iron Angel* knew where I lived—let alone where I sought peace in a huge park. I can be so freaking dense.

As Anna recovered, she gasped an apology for having confused me for so long. She even confessed that she'd wanted to join me as I greeted the sun. She'd been reading my blog. From the start.

Will it surprise you to learn that Anna is my most devoted reader? *Evelyn*.

She's been hounding and provoking and counseling and amusing and befriending me through a round and a half of bird flu. She sent me *Robinson Crusoe,* the Lenny Bruce 'toon, diatribes against Ayn Rand, advice about how to handle Nina's Relenza pregnancy, and Bruno to spring me from my house-trap.

Mindful of my zeal for self-sufficiency, Ric encouraged Anna to pursue me in her peculiar fashion. He wanted us to come together at the right moment—ordained by fate alone—in what she says he called *the inevitable collision*. Now we had met in the wake of his suicide. If there *is* an afterlife, Ric's joking to his new companions about how cozy his friends are now that he's bugged out.

While we hunched against a cold stone wall, staring into shadows. Anna apologized for what she called "enjoying [me] from a comfortable distance." She explained that she's been in a state of "*hyperactive post-traumatic anxious depression*" (Google has *nothing* to say on this particular condition) that could be salved only by working—or playing computer games with my mind.

That tide of jargon led to the twin revelations that she was studying psychology until her studies were interrupted by pregnancy and that she harbors a bizarre sense of humor. Anna's work at the LES DIY was a laudable response to her daughter's death. I understand her ensuing reluctance to flirt with strange men. Her emails didn't start as a game. She does cry a lot. Her efforts were never wasted: She got me to donate protective gear and post her manifesto.

She, too, feels that she neglected Ric in his last days. She was extremely busy with the LES DIY. She was kind enough not to mention that she took a lot of trouble to get me out of my apartment and over to his, after which I dropped the ball.

I felt Anna's (Evelyn's?) pain envelop mine as she pressed into my damaged spine. We were both stiff with cold by the time the birds welcomed the light and the wind shifted to bring up a warmer breeze.

With it came the sickly sweet odor of at least one human body in the gully below.

By then we felt sufficiently safe to look (in vain) for the backpack I'd left by the lake and to dispose of the gun in its waters. We trudged home slowly, reluctant to risk the subway without protective gear. We held hands with raw flesh as the last rays of summer poked through clouds. I didn't care about bruises.

A Mobile Meeting of Minds

As we talked for miles, we discovered we both like Chicago. Though she's from Oregon, Anna knew about the radical visions that long ago led engineers to reverse the course of the Chicago River and to erect the first skyscraper. It turns out she agrees with Ayn Rand that contemporary architects employ a mishmash of period styles to no sensible or esthetic effect. (Would you like some columns with your towering pizza?)

As we passed the site of Rand's 1960s salons, I was verbally demolishing the new buildings in this city, where land itself has become the best store of long-term value. Buildings are just a temporary delivery system. Where architects once dreamed of constructing striking, memorable towers in Manhattan, they now design buildings that make money till they can be replaced with more lucrative structures.

Any hint of compelling beauty is erased in the planning stage. Owners who look forward to tearing down their new skyscraper in a few decades don't want the public demanding that the building be preserved. Architects find it prudent not to suggest anything worth keeping in the skyline. Mediocrity pays better than Rand imagined in *The Fountainhead*.

As I was going on and on, Anna stunned me by pointing out that Rand left architecture off her list of the arts, designating it as a mere utilitarian practice. A flash of Evelyn! Is this woman going to google me into submission?

Once home, we wolfed down hot soup and crackers while we fed a ravenous—and curious—Sneeky. We soaped the gas off. She iced my spine.

We rested well.

Before she went home, Anna made me confess that I had consciously invited Evelyn to the Ramble by posting that I wished I could share it with someone, *hint hint.* "You were looking for more than trouble," she said coolly.

I feel as if my life has abruptly rebooted. Parts of me are aglow. Then I remember that my best friend's corpse needs attention.

I've lost the Ramble. I can't run into those thugs again. My bike is obliterated.

I should probably quarantine myself. That tough little creep has H5N1. So far I'm resisting temptations to inhale Relenza. Anna says she doesn't need to lie low because she caught H5N1 in the first wave. That would be after her daughter died. She wears masks only to set an example.

DAY 164-165

FLU YORK CITY'S CIVIL WAR

I'm neither insane nor sick nor murdered. Just bruised and exhausted. I've been sheltering Anna from contagious turbulence since I ran down to fetch her from Ric's Place.

It's no secret there's been rioting all over New York and the power system is coming apart. The Internet is so shaky that I'm nostalgic for the dialup days, when everything was *reliably* slow.

I haven't much to report. I saw people scared and bleeding and I saw other people armed and feeding. I put on my trademark Ramble face (a blank scowl, I hope) and ran with Anna through streets of glass and metal at a pretty good clip. Once safe at home, I've wallowed in whatever rumors I can dig up. It would be irresponsible to share them with y'all, however.

Activity in my 'hood was rated moderate to intense, which sounds bad. Then—just as a tabloid said the East Village was under siege from depraved mobs—I spotted a tall woman in elegant sunglasses walking her dog, trying to reach someone on her smartphone. Her escort looked like a Husky. She owned the curb.

I doubt she got through, however. Mobile phone service has completely crashed. I wonder if the authorities shut it down so looters can't correspond while the police chase them. The air quality implies that smoke signals have replaced texting.

NYPD doctrine has long been to overwhelm troublemakers by outnumbering them—to roll them up in a big blue blanket. But the flu leaves the brass without numbers or proven tactics. Here's one rumor: Private contractors will fill in. Guys who fight for profit in the Middle East will quell disorder here. *We the People* will be paying double for homegrown mercenaries. Restore America's Hessians, RAH!

Tribulation Beat says 'New York's Finest' are tasing and gassing everyone in sight. I heard shots and shouts an hour ago, so your faithful eyewitness now shuns windows. If you can, watch our mess online. My fave clip was from a woman who—mugged by armed eight-year-olds—persuaded them to pose for her. They even sing!

I maintain a landline with a plug-in phone, which would be more useful in emergencies if most of the people I know weren't solely dependent on cell phones—or cordless home units. Telephone companies have giant batteries to support service during brief electricity lapses. They maintain power stations to keep the system up for weeks, if necessary.

It's great that we still have juice in the East Village. The Midwest is running out of coal and Hawaii is out of oil. I expected New York City would be spared blackouts, assumed the Feds would somehow keep electricity running because of the financial exchanges, the city's global symbolism. I knew they'd let Philly and Baltimore burn, but the Big Apple? Wall Street would see to it that Manhattan was secure. Now I see that those guys can't do anything right.

Con Ed gets 40% of its energy from natural gas (whose pipelines seem secure enough if Canada keeps functioning), and 33% from nuclear power, fuel for which is well in hand. Only 20% comes from coal and oil, and the rest is a mix of biomass, wind, solid waste, and Canadian hydropower. Not so bad, so long as the nuclear plants 30 miles from here keep running. In general, the U.S. derives more than 60% of its energy from oil and coal, both extremely vulnerable these days because of sickly coal miners, ailing transport, and spotty oil shipments.

Given that local demand for electricity collapsed because offices are shut and commuters are all staying home, Con Ed has been able to lose a portion of juice without anyone noticing. I feel for city residents who fled to country homes to escape the flu. How will they get heating oil? I may be safer here than I'd have been in that bungalow I rented. Some lucky soul may already have looted it.

Anna and I have plenty of energy.

DAY 166

CHAOS—NOT QUITE PANDEMIC

My sinuses are killing me. There's smoke everywhere—tear gas, fear—everything but FOOD and HOPE. Sneeky shook like a kitten for hours last night, unless he was faking it so Anna would cuddle him. I'll keep an eye on those two.

As I'd heard, it turns out there was a blackout three days ago in most of Brooklyn, where the mood quickly turned nasty. Hungry people faced with a depleted police force broke store windows and helped themselves. (That must have been when cell phone service was cut.) So far as I can tell, poor people acted first, but the middle class jumped in.

The diversion of cops to Brooklyn left the other boroughs further understaffed, inviting all New Yorkers to fulfill their needs. Some neighborhoods burned; others experienced more civilized 'disturbances.' I wish I could have seen the khaki-clad mobs on the Upper East Side. (On second thought, they were probably the dullest-looking looters in history.) People in most places took what they needed without resort to injury or fire. Violence seems a generational thing, with kids of all ethnic groups more inclined to raise hell.

Has the proliferation of chain stores made it easier for people to pillage? Photos of old-time riots show proprietors guarding their stores with baseball bats or worse. Neighbors recognized their passion of ownership—the local roots. How can chains elicit empathy? They don't pay guards enough to die protecting band-aids and oxycontin.

I stayed inside with what I can't afford to lose. It's easy to feel powerful if your reality is small enough. Sneeky thinks he controls the world by sprawling in a doorway.

But I needed to see if the city had fetched Ric's corpse. There was so much noise on Avenue B that I called Bart's newspaper landline to see if conditions had turned much more dangerous. He said it was just a big fire and added that he won't talk to me in the future because I talk too much.

"You bloggers think they don't read you like they read us," said the professional newsman. "They scan everything. They know I'm talking to you now, and they will know I am not talking to you in the future. Good luck and goodbye."

Had Bart not hung up, I'd have responded that I know what appalling things the state can do. I know far more about <u>Randy Weaver</u>, <u>Fred Hampton</u>, <u>WACO</u>, and <u>Gitmo</u> than he does. I know what *habeas corpus*, and the lack thereof, *means*. I've watched my rights shrink all my life. In the '70s, stoned Americans ran naked at public events. Now we get strip-searched for admission.

Under throbbing helicopters, amid whiffs of tear gas, I took a stroll. My immediate neighborhood has lost whatever was available for sale. A lot of honest people must be close to starving. The weak are ever more vulnerable to disease. Exhumations of <u>corpses left by the Black Death</u> show that most were badly malnourished by the time they fell ill. The LES DIY will face record demand when they reopen tomorrow: *Ric's Place was untouched* in the violence!

Kidnapping the National Guard

It would be nice if New York's National Guard were to truck in food and water for us. The governor sent soldiers to secure blacked-out towns and cities upstate, but the NYPD is said to have argued against stationing troops here. I'm not sure how much longer they'll be available, anyway. They say the president is about to assert Federal military authority.

A little-noticed statute passed in 2006 gave the White House unprecedented power to federalize the National Guard. The legislation permits the president to send in the Army whether or not a state's governor requests military help. And it broadened presidential authority to suspend *habeas corpus*—our right to know the charges against us, to confront our accusers, to claim a fair trial.

The Insurrection Act of 1807 (slightly amended a century ago) let a president deploy troops *only* to deal with "any insurrection, domestic violence, unlawful combination, or conspiracy." The 2006 revision added "*natural disaster, epidemic, or other serious public health emergency, terrorist attack or incident.*" It called for "coordination" between DHS and the <u>Pentagon's Northern Command</u>, which oversees Defense Department activities inside the United States. <u>Governors have never been convinced</u> that giving domestic law enforcement missions to the military is a good idea.

A demonstration has been called to support New York's governor against the president. That could include everyone from those who hate federal power to those who want to see the National Guard on the streets *now*. The governor says anyone who shows up will be arrested: Demonstrations are illegal now. I've never been much for marching, but I hate seeing time-honored Constitutional options blotted out.

Pass the Pepper (Spray), Please?

Still, I say the East Village can survive all this. It survived crack and yuppies. I didn't even feel extremely afraid when I went out. The worst thing that happened was that I seem to have exacerbated my back injury climbing over debris on B. It hurts like heck. No, worse: It feels *unprintable*.

I should breathe easier, but my throat is heavy. I feel light-headed. I'm certain there's something in the air. The cops are spraying all sorts of stuff. They're always looking to test exotic crowd-control chemicals. I hope I can sleep.

Ric still lies on his bed. Sure, I called to remind the city. We both have landlines.

He waits in silence. Someone took his stereo.

DAY 166 (#2)

HELP!

Anyone out there who knows where Ric's Place is, please get there fast. We need people to prevent looting.

DAY 166 (#3)

COMMUNITY SPIRITS!

Talk about DIY: Defend It Yourself! Three bandits tried to steal the food and medical stuff at Ric's restaurant. Bruno and two other volunteers were in the kitchen when a guy waving an automatic walked in and told them to put down those carving knives and pack up the goodies. (Fortunately the clinic was closed.) A second robber stood by in the front room. Neither spotted Anna in Ric's basement office, calling people with landlines. (She keeps a list.) Everyone responded fast ... except the cops.

By the time I arrived, breathless, about a dozen men and women had gathered on the sidewalk, next to where flowers and religious and cultural artifacts commemorate the deceased *patron*. The partisans were yelling through their masks and throwing street trash at the driver of the getaway SUV. The third guy had just locked himself in the restaurant with boxes of food and wine he was supposed to be carrying to the car. The driver was craning his fat neck to figure out what the kids huddling behind his car might be doing. He never saw the little ones in front.

As neighbors, members, and passersby turned up or paused out of curiosity and respect for the LES DIY, the throng grew to number about 30 people. Once four kids were in place, the SUV began to sway and settle, its tires deflating simultaneously. The driver started honking and waving at the restaurant door. No sign of his partner. We considered smashing the windows and dragging him out, but he likely had a gun. None of us were armed. He was sweating lead pellets until Vanquisha, the LES DIY's transsexual Amazon, arrived with keys. When she unlocked Ric's front door, the crowd streamed inside, eager to free Anna and Bruno and company.

It all ended in seconds. The driver burst out and ran east as little kids called him politically incorrect names and pelted him with my Village's bounteous refuse. The robbers in the kitchen bolted for the back garden and climbed over a wall. Ric would have been in stitches. Purposeful chaos was his M.O.

I was a lesser performer. All that running inflamed my injuries. I yelled myself hoarse to psych-out the getaway man who got away. It felt great to vent after all these fearful months. Those guys feared they'd get ripped to pieces. They're accustomed to respect, not contempt. I think I tore my lungs.

In the end, a few of us toasted Ric with his cognac. It was a hyperactive dream, a happy hallucination. Bruno and Anna and the others showed great courage. You could tell they'd been very scared. Anna was drenched in sweat, nearly shivering. When the cops showed up, they seemed excited about the SUV vehicle check, said it wasn't stolen, vowed to find "the skells." (I looked it up. It seems inaccurate: Skells don't carry Glocks.)

Hearty thanks to any readers who came. Imagine how many would have turned out if Anna could have texted and called all the supporters' cell phones!

DAY 167:

I'VE CAUGHT BIRD FLU

I don't feel well. Everything is sticky, sludgy. I am dumb as heck. Iced coffee isn't helping—a sure sign I'm sick.

You know its flu. Death is in the house— heat, wetness, dryness, scorching, burning. You see things, awake and dozing. Big colorful strange bad things.

How many people ever died here? Its an old building. Maybe overdoses too. Crack murders. This room has seen things way worse than I have

I see people I didn't know I cared about. Or remembered. An airline guy was kind to me in Mexico though I was rude. I saw his eyes amused at my panic and then he helped me out of it. I hope he's OK. I never knew his name.

My head burns. my back is killing me, especially where that guy bashed me. I can't breathe.

Sure I'm taking Relenza—hope these lungs are still open enough to benefit. Farmers in Uganda said <u>feeding pot to their chickens</u> helped fight bird flu. Making that link nearly did me in. Would Sneeky even want to eat me?

I can't stop. What if I never post again? My last words are dumb.

You guys keep bugging me about being complacent. You cay I am smug So what people called me alarmist a year ago? I was right.

That doesn't make me like the flu deniers.

Its here, in my damn lungs. I dont see any cops here. I dont' see the state doing anything.

I'm sick of the whole thing. The police arent bothering me. They are dying too.

DAY 168:

GOD THIS FLU IS BAD

Theres a mirror nect to my bed so I can see if I turn blue.

Can't wait. Its cold enough for sure, is gthis winter ior what?

DAY 169-170

THIRSTY

Still here, this is her laptop. She made me drink more. I peed my bed. She didn't care, had a kid. She gave me fresh fruit like a cool fire.

DAY 171-172

BORN-AGAIN 'BANANA BOY'

I'm better, thank you, though I haven't read much mail yet.

Anna stopped in twice a day to make sure I was taking my Tamiflu and was hydrated and eating *fresh oranges and apples*! I don't know where she got them. She won't tell me. From heaven, where she lives?

I was so greedy I apparently asked for a banana. Thankfully I don't remember, but they're apparently impossible to get. When I was little, my dad called me 'banana boy' because I'd gobble a week's supply in an afternoon. When I told her that, Anna said she'd see what she could do….

Two of Anna's cooks came down with bird flu, too, so she had to cut back food services. One died, a very nice woman from the projects. Some of the other volunteers panicked. Things almost fell apart.

Anna took Sneeky home with her because she was working 22 hours a day and I couldn't feed him and she knows I'm afraid he'll catch H5N1. He seems restless and lonely, she reports. Sneeky is accustomed to having me to kick around most of the time.

Ric's landlord is trying to get the LES DIY out of the restaurant, but a lawyer is helping them fight to stay till the rent runs out at the end of this month. The lease says rent must be paid three months in advance. I can't believe the courts are processing this stuff while people risk their lives to feed starving kids.

The Betadine Solution

While I was feverish and crazed, the city called to say they've picked up Ric's corpse. I thought I'd dreamed it. My answering machine—which picked up before I did—replayed a shockingly civilized voice assuring me he was in good hands. She never asked if I was okay, though I must've sounded at least half-dead. They don't need to solicit business.

Now I'm wondering if the landlord and the city spurred them to get the body so Ric could be declared dead and the LES DIY evicted. As Our President boldly enunciated while I was hallucinating, "America has no room for cynics who'd rather scorn good works than perform them!" Huh?

A doctor from the LES DIY (one of several saintly medicos purged by the system) called today to ask how I'm doing. He apparently kept tabs on me through our friend, *Silent Nightingale*. I suspect he visited, but they both deny it. I'm told he's writing a faux mystery novel about the destruction of America's public health system—it's called *The Betadine Solution*.

I already feel like cleaning my apartment, a delicious impulse. I'll let it ripen.

I wonder if the Pneumovax 23 shot saved me from catching pneumonia. Who knows? Maybe the Relenza I took at first helped. Or the Tamiflu they gave me when I was too weak to breathe deeply. Fighting flu is a strange war in which you feel terminally passive. It's like watching someone try to beat you to death.

Fitch came by to process orders for protective gear after I assured him I'm no longer contagious. He's furious at how the Feds and Washington police gassed and busted mothers and kids who showed up at the White House to demonstrate against "toxic vaccines" and for "pandemic transparency." No one expected thousands of moms to materialize without notice.

Fitch says N.A.T.U.R.E. (Nation Against Toxins Under-Researched Everywhere, an acronym I truly hate) quietly switched the dates and caught the Feds flatfooted. While I sweated obliviously—wishing to heck I could have been vaccinated—intrepid "flu moms" were unfurling portable ladders to scale the president's fence. Some made a good run to the White House. (Soccer moms, no doubt.) The videos become hard to watch when dogs and clubs are unleashed. It made me feel sick again.

It's interesting that protesters no longer need TV stations and networks to cover their events, provided the government adds sufficient drama. When a protester's video finds a Web audience, the media buy it and run the footage for all it's worth. The government first enraged a lot of people by bashing these women and kids. Then it lied, tried to say they were violent subversives who attacked the troops guarding the White House.

The videos prove that these women were just impassioned trespassers.

They didn't deserve to be caged on an Army base while the government investigated their fitness as mothers. Hell hath no fury like a beaten, arrested, incarcerated American mom. The antivaxers are really fired up. Judging by what Fitch says, they don't believe anything the government says about anything any more. Who does? For days Manhattanites weren't even told about a blackout across the river, in Brooklyn. (As a rule, we don't peer over there.)

The Last Book on Earth

While sick, I was haunted by images that must have taken root in my mind from *The Last Town on Earth*, Thomas Mullen's novel about when the 1918 pandemic strikes an extremely independent logging community in the deepest woods of Washington State.

In most books I've read about bird flu, the language is so clinical that the symptoms seem abstract. But there's nothing distant about this disease: It explodes inside you for days like a hot sticky chain bomb.

Mullen's vivid portraits of flu victims and the tensions and hardships that surround them cropped up when I was burning with visions. Once I thought I was cutting the biggest tree in history. I realized I was kneeling in bed trying to saw something. Anna says I was funny a few times, but she's too kind to provide details.

I coughed blood early on, before my mind fled the premises. That was the scariest moment I've ever experienced. It must have been crud from my sinuses, irritated by all the gas and smoke in the air, but it looked to me like the first drops of my last gasp.

I lurched up to pour out a week's worth of kibbles for Sneeky when I saw red. There weren't many left when Anna took him away, but my toes are accounted for.

Not least, belated and limitless thanks to the woman in New Hampshire who sent me her priceless copy of Dr. R. Edgar Hope-Simpson's *The Transmission of Epidemic Influenza*. She thinks they're publishing it again. I'm thrilled. Thank you!

DAY 173

SWIMMING IN ANTIVIRAL WASTE

I worry about reports that Britain's rivers and lakes are full of Tamiflu and Relenza, which means ours are, too. Heck, I contributed my share—when I could stand up.

A flood of medicine that collects in urine has flushed into sewers since the pandemic struck. Human pee accounts for 1% of wastewater, but contributes more than half of all waste nutrients via stuff like vitamins, pharmaceuticals, and contraceptive hormones (as opposed to New York's famous _Coney Island Whitefish_, the plastic kind).

No one knows how the antiviral surge will affect wildlife or essential waterborne microbes. _The question has never been researched._ Vincent Racaniello long ago suggested that sewage from extensive use of Tamiflu might cause recombinant resistance to the antiviral. A tide of antidepressants unquestionably messes up fish and frogs. (Federal regulations force medical institutions to flush narcotics, stimulants, steroids, and depressants—any controlled drugs—down drains, rather than bury them in landfills.)

For the sake of those still uninfected, I'm now hoping the pharmaceutical-industrial complex gets vaccine out soon. I see reports that the first batch of bioactive chicken eggs is rolling off the line after many delays. There won't be that many and they won't go to regular folks. DHS and DOD will grab the lion's share. If there are black or gray markets, a lot of corporations will pay any premium to stave off a complete collapse in operations. (Have you tried _telephoning_ any companies lately?)

In case any of you snag some vaccine, you should avoid popular pain relievers known as NSAIDS (non-steroidal anti-inflammatory drugs such as Aspirin, Tylenol, Aleve, and Ibuprofen) before getting any shots. A University of Rochester study says they may inhibit your ability to produce the antibodies you want; for an excellent translation, read the explanation at Effect Measure.

It stands to reason that quelling inflammation reduces our immune response; inflammation _is_ an immune response. Taking a pill any time you feel lousy essentially stops your body from fighting what ails you.

Fever We Can Believe In

This is one of those medical "surprises" that keep cropping up because people don't want to believe it. Years after that Rochester study, the CDC urged parents not to give children Tylenol before their swine flu shots, citing what AP called a "surprising study" in Europe that found it useful to let children suffer a little fever after a vaccination. *Duh.* It meant they were building up antibodies to the virus. NSAIDS aren't so hot anyway: A Norwegian Institute of Public Health report says they seem to diminish driving skills.

When an H5N1 vaccine proves out, how will they inject the chosen few? Telekinesis? There's talk of sending EMS workers with shots, but it's tough enough for them to tend the sick, let alone deliver meds to those who remain well. I probably won't need a vaccine unless the flu keeps mutating, in which case it wouldn't work.

On the plus side, I feel as if one fever has replaced another. I'd like to see Anna soon, thank her with conviction. She'd make a great doctor, but she prefers to study psychology at what she calls "The Endorphin School of Mental Health" because she believes that stimulation through what wiki calls "excitement, pain, consumption of spicy food, love, and orgasm" is an effective way of putting people who are breaking down back into motion.

Having stimulated my natural opioid peptides, Anna has left me to recover while she lines up an alternative eatery in case Ric's landlord succeeds in evicting them. I picture her smiling innocently under wide, slashing brows, daring *anyone* to try to stop the LES DIY.

DAY 174

FIDDLING WHILE THE WEB BURNS

Count Blogula is in the house, yo!

I feel really well tonight, marvelously patient, pleasantly manic, purified by the virus. In contrast, the Internet remains so slow—at least on my block—that I managed to clean my house waiting for it to relax.

Everyone's downloading movies and shows off the Web when they're not drowning in image spam that drains capacity. They should kick back and consume low-bandwidth blogs like y'all are doing. Reading me is a public service! (Around now Count Blogula should thank you all for the fan pages you've set up for Anna and me, proudly AKA Maskman. I'm honored.)

Before the pandemic, it was forecast that the Internet wouldn't measure up to demand when tens of millions of workers tried to work from home. Indeed, corporations expecting their internal communications traffic to flow easily onto the Web wound up getting less from stay-home staffers whose messages sometimes moved at dialup speed.

This let workers direct their attention to more important matters, such as the hot new home-porn industry that's sprung up. "Tape my wife, please" has become the password to a home-cam craze that features trapped and bored Americans subscribing to one another's pandemic exhibitions. It's not just wives, of course: Plenty of hubbies and in-laws are exposing their deepest yearnings to strangers. *Missoula Housewife* has rocked the Web, but *Laramie Lumberjack* is hot on her tail. Rocky Mountain fleshbloggers are making serious money.

Domestic digital smut inspired some Flagellants to attack cable maintenance trucks while I was sick. (The driver they whipped wasn't amused.) The government says it's taking names to prosecute when bird flu subsides— porno celebrants, not Flagellants.

Even chat rooms of a sexual nature have been near-impossible to enter, crashing for days at a time as proprietors race to add servers. The telecommunications industry didn't plan much better. I'll never forget the executive who said ISPs would route traffic away from areas whose inhabitants were very ill and toward those that registered better health. Pandemics don't work like that. Sometimes people get sick everywhere.

Those who said the Internet would regulate itself in line with the tenets of supply and demand were closer to the truth. The slower it got in recent weeks, the more people logged off. Or worked late at night, like me. I never know if you'll be able to access my lines, but I'm reasonably confident I'll be able to post them between 2 am and 6 am. (Which is why I'll post my reaction to Hope-Simpson's opus later, when it's *really* calm.)

So far, the Department of Homeland Security—charged with keeping us all connected in a crisis—has pursued its customary dithering. Back during the mellow days of swine flu, Congress' General Accountability Office determined that DHS hadn't developed a plan to do much in case the Web frayed. DHS was indignant, according to Reuters: "The report gives the impression that there is potentially a single solution to Internet congestion that DHS could achieve if it were to develop an appropriate strategy," a department spokesman wrote the GAO. *"An expectation of unlimited Internet access during a pandemic is not realistic."*

What then is realistic? IT expert and flu blogger Scott McPherson has issued detailed warnings for years that the Internet would never hold up under a prolonged emergency. In predicting that the government would ultimately have to shove the rest of us aside, McPherson disclosed that key government operatives already carry cards enabling them to ensure priority access by calling a secret number once they've gotten a dial tone. "Eventually, if there is dial tone to be had, you will get dial tone," McPherson assured. "Hanging up actually means you'll lose out in the hunt for dial tone."

There Go the Little Guys

As big companies—including all significant Web vendors—pay huge premiums to boost incoming capacity, it's getting tougher to access sites like this one. Whatever remained of Net Neutrality is doomed. I'm watching Congress lure campaign money during a pandemic by vowing to toss out what's left of equal Web access. A lot of libertarians hated Net Neutrality, but entrepreneurs and bloggers aren't going to be able to find their own sites at this rate.

Want to reach missionimpossible5.com? *No problem!* Want to read a blog about some obscure disease that might kill everyone next year? *Write it yourself.* Want to launch a wiki? Get some pigeons. (*Doh,* I forgot!) "Freedom of the press is guaranteed only to those who own one," said a dead boxing writer named A.J. Liebling. It took 36 seconds to look it up *free* and it's still true.

The 'reform' won't even help consumers. A lot of the slow-mo timing issues we face are caused by *local* jams. In other words, selling elite Web access won't necessarily enable *us* to download faster unless and until the telcos and cable companies rewire our neighborhoods. We'll merely pay more for whatever the ISPs see fit to pipe in.

No matter that the pandemic will have ended by the time the proposed Internet Security Act throws us under the wheels of big carriers and vendors—and incidentally makes our private communications accessible to any official who cares to look, even for unofficial reasons.

We won't be able to sue for *any* privacy invasions. A cop could virtually hack your pc and loot your bank account without consequence, the way some experts read this thing. (I particularly recommend anything from the

<u>Electronic Privacy Information Center</u> in Washington.) Quick, let's trash our remaining freedoms before H5N1 goes away!

The president's half-baked denunciations of 'naysayers' and 'peddlers of mistrust' offer none of the usual assurances that dissent will always be welcome in Washington. (Still no comment about the recent violence on the White House lawn.)

Americans always think *now is forever.* This is a great time to buy stock and real estate if you have cash—and a rotten time to start a blog no one will be able to read once commercial traffic buys priority.

Power-wise, major chunks of the country are falling into blacked-out chaos. There are so many stories of people being shot for sneezing on other folks that I smell an urban legend. When it can get through, spam throughout our proud nation has turned into a lofty variant on Nigeria. *Hey sir, send me your money & I send you miracle protection!*

Dang, that's what <u>I do.</u>

DAY 174 (#2)

H5N1 & HOPE-SIMPSON

The following book report was composed by your humble scholar in a state of excited delirium triggered by close theoretical and historical contemplation of the virus that nearly killed me days ago. R. Edgar Hope-Simpson's *The Transmission of Epidemic Influenza* was my ultimate page-turner.

I begin by digressing: Shortly before his death in 2005, vaccine pioneer <u>Maurice Hilleman</u> told his biographer in <u>*Vaccinated*</u> that only 3 of the 16 (HA) hemagglutinin subtypes transmit flu easily among humans. Each, he said, does this every 68 years, and they do it in order, cycling H1—H2—H3. The H5 subtype, he said, was only for the birds. He'd have us battling a resurgent H2 in 2025 after a long pause between pandemics. Ominously, H2 is the one <u>Missouri pigs</u> share with people and birds.

Hilleman was cheating. His chart of outbreaks doesn't jibe with most others. For one thing, he skips the (non-pandemic) revival that 1918's H1 staged in 1977, choosing instead to claim a "mini-pandemic" for H1 in 1986. Otherwise he couldn't claim that flu subtypes follow a 68-year cycle.

Just about everyone in the flu business has pet theories, scientific convictions, and logical holes they try hard to overlook. As I showed months ago, prevailing flu dogma is deeply flawed. In summing up decades of his work in this book, Hope-Simpson effectively undermines preexisting theories as he attempts to establish his own *New Concept*. He seems admirably open to new data and I find his questions compelling, his arguments fascinating.

How I wish this spunky maverick were here to explain how H5N1 broke out, or at least to pose fresh challenges to the received wisdom that smothers us in useless expert babble.

Hope-Simpson made his name establishing that a virus could long lie dormant and then reemerge ferociously with a new set of symptoms. In assessing influenza, he didn't much look to the animal world as a source for pandemics. He believed that human beings serve as a repository for what he considered a master viral genome. He thought *we* carry the entire code in generational waves.

Original Antigenic Sin

The first subtype of Influenza A to which each generation is exposed causes a primal immunity that <u>stamps those carriers forever</u> in a phenomenon called *"original antigenic sin."* (Here, I pause to contemplate those kids who quietly came down with very mild H5N1 all over the world.) This subtype goes on to infect people for decades, with each survivor reactivating without symptoms for up to two years to infect others.

Eventually our subtype begins to run into too many specimens with primary immunity to it. In a process that remains mysterious and grand, the subtype vanishes all over the world, to be replaced in a *pandemic* by another subtype to which only old survivors of *that* flu carry immunity.

But only the first three listed hemagglutinin subtypes were previously known to transmit easily among people. Like Hilleman, Hope-Simpson believed H1, H2, and H3 comprised humanity's infectious flu genome, though he ordered their appearances differently (H2-H3-H1...). What would he make of H5N1's leap into the sequence? How did an upstart flu virus seed the world (all the way to Saskatoon) while the WHO was dogging it with Tamiflu blankets?

In his book, Hope-Simpson cites a 1979 letter to *Lancet* from China's Dr. Wang Mau Liang, who suggested that a noninfectious subtype could recombine with another animal- or human-based influenza virus to create a new pathogenic strain. But H5N1 is not a reassorted virus, or even a recombined one. It's a familiar one, located very close to H2 on an Influenza A family tree in Hope-Simpson's book (could this somehow address why pre-1968 H2 carriers seem to bear some immunity to H5N1?). All we know is that the upstart H5 suddenly turned virulent and crashed the human cycle.

I'm guessing that Hope-Simpson would begin by theorizing that H5 was in us all along, a quiescent part of that genome. (The WHO concluded [in final reference to footnote #6] in 2008 that 15% to 20% of people over 40 bore "baseline" antibodies to H5N1.)

Given that those H2—H3—H1 cycles are known only to have operated since the late 19th century, our visionary doctor might wonder if H5N1 is an element of a much bigger cycle that runs over a greater stretch of time. Were people long ago dying from H5 strains? Could an H7 (or H16) follow in a new centuries-long cycle? Is there a genomic pattern so big that puny modern mortals can't yet see it?

He might also ask if human beings have done something revolutionary to vault H5 into the subtype cycle. Did any prepandemic vaccines contain live elements that seeded the world, enabling H5N1 to jump a line it was never meant to be on? China tried plasmapheresis—injecting people with antibodies from survivors in hopes they would acquire immunity. Did some government(s) or corporation(s) try this, too? Did a bird flu correctly dismissed by Hilleman spook us into spreading it ourselves?

Just asking, folks. I don't have a clue. I'm merely danged glad to be alive. I wish the old doc were, too.

DAY 175

FLU YORK CITY BLUES

I haven't much to report. New York's streets are quieter. The government's food giveaways have gone pretty well. Little further violence has been reported, with no hijackings. On the other hand, bloodshed is rarely recounted, except by bloggers whose credibility you are continually urged to doubt by big media.

Readers who aren't prodding me for inaccessible details of my personal life have sent tales of their own communities in crisis. Those from places like New Zealand—where the government and private sector prepared contingency plans for just about everything that could arise in a pandemic—tend to revolve around personal tragedy and loss, plus complaints about Big Brother advising people what to eat. (Our government warns people what *not* to eat of what little is left.)

Europeans, Canadians, Australians, and such have seen lots of unrest, but governments have kept up fundamental services. National parliaments have been quick to debate and pass new measures as needed. *Social democrats will be insufferable after this pandemic!* They're doing pretty well, according to foreign readers transfixed by the spectacle of a National New Orleans in the U.S.A.

The rest of the world seems a mess, though India's melodramatic press may be exaggerating unrest there. I check <u>Boxun</u>—the shadowy, independent agency that blew the whistle on SARS and claims disorder is endemic in China—but it, too, favors the grimmest reports. (I welcome any insights from China.)

Here, we roam rubble that sprouts like weeds. My 'hood, long a hive of gentrification, is devolving. Yuppie eateries have been cooked. Armed men staff what remains. The peoples' gardens are locked.

A friend came home this morning from walking the dog to find two men in his kitchen next to a broken window, devouring his dinner. They beat and robbed him, took his golden retriever. *Do they intend to eat the dog?* He's looking for a gun, aims to hunt them down before they can harm his pet. He'll recognize them because they looked … Hispanic. Like almost everyone just east of here.

Looters, Looters, Everywhere

From what I hear, the death toll in the projects is awful. They weren't the only looters, though in white neighborhoods it gets reported more as "desperate parents saving their families." I've heard, seen, and read white people boasting about having made the most of a bad situation—including a zealous environmentalist pal who nabbed a pair of energy-conserving air conditioners for her apartment. Two courteous looters carried them for her. (She tipped them well; my friends aren't cheapskates.)

Three hardcore LES DIY members have died—a loss to our species. I like to think that relatively few people I know caught H5N1 because my friends are informed and have protective gear. Hope-Simpson would probably call it luck.

The Committee of Public Nutrition—as the lawyers have restyled the LES DIY—continues to serve food at the restaurant. The shrine to Ric takes up half the sidewalk. Two white-collar members just quit, however. Their employers let it be known that only groups sanctioned by RAISE should be supported in thought, word, or deed. How did they even know these people were involved with the LES DIY? Who said you need RAISE's permission to give people food?

Ominously, Tribulation Beat says <u>InfraGard</u> (that FBI-business collaboration controlled by DHS) has turned companies big and small into snoops that spy on their customers. I swear, your secrets are safe with *me* (and the credit card company you used, UPS, your bank, your ISP)—if not with InfraGard, which <u>got hacked</u> in 2011….

Happily, I'll dine at Anna's apartment tomorrow. She predicts my appetite will have recovered by then. This will be our first date.

Hope-Simpson converts are asking if I think she gave me the flu because she had it in Round One. Who knows? Anna gives me fever. She probably saved my life for the second time in two weeks when I caught bird flu. I think I saved hers in the park—just before she saved mine.

Y'all ask so many questions about Anna. I'm not holding back: I don't understand her myself. Turns out that can be a wonderful thing. Every moment contains surprises. Sometimes I'm doing new things—or old things in new ways. Seeing things freshly. The Month of Living Dangerously has only just begun, paced by this fierce old song she played for me: *Isis* from the Yeah Yeah Yeahs.

DAY 175 (#2)

AN UNHOLY STEW

I was awakened after only a few hours by fighting in the street below, but it turned out to be mere fisticuffs. Comforted, I headed to Ric's Place to mooch leftovers.

While I was chewing, a priest who was a big LES DIY fan three months ago barged in and demanded in Spanish that an elderly woman who was making pasta leave with him. When she looked down and kept working, I saw that her hands were shaking. Then he started yelling that we were doing the devil's work. I've never seen a priest act so medieval. Everyone was speechless.

The priest's relative youth, unusual accent, and black clerical costume caused two recent LES DIY recruits—kitchen staffers—to think it was a joke. They hooted and tossed stale rolls at him, which provoked the older woman to scream at them in Spanish. (She belongs to the parish in question.) They thought that was funny, too, till she flung boiling water at them. This accidentally scalded a DIYer who was scrubbing an oven. It was a domino run of sociopolitical catastrophe.

By the time Anna came upstairs to reestablish order, the priest wasn't interested in listening to a younger woman a third his size. In a voice that grew heartier and louder with each syllable, he denounced the LES DIY's sinful, sinister ways and its lack of standing with the government. (The LES DIY did, in fact, register with RAISE; because the group was not licensed as a charity, it wasn't taken seriously and never received a response. This was fine with Anna & Co., who sought neither subsidies nor approval, but left them open to the preposterous charge that they are not authorized to help anyone during a national emergency.)

When the priest ran out of rhetoric and paused for air, Anna told him to get out. I was shocked. She pointed to the door. Lifting his own finger to the heavens, then leveling it at Anna as if she intended to abort the Second Coming, the priest called on the Almighty to crush the LES DIY and anyone who sought the group's help. He was cursing us all—even the families we feed.

Anna stood her ground. She wasn't raised Catholic. She said he'd said enough. She was right, but I would never have said that to him. It didn't turn out well.

A dishwasher headed for the door, followed by the cook who had thrown water. Anna took the women's hands to thank them for all they had done. The older one was crying, The priest watched, expressionless in victory. He used to enjoy joking with Ric. They drank cognac together at least once. How could this have happened?

DAY 176-177

MY DINNER AT ANNA'S

Sorry, people, I'm fine. I appreciate your alarm when I fail to post. I apologize.

At Anna's insistence—even after the priest's earthly intervention caused so many staffing problems—I kept our dinner date. I hated relying on her to cook after all she does, but she can't legally (or safely) walk home late, while I can. And I'd been waiting to taste what she'd make just for me, on her turf.

Anna lives near the Manhattan Bridge in a slummy neighborhood that looks like mine did years ago. It's the last unspoiled nook of downtown Manhattan, where cheap but authentic Chinese eateries still flood the streets with thick, piquant odors that sing *dim sum, congee, salted pepper squid*....

Hers is a typical rent-stabilized flat, old and small with decrepit fixtures her landlord will never replace until rehabilitation expense accounting can free the apartment of regulation by lifting the monthly rent over $2,500. (My place was liberated shortly before I arrived.) As long as rent is cheap, owners treasure shabbiness.

Why is this ungrateful critter saying this about his dear friend's home, you ask?

Because her space is a timeless refuge I couldn't have imagined in that drab walkup. It's colored in aqua and magnolia and hung with fabrics that suggest a tent in a desert breeze. The vibe is both restful and stimulating. It was a dream to sit there, sampling cognac and herbs amid hushed, wailing chamber music.

I reclined in her dining area while she fetched appetizers she must have conjured: There were two good cheeses and an original dip redolent of garlic and ginger, with strips of celery, avocado, carrot, and asparagus.

We didn't talk shop, never mentioned the priest after she asked if I thought she'd go to hell. (No way.) I was dazzled by her world and her _Hot Black Silk_. (Thanks, Jason Molina & Songs Ohia.)

Then I noticed photographs over the stereo—a little girl with a shy smile and wide eyes, dancing in a red fairy outfit. For a moment, I thought it was Anna as a child, and then Anna explained that she and her daughter used to hula-hoop together in this room. She seemed happy to remember.

Anna asked me to open a malbec as soft and intense as her gaze. Wherever he was last night, Ric toasted her. He probably gave her the bottle.

Triumph of Good Will

We sipped wine and ate almonds. I could have imagined we were picnicking as we spoke of how we'd grown up, where and when—and why she waited so long to reveal herself to me. Readers have asked: *Is she really so shy? Sadistic?* I was curious, too.

We weren't ready, Anna told me. She thought she was months ago, but I drove upstate the day she was planning to introduce herself. One pandemic wave led to another. I cooped myself up. She decided I had simmered long enough when she read my longings for a partner to join me by the lake in the park. It spurred her own development. Within days, Ric's death slammed us together in that very spot, fighting for our lives.

Before anyone suggests she be toasted for sorcery, let me add that Anna is one of the most innocent people I've ever met, someone who follows her impulses with consummate integrity. If she doesn't feel like talking, she can't. But she's brilliant at anticipating how others will react. When she needs something, she's like a gifted fullback approaching an alert line: Though her target is clear to everyone, she'll get there.

She says *power* is a mirage that helps others accept what you want.

Will Anna mind my posting this? She says she doesn't care, so long as I tell the truth.

Frankly, dinner turned out to be a ravishing pesto oozing a fine blend of pine nuts and garlic and basil and arugula. I've tasted nothing like it since long before the pandemic. Ric taught her some tasty tricks while they were whipping up batches of blander food.

Want me to keep going? Is this too painful to read? I can't help myself: Dessert was *chocolate-covered bananas* and *espresso*. She was sad not to offer lemon peel.

Days ago, I feared I was dying. Now I was in heaven, *her* world. I'm still there in spirit.

DAY 178

A STIMULATING Q&A

Mail call!

Hey, I never claimed that our pandemic was propelled by an errant vaccine. I merely suggested it was an interesting possibility *if* H5N1 was indeed genomally incapable of serially infecting many people. The point I'm always trying to make is not that I know so much, but that *we know so little.*

A number of hysterical antivaxers (not including Fitch, who protests in person) have written to try to persuade me that the big pharmaceutical companies will turn babies into repurposed drones via the impending H5N1 vaccine. Ladies, you'll be lucky if your babies *see* a vaccine this year. (And please note that they no longer use <u>thimerosol</u> in any <u>vaccines for kids</u> under seven years of age.)

Still, I vigorously oppose legislation to force vaccinations not only on health workers, but all public employees. Such measures induce resentment and panic. The fact is that most Americans want to be vaccinated.

Yes, I still wear a <u>mask, gloves, and goggles</u> when I go out, and I disinfect when I come home. Even if I did catch H5N1, the virus may evolve other strains that could come back and bite me. Not to mention that I might infect others, per Hope-Simpson. And track microbes indoors for Sneeky to absorb.

I definitely dread the prospect of emergency legislation that would enable the government to draft Americans who have survived bird flu. If Hope-Simpson was right, flu survivors spread it no less than current victims do—possibly *more.*

I detest conscription anyway. The LES DIY keeps a list of flu survivors who could help others. (Only Anna has heard of Hope-Simpson; she reads this blog.) The people on the list *volunteered*, which is what the government and DHS and FEMA and RAISE ought to *ask* Americans to do—instead of drafting them to work for contractors and subcontractors hired by the government for fat fees.

I hope Congress comes to its senses (it's tough not to *laugh out loud* at the thought, but I vowed never to use Web jargon) and chooses to help citizens help themselves.

In the Food for Love

By now, more than a few readers are saying hmmm, what about *my* question? You know, *the culinary one.…* One reader put it best: "*Young man, I don't know you, but your hostess wasn't taking any chances on her menu. By my count, your dinner consisted of nearly 100% aphrodisiac foods. I'm shocked—shocked—that she didn't serve oysters!*"

Prompted to look into this unseemly allegation, I'm astounded to discover that almost everything Anna served is known or rumored to have a libidinous effect. I suspect she couldn't obtain oysters, which are laden with zinc and dopamine. (Both have an established effect on arousal.)

But she did pretty well. Take our dessert: Bananas have an enzyme called bromelain, chocolate an alkaloid called theobromine and a chemical called phenylethylamine. All have sensual effects. That was just one course. I could go on and on.

I did, but I would have anyway.

Anna provides very well for herself and her chosen beneficiaries. She's Mother Earth in gauzy fabrics, inspired and inspiring. In return, *she needs to be consumed.* It turns out we're exceedingly well-matched. Am I smitten? You bet.

Anna's world is rich because she imagines it to be, then makes it so. She says she imagined I was pure and ferocious. Reporting for duty, ma'am. I always knew she was ravishing.

Special thanks to the woman who sent the hot tip about celery. It turns out to contain androsterone, an odorless hormone men release when they sweat; it's said to excite women. If I find some celery, I'll see what happens. I doubt I could tell the difference.

DAY 179

WAR ON THE PEOPLE

Sheriff's deputies have seized Ric's restaurant and the adjacent storefront clinic. They wouldn't let the LES DIY take their stuff. Stores of food and beverages and medical supplies are missing—stolen by the landlord and his state goons. They're probably parading around in my protective gear, right arms twitching, braying about *order.*

The NYPD showed up in riot gear so <u>the First Amendment</u> wouldn't be exercised. They carried writs that threatened to arrest Anna and the LES DIY doctors for *"operating an unlicensed medical facility"* and for *"operating an unpermitted place of assembly that serves as a public inducement to gather, thereby spreading disease."* Sounds like those public schools they've stuffed with sick and hopeless New Yorkers on cots.

They busted Bruno, the tattooed drummer and delivery coordinator. He turns out to have been wanted for years on some old <u>pot</u> charges.

Someone went to a lot of trouble to obliterate a volunteer community service in the middle of a national catastrophe. *Incomprehensible.*

Anna intends to continue preparing food from her tiny apartment. She can't stomach the thought of telling the old folks and little ones that they're on their own. They're *her* grandparents, aunts, uncles, cousins—some sick, others merely weak, all helpless. It's not just about food or doctors. She doesn't want these people to feel alone.

She's lovely in battle, even when hopelessly outgunned. I want to share peace with her. We've both survived H5N1. If we can endure how other people respond to it, a grand future awaits us.

DAY 179 (#2)

EXERCISE YOUR RIGHTS & LEGS

There will be an emergency demonstration at City Hall at noon later today. I urge my NYC readers to attend. Be sure to wear protective gear.

Health-wise, that is. I've been told to emphasize that no one anticipates civil disobedience. That means no one intends to get arrested. I know I don't.

Join us, as they say.

DAY 180

UP IN SMOKE—CHINATOWN

I feel like I woke up in the first row at an action movie and the screen opened up to pour forth a screaming cast of thousands.

The day began with climbing, swirling noise—fire engines and patrol cars and helicopters racing around our pillows. I was at Anna's place near the Manhattan Bridge, on the northeast edge of Chinatown, and there was a major emergency not far away. We couldn't see anything from her southern exposure but when we heard explosions, we threw on some clothes and headed early to the demonstration at City Hall.

There was a strong eastern breeze and the noise was to the west—like the chaos we all heard on 9/11. Had New York been attacked again?

Before Anna and I got to Park Row, we started to see people milling around. They were Chinese, wearily sitting on stoops and cars with arms full of stuff, trying to keep track of old people and children. Many were weeping. People carried water to them. Everyone was holding cell phones but no one was talking or texting. Had the city shut the transmitters off? Had terrorists blown them up?

There was a lot of smoke. Cinders circled like snowflakes.

We didn't want to stare, so we tightened our masks and moved on.

A convoy of National Guards rumbled past us to head up the Bowery, weapons ready ... for what? The crowd hadn't looked criminal.

The uniformed men and women were craning their necks like tourists, pointing out sights. They looked more surprised than sanguine. Had the city come unraveled while it closed our little food service? Was there a mighty displeased Almighty up there?

Our cellular circuits were indeed jammed. No headlines, no messages, no voices.

Near City Hall we found office workers chain-smoking cigarettes. They said that the heart of Chinatown was burning and the city had quickly run out of firefighters. The National Guards we had seen were deployed from Connecticut to fight a mega-alarm fire in the warren of tenements and crooked streets between Canal Street and Park Row, from Centre Street to the Bowery.

Untrained and poorly equipped, those Guards are said to have tried valiantly. What could they do in narrow lanes full of melting parked cars as flames vaulted overhead from block to block, igniting century-old tinderboxes—each of which might contain hundreds living in bunked cubicles? Fourteen of the Guards we saw are missing.

Of course there was no LES DIY demonstration. Not even the cops showed up.

We stood around East Broadway in a daze, trying to stay out of the way. Helicopters were dumping water as if on one of those fiery windstorms that are devastating Southern California. Chinese women wailed or stood silently near us. Then a brisk line of emergency workers carrying black bags emerged from the ruins: *body bags*. They were clearing dead victims.

I held Anna as the grim parade approached us. After a few men came a woman holding a small white bag that must have contained a child. Anna twitched as if she'd been shocked and then crumpled into unconsciousness. I carried her to a stoop on Hester Street as if she were a child. We rested as she cried. I couldn't hear her amid the noise but she trembled like a bird.

A few of the survivors have taken shelter in schools that haven't yet been turned into flu wards. The East Village is full of smoke and *flugitives* bearing little bundles. Today, I cherished mine, even as she pleaded in vain for me to take her home so she could prepare food for the old people. Sorry, no LES DIY tonight.

DAY 180 (#2

THE EDGE OF DESTRUCTION

I can't sleep. I'm haunted by the fatalism of those city workers who puffed so placidly. *They weren't at all surprised* that one of earth's great Chinatowns was turning into a gargantuan charred pit several blocks away.

There aren't enough firefighters and their equipment is falling apart. Those school buses the city sends to the suburbs must be returning empty. Mountains of garbage and armies of rodents show how well the Sanitation Department has fared. The handful of cops is preoccupied with busting a community group—the LES DIY. The next time I hear people yelling, I'll keep my eyes peeled for the Idaho National Guard.

I'm scared. After six weeks of Round 2, the pandemic seems to be intensifying. Is it time to try to flee to my bungalow? The volunteer firefighting system upstate has faltered with so many key members ill or dead. Ambulance corps rely on untrained volunteers. Some counties lack ventilators. Deep, sustained snow could bury them. Tens of thousands of otherwise-healthy folk could die for want of fuel and food. That's just in one state. I don't want to drag Anna off to die in an icy bungalow.

If H5N1 doesn't blow over soon, everything we've seen so far is the prelude to *a catastrophe no one pictured*. (Except two artists did in 2009: Here's <u>Joseph Nechvatal's video study of a virus on America</u>, with Stephane Sikora.)

DAY 181

AN EPIDEMIC OF DANGEROUS MANAGEMENT

The media are bursting with reports of disorder, like cells unleashing ripe viral particles. It's as if the emperor's clothes dissolved overnight—at least in the eyes of elite bloggers and reporters who thought till now that half-dressed sounded better than half-naked.

Foremost are big-media reports that "a shadowy group" of antivaxers (whose name the government doesn't even want to disclose!) has threatened to unleash a doomsday denial-of-service attack on the Internet unless the world's governing bodies agree to answer a very long list of questions about H5N1 vaccine research and development. If this is true, could a group of techies break the Web?

Skip the somber expressions and corporate blather on TV and <u>watch this lively discussion</u> of how a catastrophic Windows blowout, a denial-of-service attack on the DNS system, or even general failure by a key ISP could impose a global blackout on all human systems. In theory, nothing might work after such a collapse—not even telephones. Unless our leaders can rehabilitate the carrier pigeon, they might have to meet up in person to begin talking about how to restore the Web. How would their flights even take off and land without the Internet? (Don't miss the ending, in which three visionaries try to keep straight faces while they try to imagine that the American Internet Czar saves the day.)

Until a digital cataclysm takes place, we'll all just surf a tsunami of stories about crime. Heroic accounts of medical workers and bureaucrats scrapping to keep us alive have been replaced by yarns about opportunistic criminals, smugglers, black marketeers, thrill killers, and especially that Oklahoma mother who advertised on Craigslist for someone to infect her children because she thought God wanted them more than her husband did. Suddenly *people are the problem*, not some virus.

Mayors and governors are issuing *shoot to kill* orders. San Francisco ordered that its citizens be gunned down after the <u>Earthquake of 1906</u> (which real estate promoters quickly rebranded as *"the Great Fire")*. During a <u>small-pox outbreak</u> six years earlier, San Francisco authorities moved to quarantine only Chinese people. They forced Chinese-American travelers to undergo an experimental vaccine.

But why are grim tales replacing promises of aid and vaccine distribution? Is it because no one wants to read about things that never happen? Few believe the government's claims and promises these days.

Fear is the ticket. Immigrant bashing is Page One. (Make that *home page.*) I'm less scared of desperate foreigners than I am of American citizens who work so hard to make aliens sound worse than H5N1.

Souls on Trial

The state is reacting to stress like a bad immune system, breaking out in hysteria and hives instead of solving problems. We get mobilizations, rules, uniforms, complaints about enemies near and far. People become uneasy. This is what Germany must have been like in the 1930s.

I wish <u>Tom Paine</u> were here. This great revolutionary—who gave our country its very name—began *The American Crisis* with the chilling line: "*These are the times that try men's souls.*" He went on to argue that *"panics, in some cases, have their uses; they produce as much good as hurt. Their duration is always short; the mind soon grows through them, and acquires a firmer habit than before."*

God, I hope he's right. An uh, esteemed Congresswoman from New Jersey just condemned me as one of 10 "extremist antivaxers" on her shortlist of Americans who ought to be silenced. This rabid Stalinist robot disguised as a conservative compared me to that loutish character Alan Krumwiede, from the movie *Contagion*. She didn't even *read* what I said about H5N1 and vaccines. Antivaxers who sent me angry emails at that time will recall my saying that I looked forward to a vaccine. You might want to forward her a friendly copy of your irate email. Better yet, call her up and read it aloud. She may need the help.

I've heard from Nina's friend from Tennessee. It turns out that she was laid off months ago, so my plea for help was sitting in the bank's voicemail system until a friend who hadn't been purged hacked her accumulated messages as a favor. Evidently everyone at the bank was so stressed and scared by the pandemic (plus cascading market crashes and layoffs) that no one noticed Nina was breaking down until her paranoia erupted at work. She accused her boss of poisoning the weekly cupcake harvest.

After 46 minutes of her wild talk, the bank escorted Nina out of the building. (It dumped the rest of her group two weeks later, keeping only the sweet-toothed boss.) Nina has since called her friend twice, saying very little from an untraceable phone. I'm told she doesn't sound better but hasn't gotten worse. She's said to be "certain about all the wrong things." It's horrible and sad.

DAY 182:

PHANTOM VACCINE FOR 'IMMUNOCRATS'

My apologies to those who couldn't find the site earlier: ISP issues.

I wish I were in Salt Lake City. It's probably the only way to determine how and why a number of citizens there burned a library two days ago. My TV says unrest had been brewing for months as people ran out of food and patience. Unfounded tales of a clinic operating in the library lured an out-of-control mob to torch it. Somehow it's the mayor's fault.

Bloggers, however, are saying the populace went ballistic because they noticed that well-connected and well-heeled residents were turning up at a library that had been closed for years. Word had it that Federal workers were vaccinating them with H5N1 shots freshly trucked in from the airport. The Web says questions weren't answered, and that the police were neither polite nor numerous enough to get away with being rude.

A latter-day hell broke loose. People were beaten, killed, run over, burned, and dragged off to Hill Air Force Base 30 miles north, where they're being held without charges.

I'm inclined to believe the Internet on this one. I can see where folks might find selective *vaccinations* compelling. We all know that cops and soldiers are getting shot up. We remain free enough to imagine who else is getting jabbed. America throbs with mistrust. People are said to be demonstrating from Tacoma to Tampa, demanding access to instant liquid security. Some chant "*Death to the Immunocracy.*"

That makes N.A.T.U.R.E. today's 'moderate' antivaxers. The group's partisans are merely hijacking big shopping websites to post informational videos about how the longed-for vaccines might kill us all. A lesser-known antivax group is threatening to shut down the U.S. transportation system with targeted Web attacks, as has been happening in Poland, Greece, and (wow) Norway. They demand to see concrete testing data on whatever the pharmaceutical sector has devised after all the problems it had cooking up H5N1 vaccine in eggs.

Enter al Qaeda. That *chatter* we always hear about at the oddest moments—particularly before elections—is back. So we're told.

The Limits of Terror

I'm not sure a terror attack would make much difference. We're already scared out of our wits, the stock market has crashed, no one is working, and people are dying in surreal numbers that clearly aren't being reported. What more could terrorists want? Would anyone notice if some schmucks blew something up?

I suspect it means elections will be held on schedule, though it's too late for them to be fair. Few will have heard of the challengers, who must find it impossible to raise money. Only very rich candidates will have a chance against the insiders. I never vote or tout candidates, but I suggest y'all bear in mind that politicians who salivate over crushing illegal aliens and looters are unlikely to work at keeping us stocked with food, water, and power. Their priorities are penal, not medical.

The president takes no chances. Anyone who disagrees with the White House is "undermining public order" and "inviting chaos." I doubt anyone is listening. Threats and bluster do not constitute leadership. Nor are they entertaining. A pox on Washington.

Anna is hard-pressed to keep the LES DIY going. Key volunteers from the community keep dropping out to work at religious facilities approved by RAISE. They're under a lot of pressure to quit. Plus the work is easier on the other side. That leaves Anna toiling 18 hours a day in her tiny kitchen. She and her dwindling band give out food late in the afternoon at Tompkins Square Park and then rush home before curfew (to work on tomorrow's offerings) because the LES DIY can't get permits. My pass and I are on call for twilight emergencies. I spend every afternoon hoping a crisis will arise so I can help Anna save the day.

Do I have to join these dangerous radicals to spend more time with her?

DAY 183

A RITE FOR STEFAN—*CANDY*

Tonight I discovered what an idiot I've been. Climbing the stairs—relaxed after visiting Anna's tight little delivery operation—I heard a noise in the old Ukrainian's apartment. It was a grating sound, respiratory tissue grinding together to no effect. *The cough we all dread.* I hadn't looked in on Stefan for at least a week.

It took him five minutes to reach the door. Only a hard-bitten man who'd survived wartime winter on the Ukrainian steppes could have managed to let me in. His sofa was piled with filthy garments. He had packed himself in a welter of old sweaters, wisely inviting fever to cleanse him of virions.

The clothes were clotted with blood. Stefan is dying.

I immediately administered Relenza—too late by any standard I know. Stefan's a tough guy and he loves life, but it may have killed him to let me in.

Of course, I called 911. They advised me to bring him to a school in Chelsea because the local ones are overrun. I have no idea how I'd carry him that far, but I'd get it done if they could promise the place has ventilators. Not that they'd necessarily give him one, but we all feed on hope.

"We don't have that information. Is there anything else?" *Nope.* I thanked them.

My Traumatic Reading

I hydrated Stefan, covered him with clean blankets, and cooled him with wet cloths. Then I consented to read to him from a tattered paperback he treasures like an heirloom: *Candy*, a novel by Terry Southern and Mason Hoffenberg. I'd never heard of it.

We live to learn—and google. Turns out *Candy* placed 22nd on *Playboy's* all-time list of sexiest novels. Southern wears shades in position No. 20 on the Beatles' *Sergeant Pepper's* cover. He co-wrote the screenplays for *Dr. Strangelove*, *Easy Rider*, and *The Cincinnati Kid* (all now available for purchase on this site).

I now suspect my ancient buddy made up for the savage deprivation of his early years by running amok through the 1960s in that room and on the streets. *Candy* may have been Stefan's guide to New York.

Since I wouldn't let him drink vodka, Stefan made me down two shots at a time so he'd feel alcoholically represented. Eventually he had me leaf ahead to a particularly crazed scene wherein the naive heroine generously humps a hunchback to the stately medieval tones of the <u>Gregorian chant</u>. I couldn't help but detect some unorthodox movements under his blankets.

I continued reading in shock. I guess I'm still not quite a New Yorker.

I was wondering how to flee politely when Stefan gasped deeply and broke out laughing as best he could, his eyes streaming tears of delight into deep grooves under his cheekbones. I wound up hoping this wasn't the last fun he'll ever have, and feeling desolated that I'll never hear the tales he should have been telling me in all the years I've lived next door.

How many great stories have I elbowed past in my time here?

When I was leaving, Stefan woke up to insist I take a rough painting he made decades ago. It *looks* like a charming snow monster chasing little girls. Unless it's abstract. I couldn't ask. It's Stefan's bequest to me, in case he dies before I come back. Or I don't bother.

While he lasts, I'll give him my time and Relenza. Maybe I can find him some relaxing literature. Anna suggests something French called *Story of the Eye*.

DAY 184

OUR POLITICIANS ARE MAD (ANGRY, TOO)

Disorder has turned universal. Armed hospital invasions are common in blue states, red states, border states, states of anxiety, hopeless states. Is the State itself in danger?

It's our fault. We didn't prepare. Sucks, doesn't it?

Who wants to read *that*?

No wonder politicians hate this and other blogs. Since bloggers are the ones calling them liars and presenting the truth about our national mess, it must be our fault that no one believes anything they say.

But I wasn't uptown last night when people broke into Lenox Hill Hospital looking for vaccine. I didn't shoot it out with anyone along Park Avenue. I can't even tell you how many people got killed—or how many patients were scared to death—because the city won't say and the press won't demand answers. Anyway, I was *here*, working to inform my fellow Americans about peaceful ways to survive.

Which can include what to guard against. I'm hearing stories of flu survivors making trouble—gangs of toughs who endured H5N1 robbing those who still cower from it. One report said they look for targets in masks. (Never let it be said that my need to sell things prevents me from sabotaging sales.)

According to some DC speechmakers, *I'm* the real problem: They are willfully misinterpreting my fanciful discussion about H5N1 antibodies and genomic subtype cycles. Why? They want to justify barring anyone who's not medically trained and/or institutionally certified (*connected*, in other words) from criticizing the government's failure to function properly during this oft-forecast emergency. Holding poor Hope-Simpson and his New Concept up for public scorn, they propose a bipartisan bill to outlaw "any effort to spread panic, conscious or otherwise."

In other words: Shut up! I call this bipartisan authoritarianism. It's been brewing for a long time, but it picked up speed and mass on Sept. 11, 2001. Few politicians of any stripe bother to stand against it.

Any such repressive statute would benefit only lawyers who can't find work after the pandemic subsides. I've got better things to do than give Congress a free consultation, but that thing needs a rewrite. What constitutes—a loaded word these days—*criminal unconscious effort*? Are Freudian slips to be criminalized?

Fortunately, I've been trying to help *avert* panic for six months. It's all documented, right here. *Click, click, click*: Case closed!

Blame the Lame

So I have nothing to '*retract*.' I'll go back to watching these demagogues grind their gums about immigrants—wretched, maskless, jobless people who are dying like bugs. Who dare not shout back like us natives when big taxpaid boots kick their doors in.

This is what scapegoating is about. When the Black Death came to Europe in the 14th Century, Christians murdered Jews for allegedly poisoning the water supply. The god-fearing majority stole Jewish property, sacked the ghettoes, incinerated babies.

Blaming a weak element of the populace still satisfies man's dumb need for the illusion of control. If we can believe that our problems derive from certain people, we can pretend to solve things by punishing the culprits—even liquidating them. That was Adolf Hitler's appeal.

If today's enemy is *us*—the poor fools who failed to prepare for a pandemic despite years of warnings—we've simply got to find a better adversary. We can't punish *ourselves*. Things are bad enough. But *someone must pay.*

I don't want to argue the merits of immigration. I moved to a city that celebrates it with every beat and every screech. Our country is founded on it—voluntary ("Give me your tired, your poor...") or not ("This most rotten branch of human shame..."). Americans can certainly burn the welcome mat if they choose.

But foreigners did not invent this plague and Americans haven't figured out how to end it. Nature is taking its course. Human nature isn't helping. *Don't make things worse.* Save the rhetoric for the next election, whenever that might be.

Scapegoating: If you're not against it, you're with it.

DAY 185

BLOG BURNING IN AMERIKA

I had no idea so many collectivist brownshirt types read this blog. I guess the reposts by all those liberals (you love me, you really *love* me!) on *their* blogs stirred up the bullies and directed them here. I've received formal threats from people claiming to live in New Jersey, Long Island, even one from Manhattan. You know what they say: If I can get dismembered here, it can happen anywhere.

Maybe the *emergency* termination of what was left of equal Web access a few hours ago will leave the idjits stranded in a morass of glittering corporate websites that won't listen to anything they say—except ADD TO SHOPPING CART.

Heil Visitor, Haf Ve Gott Ein Deal Fuhr U!

Is it coincidence that my noisiest Congressional critic of late looks like a reincarnated Reichmarschall Hermann Goering? Both love to hunt, fly, and bully people.

I ain't scared. Scanning a few of the thousands of flu blogs that have sprung up, I note that New York is relatively safe. I just saw my dentist, whose staff survived but for a very nice hygienist, whom we'll all miss. She deserved a long life.

It's the cities without water—Tucson, for example—that seem most out of control. Phoenix and Las Vegas are fighting over Lake Mead's diminishing waters. The West is aflame, whole tracts with nothing left but angry homeless survivors. It's as if a gigantic meteor shower spewed fireballs on a third of our country.

After all those prayers, Georgia is out of water, too. Lakes Lanier and Allatoona contain little more than muck from decaying animals and plants. (*Do not drink tomorrow's oil!*) The Chattahoochee River that Lanier feeds is running dry, too. Atlantans are being evacuated to Federal camps. I feel particularly sick for the Katrina survivors who were driven into this urban desert and are now being herded into *what*, <u>FEMA trailers</u> again?

Not that the water is much better back home. <u>Cholera</u>, that quaint 19th Century disease, has returned to New Orleans. *Heckuva job*, faceless bureaucrats!

Hawaii has been blacked-out for weeks. Private weapons are said to be priceless since the state's National Guard was deployed to Los Angeles. There, the Hawaiians stand with troops from Oregon in protecting the Hills from gangbangers and anyone else cruising around looking for loot and trouble in the better-endowed 'hoods. Guard units from California, Arizona, and Nevada have their fists more than full at home.

National Gangrene

I get emails from all over. I know what people are going through. I have one from a 50-year-old Texan, a Web entrepreneur whose wife and four children died. He's desperate to figure out why God let him live, saved him. I hope he comes up with a good reason—or that fate grants him one. He sounds like someone worth knowing.

Then there's the woman whose husband shot and killed two kids who tried to climb into their house in Kentucky. He thought they were the men who had raped his teenage daughter. But it was her loyal boyfriend and his buddy, trying to cheer her up by playing Romeo and Mercutio. Now dad's in jail and mother and daughter have neither protectors nor friends. Just firearms. They practice a lot, she writes. Maybe the shots keep criminals away.

Further emails recount the tale of thugs who terrorized a hamlet in

Pennsylvania's Pocono Mountains, 90 minutes from here. They butchered five residents in three weeks before someone got the state police to look into it. Two troopers were killed before the criminals got theirs.

Forty miles from here in Long Island, writes a woman who pleads that her name not be mentioned, someone firebombed a house crammed with Salvadorans, killing five children and two adults. I read last week about the unexplained accident. My informant says local lads boast that it wasn't one.

Three buildings west, on my block, they just discovered a mother and her little boy dead from flu. A neighbor looked in when he saw that their door had been kicked open, found that their ripe corpses hadn't deterred looting. Someone ripped the woman's wedding ring from her decomposing finger.

The luckiest Americans fear someone will commandeer what they've got. The least fortunate are dying in droves from injuries and illnesses the medical system normally handles with ease. People are coming down with *gangrene* because they can't obtain antibiotics. All those disabled veterans with state-of-the-art moving parts are breaking down. And this is *my* fault?

Did I mention that someone painted the word "PROFITER" on my building's front door? I suspect they meant profiteer. Should I take it personally—or correct it?

DAY 185 (#2)

LOOSE LIPS GET CLIPPED

Our old *mystery mailer* has resurfaced! It's been too long—evidently long enough for her to have acquired some legalistic skills.

Having found an occasion to catch up on my narrative, 'Evelyn' demands I retract something I posted a week ago. It was unduly salacious, she charges, asserting her historical right to respond, "a perquisite established in almost six months of well-documented public intercourse, etc."

Ominously, my *corrective correspondent* warns that she shall otherwise elect to exercise said privilege to publish in this venue an accounting of my person, including—but not limited to—my "carnal propensities" and "the particulars of [my] physical endowment." *Top that*, she adds. Did anyone out there suspect I had hooked up with a legal fetishist?

Dang this Internet thing. It never fails to go too far. Those Congress-people were right.

Oh well, here goes: *I'm sorry, my love. I won't do it again.*

If my ISP has anything to say about it, I won't be able to. Due to "numerous complaints" about my site, I've been told to find a new host within 72 hours or face a shutdown until the company has completed an investigation, which could take months. Suggestions will be appreciated, although further snickering from *Story of the Eye* fans is banned!

DAY 186

SERFDOM'S UP!

I'm not sure what rights we have left, but we sure have more laws. We are to be drafted into the Regeneration of American Liberty. (Clumsy acronym, but we can complain later, in theory.) For now, flu survivors shall serve the state at minimal wages. Unionized workers, too: Labor contracts that "limit emergency deployment of human resources" are suspended.

Turns out Restore America's Independent Spirit & Enterprise will supervise the new arrangement. No wonder *Enterprise* comes last.

Will RAISE outlive the pandemic? Is it a new incarnation of the War on Terror—an Orwellian bureaucratic device that will compel us all to 'volunteer' for many years to come? I begin to comprehend why its creators left the operative word *Health* out of the verbal lineup. It would limit this bureaucracy's grand mission to something useful.

This looks like a long-term effort, a bureaucratic spearhead. Suppose America's Independent Spirit needs apples picked next year, immigrants being scarce…?

I see, too, that Congress and the president have agreed not to stand for reelection until they concur that it seems safe. For whom, you English teachers ask? For the folks who presided over what *the New York Times* calls "*this unprecedented national catastrophe.*"

The rest of us can march around, singing *Born To Be Servile:*

> *Get the water running*
> *Serve the state for no pay*

> *We may have found employment*
> *That'll never go away....*

If the estimable Dr. R. Edgar Hope-Simpson was correct, *those who had the flu will now be spreading it far and wide.* I see this as a great reason for y'all to buy even more <u>masks, gloves, and goggles</u>: If you never get sick, you can't get drafted!

Otherwise, I consider it prudent to lie low. I've helped plenty of people. I'll continue to do so. On a *voluntary basis*, as a *free man*, in a *free society*— well, scratch that part. Or parts. Heck, they know where to find me. *Follow that UPS truck!*

Meanwhile, has the Internet Security Act improved your access? Do you like your new homepage? Those yummy corporate preferences? What, you can't find your old favorites since they reformed the address protocol priorities? They were dull, dude!

My telephone never tried to tell me whom to call.

I'm talking to an indie-minded company that wants a lot of money to host my domain because of the denial-of-service attacks you have undoubtedly noticed. *Psst, media giants*—I got these suckers to hunt me down for free! Wanna sponsor my rants? Maybe speed up access to this thing? Call me. I'm home a lot, when I'm not swabbing the indomitable Ukrainian next door.

Stefan's Confession

He's been telling stories. Yesterday, in a voice frozen with more than half a century's weight and dust and regret, Stefan growled that I should sit and listen. "On a sunny day they told me to pull out the teeth and I did," he began. It took a moment to realize he was describing something I had wondered about, but couldn't bring myself to ask.

Stefan was saying that he had worked for the Nazis as a youth in the occupied Ukraine. He had done whatever they asked of him and he had become proficient at yanking gold teeth from Jewish corpses. I was horrified, but Stefan was just beginning his account.

"She was alive," he was saying. "A young woman, pretty, holding a dead baby. She woke up when I was getting a molar." The woman watched, eyes wide, as Stefan throttled her so she couldn't call out while he finished the extraction. The Germans were watching, lest he steal a precious tooth, or take too long.

Gold still flashed in her bleeding mouth. "I left it." He shrugged under those matted covers. (I change them, but the blood returns at night.)

I had to ask: "What happened to her?"

"Buried with the rest."

That's when I realized that the Holocaust was a sociopolitical pandemic. People were seized by—acted like—the worst viruses ever. The Nazis were the Black Death with flags and ideology and grotesque human intent.

Unless they were the cytokine stormtroopers of an immune system gone haywire. Imagine being caught between the disease and the response. I'm trying to forgive Stefan. At least he feels bad about it.

DAY 187

RAISE THE DEAD, LOSE YOUR RIGHTS

I always thought New York would do okay in a pandemic, that this city is so organized, so heavily policed, so rich, so important, and so proud that nothing too nasty would occur.

I thought we'd have seen the pandemic recede by now. I'd be pounding out warnings about the next wave, next year. It wouldn't be as bad as this one, merely god-awful. People would go back to ignoring me during the second hiatus. I wouldn't take it personally. I'd be traveling with Anna.

Instead I'm living in a city whose death toll is rumored to have reached a third of those who catch H5N1. There are still lots of untouched subjects. *No one* planned for this.

What broke the camel's back? New York's snappy, can-do façade melted down in a four-story Bronx tenement. A grieving dad is accused of torching his apartment because the city never picked up the corpses of his wife and two kids. Understaffed firefighters got a few folks out and cleared neighboring buildings.

The next day they discovered five additional corpses presumed killed in the blaze. Yesterday they found three more. That's 11 bodies in a total of 36 apartments.

Now we're told they *all* seem to have died before the fire. There was no smoke in their lungs. Most were decomposing.

New York City is full of corpses. The difference between the Middle

Ages and our exalted moment is that they used to send wagons around to collect the dead. Even in the morbid mess that was Philadelphia in 1918, a Catholic priest revived the death-wagon to useful effect.

What shocks me is that the mainstream media is reporting the Bronx "tragedy." Editorials shriek for accountability. Why the sudden concern? Where were they when the LES DIY was spiritedly debating what to do with departed East Villagers?

Our leaders promise that the RAISE conscription program will solve everything, and not a moment too soon. (Is that why this mess is being reported?) It will be managed by the ubiquitous contractors that bilked the government for so much—in exchange for so little—in Iraq, Afghanistan, and New Orleans. Contractors will even police the drafting of American citizens for RAISE. They will assemble fresh databases on us. No doubt they'll sell them to big corporations when marketing is back in vogue.

I'm staggered at the thought that the government will *force* us to work for companies. Even in <u>privately run prisons</u>, labor is still considered 'voluntary.' (Inmates are <u>exploited for profit</u> in public prisons, too.)

The grand prize awaits prison contractors that branch into administering *and* enforcing RAISE's flu draft. If we cooperate, we work for them. If not, they get to lock us up at government expense. No American left unmonetized.

I propose a far simpler plan. If New York can find some oats, Central Park's idled tourist carriages could fetch our loved ones. They could begin by trotting over for Stefan, who expired just when I had begun to think he'd make it. (Of course I informed the city.)

The LES DIY: Anarchy With Purpose

They'd better be careful if and when they come for him. Front doors in my neighborhood carry warnings that strangers found inside will be killed. One screams *NO QUESTIONS* under a vivid skull crossed with AK 47s. It's nice to see that artists still breathe here.

The LES DIY proceeds as best it can, without fear or resources. The medical side has gotten stronger. Doctors and nurses who were decertified for "unprofessional activity"—helping ordinary people in an emergency— are still at it in an undisclosed location. People from the projects and some idled yuppies have infused fresh blood. Cultures have melded unbelievably well. This squad fights flu like a complex animal, a living unit. When someone falls ill or is forced to withdraw, a newcomer springs up to kick butt.

Members who fall ill know that the others will watch their kids, pets, or parents. Trust has become contagious. I've never witnessed anything like this.

There's none of the usual East Village bickering or tardiness or excuses for nonperformance. They talk a load of crap sometimes, but if I were ever in a war, I'd want this motley gang—freaky men and women, and teens, too—at my side. And behind me.

There are similar groups in the suburbs, cities, small towns, reservations. They are democratic manifestations of what is best in all of us. *Anarchy with purpose.*

Screw RAISE. They're a fig leaf for state expansion.

Self-help groups need more members, more resources. Look over your home supplies for things you may have overstocked. Give them to folks who will make you proud to have been a part of your community when this thing ever ends.

DAY 188

HOUSTON

How can we talk of anything but Houston? *What is there to say?*

At least 10,000 killed by chlorine gas after an explosion that makes no sense. The company says it was impossible and no terrorists have taken responsibility.

I get the feeling that understaffing has caught up with us. Those train wrecks failed to impress. Every high-tech endeavor is at risk as society cracks and crumbles.

I hope the soldiers that the president dispatched to Houston have good masks. Chlorine rather mimics bird flu in that it destroys the respiratory system and asphyxiates its victims. Both sides used it as combat gas in World War I.

I sure hope this wasn't a terror attack because every population center has loads of chlorine to detoxify drinking water. There's nearly 1,000 tons of chlorine gas in an old tank under an overpass just across the Hudson in New Jersey. *Oops,* I've just remembered that something called the National

<u>Cyber Response Coordination Group</u> has staged <u>simulated 'Cyber Storms'</u> with one of the targeted 'problems' being bloggers who discuss vulnerabilities in the system. (*But I saw that chlorine tank on TV….*)

Houston is full of plants that could blow up and kill everyone. Always has been, long before 9/11. Long since, too.

DAY 188 (#2)

MAKING THINGS WORSE, ASAP

Now it's a full-blown terrorist event, if we are to trust al Qaeda—or some digital shadow that claims to speak for it. (I don't remotely buy the report that antivaxers blew up Houston.)

Troops have been dispatched nationally to secure some of the hundreds of chemical sites that could kill at least 100,000 Americans. We may be approaching that *unthinkable* number in Houston. One thing I want reminding me of 9/11 is a casualty estimate that drops sharply with each passing day. Houston's is rising.

No one I know is convinced this is a terrorist act. Who cares what we think?

TV screeches scary stuff. There's blather from people who hate us, nonsense from officials who were supposed to protect us, and doubletalk from chemical companies that blocked efforts to heighten our security after 9/11.

To agree that Houston was an act of terrorism would emphasize that the company failed to secure the site. To admit that Houston blew up by accident would prove the facility should never have been located there. *Act of God*, anyone? Maybe—so long as it's someone else's god.

Witnesses, of course, are all dead, surveillance cameras blown to bits. I can't wait to see the *Emergency Indestructible Surveillance Camera Control Bill* that will undoubtedly be breathlessly introduced in Congress this morning.

How many pre-deceased corpses will they find during Houston's house-to-house inspections? How many Katrina victims who wound up there are reeling from post-traumatic stress? I wish Houston's survivors the very best air, security, medicine, and love our country can provide.

DAY 189

BLOWING UP THE CONSTITUTION, TOO

This looks like a fuzzy kind of nationwide martial law.

Army units have been spotted by bloggers in Chicago, Pittsburgh, Wilmington, Los Angeles, and North Jersey, key areas vulnerable to chemical sabotage. Unless they were National Guard units, which are officially reported to be in motion everywhere. It's a tapestry of state flags no one can recognize. No matter. There's a media blackout on troop movements, *specifically including blogs.*

I'll bet the soldiers are confused, too. At least they have masks.

Mine won't stop chlorine, or hydrochloric gas, or the stuff that killed at least 20,000 Indians (so far) in Bhopal. My protective gear assumes that people are inherently dangerous, but not because they *mean* to poison us.

So has the president quietly called out the U.S. Army for what seems a shaky terror claim? Al Qaeda franchises have occasionally used chlorine trucks and tanks for extra oomph in the Middle East, so the connection is thinkable.

I'm not convinced by that 'martyr's video' allegedly posted on behalf of a dead worker who allegedly blew up the chlorine plant. The image is really shaky. The man's family insists that the speaker's voice, face, and ideology are alien to them.

Loved ones always want to believe that. But the man in the family videos that were posted, then seized by the government and taken down as 'evidence,' looks different to me, too. Sure, both guys have black hair, but their lips, eyes, forehead, and hair quality are different.

Dead men have certain charms in a pinch: Lee Harvey Oswald will never rise to challenge anyone's convictions about John F. Kennedy's assassination in Dallas.

Consider also the enduring mystery over the post-9/11 anthrax mailings. At first the White House pressured the FBI to blame al Qaeda. Then the U.S. government spent years hounding Steven Hatfill, a bioweapons researcher who eventually won a $5.8 million settlement clearing his name. Finally the FBI pinned the attacks on Army researcher Bruce Ivins, who had committed suicide while they were pressing him.

Few were convinced he did it. A panel of the National Academy of

Sciences concluded that the FBI lacked proof of Ivins' guilt. (Read the text and/or watch the video presentation of its impressive report.) And the Justice Department admitted in 2011 that it had no idea how Ivins could have dried and weaponized the anthrax because Ivins' Federal lab lacked the necessary equipment.

Laurie Garrett, prized journalist and author of *The Coming Plague*, put out *I Heard the Sirens Scream*, an e-book detailing her experiences and thoughts regarding the 9/11 attacks and the subsequent anthrax mailings. (Both on sale here.) Garrett suspects that al Qaeda is as likely as anyone to have launched the virus and that Osama bin Laden probably enjoyed the U.S. government's response.

Then again, I'm still not convinced a crime took place in Houston. Chlorine plants are extremely dangerous. They're meant to be inspected regularly. Journalists in Houston were preparing a story about inspection lapses amid 'accidents' and 'incidents' that caused injuries and production delays at that installation. The government has just seized their work and barred them from discussing it, declaring it part of a "criminal investigation." There's no role for al Qaeda in an industrial accident facilitated by sloppy inspection practices, so *let's not go there*.

It worked! Now that the journalists' videos have vanished from YouTube, Houston is all about terror.

DAY 190

MARTIAL LAWLESSNESS IN NEW YORK

I'm recovering from that bloody demonstration against Martial Law. I don't understand why no one simply tells us we are under the boot. This is surely what it would look and *feel* like.

Anna and I went to Times Square at noon to join thousands of New Yorkers in protesting the imposition of Army troops on the city. Not that we didn't already have National Guards from who-knows-where, but suddenly a lot more people are being searched and taken away for questioning by guys operating under the U.S. flag in full battle gear. No rights, no lawyers, no papers.

Middle Easterners, of course, are hotly pursued. Stretches of Brooklyn are said to be deserted day and night as Muslims and swarthy residents in general hide from the authorities. I get emails from people who say their kids were snatched off the street.

To cut a long story short, the NYPD would not authorize the protest. Some big shots came out with military backup and read a riot act that entitled soldiers to shoot us.

That put me on high alert. I'm not accustomed to demonstrating and this didn't look much like photos from the Sixties. No flowers in M16 barrels.

The announcement that we were all criminals set off raucous protests from the 9/11 Conspiracy people, who tend to be young and excitable and who don't realize that *the people united* can not only be defeated, they can be corralled and massacred.

I've never been drawn into the mystery over 9/11, an unlikely event by anyone's standard. I am more prepared to believe that a bunch of fanatics did it than that the U.S. government could pull off such a neat and complex set of activities. I think people prefer to think that a president whom *they* might conceivably control (though they never did) was responsible. By personally sorting out the lines of a mega-plot, they feel that they are battling the forces behind 9/11. How do you fight the idea that some nondescript guys with box cutters can wreck your life? You grant them special powers.

We can all agree that the vaporization of the World Trade Center helped lay the ground for the state to deprive us of all liberties, whether or not the White House engineered the event. I'm confident that our administrators weren't sorry to see it happen. I see no reason to fret over past details. (Still, I can't resist <u>The Children</u>'s gorgeous elegy, *September.*)

We milled around as I sized up the security. There was a lot of military gear behind the barricades. Big trucks with strange equipment loomed over the crowd. A pair of military trucks alongside the demonstrators featured bulky plates tilted gently toward us. Closest to the crowd were dense packs of New York cops in riot gear, backed by soldiers. Was the military's ammunition live?

People chanted all kinds of crap, from flu-related stuff opposing vaccine adjuvants and suggesting that bird flu was an experiment gone wrong to calls for U.S. troops to be withdrawn from various combat missions. (An Asian guy next to me found that one funny: "Bring 'em home so they can shoot us instead," he yelled.) He had a point.

After yet another declaration that we were breaking the law, I noticed that the cops were all donning ear packs to muffle sound. Sure enough, a pair of NYPD trucks mounted with black screens had drawn up on our left. I took these for <u>LRADs</u>, long-range acoustic devices known as 'sonic cannons' that were developed for the Navy after the attack on the U.S.S. Cole in 2000. One was used against protesters in Pittsburgh in 2009—successfully, <u>as seen on YouTube</u>. Somali pirates block them with headphones.

It was time for an exit strategy but Anna wouldn't hear of it. "They always do that," she said. "I've seen those trucks before. But not those," she added, pointing at the Army trucks with the big plates.

The cops began making forays into the crowd, snatching individuals to haul behind their lines. (How long had they been watching these people? Hours? Days? Months?) A platform supporting journalists documenting the protest was clumsily cleared. The police knocked a photographer down. Were they removing witnesses?

Anna was intent on staying. I hadn't seen her in a week. Her tough little fingers, honed by unrelenting altruism, felt safe in mine. Fate had plunked me in an arena with thousands of defiant leftists I generally disagreed with. I started kissing the one I loved and respected.

The crowd erupted in whoops and jeers. The police were withdrawing. The people pressed hard against the barricades, chanting "shoot the rich," which probably wasn't about vaccinating them. Facing us were soldiers, who must have been wearing earphones inside their ear guards. I heard no command when they sliced neatly into the 9/11 Truthers.

No Quarter for American Citizens

I dragged Anna away in my arms as she cursed, appalled at my cowardice. She must have seemed like a victim of police brutality, prompting the crowd to part for us all the way to the rear. I felt like Moses going the wrong way, but it worked. We wound up squinting at the confrontation from a subway entrance. Vigorous chanting resounded among the sunlit skyscrapers as the people defied the state.

Then the rhythm broke into fragments, as if 5,000 folks had run short of breath. There came a giant stomping, churning noise. It was the sound of soldiers charging demonstrators who grunted under blows that echoed like the work of woodcutters.

It was the kind of thing we expect from St. Petersburg or Moscow or Beijing, presented disapprovingly on good ol' American TV.

Then came horrible piercing sirens and a torrent of screams. The stampede was on.

I pulled Anna down the stairs past a bunch of cops who had missed their cue. We raced to the crosstown shuttle and caught it just as the doors were closing. I looked back to see the police swinging into motion. A middle-aged redhead took a club to her face as our train lurched eastward.

Anna was pretty shattered. To cover my dignity, I'll call my condition *helpless rage*.

Videos appear briefly on YouTube under ever-more senseless keywords, lest they be taken down immediately. They show that the cops got to use those sonic cannons and that the Army deployed what turned out to be 'pain ray' trucks against the most stubborn protesters. They arrested hundreds, at least. People were fatally crushed.

We were lucky. None of what I saw made sense. Why did the police withdraw? Why did the Army attack? Who was in charge? How many were killed? Who are we supposed to ask? Are inquiries even legal? Or is the law simply irrelevant now?

DAY 191

THE REAL SACRIFICE—OUR FUTURE

The surreal is made real. The massacre in Times Square isn't New York's lead story. The fatal stomping of nine protestors during an encircled charge by the NYPD and U.S. military units is playing second fiddle to the ghastly crime at St. Patrick's Cathedral.

You undoubtedly know about the bearded man who announced that God wanted him to save the world from man's misdeeds and then killed his son on the high altar. You've seen him shout "I fear God" on the Web while he waves that bloody blade, courtesy of the phone cams that must have lit the Cathedral as if it were July 4th.

The gory images went global in minutes, thanks to an inviting Google.

They sound more striking than they look. The lighting was poor, the framing wide, and the man's white clothing confused the sensors, so the unfortunate lad's moment of death is more conceptual than real. The scene looked better on the TV news after some high-tech light therapy.

But hey, the sacrifice was not in vain. There's much less fuss about those dead demonstrators. They were, after all, gathering illegally. I must have dreamed <u>Freedom of Assembly</u>. Was it old-fashioned of me to think that *if the will to control is human, the will to resist is divine*?

There are no vivid images of the state riot on TV, nothing to hold a candle to the 'St. Patrick's Sacrifice.' Just wide shots of demonstrators chanting, some masked punks in black throwing things, and the unavoidable stampede when cops and soldiers followed orders.

Now that Google is barring 'disruptive' videos from its sites, the good footage is on the Web, overseas, still viewable if your ISP allows access. I'm not certain about the image that claims to show the late lab technician standing politely as a line of robo-clubs engulfed him. Practically speaking, it could be someone else being brutally assaulted.

Or it could be evidence of outright murder. It certainly shows what happened to people who didn't run in panic over the mashed bodies of their fellow demonstrators.

The aftermath was a generously photographed press conference. Our mayor looked stalwart, solemnly flanked by the Commissioner of Police and the Generalissimo of Whatever, those imposing columns of state firepower. The citizens they killed weren't *victims*, went the unmasked lecture. They brought death upon themselves by not respecting the law and our need for order. That's what they get for chanting in public.

Incensed by Sanctimony

The official eye-wiping came moments later, when the masked media breathlessly solicited responses to The Sacrifice. An innocent boy lost, a deranged dad in custody, so sad.

Tomorrow will be a citywide Day Of Mourning. Not for flu victims, or police victims, or justice, or common sense, but for the *kid*.

Like everyone, I'm sorry for the boy. His father betrayed him.

Not that the lad got much help from churchgoers, who flooded the altar for close-ups and then oozed outside to post them online while the murderer waved his bloody bayonet and raved that Abraham caught a break when God called off *his* attempted sacrifice of Isaac. This guy thought God was just kidding.

The miracle is that no one killed the man. Will a jury find him insane, infuriating, or both?

Meanwhile talk shows pretend to debate God's role in the pandemic while sneakily wondering why the boy lay still as his father wielded the blade. Was he hypnotized? Drugged?

I suspect the father and son had practiced performing _Genesis 22_. The kid thought it was just an exhibition. Dad expected _The Word_ to call off his shtick at the climax.

Maybe Americans think the president will stop just short of dismembering our Constitution. When a voice from above says we've suffered enough, the authorities will relax.

Me, I see my people prostrate, licking the blood off their screens, fearing one another more than any God—and bowing to Caesar.

DAY 192

SMASHING THE LES DIY

I'll grit my teeth and keep posting one letter after the other.

The cops raided Anna's apartment while I was posting last night. They busted a lot of LES DIY members, took their documents, computers, tablets, smartphones, and humble cell phones. They took the volunteers in for questioning, too—but not for long. They released Anna before I could figure out where she had gone.

Her door was removed, her daughter's things scattered, her kitchen smashed like an old still after a revenuers' raid. No more food for the needy, RAISE be praised.

Anna is here with me now. I drafted Mark to fetch her and her things with his new car. The idiot tried to flirt with her.

Unlike me, Anna fights hard not to judge others. I'm afraid she'll implode if the government keeps pushing her. She's furious that they arrested the group's doctors and nurses and told the media that her free medics were quacks exploiting the poor and ignorant. The doctor who saved my life is in jail now, at risk of losing his. Contributions to the group's efforts by a few people they treated are being pitched as illicit fees. This is what they do to Howard Roark in _The Fountainhead_.

Anna and I drank whiskey and held each other: Still breathing, still real. How can anyone make me so glad I'm alive in the midst of such a nightmare?

In my panic, I called Bart at his newspaper. No answer. He did warn me. *Good for him*!

Now to sleep off the shock—together at least.

DAY 192 (#2)

AMERICA'S AUTOIMMUNE DISORDER

I can't sleep. I think I know what's going on. The body politic is overreacting. And to the wrong danger. It is targeting *people*—not the virus—with deadly force. As if America has been seized by a cytokine storm.

Since 9/11 our government has hunted enemies at home and abroad, tracking potentially disagreeable thoughts, words, and deeds. Vast resources have been devoted to data-mining our lives and transactions, the way an immune system tries to detect the presence of alien cells.

Public safety bureaucrats have vied to fulfill the security mission. The CDC refocused on preventing terrorism more than disease. The DHS took border inspection duties away from the Agriculture Department, slackening food-safety enforcement—unless a poisoning seems political. The DHS also engulfed FEMA, reshaped it to contend with dirty bombs instead of hurricanes, fires, earthquakes. People replaced nature as the primary adversary.

Our reward was Katrina.

I'm sad to note that the private sector wholeheartedly embraced the War On Terror. Big telecommunications companies invited the state to spy on their customers. Our greatest aircraft manufacturer conducted secret flights to convey kidnapped captives to be tortured. The Pentagon privatized warfare, shoveling tax dollars at paramilitary companies to pay contractors generously to die off the books. America's glowing Web-search pioneers consented to stifle thoughts and words.

Now the popular social networks have just shut down antivax pages, groups, and circles. They banned certain antivaxers, including Fitch, without explanation.

State corporatism is no improvement on Big Brother. It's worse. Look where it got Hitler and Mussolini and Tojo. Look what it's doing to the individual, left and right.

More recently, it failed us against H5N1. As with Katrina, America proved helpless against a *natural* threat that Washington itself had warned was "inevitable." In the wake of the cynicism stirred by the swine flu pandemic, corporations saw little profit in preparing for bird flu. When it came, they fired millions of workers. The government was so obsessed with finding and countering the dangers posed by human beings that it did little more than recite: *Stay home & wash your hands.*

Left without reliable water, power, food, medicine, and security, citizens took survival into their own hands. In keeping with our society's finest traditions, many acted sweetly and effectively. The LES DIY, for instance, served as a kind of immune response to bird flu. The group put forth social antibodies to the helplessness, fear, and sickness that H5N1 was spreading.

A Better Enemy than Flu

Now Washington began to recognize a peril for which it *had* prepared: People. That would be *us*. We can be seen, defined, *controlled*.

The government desperately moved to assert itself. Washington nationalized the state militias, handed total power over our most useful communications medium—the Internet—to giant corporations, and started conscripting flu victims. *Hup two three four* became the state's latest mantra.

H5N1 wouldn't listen.

Then came the *shape* of a familiar adversary—terrorism. Like an old microbial foe, the horror in Houston triggered the organized fury of American bureaucracy. *Here* at last appeared the enemy the state was geared to fight.

There was no time or need to determine if God, man, or incompetence had brought us Houston. Agents activated everywhere to fight terrorism by any means necessary.

Now America is aflame, flush with political toxins. We know they can't kill H5N1. Will they kill us?

'Nina' just called, using a concealed number. She wouldn't say where she was but sounded pleased to have heard from her friend that I'm concerned about her. Her voice was cool, suspicious—maybe a little weak. I said I'd be happy to have tea with her if she's around. That made her laugh. I didn't know what to say when she asked if I'm living with someone. I told the truth—to Anna as well. That ended both conversations. I hope Nina calls again.

DAY 193

GROUNDED AT ZERO

The NYPD is staffed with gifted readers. Having obtained the LES DIY's list of members who had recovered from bird flu, they managed to tip RAISE to conscript them all in less than 48 hours. These guys should probably be running RAISE (whose food distribution system broke down in Boston for reasons that are *classified*).

Or is RAISE already running *them*?

Anna intends to comply. She's to report in the morning for a test that will show whether or not she has antibodies to H5N1. It's fair to worry that <u>the lab screens won't be reliable</u>. Our society is in shambles. What's one more flu victim as long as the garbage gets picked up? What was a volunteer worth when they wanted to get Ground Zero cleared fast?

The good news is that we're getting used to the telephoned death threats from people who mask their numbers. Anna recognizes a persistent Philadelphia accent.

DAY 194

TURTLE ENVY

I don't know who reads this thing. The Web is slower than ever. Still, I'm trying to get my site and blog listed for what they're calling "enhanced access" so you can reach it. The expense isn't the biggest problem. The new Digital Code Of Conduct invites censorship and expulsion—after they get my money.

The authorities are afraid people will post irresponsibly.

We need Americans to march out of their hidey holes into the streets – naked, sick, frightened – and shout at the evil bastards who are exploiting our misery to grab more power & wealth at the expense of innocent and honest, unconnected folks.

That sort of thing, ya know? We just can't have it here.

Are any leaders out there using their power to help people? Are they all bent on wrapping us in fear—turning us into human tacos to be gobbled by an insatiable state and its corporate partners?

If you're still reading this, please let me know how your communities are dealing with the repression. I can no longer reach lots of blogs I've come to rely on for *unmediated* information. The fog thickens.

To dispel the murk, I took a long walk with Anna through the East Village. Tompkins Square Park looks about as bad as it did when I first moved here. People are camping under a sign that says their buildings burned down, *thank you very much*. The lawns have been torn up, presumably for graves. Or are *the soldiers of RAISE* digging up corpses? We didn't stop to ask.

Anna and I wandered past countless shuttered shops down to Houston Street, where we turned west because it felt safer. When we passed Second Avenue, we realized we were at a spot we've never discussed, but which it turns out we both love: Liz Christy Garden.

Created in 1973, it's considered the area's first community garden. Stone paths wind past a busy little turtle pond under a cypress tree. And it's supervised by cats.

We expected the spot to be closed. But one of those remarkable creatures—a masked *volunteer*—was tending the greenery as we peered through the fence. She and her companion waved us inside.

It didn't take long to unwind in there. We kissed to the sounds of trickling water and of tools turning earth that cares nothing about influenza and injustice.

DAY 195

THE BEAT GOES ON

Anna is now a certified bird flu survivor, having tested positive for H5N1 antibodies. She's pleased to have been assigned to a sprawling shelter for prospective foster children. This sounds like a temporary orphanage, but it's more complicated.

There are enormous numbers of little kids whose single parents died of flu. They're being warehoused in elementary schools that serve as dormitories—and theoretically as schools, if staff could spare time to teach them.

Anna's excited about caring for them. Tomorrow she will hand out her daughter's favorite toys, which we've rescued from Anna's ransacked apartment. I'll rise in a couple of hours to help her carry them, brightening the lives of about 50 children.

I'm delighted she feels useful so quickly. Her spirits have improved, though she remains frighteningly close to fatigue. Her little form needs to rest.

Of course I've argued fervently against cooperating with conscription. Anna opposes it in principle, but she'd rather not stay home and mope. Her mind and heart disdain longwinded reasoning—and hopelessness.

It's not that she aspires to sainthood. She's a brilliant schemer when she finds it necessary. She'd make an exceptional criminal. Sneeky never takes his eyes off her.

Anna has revitalized this apartment. The air reverberates with strange foreign sounds, or the music of bands I barely knew, like the Yeah Yeah Yeahs' ferocious, squealing logic or the Kills' *Cat Claw*. I'd always figured Fiona Apple for some fluffy princess; I live to learn and love, she to make a *Mistake* and rhapsodize about it. There's always room for Gene Clark: Anna played *No Other* last night—prime kissing music.

Happily, I've found a car to borrow. I'm going to drive Anna to my mythical bungalow on her weekend break, hang out with her in the autumn woods for two days. If it's warm enough, we'll picnic and tumble amid red and gold leaves in a forest glade. I want to help the sun paint that broad smile back on her face. She deserves it, needs it.

I'm glad I safeguarded Ric's kitchenware when his neighbors started looting his possessions. The thieves acquired well-deserved bedbugs, but I rinsed off any pests as I salvaged his pots, pans, dishes, and cutlery. Ric joins us in spirit when we dine. My home cuisine has improved immeasurably since RAISE made me the surrogate for hundreds of hungry New Yorkers.

DAY 196

'CONSTITUTIONAL CANCER'

Not to get too Biblical about it, but this War on the U.S. Constitution began as the War On Terror, itself descended from the War on Drugs, which had followed the Cold War, World War II, and the War to End All Wars.

The current hostilities follow the legal shortcuts pioneered in the 1980s and expanded in 2001 and thereafter. America's Founding Fathers never countenanced a justice system that allows the state to seize your property before you're convicted, depriving you of funding for a lawyer to mount your defense. They never envisioned letting all Americans be considered potential 'enemy combatants' because some politicians feel like it.

These are struggles ordained from on high. They feed the state as it purports to fight an invisible enemy, engorging the police and bureaucrats and military with special resources and rights at our expense. *Even as they fail to achieve anything useful.* Check out <u>Goya</u>'s painting of Saturn chewing his son.

Will the state's overreaction to 9/11—compounded by the high fever it has sustained from bird flu—kill *us*, the tiny cells that enliven the body politic? A cytokine flood has Americans pleading from their rooftops for food and freedom.

A spark of hope emanates from the band of Senators who stood together yesterday to demand statistics from the Attorney General about how many Americans have been rounded up and what is being done to them. The politicians come from both political parties, from left and right, and some of their rhetoric pumped my pulse.

"*Freedom is not a virus and draconian laws are not pills our system can automatically flush away after a fever,*" said one. "*We flirt with constitutional cancer,*" warned another.

Sure it's just talk. There aren't enough of them to approve any bills, and anything they ever passed would be vetoed. But let me dream. As long as people talk like that, *and I can read their words in the mainstream media,* I breathe a little.

People want to know how I can meet Nina tomorrow while I'm living so happily with Anna. Happiness is a terrible thing to waste. I've been blessed with an upgrade.

I once fell in love with Nina and she fell apart. I was hurt plenty, but I've tried not to take it personally. I still care about Nina. She's a good person who needs help. I hope to be useful. And I'm certain Anna will understand because we are happy and she is strong.

DAY 197-198

HELP—PLEASE

This is a note from the woman known here as Anna. I hope one of you can help me figure out what happened.

I am sorry to have to tell you Blogula has disappeared. I came home from work yesterday to find the door on the floor and the apartment looted. His iMac and papers are gone, so it might have been an official raid. All his protective stuff and cash and food are missing, too, so it could have been a big burglary. Whoever did it would have needed a truck.

Where is he? Why would robbers take him away, too? Where's Sneeky? Even the cat food is missing.

He was supposed to meet his old girlfriend for coffee at 3 pm, but I doubt she kidnapped him. The door was removed by the kind of system the police used when they raided my apartment. When I called the local precinct, a detective asked me who the missing man talks to and who would want to harm him. No cops came to view the mess or take a statement about the break-in.

His nearest neighbors are both dead. No one else heard anything. A couple shrugged and looked away. Two block residents saw a lot of police cars parked here yesterday.

I'm scared for him. If you know anything, please write his business email. If you know anyone important in New York or Washington—anywhere, really—please get help.

DAY 199-200:

PLEASE JOIN THE HUNT

Anna again. Thank you all for your concern. He really is a good person.

I wish I had good news. His disappearance has been reported in a lot of blogs and even on a paper's website. We launched an online petition to make the New York Police Department account for eyewitness reports that the police took him away in handcuffs three days ago. A man just released from custody says he thinks he's positive he saw him in jail with his face banged-up.

The neighbors still saw nothing.

Thank God for the Internet. Please help in any way you can. Sign our petition and tell your friends about it.

DAY 201-202

GETTING WARMER

The city admits they were holding him a couple of days ago, but they say the trail goes cold after that. As if he went to get a beer from the prison commissary and disappeared like a ghost from the old "Tombs." Blogula's no quitter.

We collected around 20,000 American names on our Web petition plus many more than that from overseas. Please keep circulating it. We are getting close. I know it.

THANK YOU!

DAY 203

BE PATIENT—THANK YOU!

He is resting here at home! He'll be okay, I think. He wants to tell you about it. He hopes to start tomorrow. He hasn't told me much. I'll be reading, too.

Thank you ALL for raising such a fuss. I'm proud to be an American right now. Maybe we *can* make a difference.

We have to, don't we?

Sincerely, Anna

DAY 204

AWOL (ABSENT WITHOUT LAW)

I apologize for my absence. I was enjoying board (not much food) in three repellant joints, highlighted by reluctant conversation with psychotic bullies, official and otherwise. I was raided and locked up and physically abused. A U.S. passport is no impediment to America's cytokine stormtroopers.

I'm already tempted to sign off. Count Blogula is bone-weary and whatever's in my lungs doesn't seem to be flu. (I sure hope it's not <u>drug-resistant tuberculosis</u>.) I'm trying to get used to this borrowed pc laptop. My fingers are sore from the application of coercive force by two cops, a civilian, a machine, and a comrade prisoner. I'm literally beat.

But postponing my account isn't an option. It has ceased to be predictable that I'll be able to put it online, ya know? Gotta strike while the iron is handy.

So let's say I face a bunch of charges, some of which would be quite serious in ordinary circumstances. I reckon *any* charges are grave these days. I'm in deep dung.

The cops burst in six days ago while I was expecting Nina, who had contacted me after coming across one of the YouTube videos about the LES DIY, which featured me praising the group at Ric's Place. I was wondering if she would knock hesitantly or aggressively when the door blew out and my apartment filled with uniformed men in crappy masks, pointing guns and bellowing like high school football players as I emerged from my bedroom.

I did what all New Yorkers are trained to do when mugged: raised my hands and vowed to cooperate.

Anna was off doing forced labor. We can picture her shock on returning to my trashed apartment. Having herself just been raided and detained, she recognized the signs of state pillage—the absence of documents, communications equipment, and storage media. Thieves might overlook old files and a thumb drive or two, but today's public servants leave no thought unexamined.

She was briefly confused by the fact that most everything else I owned was missing, too. That's where I suspect the neighbors came in, at least as far as my food supplies went.

I think I must've gotten more sleep than Anna did while I was gone. She tried relentlessly to locate me, but of course she had to keep reporting to work *under pain of arrest.* That left lunchtime for telephoning a system that took her inquiries for an excuse to ask what she *thought* I might have been arrested for. *"Well, I don't think he told anyone about that murder, so it must have been the bank robbery Thursday...."*

During the evenings—when she wasn't stirring up support and interest among local punks, yuppies, artists, musicians, and politicians—Anna was searching for Sneeky. He vanished in the ruckus, along with all of his food. She also recruited friends from the LES DIY to replace my door. They're getting mighty proficient at this. With fresh customers in abundance, they should incorporate as *Doors R Bust.*

Guns & Money: Send Lawyers

In tossing my possessions like baboons, the cops claim to have found some illicit items. These allegedly include a taser and some marijuana. That adds up to real trouble. The cash from local mask sales could further complicate the picture, though it's fair to wonder if my money will turn up—as evidence or otherwise.

Like all good Americans, I had prescriptions for the Ambien and for the Relenza that outlasted Stefan. (Oops, giving it to a sick person could be criminal, too.) As in so many busts, all meds have disappeared.

The raiding party also said they found a handgun in one of my boots. It closely resembles the one I captured from the guys who attacked Anna and me in the Ramble. Steadfast readers will join me in recalling that I tossed the semiautomatic into the lake. I regret any confusion over this.

Since the alleged weapon wasn't loaded and was in my home, possession would be a relatively light offense under state law. The city, however, has stricter statutes and maintains a <u>registry</u> that requires gun offenders to report frequently for years, like pedophiles.

Suddenly I was being called a well-armed miscreant in possession of a commercial quantity of pot. My blood turned cold, kept me cool for days.

I pleaded to take a mask or two with me. "*Sure,*" came the sardonic reply. "*We always let our guests pack.*"

They must have come back later with a truck to collect my masks, gloves, and goggles.

Hence, I no longer purvey protective gear. Refunds to anyone whose order hasn't been filled, unless they seize my bank accounts, too. This page is the only part of the website that will remain active, *so long as blogging is permitted.* I still turn up on Google.

Slow Ride to Hell

I was driven around in a caged bus for hours while the cops picked up more prisoners. These ranged from everyday criminal types to an elderly schoolteacher who was arrested for refusing to leave her local precinct without her daughter, who hasn't been seen since that demonstration in Times Square. The woman, who must be at least 60, said she watched the desk sergeant while he looked into it by telephone. She swears his eyes flashed recognition when he called headquarters and queried them. The schoolteacher got herself arrested in hopes of finding her girl. I wish her luck in that urban Gulag.

For old times' sake, our mobile crate even contained a busted graffiti writer. Too bad they didn't use it to pick up corpses instead.

As on the subways below, the color of the people joining our population got darker as we rolled north in a haze of sickening exhaust fumes. Several battered souls climbed aboard in Harlem, where they'd been beaten and busted at one more demonstration that will never be reported.

Eventually we reached a gigantic prison barge, where it took all night to process us. In the morning they handed out stale bologna sandwiches on white bread. I couldn't taste anything but refried bus air. I ate because hunger makes you stupid. (Whereas food poisoning keeps you on your toes.)

I spent dawn on the barge, waiting to be arraigned. A lot of people had been there much longer. It used to be illegal to hold Americans without charging them.

No one had masks. Many were ill. Impoverished prisoners had been doing without their normal meds for months; middle-class ones were withdrawing from whatever pills they'd stockpiled for Round 2. A lot of people had stomach problems, skyrocketing pulse rates, anxieties, and of course, flu.

I saw one man die and several others fail. There were pools of blood where people had coughed up vital juice—red stains all around.

The PA constantly urged inmates to volunteer to clean the place up and tend the sick in exchange for better food and semi-private cells. A prisoner awaiting burglary charges said he had helped out for a few days in hopes of getting quicker access to a judge, or at least asthma medicine (which is what he said he'd been caught trying to steal), until he realized his jailers would never part with someone so useful.

Ten days later, the man was still there, gawking at seagulls as they picked at a nearby dump. He considers bird flu a fraud unleashed by the rich to kill off workers they don't need anymore. *They look fine out there, yo,* he said of the flying scavengers.

A Fight to Forget

I couldn't help but start explaining about H5N1 till an extraordinary prisoner turned on me. He was a tall man with dreadlocks and whiskers that angled to a precise Fu Manchu from fierce sideburns directly under his cheekbones. I had previously noticed twin scars underneath the whiskers, which he'd apparently shaped to camouflage his flesh. The original wounds looked to have been cut to match, as if in some coming-of-age ritual, but the guy wasn't proud of these scars. He was hiding them.

Maybe I stared too much. I told you I wasn't feeling well.

He called me a *snitch* and punched me till I contributed blood to the cell's evolving design. I tried to fight hard enough to dissuade anyone from wanting to emulate him later, but I never had a chance. It ended when he held me up by the neck with one hand, winked, and dropped me.

I just stayed put, slept with my head against the wall. I didn't move till they took me to the Manhattan Detention Complex, the underground fortress known as the Tombs, where my bruises made me look mean enough not to be bothered. I managed to miss meals at both ends of the trip.

The Tombs was full of prisoners who said their terms were up, even without time off for good behavior. Early in Round One a guy had been sent to the big joint at Riker's Island for three months. Five months later he was back downtown, awaiting release, swearing passionately that the only thing he'd done to extend his stay was survive a flu attack in a block full of dying men. "*My death sentence, ya know, is turned into a life sentence.*" (He gave me his girlfriend's number to call and offer empty reassurance on his behalf, but the paper was taken from me a day later.)

Just as I began wondering if I'd spend my life there, too, I was off to be interrogated by a good cop/bad cop combo. Except they both sucked. Each was wearing the protective gear I used to sell, presumably from my inventory. They evidently wanted me to notice, so I chose to let it pass.

I demanded an attorney. I don't know any criminal lawyers, but I have money in the bank and I have credit and I wanted one. "*They're all sick,*" said the 'bad' cop, who looked friendlier for some reason.

The 'good' one was fatter and looked bored. He literally shrugged at my request. "*They don't like to come in these days. You need a doctor more,*" he added, nodding at my colorful complexion.

"*They don't come here either,*" grinned the nasty one, blue eyes twinkling.

When I clammed up, they explained that my charges could be deployed in combinations to ratchet the penalties up—drugs and guns, for instance. I could get from 35 to 80 years.

I knew this was BS. I've never been arrested and I didn't use a weapon to commit a crime. They hadn't claimed the gun was loaded. Even the alleged pot possession amounts to less than a quarter-pound, which New York City judges have historically regarded as a personal stash.

So the rotten one suggested they had a witness who had purchased pot from me.

I instantly demanded to be arraigned. If they were going to throw phony charges at me, they might as well book me for murder. *Bring it on*—lawyer or not.

So the nice cop mentioned that the gun had been used in at least one shooting. This was a new threat with ugly possibilities. *Why were they so bent on screwing me?*

Rope-a-Dope, My Way

I told them what had happened in the Ramble and asked them what they wanted, besides the masks they'd stolen. That was when the nasty one punched me right where the inmate had struck. He kept at it till the plastic gloves he'd appropriated were bloody.

Did I mention that I was cuffed to a pole? My lips are still mashed, my nose swollen. I still have twin black eyes.

It took the wonderful cop a long time to get me to talk again. He got me some lukewarm soapy water, a cleaning pad, and a bottle of drinking water. He also dialed up a warm meal and admitted he could see as to how I might not be the tall Dominican guy who'd shot up a bar in Washington Heights four years ago. I appreciated the *un*-recognition.

They wanted to know about Mark's friends, the men he'd introduced me to in the nightclub during the hiatus. My Relenza disks had checked out, unlike the ones these guys allegedly sell on the Web, *using accounts the cops claim were created on my iMac.*

This was an alarming concept. Mark had tended Sneeky as I drove upstate over the summer. I remember being thrilled at his generous and responsible performance. Now I picture the gang cooking up schemes on my account, my beer, my reputation.

Like it or not, I'm an informational dead end for the cops. I don't know those guys. They may be as innocent as I am. I've never known them to do anything but buy booze in a bar and call up to ask what I think of the flu. Mark might be in profound trouble, but I couldn't cover for him. I suggested one of the guys might have used my machine for criminal purposes while Mark was getting cigarettes.

By then the brutal cop seemed bored and the beneficent one was getting cranky. I was useless. The food never came.

I asked if I were free to go. The LES DIY had been released in hours. That amused them both: "*Not quite…*"

Now I'm going to sleep. If no one kills me or drags me away or takes this laptop or cuts my power or my URL, I'm certain to continue tomorrow.

A lot of *ifs*, I know. Your assignment is to read the <u>Bill of Rights</u> all day. Good night.

DAY 205

AMERICAN NIGHTMARE

I expected to be booked on the charges I faced. <u>The Tombs</u> connects to plenty of courtrooms via a cantilevered walkway called the "Bridge of Sighs." Instead I was taken from my session with the NYPD to a patrol car. Were they driving me home? Had that whimsical beating been some weird *Get Out of Jail* interview?

My hopes were smothered when two uniformed cops put earmuffs on me and slipped a black hood over my head. I think they drove around in circles so I couldn't tell where we were going. I could taste other peoples' fear. Had that hood had ever been laundered?

I wound up at a detention center that probably doesn't exist, somewhere in downtown Manhattan. I had been *rendered* for secret investigation—dissolved like the World Trade Center, but without witnesses.

I was handed off to people who never spoke. I figured they worked for the Department of Homeland Security, perhaps even for RAISE. They walked me a short distance and stripped off my clothes. They attached my cuffed wrists to an apparatus that forced me to bend as they deeply inspected my filthy butt. I mumbled that the process would be easier if they let me shower. No answer.

Next my hood was removed as I stood spread-eagled in a white room.

Someone in a streamlined Darth Vader helmet swiftly cut my hair and shaved my head and face as a camera clicked. It hurt whenever the razor encountered bruises and cuts. There was a delay while someone soaped my eyes and checked the damage. Apparently I didn't need stitches: A hand held my eyelids wide, one by one, so sensors could scan my face for what I presume is <u>a wealth of biometric detail</u>. I'll forever be known by biometric readers, though my features with whole, healthy flesh might confuse them.

After restoring the hood, which smelled worse over my cleaned face, they elevated me to another floor, walked me to a door, and brusquely guided me inside. My earmuffs and hood were stripped off. When the cloth sack was yanked, the door locked almost instantly with a deep, conclusive *thunk*.

The cell was about nine feet by six, gleaming white. It was empty but for a hard plastic bed and a stainless steel toilet. There was no window. Strong light beamed down from several locations, as uncontrollable as the cameras that scanned every angle of my box. The hood and earmuffs waited by the door.

Gradually I detected random percussive beats and clicks at a haunting volume, occasionally punctuated by mechanical whistles. No heavy metal for me. They must have known Motorhead or Metallica would have lifted my spirits—at least till 5 am.

The place smelled better than anywhere I'd been for days—until my stench caught up with me. There was no sink in which to bathe. Just a tiny plastic water bottle. I chose hydration over hygiene. The water tasted weird. I suspect it was medicated.

The food was mostly <u>refined carbohydrates</u>: oatmeal and bread, bland pasta and bread, or white rice with a few beans, hold the bread. I would try to catch them leaving it but the pliable plastic tray seemed simply to appear. (Did they have some way of making me fall asleep?) The water bottles were near-frozen. I never saw a shower.

There was nothing human about the space, no way for me to adjust lighting or sound. It was always cold and I had no covers, not even a sheet. I shivered for hours, naked, my hands cuffed in front. This would be my life 24/7. I'm told I must have spent five nights there. It felt like weeks. I'm still there.

Naked, Hooded, Questioned

Did any of you imagine an American could be treated this way in his own city? Of course I warned about the prospect in my libertarian way, but I don't think I ever really *expected* it. Some of you will say *I asked for it*. Better me than you, eh?

My reward was an interrogation. Before my captors entered the cell, I was instructed to hood and earmuff myself. In spite of the handcuffs, I complied. Then I was escorted to an elevator that seemed to drop. We walked into an even colder room that echoed when they removed my earmuffs. I was still nude. I felt the presence of others.

A man asked if I'd been comfortable. "No," I said, as flatly as I could.

"Is it cold down there?" (Funny, on the elevator I had felt that we were descending from my cell, not rising.) "Sure," I said.

"Too bad," he continued. "Maybe we can make things better today." The voice of the state was assured, even condescending. As if I were a bit defective and could be fixed if we both made the effort.

He started with a reasonable opener—if one of *you* had asked it: What made me think I was an expert on bird flu or public policy?

I asked who was asking. No answer. "What is this, RAISE?" No answer. I replied that whatever agency he represented, the government has no right to ask. He chuckled. "We're here, aren't we?"

I don't recall how, but the man managed to get me rattling on about H5N1. I was charmed that he didn't quarrel with my assertion that I'd been correct about more things than the experts had been. I started showing off, said that the cool, dry atmosphere reminded me of a 2007 study (forgive me—I can't be hunting links just now) that claimed flu thrives in the winter because it hates the heat and humidity of places like that prison barge—or *Indonesia*. He thought that was cute, ho hum, so I pointed out that the 1918 bloodbath wave began in August and peaked in October. So 'cool and dry,' ya know?

He abruptly told me that I am accused of indulging in terrorist activities. *For profit.* "No virgins for you," he laughed.

Consternation must have registered through my hood. A woman's voice surprised me with the news that New York State law defines terrorism as an act intended "to intimidate or coerce a civilian population." She said simple gang members had been convicted under this statute. (She neglected to mention that a sensible judge later threw out the terrorism charges as unmerited.) These two were citing some hysterical post-9/11 law as if I'd single-handedly and deliberately panicked y'all into buying masks. As if people haven't been burying their kids in Central Park! If there were two of me, they'd make us racketeers under <u>RICO</u>.

It didn't take long to persuade me that the Feds could charge me with anything they liked—and make it stick. Courts, Congress, and Presidents have spent so many years gutting the Bill of Rights that all that's left is a house of cards that can serve as a giant prison.

The woman read me a list of Web searches I had conducted for a week before making some comments about flu vaccine. Words like "danger," "risk," and "harm" abounded. Searches of a more personal nature were tossed in, inviting me to imagine what a jury might conclude from my googling.

They played tapes of things I'd said in my apartment over the past few months, edited so that I couldn't hear Anna (or Nina) responding. You can imagine stuff I said after we escaped that bloodbath in Times Square or after Anna's home was raided. I reckoned the Feds must have been spying on me through my computer. I wondered silently if they had pictures, home video. "We have visual corroboration of everything," the man volunteered.

I had to relieve myself blindly in front of them in the interrogation room. It bothered me that there was at least one woman present. I reeked. I swear I could hear discreet coughing, as if someone were too disgusted to breathe fully.

Our first session ended when I conceded I might have been wrong in speculating as to how H5N1 had become a human disease. Every vaccine might have been perfect. No matter that I had posted this.

Everything but Bedbugs

I was so exhausted that I was sure I'd sleep splendidly on the cold platform in my white room, but they cranked up the noises in my cell. I swear I could hear mosquitoes, even though it was too cold for them. Then I felt something bite me. Rodents seemed to be scraping around, squeaking and chirping—not that there was food for them. The lights seemed brighter. It had to have been nighttime, but who knows? Maybe these people wangle overtime to bug detainees who never see a hint of sun anyway.

The only time I could see anything came inside the cold hard whiteness of my cell. I was miserable. I wondered if they had arrested Anna—if she too were freezing in some taxpayer-funded box for having tried to help neighbors after the flu killed her daughter. I felt I had known Anna for years, forever. I longed for her terribly. What did she think had happened to me? Would I see her again? I played songs in my head that she had turned me onto, especially _Isis_. Alternately, I imagined traveling with Anna to a warm place, holding her in sunlight, rejoicing that we were alive, together.

At some point I remembered that Nina had been due to visit me when the cops broke in. It was excruciating to imagine her arriving at my pillaged apartment. What if she had arrived when the cops were still there? Had they taken her away, too?

Nina's in no shape to contend with Federal goons. They could crack her psyche with a question. I shivered at length on that plastic shell, surrounded by unnatural sounds, imagining I could hear her sob and gasp.

I thought about how tormented Nina must have been while she lived with me, quietly certain I was cheating on her. She must have tried so hard to be happy, to trust me, to enjoy life—only to lapse into torture whenever her doubts gathered strength. I appreciate anew how much fun Nina was to be with, how much pleasure and companionship she gave me in her crippled paranoid state. If I ever hear from her again and she seems to understand what happened, I'll know she has recovered.

I hope Nina never showed up, that she called to postpone. The cops probably have my phone now, unless the Feds have it. Does anyone answer? What happens to people who call me?

When the keepers eventually returned to fetch me from my cell, I was excited to think further talk might clarify that I was innocent of political crimes. The boss started by telling me that they had evidence of my links to Mafia drug dealers and pharmaceutical counterfeiters. Not to mention left-wing rabble-rousers and antivax radicals involved in antigovernment activities. I was a diabolical blend of crime and subversion.

Still, there were questions. He wanted to know if I was motivated more by greed or revolutionary zeal. Why had I gone to so much trouble to build a global audience? When I said it had come as a pleasant surprise that people liked my posts, he said I'd be his guest as long as it took to learn the truth. I said I could tell he meant as long as it took for me to agree with his version of my life.

Uncle Sam Needs ... Me?

Now he surprised me by saying he wanted my help. No, he _needed_ my help. America needed my help. There were enemies everywhere that must be monitored and neutralized. I was in a remarkable position to help him safeguard the nation's health and security. I needed only to tell them everything I knew. He was trying to get me a pillow, a blanket, a shower, a robe. Wouldn't I help?

I kept saying it was all in my blog. He didn't seem to have read anything but a few quotes someone had transcribed and handed him. I told him he should go read it. I recited my name and URL.

A punch to the gut knocked the wind out of me. While I wheezed and tasted greasy fabric, the man asked about a telephone number I was carrying when I arrived at "this facility." It took further blows till I recalled that I had agreed to call a prisoner's girlfriend if I ever got out of jail. Now I was being told he's a crack wholesaler. So what? He seemed sober and pleasant. Who did they think I'd meet in the Tombs?

Now our costumes were reversed. My hood was removed, revealing a room that was much smaller than I'd imagined. I was facing a screen that seemed to reflect a guard, three men, and a woman—all wearing hoods and sitting behind me. A man started showing intimate images Nina and I had recorded of love play. I had scrubbed the stuff from my old PC's hard drive, but the government must have recovered the machine after I gave it to Lisa's cousin (who never used it) ... unless they got or stole the video from Nina. (If I ever see that poor paranoid woman, how can I tell her the Feds have a dub?)

I had no interest in discussing any of this. It was embarrassing as hell. Hooded torturers were watching me blush at myself. Was all this an implied threat to blackmail me? I mostly kept my mouth shut.

They showed a number of images of me hunched on my bike against a storefront as I watched the DHS unload Relenza at Penn Station. You could see my feet twitching as I tried not to wet myself and the sidewalk for what felt like the longest and dullest Andy Warhol movie ever.

The peoples' cameras must have missed my blissful urination and the off-loading of the mysterious pallet because the show shifted to a long, wide shot of me biking across the highway to the party boat. Thereabouts, I could be seen aiming my cell phone at something on the riverside. They then cut to the pictures I'd taken, which weren't much good. I agreed that the printing on the boxes in my photos could not be deciphered.

They blew the images up again and again until the pixels ate my brain. *Nope, can't read 'em.* I was shaking.

They started cursing, asking why I'd sullied the Department of Homeland Security with phony accusations. And why I'd recruited a reporter to ask questions....

Bart had actually lifted a finger, dialed DHS! They wanted to know a lot about him—a dead end, like all my connections. I met Bart once. I hope he survives that.

My life proceeded in a flow of scruffy footage they must have collected with <u>facial-recognition technology</u>. Here I was, watching the flagellants at St. Patrick's, coming and going at Ric's Place, selling masks out of a backpack in Tompkins Square Park, peering out of Sneeky's window, obscured by a furry lump. I watched crisp images of Anna and me demonstrating in Times Square, then cringing on the subway steps as the cops and military charged the marchers. It felt good to see us dive onto that shuttle, though the footage of us hugging on the moving train was chilling.

Risqué Viewings in DC?

The creepiest images were of me walking through the Ramble at night. I had looked for cameras there, out of curiosity. Are they disguised as lumps of bark, bird's nests? Do the cops bootleg the hot stuff as porn? Do they blackmail men who go there?

The government had even (fuzzily) recorded my fight with the men who attacked Anna on my peninsula. You could sort of almost see a gun pointed at me. By now my jaw must have sagged open. (They can show that to me at my next interrogation.) I was deeply bewildered, stupid.

"You can see we know everything," a short man said. I recognized his voice as that of the man I had presumed was running things.

"Then you know I'm innocent," I said. The guard boxed my ears till my head rang. I slipped into darkness, wondered if I was fainting. It was probably the hood coming back.

I don't remember returning to my cell. I found myself in a kind of monkey hell paced by hyper techno music and flashing lights. Who cared? I was a disco hero. I won't be giving much away to say I was feeling good in a weird way. I had kept my dignity. They were trashing theirs to torture a fellow American for nothing.

Suddenly—it seemed to me—I was back in the vault, exhausted. I would have confessed to anything for a hot cup of coffee. I was sneezing a lot inside the hood. The fabric grew slimy. They yelled at me to speak up. Someone slapped me. They bound me to the chair after I fell off.

After some murmuring, I was wired to something by an enthusiastic newcomer who was either a man with a soft voice or a second woman with a hoarse tone. The prime inquisitor was annoyed. He seemed uncertain how to get anything useful out of the system. Perhaps he doubted it would break me, or considered it a distraction. He muttered as the young expert fumbled to fit what felt like a metallic cap on my head, with additional connections on my wrists and ankles. All this, I gathered, was plugged into some kind of analyzer that would present highlighted, color-coded images of my brain activity on a big screen.

After some disturbing test shocks, they adjusted the zapper.

As I figure it, the contraption was designed to do more than detect lies. They wanted impulsive, unthinking responses. The machine was meant to scan my brain for evidence of certain activity—*thought*—and to punish me instantly for it. It proposed to eliminate contemplation, prevent captives from considering how to respond to questions. Forcing prisoners to cough up their first thought could be useful.

Newfangled Thought Detector

The round began with technical probes about the quest for a universal flu shot that wouldn't have to be altered every year. Of course I had to think. I was being asked about something I hadn't contemplated for months because it wasn't going to affect H5N1. *Zap. Zap.* I don't think they really cared what I said so long as they fancied they were watching me think. I was getting conditioned to it. So were they.

The next round of questions was ridiculous. Most concerned the LES DIY, which the government apparently views as *New Improved* <u>Bolsheviks</u>—highly motivated activists whose membership reflects every ethnic and interest group in the community. Bruno's alleged past as a pot dealer, not to mention the charges I face, made all the LES DIY members likely drug pushers. A couple of aging Marxists who made food deliveries and the Navy veteran who made vats of rice meant that Anna and the woman who ran the community garden had been plotting armed revolt.

I tried to provide clean answers. Then a question would require principled consideration, some informed judgment on my part. I'd pause.

Their apparatus homed in on indecision. It demanded certainty. I started to feel it coiling, gathering juice whenever I started to think: *Zap.* The kid—as I'd come to think of the sexless assistant—typed copious notes on a keyboard whenever I jerked or cringed. *Zap: Tap, tap, tap.*

There was a long pause filled with murmuring and beeping. The young techie wanted to continue—must work for the company that developed the system. My interrogator said they'd done enough testing; he had work to do. He was told it was company policy to proceed. Phone calls were made, answered.

"All the more reason to go full-force," a woman was saying. "It's her or him. A bird in the hand...."

Finally the boss emitted a lackluster "roger."

Six Degrees of Subversion

I was barraged with queries about Fitch. According to the boss and the vendor, my partner is far more active in antivax activities than I had suspected. Could this be true? Wondering if these people were crazy—or if Fitch might truly have articulated something alarming, even as bluster—brought me considerable pain.

The government seems to believe he's concretely involved in the threats to scuttle the Internet with denial-of-service attacks. I'm not convinced that antivaxers want to destroy the known world, but I'd guess surveillance shows that someone the government thinks is central to the plot is 6 degrees or fewer from Fitch in some digital chat circle. I reckon he'd be shocked, perhaps a little thrilled. In any event, I don't control Fitch. I barely understand him sometimes. By then I was responding quickly, with conviction, so jolts were minimal.

I gained a tiny respite when I slipped in that <u>Charles Lutwige Dodgson</u> (AKA Lewis Carroll, author of *Alice's Adventures in Wonderland)* campaigned feverishly for smallpox revaccination. This prompted a little huddle about how to crack me.

They returned with simple questions about Karl Marx, only to find that I loathe Marx at least as much as they do. "I am an entrepreneur," I insisted, "selling useful things to people who need them. You have no business punishing me for it." This further discouraged the chief interrogator, who countered desperately that I'm a nonbeliever. The government was complaining about my disinterest in religion.

I threw the book at them—Ayn Rand's whole *oeuvre,* in fact. "Ayn Rand was a militant atheist and half the Congress claims to worship her," I snapped.

The boss was dumbfounded to discover that I consider myself an <u>Objectivist</u>. Having still not read my blog, he was content to zap thoughts he hadn't even researched. I realized he fancied himself a Rand follower, too, even though <u>she opposed torture by any state</u>, left or right. He asked how "an alleged" follower of Ayn Rand's philosophy could ever have collaborated with such unsavory socialists as the LES DIY. I replied that Rand had plenty of dealings with people who didn't share her beliefs, so long as she felt (bad word choice, I know) her cause would be promoted: *Atlas Shrugged*'s <u>pub-lisher was an outspoken liberal</u>.

I wondered if my tormentor had ever afflicted a fellow Randian. Amid a welcome absence of shocks, I told him what she would have thought of his profession. He replied that Rand was a patriot and <u>had enthusiastically testified</u> at the Congressional hearings about purging communists in Hol-lywood. Then he paused—possibly because debating Rand's work was mak-ing me feel better while it paralyzed the machine and confused the young techie charged with interpreting its judgments.

"A waste of time," I heard him tell the minion. The magic machine had basically confirmed to him that I wasn't a socialist. Worse, I was someone he would expect to agree with. The woman said something I couldn't hear.

"The genius of capitalism," I said, "is that it recognizes the human urge to extract personal benefit from anything that happens—good or bad. That's what I did with bird flu: I sold equipment to fight it. I also gave away information to fight it." No one answered. The machine concurred.

"I'll tell you something else," I interrupted. I told them that the per-son my readers know as 'Anna' is a Randian heroine—a fierce partisan of moral values, honesty, strength, vision, and perseverance—someone who has elevated the role of the individual to glorious heights during a time of grotesque social decadence. Heck, even her persecution of me as the mystery mailer was Randian. My timing in praising her was dreadful, however, given that Anna was at that moment causing them a lot of problems by stirring up the Internet over my disappearance.

The machine no longer minded what I thought, so they took manual control of the voltage. They all began shouting at me, zapping me harshly for advocating reckless theories even as they urged me to cooperate. After some time, the older guy actually ordered me to "let nature take its course."

So help me, I did. My bladder and rectum simultaneously capitulated.

My brain exploded, too. "Doesn't DHS have more important people to torture?" My voice squeaked like the audio mice in my cell.

Just Following Purchase Orders

"Ask them," he replied. "I'm just doing my job."

"But you *chose* to work for DHS." I sounded like a cranky 12-year-old whose maturing voice couldn't handle the load, but I couldn't let him pass the buck.

"I serve my country," he answered, "in a private capacity. I wish you'd let me help you."

What a joke. The guy wasn't even a Fed. I was being zapped to bits by contractors. Some jerks—maybe veterans, or ex-cops, well-connected sadists—had been hired to make me admit that I had been scaring people for profit and that the LES DIY hates the government. This was a pointless atrocity by clock-punching cheeseballs who were collecting overtime on my innocence.

I tried to stick to my guns. I croaked that it was I who was coming to hate the government and that the LES DIY is a bunch of swell people.

The main interrogator was extremely unhappy. He wasn't at all sold on the technology. The young vendor pleaded to continue. When the boss replied with words I won't repeat, his female counterpart told the kid she'd handle the next session. The techie sullenly unplugged me and then someone hosed me off. The water was thrilling!

I caught some sleep in the white room, half-buried in a jungle crawling with bugs. Anna was out there, calling my name. It's amazing what the human brain will make of a little rest when it's desperate. I felt blessedly connected to her—until I'd remember those people in the hoods and how much they hated her. *Had I helped them?*

At some point I ate whitish paste. By now meals seemed scarce. There was no feeding pattern. I wasn't hungry anyway. I was drifting, trying to focus on whatever seemed real at any given moment. Mush, tooth pain, a red stain on my knee, a pause by my inquisitor. My face was swollen, my midsection inflamed by poor hygiene.

Downstairs/upstairs, it was different. This time my interrogators seemed to be in a big hurry.

The woman was in charge, though I heard the boss grunt now and then. She began with a series of questions about Anna. I remembered reading that businessmen negotiate more fruitfully after women lap dance on them. A wrenching shock that followed a question about Anna's politics seemed to bond my tormenters. I sensed shared gratification across gender lines.

According to them, Anna is subverting the other RAISE conscripts at the day care center. The government wanted me to explain what she preaches. I insisted she takes deep selfish pleasure in helping people because her daughter died. I know she feels strongly about things and I know she votes, but she doesn't lecture anyone about anything, unless they're late. She was never one of the LES DIY's socialist loudmouths. (I knew she wouldn't approve of my telling that to the Feds.)

When pressed for detail, I must have registered enough ambivalence about her ideology to trigger the shock mechanism. Their machine was registering a libertarian's confusion at having fallen for a liberal.

Shockingly Awful—No Joke

Someone pulled me to my feet—a big guy, unfamiliar. Hands started messing with my crotch. I yelled, only to be pinned back in my chair, legs held apart. They were wiring my testicles. I was heading full force to <u>Abu Ghraib</u>. Next stop, <u>Bagram</u>?

Now they cranked up the power and the queries about Anna. I was shouting 'No" to everything they asked, then just bellowing.

They stopped. For some reason, this made things worse. I was writhing without stimulus, nerves firing chaotically, waiting for the next jolt.

"Is she a subversive?"

"No!" *ZAP.*

Again and again and again … until I lost it. "YESSSSSSSS," I screamed. But they didn't stop. "She is?" "YESSSSSSSSSSS!" "Are you sure?" "YES-SSSSSSSSSSSSSSS."

I was a screaming blur of pain, punctuated by precise jolts that linked my scrotum to my brain. My spine was a fiery passage to hell. I know I fouled myself, but we were all getting used to that.

A few times they emptied buckets of water on me. Refreshing.

Once I heard a door open. Someone examined my pulse and lifted my eyelids. Then a woman's voice asked if I would sign a document saying that Anna was a professional agitator who used the pandemic to spread social disorder, using me to undermine public confidence.

I wish I could say I refused. I can argue only that no one in his or her right mind would accept such nonsense as anything but what it is—the fruits of brutal torture. Then I remember that juries commonly convict suspects who have been interrogated by cops like the two detectives who had questioned and beaten me. These folks had more time and better toys.

I'm not sure what I did. How can I not remember? Did I sign that thing? Would that invite them to do this to Anna?

I don't recall being taken back to my cell.

I haven't told Anna about this yet. I couldn't. She was so glad to see me, so kind. She bathed me for hours, fed me soup and soft kisses while I sobbed into her instead of telling her.

I can't write.

Forgive me, Anna. *Please.*

It's all I want.

DAY 206

OUR PATIENT IS RESTING

I'm sorry to have to tell you he can't post today. Of course I forgave him. He's not even sure he did anything. If he did it wasn't him, but a man zapped out of his mind.

The torture is still going on, but he's doing it to himself. He breaks things and curses himself and wants to work all the time. He feels guilty about me, Sneeky, guys he met who are still stuck in jail, and people who paid to buy masks and whose money the government grabbed.

It's healthy to get it all off his chest, but he is exhausted and damaged and he needs to heal. One of the ex-doctors says Blogula needs to spend a month at the beach in a country with no flu and no cops.

We'd need a time machine for that, so I persuaded him to take the day off.

He's sleeping, which lasts about an hour at the most. I want to be there when he wakes up, so wish him well and I'll sign off.

Best, Anna

DAY 207

WHAT WAS MY CRIME?

I'm sorry about the delay. I was just dreaming the same thing anyway, so here goes.

I have no idea how long I sprawled amid strange growls and light flashes. Mosquitoes droned around my head as dogs barked, even howled. I was surrounded by ravenous bugs and canines. A talented and degenerate sound designer who should have been turning out great recordings had taken loads of tax dollars to drive me insane. Could it work?

By luck, I managed to shape the cacophony into a bizarre, looping rendition of the Yeah Yeah Yeahs' _The Sweets_ (from _Show Your Bones_—you can still buy music on this site!), transforming governmental growls and threats into Karen O's honeyed yowls as she demands in a cycle of violence and repetition to know what my crime is.

Good question! I should find out what they were formally charging me with. Admiring Hope-Simpson? Preferring Gene Clark to Gram Parsons? Loving Anna?

Awakened, strapped back, and hooked up without a hood, I tried to question people I couldn't see and was zapped for my pains. I was confronted with piles of papers about my life, which they had extensively data-mined. With the state privy to all our spoken and written thoughts in phone calls and emails, we might as well share our ideas and feelings with others we actually like, respect, care about: _Post away, people!_

They established that I'd telephoned members of the LES DIY, and Bart, and flu fatalities I loved, and my folks, and Mark, and UPS. My google query lists cracked them up—imagine the topics I've plugged into. I laughed, too, as they recited the searches that led me to toxoplasmosis, as well as blind googles I never wrote about, like plague sex. The climax came with the search that led to Hungarian researchers positing that ducks with small penises spread bird flu when they rape female ducks.

They asked me to quack and I did. I can't explain this, but it was comforting to feel like a pretty good duck. The machine liked it, too.

The glorious terrorism inquiry devolved into questions about whether or not I was licensed to sell masks and if I had lied to get my Health Security Certificate. Finally they accused me of tax evasion. Yeah, Al Capone here, banging away with sore fingers on a borrowed keyboard.

They tried to assume that, as a libertarian, I had refused to pay taxes. But you know me: I filed. And paid. No _zap_. You would think they'd have the records, right?

Just as I was thinking I'd get out of the session without too much damage, up stepped the woman who had been so cruel the previous session. Tall heels paced behind me. She started demanding I admit to vending bogus Tamiflu with Mark's strange friends. The machine backed me when I pointed out that I told my readers not to buy Tamiflu, even warned them against counterfeit antivirals, so she arranged to zap me directly. It was bad.

Eventually I fell apart again—cried, vomited, whatever. I was soaked in waste. You can't imagine what it's like to exist only as an object of abuse. I was drowning in high-tech bureaucratic brutality. No one decent knew where I was or had the power to find out. If I were to keel over and die, the government's well-paid corporate flunkies had plenty of ways to dispose of me. No need to sully a community garden.

I have no idea how long that went on—or what I said. If I did confess to anything, we may someday see footage of it on TV, or in a courtroom. Prosecutors would need deft CGI to cover all-too-obvious signs of abuse, but taxpayers have deep pockets, don't we?

I don't recall what they did to me after that. They may have drugged me. Or simply lost my attention. I came to in a patrol car, hoodless. The door was open. I smelled of soap. I was dressed in new jeans and a Coldplay t-shirt that I thankfully had never seen.

Some lawyer met me and encouraged me to sip water from a bathroom faucet. I blearily pleaded not guilty while I tried to note my experiences on a legal pad with shifting lines. A friend of Anna's turned up with my credit cards to cover one tenth of my $100,000 bail, which I'll never get back. I don't know what the lawyer cost me. I can't read her signature on my release order. I hope she calls to explain herself. *Who was she working for?*

I still have to pick up the mess here. Sneeky would have enjoyed it. When I used to chase him, he loved taking shelter on pieces of cardboard and plastic, thinking they'd protect him.

DAY 208

HOMELAND INSECURITY

Anna and I take turns reassuring one another, cycling between anxious hope and confirmed paranoia. I still haven't asked her what she thinks of what I said about her. She acts as if nothing matters but the present and future.

Perhaps to make me feel better about the words we find painted on our apartment door ("TRAITOR" and "PROFITEER" being two I can post), a homecoming present appeared today to brighten the wall in my suddenly spacious kitchen. Where boxes of personal protective gear once loomed, an extravagantly framed tapestry proclaims in red, white, and blue: *AMERICA — LOVE IT OR LEAVE IT!*

Anna won't say how or where she got my homecoming gift—only that she's happy her notorious "unemployed architect-blogger" is back.

Danged if my presence isn't her doing. Anna worked tirelessly to spring me, as you all knew before I did. I thank her and I thank those of you who stuck your necks out. *Home Sweet Homeland*!

Blogula's still not quite here, to be honest. I've been crawling through mind tunnels trying to recall and record everything that happened to me in that place. I feel empty and sick. Now that I've shared a lot of them, the memories are no longer any use to me. They're like rocks weighing me down in quicksand. I wish I could cut them loose, forget it all. Anna keeps saying that writing about it might help.

I hope no one gets angry with me for saying this, but I wonder if this is how women feel after they've been raped. I'm numb, walking heel-to-toe in the fog, trying to fulfill tasks, hoping no one can tell I have flaming holes in my brain and body and soul and heart. I've been rendered helpless and hopeless by unthinking hateful brutes. What makes me safe from them now?

It wasn't sexual, but I feel thoroughly violated, like someone penetrated my cerebral cortex with a toilet plunger. I feel like shit. I'm not sleeping.

I'm still here, writing. I miss my iMac, but I'm really grateful to the person who donated their plain old Mac. Even though I feel as if someone else is doing the typing, it's a start. I'm awed when a sentence turns out to make sense. The words link to form nice-sounding logic that might even be true. *Gee.*

The Shock Doctrine

I can read, although it triggers headaches. I've been locked into a book Anna gave me: Naomi Klein's *The Shock Doctrine*. It begins with torture and it pisses me off immensely, but it explains what happened to me.

Many of you will have heard about the CIA's experiments with <u>LSD</u> in the 1950s and '60s. In fact, the agency's <u>Project MK-Ultra</u> deployed a wide variety of drugs and non-pharmaceutical pressures in mind-control experiments that traumatized, even killed, an unknown number of Americans. One likely effect was the violent eco-oriented career of <u>Unabomber Ted Kaczynski</u>, who participated in <u>MK-ULTRA experiments</u> for three years while a student at Harvard.

Some of the nastiest known work was conducted for seven years in the <u>Allen Memorial Institute</u>, a Montreal mental hospital, by <u>Donald Ewen Cameron</u>, a former president of the World Psychiatric Association and the American and Canadian psychiatric associations. As Klein details very well in *Shock Doctrine* (buy it on this site), Cameron used an intense array of legal drugs, environmental controls, electroshock treatment (<u>ECT</u>) brainwashing tapes, and LSD on patients who weren't necessarily so troubled when they entered his office, but who fared very badly later on in life.

Why would a psychiatrist who had served at the <u>Nuremberg Medical Tribunal</u> that sentenced German doctors to death for having conducted Nazi experiments on prisoners do these things? Apart from hating communism, Cameron wanted to prove the <u>'psychic driving theory'</u> he had pioneered, whereby you could blow someone's mind to bits with drugs and shocks and then play audiotapes to condition a new him or her. None of his patients knew what they were getting into.

Cameron, Klein writes, focused on "regression, the idea that by depriving people of their sense of who they are and where they are in time and space, adults can be converted into dependent children whose minds are a blank slate of suggestibility."

I *quacked* for those freelance Fed torturers. I liked making them laugh under their hoods. It felt really good for a moment.

What if Anna hadn't gotten me out of that place?

I'll cut to the chase. The CIA's MK-ULTRA experiments surfaced in a tide of government scandals in the 1970s. The CIA claimed involuntary drugging and torture were the doings of 'rogue agents' who had achieved nothing of value. Ho hum. I mean, why would any government ever want to turn dissenting adults into frail, trembling children?

Then something called the <u>KUBARK Manual</u> surfaced in the 1990s. (KUBARK is the <u>CIA's cryptonym</u> for its own headquarters.) A series of CIA documents that began in 1963, the KUBARK Manual (read the entire text <u>here</u>) is the spy agency's evolving blueprint for torturing people. It's full of stuff Dr. Cameron did. It describes what the U.S. government trained Latin American military units to do to civilians in the 1970s, '80s, and '90s. And what our government did to people it seized in the post 9/11 Middle Eastern conflicts: <u>brutally administer drugs</u> at Guantanamo and <u>abuse prisoners</u> at Abu Ghraib. (Some people probably shouldn't look at these <u>photos from Abu Ghraib</u>—nudity being the least problem).

A word about forced nakedness: It's a way of breaking down a prisoner's character, cracking his or her psychological integrity. Nakedness has been a significant feature of torture since the CIA revived it. *If they know everything, we are nothing.*

Sometimes I just want to sit in the bathroom, alone. I come out when Anna needs to use it. I write better in there.

I have to stop. I feel sick that I didn't complain when this was happening to far-off Iraqis. Now would be a very good time for us all to speak up. It's never too late.

Is it?

DAY 209

CAPITALIZING ON CRISIS

Anna is being very nice to me, even though she wishes I'd slow down on the blogging. How can she say that? It's how we met. I wonder if she's tired of trying to take care of me. Am I too needy?

She says I should take a day off to celebrate that we've both conquered H5N1. What's a bunch of well-funded thugs compared to history's fiercest flu?

I still don't know why they tortured me, or why they broke up the LES DIY. Naomi Klein says that for decades the U.S. government and the private sector have used great shocks to break popular resistance to radical economic and political measures. *Shock Doctrine* is a compelling catalogue of disasters that turned out to be very profitable, from foreign military coups to Hurricane Katrina, the 2004 tsunami, and the Pentagon's 'Shock & Awe' assault on Baghdad.

We should all be able to agree that there's nothing wrong with trying to make money by offering solutions to things that have gone wrong. I did that with my masks. Klein shows how some capitalists cheat by fostering chaos and catastrophe so they can boost profits.

The same companies turn up each time everything goes wrong. They're like inept yakuza in a Japanese gangster comedy with a happy ending: They make lots of money making things worse.

I'm scared. Has a flu pandemic coughed up so much fear and failure that these clowns can get away with junking American democracy? Voters don't seem to care. (Disclosure: I've never voted.)

The worse things get under this government, the more power Americans surrender to it.

Klein makes a big deal about contractors performing vital government functions. She sees the state as an indispensable utility that is being hollowed out by corporate worms that are accountable only to those who own shares in them. The courts aren't saying much about any of this.

Unlike Klein, I've always been suspicious of the state. I should be heartened that the guy who zapped me with a (very expensive) penis prod works in the private sector and not for the government. But who cuts his checks? I bet I've got a penny of personal tax payments buried somewhere in his yard.

I cheered privatization for many years. Now its agents deride me as an immoral profiteer for selling a few masks while they scoop up big bucks replacing government services and busting unions. Some relentless, faceless process has begun to devour the rest of my life. I'll never understand why my existence even matters to them. Do they hate me because I believed the things they were saying?

The good news: Anna has found a criminal lawyer who says I'll be okay. He predicted today that the furor would subside by the time the case reaches prosecution. "People will want to forget all about the pandemic and the sh*t that happened. No jury's gonna want to hear your case, let alone punish you for nothing. Or for something the state has to admit never harmed anyone."

The word *jury* sounds so old-fashioned.

But he was confident that the country's, um, systemic problems will settle down. "You're like the Japanese Americans who got robbed and locked up during World War II," he told me. "Our country apologized after 50 years of embarrassing debate. You they'll prefer to forget faster."

Of course I've retained the man. Picture a cynical postwar Jimmy Stewart (with a heart of gold) doing the right thing for the little guy. He bows to the judge, tips his hat to Lady Justice, helps her get the blindfold back on. Then he skewers the assistant district attorney in *Mr. Smith Saves Count Blogula...*.

He cracked up when I said I needed to file a crime report about the masks, gloves, and goggles the cops stole. Once I explained that my insured loss is momentous—it can ruin me—he heartily agreed. He even offered to accompany me to the precinct.

If I could find Sneeky, I'd feel okay. A vision when I was sleeping spurred me to look in at Liz Christy Gardens, but I didn't see any cats. Not even the regulars. I can't believe none of my neighbors tried to help Sneeky. They have no eyes when I see them in the hallway or on the sidewalk. They sure do write stuff about me.

DAY 210

POLICE & THIEVES

No one talks to old Blogula in the 'hood. My block feels like part of the shadowy, sensitive world of *The Curfew*, Jesse Ball's fanciful novel about a kind of political plague that has stripped society of music, mobility, freedom. (Delighted to be selling it here!)

Every morning someone posts a death threat on my building's front door. Even some of my supporters have caught buyer's remorse since the Feds leaked some of the things I admitted to under torture. Fitch won't talk to me since the Feds, armed with my quotes, broke in and took away all his devices and what remained of our inventory. He's been charged with conspiracy to do things that would make you laugh.

Some American readers write to say they'd happily improve on my captors' methods. Europeans and Canadians are more sympathetic to me, though many favor the globalizing crackdown on dissent—as long as it doesn't happen to people they like. I guess that defines a liberal these days.

An older New Yorker emailed to tell me about how in the 1950s and '60s and '70s, you would encounter people with tattoos on their arms—Nazi concentration camp survivors. They'd seen the worst things imaginable, had survived as their loved ones were ground up, gassed, cooked. "Some Holocaust survivors were the loveliest folks you could meet. They were oddly gentle and happy," she wrote. "I've never understood how, but you should find out. Maybe "living well *is* the best revenge."

A couple of my countrymen (and women) call my report from Fed World illegal because I discussed interrogation techniques that are innately classified. They couldn't be *illegal* because our government cannot torture anyone. I get what they're saying: My lawyer isn't allowed to discuss the state's inquisition techniques in court. I'm glad I read *Catch-22* when it still seemed funny.

Others say I'm deluded. No such machine has ever existed; a lie detector must have malfunctioned. (*For days?*) Not to worry, anyway: Such results are still inadmissible in court (unless you're accused of terrorism; coerced evidence is admissible at Gitmo). Will the courts play a meaningful role in my case? So far they haven't.

I filed a burglary report. In the precinct house lobby, I saw one of those newfangled Internet surveillance posters. The government asks citizens to spot and forward "disruptive" emails and website URLs to a central Internet site for vetting by certified experts on influenza and journalism: *Panic is like a virus – FIGHT FEAR – Call or Click 1-800....* (Look up the number yourself if you want it so badly.)

Upstairs, one of the detectives who shredded my life was doing paperwork. He inclined his ears to hear me recite the events to one of his colleagues. I dropped my voice to a virtual undertone.

When I spotted him angling to read my lips, I surprised both of us by winking at him. The things you learn in prison.

I kept the details as bland as possible. I made no accusations. Sure, my home contained officers of the law when I last saw my inventory. The place was stuffed to the ceiling with masks and gloves and goggles, exactly like the ones those detectives are wearing. The boxes looked just like that one in the corner. *Just the facts* that ought to help them identify any perps they might encounter....

The detective focused on the fact that my neighbors knew my apartment was full of gear. I haven't seen any of them wearing my masks. They all look like ghosts.

How could I remain so calm? I avoided thinking of Sneeky.

DAY 211

SEE ME, HEAR ME, FEAR ME

My tour of local lockups showed me that America has a new social division. There are two kinds of people—those who have endured the flu and the ones who haven't caught it yet.

It was easy to spot flu virgins in prison. They were scared witless. They preferred not to breathe, avoided contact, barely looked around. Some were quietly preparing to die, praying in corners, trembling.

I empathized with their vulnerability because I fear the resistant strain of TB. But I was already a flu survivor. Unless someone pounded them out of me, I wasn't going to spit bloody bits of lung on the floor.

A burgeoning population no longer feels so endangered, at least from bird flu. You can sense this in the street. I saw a man collapse on the sidewalk today and people barely reacted, as if he were an old-time sloppy drunk. Sure I called 911—which answered from somewhere far away, but quickly. They should make phone contractors sing *East Side, West Side* till they know the difference.

The president appealed to the nation again. In cautious words I'd once have welcomed—but I now suspect may be exaggerated to justify ever-expansive powers—the voice of the state gave no sign that the flu has effectively wound down. Top gun says no effort will be spared to protect us (*from me?*), and that vaccine cometh to those who wait. Our vigorous young attorney general made a meatier statement, vowing war on criminals, illegal immigrants, anyone who spreads filth and lies to undermine our resolve.

I see more stories about terrorism than influenza. As long as we continue to dread one another and follow orders, it's all the same. *See me, hear me, fear me.*

I have no opinion on the current conspiracy theory that the vaccine release has been delayed to maintain the crisis at a boil. Nothing about that process makes sense to me.

Did I mention that my Irish pal has been detained and is presumably being deported? I'm told they ransacked his (and Lisa's) apartment for digital photographic storage media. His stash of protective gear has, of course, vanished. He had a Green Card. I'm sorry to have infected him with my special sociopolitical disease. I meant well.

There went the reserve of masks and gloves and goggles I had given him and Lisa.

This Cell Is Your Cell

Don't bother sending me quotes, links, and pastes from the Feds' study showing that 81% of the people they acknowledge having incarcerated in Houston will face criminal charges. I face plenty of charges myself. None have to do with public safety.

I suggest you all look in the mirror and ask which possessions and papers could get you busted. Long before the bug struck, this country boasted 5% of the world's population and more than 23% of its prisoners. More than one in every 100 adult Americans was in jail. Those figures must be really arresting now.

How many nations responded to the pandemic by locking up so many potential victims?

Not that they don't want to send this accused felon on vital missions to RAISE whatever they want. I'm being conscripted!

When did they take and test my blood sample to confirm I'd had the flu, you ask? *Good question.* They had certain opportunities. My work call starts next week.

Anna is feeling poorly. It's been raining a lot and she is exposed every day to myriad children's ailments. Without a mask. They give the conscripts color-coded caps and t-shirts, with armbands for the trusties—I mean supervisors.

My turn to take care of her. *Teatime, my sweet!*

DAY 212

ANNA IS SICK!

Anna is in bad shape. She's running a high fever and coughing like hell. It looks like influenza. She won't consider it.

Has a new strain evolved? Are we going to go through this again?

I've called the doctors who used to help the LES DIY, but none of them pick up or call back. Maybe they're *tied up.*

I telephoned Mark's friends—hoping and presuming they haven't been reading this thing—to see if they can get me some genuine Relenza. I didn't mention that they owe me for having sullied my name and computer with their (alleged) schemes. The group leader said Mark joined a new crowd.

Then came a promising torrent of slick doubletalk.

I had to tell him I'd kill anyone who furnished bogus pharmaceuticals to the woman I love. He seemed to admire my attitude. Here's hoping.

DAY 213

DEPARTMENT OF HEALTH SECURITY?

Anna slipped off to work while I slept. The rules for calling in sick are so convoluted that it's wiser for flu conscripts to show up ill. "If they send you home," she said last night, "it's on them, not you."

Judging from the mess I found in the kitchen, she wasn't feeling better.

I'm still tidying the papers the police scattered, recreating my files as best I can. Some of the documents belong to Anna, who brought them here after the 7th Precinct tossed her apartment. The rampaging 9th mixed our papers pretty badly.

So I squat every day in a sunbeam, where Sneeky should be soaking up Vitamin D. I sort documents into stacks he would have delighted in scattering.

Today I found the death certificate of Anna's little girl, whom I knew to have died of flu in Round One, when they both caught it. It said she was three years old and she died at home, in their apartment near the Manhattan Bridge. Of a *ruptured appendix.*

I don't know what this means. I looked up the <u>symptoms</u>. They're a lot like flu—vomiting, stomach pain, fever, loss of appetite. (Read Carl Zimmer's <u>'Riddle of the Appendix.'</u>) But it wasn't flu.

I tried to call Anna at work, though it's forbidden. No answer. I'll wait.

I called the New York City Department Of Health & Mental Hygiene to ask what specific test they perform on conscripts before they force them to work closely with potential flu carriers. Presumably it was a <u>microneutralization assay</u> that would show antibodies from previous H5N1 exposure. It seemed wise to ask. I was told to expect a callback.

The call came from a different agency. A woman wanted to know why I was asking. I explained. She said she wasn't authorized to address medical issues. When I called back the number her call left on my caller ID, I reached the Department of Homeland Security.

DAY 213 (#2)

A NEW FLU STRAIN?

Anna called me while she waited for the bus that brings her back to this neighborhood from work. They now confiscate conscripts' cell phones while they're on duty. (Do they load them with <u>surveillance apps</u>?) She took a nap instead of eating lunch, so she never got my messages till now.

She sounded woozy, which diminished the fury with which she greeted my question about her daughter's death certificate. I assured her that I was merely sorting out our papers, not attempting to snoop into hers.

Anna said she'd never claimed her daughter died directly from bird flu. The girl was a collateral casualty who had come down with appendicitis, unusual in kids under 6. The city was in the first blush of pandemic panic and no ambulance was available. Nor were taxis.

Anna had carried her daughter to a hospital just south of City Hall in the financial district, but found only people stretched on the floor inside some locked doors. The place was sealed. As she pleaded for entry, a masked patient pointed to a sign that directed visitors to a bigger hospital north of the East Village, almost two miles away. Then the woman pointed to her chest and to the other patients on the floor and made a throat-cutting motion.

An old Chinese man who didn't speak English led her to a shop in Chinatown, where he obtained some herbs for the child. He helped her home. By then she was herself gasping, hot-headed.

The little girl died horribly at home that night, when her appendix burst. Enough said.

Anna immediately came down with something she still thinks was the flu. She was feverish, achy, congested, lying for days in the apartment with her daughter's corpse. She would dream her baby had recovered, sleepwalk to her, and break down all over again.

Recounting the horror made Anna cry so intensely I started dressing to fetch her. I could hear her getting sicker as she sobbed and gasped. Her voice failed as she climbed aboard the bus.

I didn't say this to her, but I'm scared she's caught a new strain. I'm trying to get that Relenza while I wait for her to get home.

DAY 213 (#3)

A CASE FOR BRANDEIS

Anna just called to say she's being dropped at a big high school where they examine and treat flu victims. She got the name out before they shut off her cell phone. She hasn't called back.

I've heard of the place, but I had to google to find out where and what it is.

Not many of New York's high schools can boast that Edgar Allan Poe is thought to have penned *The Raven* on the corner. Founded as the High School of Commerce in 1902 and renamed for America's first Jewish Supreme Court Justice, Louis D. Brandeis High School's most famous alumnus is Lou Gehrig, the New York Yankees' *Iron Man*, whose death was so memorable that they named the disease after him.

Not a good omen for my *Iron Angel*.

On the other hand, Louis Brandeis (1856-1941) was a magnificent libertarian! He opposed central economic planning, favored individual rights. In 1890 Brandeis began constructing the legal theory for a Constitutional right that we still can't take for granted. In 1928, as a Supreme Court Justice, Brandeis spoke of an American "right of privacy" in a dissent that became law 39 years later, when the Court overturned an earlier ruling he had opposed.

"The greatest dangers to liberty," he wrote then, "lurk in insidious encroachment by men of zeal, well-meaning but without understanding."

Why am I googling and posting? I'm waiting to see if the Relenza shows up. Anna needs it *instantly.*

In 1918 flu patients were warehoused in public buildings, too. They served as rooms with food and water. There was no significant medical equipment, no care beyond that which victims with kin might have found at home. They were places in which to die.

I will not let that happen to Anna.

Here are some choice Brandeis quotes while I chew my fingers and wait to see if the guy I'm waiting for has any honor.

"Experience teaches us to be most on our guard to protect liberty when the government's purposes are beneficent."

"Crime is contagious. If the government becomes a lawbreaker, it breeds contempt for law; it invites every man to become a law unto himself; it invites anarchy."

There's even one for Hope-Simpson fans: "*Publicity is justly commended as a remedy for social and industrial diseases. Sunlight is said to be the best of disinfectants; electric light the most efficient policeman.*"

How much natural wisdom have we forgotten? In this age of triple antibiotic ointment, how many people suspect that sunlight is a disinfectant? Turns out it's <u>true</u> (as this evangelical Christian Web page about sunlight's wonders explains so eloquently).

DAY 213 (#4)

EUREKA!

My world hasn't run out of miracles.

The powder and Diskhalers look good. A handshake and a square look still count with me. *They have to.*

DAY 214

SCHOOL'S OUT FOREVER

Thanks for your better wishes. There were even some kind words from folks who had called me a rotten traitor.

I'm lying low. I have finally and definitively transgressed, added to my list of 'crimes.' My activities remain relatively victimless, though the latest was a little tricky.

Having obtained the Relenza that made risks worth taking, I went to Brandeis High School with a box that contained a few masks I was able to gather. I bet everything on double zero. I feel certain that ol' Justice Brandeis would have looked the other way.

First I arranged for a getaway car and a driver to get us to it. Then I labeled the box of masks with a phony purchase order from *A. Rand MD.* Next I convinced a National Guard with a southern accent and a fuzzy improvised mask that smelled of lemon detergent that I was delivering emergency medical gear to a doctor at the school. He was standing at the gates of a surprisingly modern building that must have replaced the original school.

An edgy moment came when he asked if I was sure there was a doctor on duty. *Are these places untended by physicians?* I reached into the box and handed him a proper mask, which he appreciated.

No one bothered me once I got upstairs. The second floor was stuffy and smelled awful, as if the world's biggest septic system had erupted like Vesuvius. The classrooms were packed with people on metal cots moaning softly, hopelessly—a symphony of death paced by wheezing and rattling lungs and occasional grunts and moans. The sturdiest souls blinked at me as I scanned for Anna.

If I'd been wearing black and carrying a scythe, I doubt they would have stirred.

The attendants were draftees in lime green t-shirts and caps with RAISE logos. They wore soggy paper masks that couldn't remotely suppress the stench of death, urine, vomit, and crap. They were supervised by nurses in white paper masks that smartly matched their uniforms. One seemed particularly fatigued as she patiently taught a clueless rookie how to keep patients hydrated. Her legs were unsteady as she rambled on.

I give them all credit for trying. No one was disregarding the plentiful misery. The staff lacked tools to do anything substantive. There was very little equipment, no ventilators or monitors.

Anna was in the corner of a big classroom at the end of the floor, sweating under a big display about French verbs. *J'irais*, it said, right over her head, which looked prettier and smaller than anyone else's. *I would go.* And that's what we did.

I dressed Anna under the covers. She didn't recognize me. She looked so vulnerable. Her face was flushed, lips dry and cracked. She was dying.

I heard a death reported in the hallway, the voice of a conscript reverberating with fear. A radio crackled as someone called for a truck. For once I hoped it wouldn't come soon.

I could feel Anna's fever through my jacket when I lifted her. How could she already have lost so much weight? It was awkward carrying her and the box, but the masks were too valuable to leave behind.

A pair of draftees approached to ask what I was doing. I hadn't thought of anything clever, so I explained I was taking my wife home. Evidently this entails visits to various city agencies for authorization.

The Challenge of Authority

I promised a doctor would see her, kept moving. They looked at each other, speechless.

Then I heard the voice of authority, barking that I wasn't taking the patient anywhere. This nurse was like a nun I once knew, a short-fused guardian of order named Sister Valencia. There could be no appeal to reason or emotion.

I secured Anna over my left shoulder and rammed my hand into the box so I could wield it like a cardboard club. I raced away from quickening exclamations into a stairwell that would drop us near an exit on the ground floor.

Downstairs, the nurse was already aiming a soldier our way. The exit was locked, a violation of the fire code. We were trapped.

Calmly, I strode toward the Guard. He held his M16 ready while I explained that I needed to take my wife home *now*, that I had medication and a doctor awaiting her. I could see this made sense to him. He was a southerner and it's what he'd want to do if his wife were filed away to die alone in a big, smelly brick schoolhouse.

He radioed for his sergeant. *There were at least three Guards on duty.*

He looked away when he started describing my situation. He felt guilty.

I moved by instinct. I think I bent to slide Anna onto the floor and then rose up under his weapon and into his belly. He was bigger than me, so he had more wind to lose. I ducked and hurled my shoulder into him again. I was celebrated as a gritty tackle in high school, making up in focused dementia what I lacked in brawn. I may have slammed him three times. He fell hard, his weapon clattering on the floor.

Shouts and bootsteps followed as I hoisted Anna and burst through the front door, past the first southerner. "She's *mah* wife," I yelled. "We're from *Missoura!*"

As we passed the gate and reached the curb, I heard more than one click as Guards cocked their weapons. I could only run eastward, hoping they'd pause at the thought of shooting an unconscious patient.

A car screeched between the M16s and us, as if to ask me for directions. A chorus of curses erupted as I leapt into the back seat with Anna in my arms like a broken doll. I heard a shot as we screeched around the corner, down Columbus Avenue.

I can say that Anna is resting in a safe place. She still hasn't spoken and has issued some blood. She can't be moved.

Wish us well. I'll do my best to keep you posted.

DAY 215-218

FREE—FOR A NIGHT

I guess I can say where I've been. I wish I could say where I'm going. If only I knew.

Vitamin D or Bust? Nothing else has worked.

Using a vehicle whose provenance I can't detail, I drove to the bungalow I'd rented upstate. I had equipped it with everything a person would need to survive three months of pandemic. Bags of cat food, too. I feared the place would have been ransacked, but the locals hadn't touched it.

I parked the vehicle in the corner of some woods in the back and covered it with loose limbs and leaves. By then the heat was up and I could carry Anna inside. She seemed to think it was a rented ski shack. It was a poignant way to find out she enjoys skiing.

I hung blackout fabric over the windows so no one would detect our presence. Then I cooked up a pot of steaming soup—chicken noodle from cans and bottled spices.

For the first time in months, I felt fully free, alive. There was no authority in sight, just four walls of cheap paneling. Only nature lay outside, harboring nothing against us flu victims but a stiff autumnal chill.

That night I clutched Anna's hot little body like a thermal pillow. Her sick sweat tasted better than Irish whiskey. But she remained insensate under the damp cooling cloths I applied. I didn't sleep for fear she'd pass away in my arms.

Eighteen hours later Anna was still very weak, but we managed some conversation. I explained where we were, who had helped us, and where we were going. She said my soups needed seasoning, a very good sign.

A Process of Communication

Anna said she knew it would come to this. I was slow to understand. She drank more soup. Her face glistened, eyes bright. She was coming back.

Eventually Anna was strong enough to explain that she'd always known she'd wind up in my hands. When she was badgering my blog, mocking my reverence for Ayn Rand, dissing my heartache over Nina, it wasn't a game so much as *a process of communication*, she said.

I had to learn what was *important*, whatever that means. (I do think I know what's important, for sure.)

Anna giggled faintly at how she'd set her account to block my emails so I could only respond publicly. She rolled her puffy eyes at how dreary I had been at Ric's reopening—until I started smoking weed and making out with the young med student I mistook for my stalker.

Ric had blessed Anna's strategy as the most promising way to crack my *"thick shell of self-importance."* Some friend, eh? *The best.*

She kissed me as hard as she could, wetting her lips with mine. I could feel her little body straining. I was happier than I've ever been, no exaggeration.

Then the door rattled, *hard.*

Pounding followed. A gruff voice vowed to blow the lock off if I didn't open up.

I hid Anna's soup bowl and covered her with the bloody blanket that had kept her warm during the drive up. Then I unlatched the door to find the man who had rented me the bungalow.

The landlord was pointing a shotgun at my chest. He didn't recognize me, but he was wearing one of the masks I'd given him. Goggles, too. And work gloves.

I told him I was glad my gear had kept him safe, asked him if he needed to see my rental agreement. He nodded, escorted me inside at gunpoint.

He stopped dead when he saw Anna, pale and motionless under that red-splattered blanket.

I asked if any friends or anyone at all had come to look for me. (*Could the Feds have overlooked this place?*) He grunted negatively and left.

I packed as fast as I could. There was a lot of protective gear and food and rice milk. I filled plastic jugs with reverse osmosis water I'd been processing since we arrived. And I dug up two safety cans of gasoline I had buried in the yard months earlier. I'm driving a guzzler.

It was far too early and extremely risky to move Anna, but we were gone in 90 minutes.

The last words I heard from her since then came just after midnight, long ago. I think I have enough gas to get her to rich sun before it's too late. It's a long way. Keep wishing us well, please.

DAY 219-20

MY BURNING TIRE

I drive very slowly and I think. The highways sing the Yeah Yeah Yeahs' _Warrior_ at me, about fleeing on a hostile road, frightened and discouraged, filled with fierce longing.

When you're on the run, your soul is singed, tender, needy—and ferocious. Like it's on fire. Like a burning tire.

It seems to me that in ordinary life, there are plenty of times when you begin to feel your spirit acutely. But there are other souls all around, bumping into yours, deadening it.

When you find yourself alone—exposed to the dangerous whims of man and nature—your spirit breaks out of the past. You need love more nakedly than you ever did.

The old substitutes could never cut it. Attention, admiration, and envy won't satisfy. Lust is empty. The ways love always scared you back into your hole—all the botched expectations and fear of disappointing—don't matter at all.

I would kill to save Anna. Post it on my tomb if it comes to that.

DAY 221

AND ANOTHER DREAM....

I've done my best to hydrate Anna, but she's flagging.

I can barely keep my eyes open, but I can't trust a motel not to report us. I don't feel secure enough to pull over for coffee. The only reliable way to wake up is for me to spot a police car—they charge my heart like an electric prod.

I must be going through digital withdrawal. I think of all the emails and photos and movies that pass through me as I drive through rivers of Wi-Fi. They talk to me.

And I picture John Galt & the Gang in _Atlas Shrugged_, fearlessly fending off pointy-headed bureaucrats as I contemplate all the corporations that are trying to track me for the Feds. (Nothing personal, of course.)

I dread to think what Ayn Rand would have thought of Halliburton—or any of the companies that foster and feed off big government today. (She'd have rejoiced in the freakish primacy of Steve Jobs—a passing exception that proved the rule.)

I realize now that big bureaucracies of any kind are the problem. Any organizational threshing machine is a menace, whether it's public or private. They all spy on us, despise us, atomize us.

What would Ayn Rand say today about her failure? Her acolyte Alan Greenspan turned the Federal Reserve into a private investment pump. The business world is run by men she would have despised. Their enterprises feed off a state whose overseers take orders from CEOs. It's a merger made in hell, corporatism without obvious ranting villains like Hitler and Mussolini.

Ayn Rand: Used & Abused

Ayn Rand would see that her life's work has been abused, that she's become a seductive fig leaf for corporatism. Her mystique, born of a hunger to escape and counter Russian Leninism, has become the face of a fraud: We fantasize about limitless freedom as we descend into the depressing reality of an authoritarianism born of the unholy union of government and monolithic 'free enterprise' that strangles competition.

Libertarians have been hoodwinked by Rand's glorious entrepreneurial romanticism into accepting a tsunami of armed corporatism that drowns us in surveillance and control.

This is worse than any virus. It would break Rand's passionate heart. Wake up!

I just passed some big grinning pumpkins. I think I'm late, but: Happy Halloween, friends.

DAY 222-225

STAY WELL & FREE

I'll post when it's safer.
Stay well & free.

ACCESS TO THE SITE WAS DISABLED A WEEK LATER.

POSTSCRIPT

HOW WE FLEW THE COOP

Now I'm supposed to present a climactic yarn about my heroic escape from the virulent clutches of the cytokine stormtroopers. I'll disappoint my publisher by sticking to the facts.

I was never heroic. The heroes are the people who stayed and fought for freedom as hard as they fought the flu. I ran.

I'm still running.

Nor was my first escape as exciting as reports would have it. How to convey the thrills of unending smelly claustrophobia?

We couldn't leave the car. Anna was sick and we were on the run in Upstate New York, surrounded by a government gone mad on the limitless power it drew from its failures.

Day after day, I gorged on granola and dried fruit, peeing into rice milk containers like an environmentalist trucker, grabbing naps in swamps and post-industrial wastelands while she kept watch. I was a Boy Scout on the run, all my pandemic prep reduced to bleary panic.

I had tried so hard to be a good New Yorker, to body surf this crashing wave of natural history, and then to rise up through the human chaos that ensued. To triumph, American-style.

I wound up as another black-and-white movie gangster squinting into the early light for patrol cars, hallucinating mugs of fresh coffee and starting to mutter prayers I thought I'd forgotten.

You should know that the final blog entries were a fraud. I used my posts to confuse the Feds as to our whereabouts. I apologize (yet again) to my loyal readers for using you, but the stakes were sharp and high. I'm not really *sorry*, but I apologize. I meant well.

A lot of people started following the chase online. Other bloggers discussed it. We were unofficial news. A Blogula support committee sprang up in the Netherlands.

Then, nothing: *Niets*.

I never intended to leave everyone hanging. I endangered some wonderful friends routing two further entries through a maze of emails and bulletin boards to be posted by someone who was living in a country immune to Washington's charms. The posts would have reassured my readers that we had made it to wherever we were going.

The Feds didn't want to read that, let alone see you reading it. They shut down my blog.

Naming No Names

Here, then, is an expurgated version of how we flew the coop. I have to skip over details that might give away the identities and methods of folks who helped us. The Feds remain hungry to know them. In trying to negotiate my return to the U.S., I have refused to implicate anyone. I'd rather spend the rest of my years underground—die in obscurity as the world's longest-running *flugitive*—than betray anyone who helped. Some kind souls barely knew us.

Okay: Back in my apartment, with Anna consigned to die in Brandeis High School, I spent hours planning and assembling the elements of our flight. These included what I hoped was genuine Relenza; phony identification; a laptop; an old car (it was no gas guzzler, another lie); road maps; and backup supplies in case the bungalow was inhospitable.

Not least, I needed a gutsy accomplice to spirit us away from the high school in a borrowed car with artfully obscured plates. We drove directly upstate in the car I'd obtained while that noble soul piggybacked on someone else's friend's neighbor's wireless account to post the decoy blog item about us resting overnight in New York.

I owe that brave spirit two lives every day. I've determined that he was locked up for helping us, and that he died of H5N1 in jail a month later. So I can thank 'Bruno,' the finest punk who ever lived and drummed and died struggling for a better world. He'd have made a great brother. Briefly, he *did*.

When our respite at the bungalow ended, I drove hundreds of miles out of our way while Anna relapsed. I accessed a stranger's wireless modem near the cooling towers of Three Mile Island in south-central Pennsylvania to post the account of our latest flight. I wanted the Feds to think we were chasing the sun—and Vitamin D—southward, toward my home state of Missouri. Or perhaps Mexico.

Around now I wish to apologize to anyone whose door may have gotten kicked in as a result of one of the wireless-tapping exploits involved in my escape. I'm truly sorry. If they ever legalize me, I'll honor bills for the repairs.

A day later, Anna was still weak. The car was stuffy with perspiration amid the high heat I needed to maintain for her. I remember hearing radio announcements saying that certain people under 40 could start turning up at selected hospitals for vaccination, *so long as they had proper ID.* No illegal immigrants or dissidents on the run. It was like being barred from celebrating Thanksgiving.

I found it tough to stay alert on the back roads and we had a long way to go to reach a place the Feds would expect me to shun because of my libertarian leanings: *Canada.* I'd begun to look into fleeing northward as soon as I emerged from that glowing box at DHS. To paraphrase Dylan, I didn't need a weatherman to know which way the wind was blowing out of DC.

Exhausted and impatient, I took a chance and veered onto the New York State Thruway, America's longest interstate highway. I made great time for a while. Anna and I spoke eagerly about our prospects up north; being with her made me feel that anything was possible, even something *good.* When she fell asleep, I was happy to see her resting like a kid—tired of the road, hoping we'd be *there* when she woke up.

Instead I woke up in the worst way—with a siren in my ears, flashing lights in my mirror, and a wheel in my hands. I wasn't so much speeding as drifting drowsily from lane to lane ahead of a state trooper who was shocking some respect into me.

CytoKind Trooper

Anna didn't wake up as I pulled over, a good thing. I needed to play the old bloody blanket trick, and her lolling head, greasy hair, and shiny chin helped it look convincing. I slipped a soiled paper mask onto my face. I'd kept it under my chin for fill-ups.

I handed a tall, gray-haired, Hollywood-looking cop my forged papers and humbly apologized for having nodded off at the wheel. I explained with tired desperation and cottony tongue that my wife was sick with flu. I was taking her to a hospital in Buffalo I'd heard was treating folks. I hoped he wouldn't ask where such a place might be, that he'd withdraw in horror and leave us to our fates. We must have smelled like death on wheels.

A rustle caused us both to turn to my passenger. Behind her seatbelt, Anna had slipped so that her head lolled forward, tongue drooping. It was disgusting and completely unnecessary. Genuinely alarmed, I turned to the cop.

He stunned me with a compassionate look and the news that we'd be welcome at a hospital less than 15 miles away. He offered to call for an ambulance or at least a car to get us there, but I pleaded to be allowed to drive there, keep our things intact. He pulled out a cell phone and notified the hospital that we'd be arriving, then wrote directions for me. He even followed us to the toll turnoff to make sure I was capable of driving safely. We exchanged honks as I turned to exit. The last American cop I met was the best—no kind of stormtrooper. (I hoped he'd never find out who we were, lest he regret being so generous, though I doubt he'd mind so much by now.)

I worried that the officer would report us when we failed to show up at the hospital. Soon I was sneaking into farmyards to look for active license plates I could attach to our car. I snatched some from a sedan mounted on blocks. Twenty-four hours later, Anna was rebounding as we hid with some people I'd been told could smuggle us over the border.

That night, I arranged for a friend to post something via a wireless hit somewhere around Missouri. The next day's entry was similarly jacked up nearby, maybe in Arkansas.

The last post was a farewell tip of the mask to DHS, whose FEMA had done so little to save New Orleans. I had reckoned back in New York that the Feds would get a kick from a doomed whimper out of the Crescent City.

I wish I could explain how we got into Canada, where everyone from everywhere had been vaccinated by then. Our immigration combined the creative and the traditional, was even a little funny. It took a while. I can say that Gene Clark's *Strength Of Strings*—a rolling throbbing soaring heartbeat of a song—filled my brain at the key crossing juncture with yearning for a new life as I overheard a wary Canadian voice turn pleasant and inviting.

We wound up settling in a hillside community, a semi-abandoned mining town that could use more Vitamin D. Land was bountiful. The people were pleasant and tolerant. I wound up designing stuff in the DIY mode they favor.

I pretended I was gleaning know-how off the Web. It was fascinating having to reinvent the wheel, justify things I'd learned in architecture school. I built a few structures, even a boat. I helped rig water-recycling schemes and I customized energy systems to liberate folks from the grid.

Familiarity Breeds Content

When you're living underground, you avoid questions. Some you answer before people can pose them. Others you gradually finesse by turning yourself into local furniture. Your neighbors whisper comfortable myths about your past. Over time you want to be like that 'new' chair Aunt Mabel got long ago.

Canadians made it easy for us. They're too polite to pry. They respect strangers till you give them reason not to. It still hurts that I lied to them. I had to pass on some promising friendships.

To avoid generating attention, I also had to learn not to argue, never to express controversial opinions. When I speak English, I still want to close sentences with that self-deprecating Canadian *eh*.

Anna and I developed the gift of debating in whispers, or eyebrow code when silence was essential. She always preferred telepathic discourse anyway. Anna never lost her taste for teasing me with meaningful flashes from her gray eyes until I was too weak to resist her sweet implacable wisdom.

Canada was very good to us. I guess it civilized me, made me a *social libertarian*.

We didn't go anywhere the next flu season. We lay low in honor of Dr. Hope-Simpson, trying not to spread whatever we harbored. You all know better than I how fearsome Round Three was. A lot of Round One survivors got reinfected. I told you viruses were tricky.

I expect to see more pandemics in my lifetime. There are currently circulating five bird flu strains that could cross over and kick society to pieces all over again. Forget the smug assurances that a big pandemic can occur only once per century: We continue to culture killer microbes in the industrial food chain.

I'm surprised that the authorities still don't know how influenza spreads among people. No one cares. That's probably just as well: If Hope-Simpson were well understood and respected, some would try to thwart the natural process of immunization. In order to keep flu survivors from reactivating and spreading the virus, people with immunity would be hunted down and liquidated by the unexposed—a biological nightmare Ayn Rand might have dreamed up.

Two years ago, Anna and I nearly replaced one of the world's billion flu victims. We had well-practiced and capable help, but our baby's birth went wrong. Losing a second daughter hurt Anna immeasurably more than it hurt me. What's more than infinity? We fell into a state of considerate depression, trying to care for one another even as we stopped caring about ourselves.

American Exposé

Then my brother's unauthorized publication of my blog forced us to separate: I had described Anna too well and Canada doesn't want illegal immigrants either. I haven't communicated with her since we left the country by separate means. Since there were no warrants out for her, I sent Anna back to New York.

How I long for her. All women remind me of Anna. They either do something she would do or they lack things I like about her. There's no way for us to communicate safely, but I'm certain she misses me, too. I can't even buy music that reminds me of her, lest I trigger some data-mining algorithm they've cooked up to catch me shopping on the Web.

The City of New York and the U.S. Government still demand that I admit to assaulting an officer of the law, possessing weapons and drugs, using false documents, tampering with the Internet at home and abroad for criminal gain, and committing a host of lesser offenses. I herewith throw the book back at *them*.

You're reading it.

I never harmed anyone. I helped people. My transgressions were verbal and they were aimed at a state that failed its citizens in a thousand ways. My 'crimes' have outlived the Great H5N1 Avian Pandemic.

I will not go to prison or see my reputation blackened further. I want to clear my name.

I don't hate the people who hound me. The DHS workers and fellow apparatchiks are merely doing their jobs, dreaming of pensions and college for the kids. Nice folks, following orders. We've all heard that before. I want them to stop.

I want *Round Two* with Anna. I yearn to stroll Manhattan with her. No masks or gloves or goggles. We'd rediscover one another in magnificent combustion. I'd taste her resolve, consume her anew. I'd learn to laugh again.

I'm trapped in cyberspace like that polar bear you all fussed over last year as he drifted to his doom on that shrinking ice floe. Please don't let that happen to me.

Don't count Blogula out!

Photograph by Miriam Berkley

Peter Christian Hall is a writer and filmmaker who was raised in upstate New York and now lives in New York City. He has written for *Rolling Stone*, the *Village Voice*, the *New York Times*, Reuters.com, and The Big Money and served as executive editor at *Financial World*.

Hall wrote, produced, and directed *Delinquent*, a feature film (with an original score from Gang of Four) that the *Los Angeles Times* called: "a highly accomplished work [that] marks a stunning feature debut for writer-director Peter Hall, who never makes a false move as he builds suspense right from the start."

Please visit **www.AmericanFeverBook.com** for live links, illustrations, an art gallery, and worlds of information.